STARGATE
AT_____

D_____

"SOMETHING'S NOT right about this."

"I share your sense of unease," Teyla said. John had spoken the words that were behind the creeping sense of wrongness she felt. "I have seen other worlds with as much, but they were in fear of the Wraith. They had precautions, plans. These people do not even seem to know what we mean. Why have the Wraith not come?"

John shook his head.

Teyla picked up a piece of fruit and continued. "There are, for better or worse, three responses to the Wraith. To hide, as the Genii do, and hope that the Wraith will not discover the extent of one's civilization. To defy them and fight, as the Satedans did. Or to disperse and give them no targets, as my people did. All of the peoples of this galaxy that I have met do one or another of these. These people..." Her voice trailed off as the barge came upon another large stone wharf, passing a barge that lay tied up beside it, cattle being loaded aboard. "These people are a puzzle."

"Something's rotten," John said. "I don't like it." He took the radio from his pocket. The light flashed standby.

"You will try to call them again?"

He shook his head. "The battery is low. And we'll hear them when they call us in range."

"Surely by now they are looking..."

STARGATE
ATLANTIS ™

DEATH GAME

JO GRAHAM

FANDEMONIUM BOOKS

An original publication of Fandemonium Ltd, produced under license from MGM Consumer Products.

Fandemonium Books
PO Box 795A
Surbiton
Surrey KT5 8YB
United Kingdom
Visit our website: www.stargatenovels.com

STARGATE ATLANTIS.

METRO-GOLDWYN-MAYER Presents
STARGATE ATLANTIS™
JOE FLANIGAN TORRI HIGGINSON RACHEL LUTTRELL JASON MOMOA
with PAUL McGILLION as Dr. Carson Beckett and DAVID HEWLETT as Dr. McKay
Executive Producers BRAD WRIGHT & ROBERT C. COOPER
Created by BRAD WRIGHT & ROBERT C. COOPER

WWW.MGM.COM

ISBN: 978-1-905586-47-9
Printed in the United States of America

For my mother

Acknowledgements

A book is never produced in solitude, and there are many people who have greatly contributed to *Death Game*. First and foremost, I must thank Sally Malcolm for getting me to watch *Stargate Atlantis* in the first place, and for introducing me to these wonderful characters. It's a pleasure to work with her, and to share the squee of writing a new chapter of *Stargate Atlantis*.

I would also like to thank my super online friends who have provided much help and feedback along the way: Rachel Barenblat, Gretchen Brinkerhoff, Mary Day, Lynn Foster, Mara Greengrass, Imogen Hardy, Mihan House, Nathan Jensen, Anna Kiwiel, Anna Lidstrom, Gabrielle Lyons, Kathryn McCulley, Anjali Salvador, Lina Sheng, Lena Strid, Casimira Walker-Smith, and Robert Waters. I am also deeply indebted to Melissa Scott, whose insights about the Wraith have been fascinating, and who I am looking forward to working with in the future, and to Laura Harper, who suggested that I write this book.

Most of all, I would like to thank my wonderful partner, Amy Griswold, who was only a little taken aback when the Team moved in!

CHAPTER ONE

LT. COLONEL JOHN SHEPPARD was sure he'd had better days. That he couldn't remember any of them right now was just one disturbing thing. Another one was the great big crack in the puddle jumper's front window. He was pretty sure that shouldn't be there. He was almost sure that the view out the window shouldn't be mostly dirt, with what looked like the trunks of several big trees in it. Also, the board of instruments under his chest shouldn't be sputtering and smoking.

The latter seemed like a really bad thing, so he cautiously pulled himself off the panel and sat back in his seat. Moving hurt, but not as much as it would have if he'd broken ribs, which was something, but there was a long wet smear of blood across the docking indicators and the tactical controls, which couldn't be good. Several droplets splashed against the board as he watched, and he put his hand to his head. It came away drenched in blood. Great. Holding his left hand to the general vicinity as tightly as possible, John looked around the jumper. What was he doing? Who was with him? He remembered the jumper descending into the gate room, the bright blue fire of the gate kindling. And after that... Nothing.

He took a deep breath and made himself let it out slowly. Some short term memory loss was normal with a head wound. He knew who he was and what he was doing, Lt. Colonel John Sheppard, with a gate team mission to M32-3R1 to check out an anomalous energy reading. He had punched the gate and...

John heard a moan behind him and scrambled backward out of the pilot's seat as quickly as possible. "Teyla?"

She seemed to have been thrown clear of the copilot's seat, lying crumpled between the pair of rear seats, her left arm twisted at an odd angle that couldn't possibly be right. He heard the swift hiss of her breath as she moved, her fingers opening and closing against the floor.

"Hang on," John said, kneeling beside her. "Careful." When he bent over, blood ran down into his eyes and he dashed it away.

Teyla pushed herself up with her right arm, half rolling into a sitting position, her left arm clutched tight against her side. When she saw him her eyes widened. "John? You are bleeding badly."

"I know," he said. "I think I hit my head on the board." He took his hand away. Yeah, it was bleeding hard.

Teyla reached up to get a look at it, wincing as she moved. Not good.

"Can you move your fingers?" he asked, reaching across to her left arm. She was wearing a jacket, and he couldn't tell if the shape of her arm looked right or not.

"Yes," she said, wiggling them. "But I cannot move my arm as it should or put any weight on it." She leaned back against one of the rear seats, fumbling in her pants pockets with her right hand and producing a dressing. "But you are bleeding. Here, now."

"Got it," John said, unrolling it and putting it to his head, holding it in place as tightly as he could stand. Not good. There was a world of not good here. Teyla's shoulder was probably broken or at least dislocated, and his head was bleeding hard — in addition to not being able to remember anything since he'd dialed the gate... A thought struck him and he glanced wildly around the jumper. "Where are Rodney and Ronon and Zelenka?"

"What do you mean, where are they?" Teyla looked at him with concern. "We dropped them off. Do you not remember?"

"No, actually." He'd dialed the gate and watched it open, said something to Rodney, and then... Nothing. Everything after that was a blank until he'd picked himself up from the board in the crashed jumper.

"We left Rodney at the gate to try to figure out what had been done to the DHD because it was tampered with in a way he had never seen before," Teyla said. "And we dropped off Radek and Ronon on the island with the Ancient ruins to investigate the energy readings because Rodney said it was a waste of time. You do not remember?" Her voice was concerned, and the two small lines between her brows deepened.

John shook his head slowly. Good to know no one else from his team was lying bleeding around here, but... "What happened?"

"We had just lifted off from the island when we spotted a Wraith cruiser. It was at low altitude and we did not see it at first, not before it got off a number of shots that disabled the cloaking mechanism. You ran hard at extremely low altitude, trying to put some distance between us, but without the cloak there wasn't any way to hide, especially over open sea. We took fire and crossed the coast, and you said we were going down." Teyla's eyes were apprehensive. "Do you truly not remember any of this?"

"No." A cruiser. That was very, very bad, much worse than a few Wraith Darts.

Teyla pushed herself up, using the seat to get to her feet. "John, we have to get out of here. The cruiser is still out there, undamaged, and it will be able to find our wreckage. We have to get as far away from it as we can before the Wraith arrive. We are in no shape to face them."

"I have to agree with that," John said, dragging himself upright. There were backpacks in the rear compartment with survival gear, and they needed ammunition and preferably the P90s, not just the sidearms they carried in the field. He tied the dressing on and grabbed for supplies, aware that Teyla was doing the same beside him, stuffing her pockets with various things as she usually did. He felt like he was missing something, but annoyingly couldn't remember what. Something he'd lost along with what sounded like the better part of a couple of hours.

Dressings. The first aid kit. They were going to need that. Flares? Not so much so. A drill? He hoped not.

"We need to go," he said, reaching for the emergency release for the back hatch. Even if he'd eluded the cruiser in the last moments of their flight, the wreckage of the jumper would be obvious from the air.

"Understood," Teyla said, making a last awkward lunge for something.

The air that poured in the back was hot and dry, bright sunlight dazzling him. John blinked, his eyes watering as he refocused on blindingly blue sky and the tall palm trees that surrounded the jumper. It had come down in a grove of trees, the right drive pod sheared off entirely by the cruiser's fire. Ok. That was pretty impressive looking if he did say so himself. The crippled jumper should have dropped like a rock instead of landing upright and more or less level, a long scar through the trees marking their passage. He must have used the trees to bleed off airspeed and soften the crash. Nice, but even more easily spotted from above. He might as well have drawn a big arrow across the landscape pointing to them.

Teyla dragged at his arm with her good hand. "Come on, John. We must go."

The trees seemed thicker in one direction, and so they set off toward the heavier cover, though there was very little undergrowth. Taller palm trees shaded shorter, but the sky was always visible, lambent and bright through the trees above. It was also hot. That was going to get old fast. But it wasn't humid. Not a jungle. An oasis. Beyond the edges of the trees were the stark lines of desert, sand and ridges of stone showing gold and white under the glaring sun.

John stopped and swore. That limited their options a lot. He knew all too well that two people trekking across the desert were very, very vulnerable, not to mention that it would be incredibly stupid to set off across it without any idea where they were going. He must have seen from the air. They'd flown this way, dodging the cruiser. He must have seen how the course lay, how far they were from the sea and the island where they'd left Zelenka and Ronon, from more hospitable areas. But he couldn't remember.

"Did we see anything when we came over?" he asked Teyla. "Towns or anything? Any idea how far it is to the coast?"

She shook her head, shading her eyes with her good hand. "I do not know," she said. "It happened very quickly and I do not know how fast we were moving. I am certain there were settlements that we passed over, and some areas that looked farmed, but I do not know how far. Forty miles? Seventy miles?"

John winced. Whether forty or seventy miles of desert, neither was good news in this heat. And in broad daylight they'd be an easy target. "Settlements?"

"Yes," she said. "I am sure we are not far from some. I thought I saw a village not long before we crashed. Though I know nothing of the people of this world."

There were voices behind them, human voices raised in shouts, the sounds of running feet.

Slinging the P90 around, John turned toward the sound. "I think we're about to," he said.

Dr. Radek Zelenka lifted his hand to screen his eyes from the bright sun and looked out over the azure sea. The ruins of what once must have been a citadel perched on the edge of a cliff above the waves, providing a magnificent view of sky and sea and a few distant islands beckoning on the horizon. A steep path led down the cliff to a white sand beach, while behind, on the other side of the broken stone walls of the citadel, lush jungle crowded up to the heights. The island was not uninhabited, as they had first thought. A few tendrils of smoke rose from cooking fires on the other side of the island, marking the location of a little fishing village. The scene was, Zelenka thought, idyllic. It looked like the coast of Dalmatia on the Adriatic. If it weren't in the Pegasus Galaxy the place would be overrun with tourists.

And if the planet weren't protected by an energy field. They'd seen that before, worlds protected by the Ancients for some purpose of their own. There was a Stargate, of course, a ground gate, not a space gate, otherwise they could not have penetrated the shield, its DHD modified in a way that Rodney had huffed over and eyed suspiciously. He had not been much interested in the shield. They had seen them before. He was all too happy to leave the investigation of the Ancient ruins and the shield generator to Radek.

"It's going to be just like the one on M7G-677," Rodney had said. "You know. The planet with all the kids. There's not much point in poking at it." His eyes had lit as he ran his hands over the DHD by the gate. "But this! This is really interesting! It seems like there's some kind of tampering with the control mechanisms…"

And so they had left Rodney to the DHD while he had been detailed to investigate the energy shield, with Ronon to stay with him in case of trouble. Now Ronon came and stood beside him at the edge of the cliff. He thought that Ronon's expression altered just a tad. Surely the man could not be impervious to so much beauty!

"Glorious, isn't it?" Radek said.

Ronon nodded slowly. "Yeah."

Someday, Radek thought, he would hear the Satedan put more than two words together. In the few months since Ronon Dex had joined the expedition in Atlantis he didn't think he'd ever heard the man utter a complete sentence.

"It reminds me of a place I used to know," Radek said. "Near a city named Dubrovnik."

"Home?"

"No," Radek said. "Somewhere I visited once. The Czech Republic has no coast." He put his hands his pockets, scanning the far horizon. "A beautiful town, and then I had a beautiful person to see it with."

Ronon stiffened, and for moment Radek wondered what he could have said that gave offense, but then his eye caught what Ronon had already seen.

The shape of one of the clouds was wrong, and it moved wrong, against the flow of wind, against the flow of the other clouds. It was a Wraith cruiser coming in over the sea, flirting with the edges of the soaring clouds, white against the blue sky.

"Get down!" Ronon yelled, grabbing Radek by the back of the shirt and all but flinging him to his knees. "Stay down!"

They huddled in the shelter of the citadel wall, and for once Radek was glad of the grays and tans of the Atlantis uniform. It was hard to spot from above against gray stone and shadow. Ronon's brown blended equally well.

The cruiser swept over at a few thousand feet, and the sound of its passage was a roaring in his ears. He watched, waiting to see if it would come around for another pass, Ronon's hand on his arm to keep him still.

"Wait," Ronon said, every muscle tensed, his other hand on the energy pistol at his belt.

They waited.

The cruiser faded into the distance. When all was once again still, Ronon unfolded and stood up. "Not good."

Radek nodded. "Do you think that the jumper, that Sheppard..."

"If Sheppard ran into that thing he had a problem," Ronon said. "Ten times the firepower."

"What are the Wraith doing here?" Radek said, scrambling to his feet. "The energy shield should prevent them from getting in, and that ship is much too large to go through the Stargate."

"I don't know." Ronon looked after the cruiser, shading his eyes against the bright sun. "But I think we're in big trouble."

CHAPTER TWO

TEYLA EMMAGAN HURRIED through the trees surrounding the oasis, her shoulder a dull throb of pain. The hot sun beat down on them. They would not evade the inhabitants of this world for long, and perhaps it was foolish to try.

"Colonel," she said. "There is little point in running. We cannot hope to elude them." Certainly if they left the trees and took off across the desert they would be easily spotted, and the cover around the oasis was by no means dense enough to hide effectively. "It would be better to seek them out."

Sheppard stopped, turning back with the P90 ready in his hands. "You have a point," he said. Sweat stood upon his face and the dressing that covered the wound to his head was already soaked through with blood. He didn't look good.

There were distant shouts and the sounds of running feet. Someone yelled, "That way!"

They stood together beneath a stand of palm trees, shoulder to shoulder, a quarter turn off each other, covering overlapping fields of fire. It was hard to hold the heavy weapon with her right hand alone, and her left was entirely useless.

"I do not sense the Wraith," Teyla said. "They are not close. All these are human." Of course, she thought, she would not sense the Wraith cruiser unless it were near. She was not certain what the range of her Gift was, but surely only a few miles, forty at most, or more likely twenty. But enough to know that there were no Wraith among the pursuers bearing down on them.

"Understood," John said, nodding sharply. "Let's see what we can do with these guys." He did not have to tell her to hold fire. Teyla knew that.

They came out of the trees cautiously, mostly villagers, wearing knee length tunics of light colored cloth, stained with work and toil. They were barefooted, and carried a variety of farm implements, stopping short when they saw her and Sheppard in the shadow of the trees.

Teyla could see the thought cross his face. "It would cost too much," Teyla said quietly. "We would have to kill dozens to break out." Possible, with the automatic weapons, but a terrible thing, to shoot villagers who had come to investigate the crash and as yet had threatened nothing.

John grimaced. "I know. I got that a long time ago." Teyla had learned that it was not the way he did things, had seen it on Athos when the men from Earth first came there. Colonel Sumner thought nothing of her people, regarded them little, but Sheppard always saw them real and whole.

"We are friendly," Teyla called out. "You see that we are human, and our ship has crashed."

John gave them his most ingratiating smile, the one Teyla had begun to think of as the Smile of Wrongness, because it only appeared when something was badly wrong. "Hi, everybody."

"Hold your hands where we can see them!" A man's voice rang out, the local inhabitants crowding back away from him as he strode through the crowd. He was very tall, his head shaved in the summer heat, wearing a tunic that didn't quite come to his knees and a bronze breastplate over it. He held a long spear in his hand, the point higher than the top of his head. "Do not move, or we shall regard it as an act of aggression!"

"The head honcho," John said in a low voice.

Teyla nodded. She didn't think the man looked particularly threatening. He seemed more annoyed than anything else, as a leader will when something spoils their scheduling and their day is suddenly interrupted by the unexpected.

"We're very friendly," John said with another ingratiating smile. "Just travelers with an accident."

"They came from the sky," one of the villagers began, but the tall man shot him a silencing look.

"We crashed our ship," John said, turning toward him. "It was an accident. See? Me and my friend here are hurt. We don't want to start any trouble."

Teyla thought his voice didn't sound right. *He is more hurt than he admits,* Teyla thought. *It must be a priority to get medical attention, or at least to get John to a place he might rest out of the heat.*

"I am Tolas, Ruler of a Thousand," the man said. "Is it true you came from the sky?"

That would be the question, Teyla thought. Probably the only ships they had ever seen were Wraith. "We have never been here before," she answered cautiously. "We came from the sky, but we are human, as you can see."

She saw his brow furrow, then relax. *Yes,* she thought. *They know the Wraith, and like all people they fear them.*

"Who are you?" Tolas demanded. "And what do you want?"

"I'm Lieutenant Colonel John Sheppard," John replied, "and this is Teyla Emmagan. We're explorers."

"We did not mean to be here," Teyla said, with a swift look at him. He looked pale even in the bright sun. "We were hurt in the crash of our ship. We would request that we be taken to a healer as soon as possible. We have things to trade, and are eager to come to agreements with you."

John glanced at her sharply but didn't argue. *Worse,* Teyla thought. *He is bad indeed if he will not balk at that.*

One of the villagers dragged at Tolas' arm, and he leaned down to speak with him.

"Are you dizzy?" Teyla whispered. "John?"

He nodded, his jaw clenched shut, his fingers white on the stock of the P90.

Concussion, she thought. *Perhaps it would not be danger-*

ous in Atlantis, but they were not in Atlantis, and she was not Dr. Beckett.

Tolas straightened up. "We have a healer," he said. "And we will take you to her in the name of humanity. We can discuss your trades later."

"Agreed," Teyla called back. "Now let us go." She slung the weapon down, wincing at the pull against her left shoulder. Away from the crash site and the guests of people — that was the best they could hope for.

It was not terribly far to the nearest village, only two or three miles, but more than once John had to stop and lean on her for a few moments, too dizzy and nauseated to go on. The village looked much as Teyla had expected, a town of perhaps forty or fifty mud brick buildings near the small lake that made up the center of the oasis, surrounded by billowing palm trees and irrigated gardens that took up every bit of available room near the water. Domestic fowl ran loose, and children came running to see the newcomers, barefoot but unafraid.

"They must not be Culled often," Teyla said to John in a low voice. "They are not frightened enough."

He didn't reply, just kept his head down and walked on doggedly.

Teyla sped up to catch Tolas, walking at the head of the party. "Where are you taking us?"

"To the Main House," he replied. "It is where our visitors stay. And there I will have the doctor for you." His eyes did not evade hers, as those of men often did, depending on the culture of their world. It was a good sign, Teyla thought, that he spoke to her comfortably, saying much about the place of women here. All too often she'd been ignored, or had the local inhabitants of a place speak only to Sheppard or McKay or Lt. Ford.

"We will be in your debt," Teyla said formally. "My friend is hurt and we will appreciate your doctor's concern."

Tolas cast an appraising glance over John, his brows knitting. "The healer is skilled," he said.

"I am glad to hear that," Teyla replied.

The Main House was larger than she had expected, three stories surrounded by a wall of painted mud brick, a fortified house of some size. Inside the walls were gardens, and she dimly had the impression of tiled floors and cool interior as they were hurried through. John staggered, and she caught him with her good arm. "Not far now," she said.

"Here," Tolas said, and threw open a door. Teyla helped John through.

It was a small room with walls washed in pale blue paint, two tiny windows high up in the wall letting in light, furnished with three carved wooden chairs, a table, and a bed piled with blue blankets. A hanging lamp of bronze intricately worked with snakes hung from the ceiling above, unlit in the middle of the day, while a small side table held several pottery jars.

"The doctor will be here in a moment," Tolas said, and backed out while she helped John to the side of the bed.

He lay back on the pillows, his eyes clenched tight as one will when the world seems to spin around. Blood had soaked through the bandage on his forehead and smeared across his face.

"Here," Teyla said, taking weapon and pack from him and putting them on the floor. "Just lie still for a bit." The room was surprisingly cool given the heat outside. The walls must be very thick to insulate so well.

"I think I've got a concussion," John managed.

"I know you do," Teyla said, putting her own things down beside his. Her shoulder was throbbing and her left hand mostly useless. "But we will not be here long. We will get back to Atlantis soon."

"The jumper..."

"The jumper is destroyed," Teyla said firmly. "But we left

Rodney at the DHD, if you do not remember. As soon as we are overdue, Dr. Weir will dial in and Rodney will tell her that we have not returned. She will send another jumper through, and our crash site is very visible from the air. Major Lorne will fan out from there in a search, so I do not think it will be later than tomorrow morning that we will see them arrive, and then we will be back to Atlantis in no time at all."

John started to nod, then looked like he thought better of moving his head. "Yeah. Only what about the Wraith? That cruiser…"

"Was not anywhere near the gate," Teyla said soothingly, trying to lift the edge of the dressing on his head without tearing the scab if it had formed. He really should not lose more blood. "And Lorne and Rodney will be alert, since they will know we must have met trouble. Tomorrow at the latest we will be back in Atlantis, and Dr. Beckett will be complaining that you are injured again." Stuck down, she thought, checking the bandage. Water would soak it free without pulling. "What is it he says? That he needs a loyalty scheme for you?"

John snorted. "Just about." He twisted a little, uncomfortably. "How's your shoulder?"

"I will manage," Teyla said.

The door opened again and two men stepped in carrying long spears, their shaved heads glistening with sweat, bronze breastplates glittering. Between them stood an elderly woman carrying a bag. She was dark eyed and dark skinned, her graying hair caught up in a multitude of tiny plaits, each one wrapped round with copper wire. She wore a floor length robe of draped linen, much finer cloth than that of the soldiers who accompanied her, and her voice was lightly accented.

"I am Jitrine," she said. "I am a doctor. I understand that you have been injured in an accident?"

"My friend has been badly hurt," Teyla said, stepping aside so that she could come closer. "He has hit his head. It bled freely, and now he is also dizzy and sick."

"Humm," Jitrine said, and slid in to sit beside John, taking his wrist in her hand with the practiced motion of physicians anywhere. She frowned over it for a moment, then cupped her hand over his eyes. "Look at me," she said sharply.

John blinked.

"You see?" Jitrine said to Teyla. "How his pupils do not respond to the light the same on each side? The left side is over dilated. That's common with head injuries."

"I see," Teyla said, bending closer. The left pupil did not shrink when the light hit it as the right did.

"Now let me see the bandage," Jitrine said.

"It has stuck," Teyla said. "I thought water to soak it free?"

"Go and get some," Jitrine said to one of the soldiers. When he stood stupidly she snapped, "Water. In a bowl. What do you think I will do while you are gone?"

She put her fingers to John's neck, checking the pulse there, then lifted the corners of the dressing again. "Who did this, young woman? You?"

"Yes," Teyla said, "And my name is Teyla. This is Colonel Sheppard, and we are travelers who have come here by accident. He was hurt when our ship crashed."

"I'm still here you know," John said. "You can talk to me."

"We know," Jitrine said tartly. "And you're not going anywhere else. Not for quite a while. You will lie where you are while I tend you."

"Yes, ma'am," John said, the ghost of his old smile playing around the corners of his mouth. Teyla thought he must find Jitrine's bedside manner as comforting as she did.

"Water," the soldier said, bringing back a bowl. He and the other soldier were moving things around behind them, and one of them edged the table closer.

"Now to soak this off," Jitrine said, dipping a clean cloth in the water. "And see if I can keep it from bleeding again. You will probably need stitches. I hate to mess up your pretty face, but there it is. Your wife here won't mind too much, if you keep your wits instead."

"I am not his wife," Teyla said.

A third soldier came to the door. "Is all well?"

Jitrine did not look around. "Tell Tolas this will take some time. And not to interrupt me every few minutes."

"Yes, doctor," the soldier said. There was again the sound of shuffling about, and he went out and shut the door.

"There!" Jitrine carefully lifted the soggy dressing off. "Beautiful."

Teyla tried not to cringe. The cut was long and deep, four inches from just above his eyebrow to somewhere in his hair, slowly seeping blood.

"Bad?" John asked. Of course he could see her face.

"I've seen a lot worse," Jitrine said. "But it doesn't matter so much what the outside of your head looks like. What matters is if your brain is swelling inside. I certainly hope not."

"You know about brain swelling?" Teyla asked. She had not seen anything to lead her to believe there was much technology on this world, certainly not the CAT scans that Dr. Beckett insisted on every time she got hit in the head.

"I am a doctor," Jitrine said tartly. "Not a village midwife. I was trained in the College of the Healers in Pelagia, where we learn the causes of decease from the corpses of prisoners. I have practiced as a physician for twenty years. I have seen a man die from brain swelling, and if it is necessary I will open his skull to relieve the pressure."

"Um, no…" John began.

"I hope that will not be necessary?" Teyla said quickly.

"I hope not as well," Jitrine said. "I lose one out of four that way. I'd rather give you better odds."

"Um, no!" John said quickly, starting to push up on his elbows.

"Lie down." Jitrine pushed on his chest. "Don't be stupid. I need to sew you up."

John's eyes were wide. "Just sewing. Not drilling my skull or something."

"Just sewing," Jitrine said with a tight smile. "You must be a soldier. Soldiers are the worst patients. Now lie still and let me work." She sutured the wound with quick stitches, and if her work was not entirely sanitary, Teyla could not fault its expertise. Well, she thought, she had antibiotic cream in the medical kit, and probably some in her pocket case as well. She would put that on when Jitrine was finished.

"That's done it," Jitrine said, tying the last stitch off neatly and putting a pad of soft clean cloth to it. "I'll tie the bandage on, and then you should rest." She looked at Teyla. "If he seems unresponsive or stops making sense, I want you to send the soldiers for me at once, do you understand? If he seems disoriented at all. There is no time to lose in that event."

Teyla opened her mouth and shut it again, and Jitrine reached over to pat her arm. "It is likely he will be fine, but we must keep close watch. It has been several hours already, and he seems himself, does he not?"

"Yes," Teyla said. "He is making sense, and he does not seem different than he usually does."

Jitrine nodded. "Then chances are it is a mild injury. But you must call me if anything changes. Right away."

"I will," Teyla promised.

Jitrine got to her feet, taking her bag with her. One of the two spearmen opened the door. "I will check on you later," she said, and went out, followed by the soldiers. The door closed behind her. Teyla jumped up too slowly. Outside she heard the sound of a stout bar being lowered across it.

John started up from the pillow. "Not good," he said.

"Perhaps they are not entirely certain of us," Teyla said. "But they are not hostile, and she has given you good care. You should lie down. I am sure Jitrine will be back later."

Her voice was soothing, but her eyes fell on the bare floor beside the door. Their packs and their P90s were gone.

CHAPTER THREE

"IT'S NO USE," RADEK ZELENKA said, laying the radio aside. "We are too far from the Stargate to reach Rodney without the longer range transmitter in the jumper."

Ronon crouched in the shadow of one of the Ancient citadel's broken walls, scanning the seas and skies with binoculars. "Can you raise the jumper?"

"I have been trying," Radek said. "They are not answering either. This is why I do not like to go offworld. This is why I avoid it if I can. One moment you are looking at a beautiful view, and the next moment you are in deep trouble."

Ronon snorted. "That's life."

"Yes, well, it may be your life. I try not to have it be my life," Radek said. He squinted out over the blue sea. The sun was definitely well past its zenith. He was not certain how long the days on this world were, but it was certainly late afternoon. It could not be so many hours to sunset. "They should have been back for us by now."

"Maybe." Ronon Dex was a man of few words. "Maybe not."

"If they found something interesting, or if the Wraith cruiser found them?"

"Either way." Ronon looked around, lowering the binoculars. "Sheppard's a good pilot. But that thing's got him outgunned. He may have decided to lay low for a while and slip back to get us after dark."

"That could be," Radek said. It was a comforting scenario, at least. Though with the cloak on the jumper surely it would not be necessary to wait until dark. The cloak should disguise the jumper far more effectively than mere darkness. He sat down against the wall and took a drink from his metal water bottle.

"In which case we wait?"

"Right." Ronon raised the glasses again, as though scanning the horizon with binoculars would somehow reveal a cloaked jumper.

"As you say," Radek said. "Sheppard is a good pilot. They are no doubt fine, yes?"

Ronon didn't seem to think that required an answer.

"Lovely," Radek muttered under his breath. "Just lovely."

Jitrine returned in an hour or so, the same guards opening the door.

"Where is our stuff?" John demanded, trying to sit up. "Give our stuff back."

"I cannot do that," Jitrine replied calmly.

"Why not?" Teyla asked, stepping between her and John on the bed. "We have offered you no threats or trouble. What kind of host takes their guests' goods without a fair trade?"

"I am not your host," Jitrine said, with a swift look at the guards. "And it is not my decision to make. How is your head? And shall I tend to your shoulder, young woman?"

"Then who is our host?" John demanded. "What's going on here?"

"You are the guests of Tolas, Who Rules a Thousand," Jitrine said. "This is his house, and things are done here by his will, not mine. I am also his…guest."

The way she emphasized the last word, her glance at the guards, told Teyla a great deal. Not only were they the prisoners of this Tolas, but so was Jitrine. The guards might be less for them than for her. Jitrine met her eyes, and she knew that it was so.

John had not seen, behind her as he was. "We need to talk to Tolas," he said.

"I am sure that Tolas will see you in good time," Jitrine said, her eyes on Teyla. "I am sure that he will make his position plain. But until that time, perhaps you will allow me to tend your hurts? Your wife's shoulder is injured, and I should look at it."

"She's not my wife," John said. "And I don't…"

Teyla turned around, her voice a little too loud and enunciated, a warning he would know. "We should be patient," she said. "And I am happy to have Jitrine look at my shoulder, if your head is well."

"It's the same as it was," John said, and his eyes narrowed as he got her message, flickering to the two guards. He shook his head almost imperceptibly. Two guards, with him injured and Teyla with one good arm. And then they'd have to get out of the house, out of the settlement, and then where? Back to the wreckage of the jumper? Across the desert? Not a plan.

All that passed between them in a moment's look. Teyla turned back to Jitrine. "I would appreciate your care, doctor," she said.

Beneath her jacket she wore a tank top, and with the jacket off her shoulder looked bruised and wrong. Jitrine examined it with practiced fingers, and Teyla's breath hissed.

"Painful?" Jitrine asked.

"Very." Teyla set her jaw. John was sitting up, as close as he could get without blocking Jitrine.

"It is dislocated," Jitrine said. "I can feel the joint out of the socket. The muscles are torn, but they will heal if I can get it back in." She looked at John. "I will need your help for this, soldier. I cannot press and hold at once, and it requires some strength."

"Do it," Teyla breathed. Her shoulder was a solid throb of pain, and it would not get better until it was done.

"Here." Jitrine took John's hands, positioning them at the back of her shoulder, the heel of one hand on the shoulder blade. "Like this and this. I will need you to hold very tight. I am going to have to press against you, and you must not move, do you understand?"

"Yeah." John frowned beneath the bandage. "I've got it."

"Hold just like that." Jitrine moved one of his hands a little bit, then looked at Teyla. "This is going to hurt, but then it will be better."

She set her teeth, and in that moment Jitrine pushed on her upper arm with surprising strength. Red swam before her eyes, and pain washed over her, her breath catching in her throat. There was a sharp pop. Pain raced down her arm, fingers cramping.

"There," Jitrine said.

Teyla blinked, the wave rushing past her, the crest of the pain already reached and subsiding.

"That's better." Jitrine felt her shoulder again, moving John's hand off her back. Gingerly, she rotated the joint, and the twinges of pain ran again down Teyla's arm. "Much better." She nodded sharply. "The muscles are injured, and it will take many days for them to heal. In the next few days your arm will be extremely sore, and it is normal for there to be some swelling and discoloration. That should pass inside of a tenday."

"Does it hurt?" John asked.

"Yes, it hurts!" Teyla snapped. "What do you think?"

"Sorry."

Jitrine reached back for a length of linen she had brought and looped it over Teyla's head, bringing it down and wrapping it around her arm. "A sling will help support it and keep it immobile. The less you use it the better it will heal. And you must let me know at once if you lose feeling in your hand or fingers." She lifted her arm with care, settling it gently in the folds of linen and tying them securely at the top of her shoulder.

It did feel better. Teyla wiggled her fingers experimentally, surprised that there were only twinges of pain. "That is not so bad."

"Good." Jitrine worked her fingers back and forth. "Nice

and warm. Your circulation is fine. That is the movement of blood through the vessels of your body," she said by way of explanation.

"Yes, we know of such things," Teyla said.

"You must let your arm rest. I will return soon, and I will speak about getting some food sent for you." Jitrine looked at John. "You should only eat very lightly at this point, but if the nausea has passed you may have some bread or fruit."

"I'm ok," John said.

Jitrine's mouth quirked. "Of course you are. Now get some rest, and keep her from using that arm." She got up and went out, followed closely by the guards. They heard the bar fall into place behind her.

Teyla sagged.

"She's a prisoner too?" John whispered.

"I am getting that impression," Teyla replied, turning about so they sat face to face.

"We need our stuff back," John said. "And I don't like this."

"I don't like it either. But they have given us medical attention and this is not a cell," Teyla replied. "I do not sense any Wraith about, and they are unlikely to find us easily in the midst of a human settlement, unless they seek us out house to house."

"It's a nice cell," John said, glancing around. "The windows are too high and too small for either of us to get through, and that door is solid. It's a real nice cell."

"I am not sure that either of us should climb out a window in any event," Teyla said. The light through the windows was different. Twilight was coming. "How far would we get if we did? Would it be better to be hunted through the desert? I think we have a better chance making some kind of arrangement with this Tolas. If these people are the enemy of the Wraith, no doubt they are suspicious of us because of our ship. They may never have seen any ship before that is not Wraith. Their caution would be understandable. They may believe that we are Wraith, or that we are with them."

"Yeah, maybe so." It was a measure of John's injury, she thought, that he was willing to accept that with so little discussion. "Let me see if I can get Ronon on the radio." He felt his side pocket, then checked the other. Then patted all this pockets down, swearing.

"No radio?" Teyla said.

"That's what I left in the jumper," John said, grimacing. "I knew there was something. I was wearing the headset and it must have gotten knocked off in the crash."

"I have mine," Teyla said, proffering it. She winced as she moved.

"How about some ibuprofen?" John said, patting his pockets again and coming out with a plastic box. "That should help with the pain and the swelling."

"Thank you." She swallowed the caplets down dry and passed the box back to him. "You?"

"I can't take it with a head injury," John said. "It's a blood thinner. If I've got a brain bleed it will make it worse. So I need to grin and bear it."

"As long as you can grin," she said.

"I can grin." John picked up the radio. "Now let's see if we can get Ronon."

Twilight was coming. That, in itself, was not particularly interesting. What was interesting to Rodney McKay was the fact that the jumper had not returned. How long could Zelenka take looking at the ruins on the island? It had been hours.

Rodney sat in the shadow of the DHD, the only shelter from the setting sun, in the middle of a barren stretch of desert.

And what was with building a Stargate in the middle of deserts? Or in the middle of forests? Or in Antarctica? Or otherwise out in the middle of nowhere? Why didn't the Ancients put Stargates in the middle of cities? It's like building an airport in Saskatchewan. Why? Wouldn't you want to put a main interplanetary terminal somewhere people could get to?

But no. The Ancients didn't think like that. The Ancients loved to put Stargates in remote and inaccessible places replete with assorted dangers.

So here he sat, in the middle of a desert, with the gate, waiting for the jumper to get back. No doubt they were taking their sweet time on a tropical island, maybe getting in a little swimming, hanging around eating pineapples or something. While he sat waiting at the gate like an obedient dachshund. Maybe it was all an elaborate practical joke, and any minute they'd show up and have a good laugh.

He wouldn't give them the satisfaction of thinking they'd gotten to him. No way. He'd be busy, like he hadn't even noticed they were gone. When they showed up. Any minute now.

Rodney sighed and checked his watch again. Nine hours. This was getting absurd. Before long Elizabeth would be worried in Atlantis and would dial in to find out what was wrong. And what would he tell her? That everybody had wandered off, leaving him with the gate? How nice.

Somewhere in the sandy hills off to the east there was a long howl.

Oh bad. So very bad. Like a wolf. Only there probably weren't wolves in the desert. Maybe a jackal. But it didn't sound good. The long sunset was fading and it would be night soon. And then here he'd be, jackals and all.

This was not turning into Rodney McKay's day.

He picked up his radio again. "Sheppard? Come in, Sheppard. Sheppard?"

CHAPTER FOUR

"SO WHAT HAVE WE got?" John asked, propping back against the firm pillows of the bed. "Dinnerwise."

It was full night, and the bronze oil lamp cast a warm glow over the room as it swung back and forth on its chains. A few minutes before the soldiers had returned, bringing a large flat loaf of bread, a plate with several kinds of fruit, a covered dish, and a bowl. The bowl proved full of some sort of vegetable puree. Teyla had wrinkled her nose at the strange texture, but John licked some off a morsel of bread experimentally.

"Kind of like baba ghanoush," he decided, and dipped the bread more lavishly.

"You are not supposed to eat much," Teyla admonished.

"This isn't much," John said, tearing off another piece of bread. "Besides, if I was going pass out, wouldn't I be unconscious by now?"

"How would I know?" Teyla said. "Do you think that I am suddenly become a doctor?"

John stopped, the bread in hand. "If I'm brain bleeding, there's not anything to do about it. If you think I'm going to have these guys trepan me, you're crazy. And if I'm not brain bleeding, then there's not much point in missing supper, is there?" He lifted the lid on the round covered dish and an aromatic steam escaped. "Some kind of tea or thin soup," he said.

Teyla lifted the dish and took an experimental sip. "Tea, I think. It is sweet." She looked at her watch. "It has been nearly eleven hours. I suppose you should eat and drink something." She handed him the warm dish.

"Unless you'd rather have me die of dehydration than concussion," he said. John was grinning, which was better. He must be feeling at least some better to be able to joke about it. He took a cautious sip, then a longer one.

Teyla busied herself with the fruit, familiar *sila* and *rannin*, rare and expensive on Athos, but common to tropical climates throughout the Pegasus Galaxy. Here, this probably registered as an ordinary meal, not the kind of thing one would give prisoners but not the way one would entertain honored guests either. This was probably the meal the household was eating. She found this obscurely comforting. It suggested that their hosts weren't sure of their status and had not decided their fate. Perhaps in the morning they could meet formally with Tolas and convince him that they deserved his help. Certainly these people lacked many things that could be proposed in trade. Jitrine had the training to understand many of the medical supplies Dr. Beckett used, and would surely be eager to try them.

Medical supplies. Teyla had put antibiotic cream on John's stitches from the tiny first aid kit she carried in her pocket, but there were only three packets. There were more in her backpack, but without it they were very limited.

John had clearly been thinking in the same direction, as he put down the piece of fruit he was eating and leaned back. "We should inventory our stuff."

"Agreed," Teyla said, setting the chewy bread aside and sitting cross-legged opposite him.

John took his nine millimeter out of its holster and laid it on the sheet. "Pistol. Two clips for it in my pocket. A spare clip for the P90, but since I don't have the gun..."

"Hunting knife and eating knife," Teyla said, putting the larger and smaller side by side. "Another clip for the P90."

"Let's empty the pockets out," John said, and started unbuttoning them. Two energy bars. His wallet, which he carried more out of force of habit than anything else. It wasn't like they were going to ask him for his driver's license. A pen. A flashlight. Sunglasses. Mini first aid kit. Swiss Army knife. Three packets of salt. Multi tool. One more field dressing. A magnetic compass. A packet of tissues. He looked at the pile on the bed. "Not so much, really. Everything was in the pack." John looked up and boggled at the pile around Teyla.

Three packets of crackers, four granola bars, two juice packets, a chocolate bar, a bag of fruit leather, a bag of salted corn kernels, a flashlight, four field dressings, a flat box of pills, a compression bandage, a box of toilet tissue, lip balm, sunscreen, rubber bands, note pad, magnetic compass, water bottle, screwdriver, pair of socks, ball of yarn, two small candles, a lighter, and a paperback copy of Watership Down. John smiled at the latter.

"I have two MREs in my pack," Teyla said. "And fifty feet of rope."

"Do you always plan for the apocalypse?" John asked.

"Usually," Teyla said serenely. "It is always better to be prepared."

There was the sound of the bar at the door being moved, and they hurriedly repacked their pockets. It occurred to Teyla that it was very interesting indeed that their captors had let John retain his pistol. Perhaps they were so unfamiliar with firearms that they did not perceive it as a threat. Surely a pistol and two spare clips for it would be enough to end almost any confrontation their way.

Jitrine returned, accompanied by the ever present soldiers. "Is all well?"

"Fine," John said, stuffing the last energy bar away.

Jitrine walked over and grabbed him by the chin, tilting his face up into the flickering light. "Not bad," she said. "Your pupil is still dilated, but you seem alert. Does it hurt?"

John nodded. "Yeah, but not as bad as before."

Jitrine looked and felt at his throat for his pulse. "You can sleep then. I have told Tolas that you will wish to speak to him in the morning. I will return and change the dressing then." She let go of John and turned to Teyla. "How is your shoulder?"

"Much better, Doctor," Teyla said respectfully. "May I ask you where we are, and what this place is called?"

"This is The Chora," Jitrine said. "We are in the Thousand of Mabre, one-hundred and twenty *auri* from the city of Pelagia on the coast."

"And Tolas? He's the king or something?" John asked.

Jitrine snorted. "He is no more than the crudest sort of local official. The king in Pelagia would not know his name, and he would wash the floors in the palace of Pelagia."

"I see," Teyla said. "And does he make trade agreements? Our people would very much like to open trade with the people of this world."

"Through the Gate of the Ancients?" Jitrine's eyes grew sharp. "How do you plan to do that?"

John looked at Teyla and she read his glance — go on, you are getting somewhere. "You know of the Gate of the Ancients then?"

"Of course we do," Jitrine said. "But it has been generations since the gate worked. Or rather, since the gate worked as it should. There was a time when it did as it ought, and men came and went from this place. But something happened, and now it is not possible to open the gate from here. People may pass through it into The Chora, as sometimes happens, but there is no way to reopen it going in the other direction. So you see, you cannot arrange trade with another world. You cannot even return to your own."

Teyla felt a cold chill run down her spine. "The gate will not open from this side?"

"It has not in generations," Jitrine said.

"Why?"

"We do not know," Jitrine said. "Many scholars from Pelagia have studied it since the time of our second King Anados. But we are not stupid enough to take it apart or break its components when we do not understand them. The King has given orders that it is to be left alone, that future generations of scholars might work on it fresh without further damage."

"And so no one comes through?" Teyla asked. "In ships?"

Jitrine's eyes wavered. "It may be that…"

"Enough talk," one of the soldiers said firmly. "Tolas said you could treat their injuries, not gossip all day."

"Of course," Jitrine said mildly, but her eyes flickered to John's and he nodded imperceptibly.

Yes, she too is a prisoner, Teyla thought, and she is telling us all she may. And she knows something of ships that pass through the gate. Wraith ships? Or some other?

"Come along," the soldier said, and drawing open the door escorted her out, her back stiff and straight.

After the bar was shot home, Teyla sat back down on the end of the bed.

"Not good," John said. "If there's been something wrong with the DHD for generations."

"Rodney said there was something strange about it," Teyla said. "Perhaps he can fix what is wrong. After all, he has much more understanding of how it works than people here do."

John nodded, scrubbing his hand across his stubbled chin. "Rodney can fix pretty much anything wrong with a DHD short of it being blown up. He may have it fixed by now. Besides, we have the DHD in the jumper. Had the DHD in the jumper," he amended.

"True," Teyla said. "And surely by now Elizabeth has begun to worry at least. She will dial in and speak to Rodney, who can tell her that we are missing. And Radek and Ronon…"

"Are still on the island," John said. "I don't remember leaving them there, but…"

"They should be fine," Teyla said. "There was a village at the other end, and it was a lush place with much water and food.

I'm sure Ronon can look after Radek until help comes." She did not add that it would be much harder for a rescue party to find John and herself. That was already evident.

Teyla got up and put the plate of food on the table, then pulled a chair over and stood on it so she could see out the window. Outside, the gardens were washed in bright moonlight, and a cool breeze whispered through the palm trees, their leaves waving together with a soft sound. It was very peaceful.

"See anything?" John asked.

"There is a garden," she said. "The moon is very bright."

"That could be good or bad." He was propped up against the pillows, and the dark shadows under his eyes were not all cast by the hanging lamp.

Teyla climbed down awkwardly. "We should try to rest," she said. "Tomorrow may be a very long day."

The jackals or whatever they were howled louder. Rodney certainly hoped they were afraid of flashlights, because that's what he had to keep them off. Ok, he supposed a pistol was also useful, but his chances of shooting jackals in the dark with a pistol seemed pretty nonexistent. And he was hungry.

Rodney jumped when the chevrons lit blue with the incoming wormhole, and got to his feet before it even stabilized.

"Sheppard, this is Weir." Elizabeth's familiar voice crackled over the radio. "Report."

Rodney slipped the headset over his ear quickly. "This is McKay," he said. "I'm at the gate alone."

He could almost see Elizabeth's frown. "Where is the rest of the team?"

"They dropped me here, oh, thirteen hours ago, and went to investigate a strange energy reading in some Ancient ruins on an island north of here," Rodney said. "Since then there's been no contact. And let me tell you, I am starting to be unhappy about that!"

"Thirteen hours?" Elizabeth's brows would be rising. "That's not like Colonel Sheppard."

"No. It's not. It's bad. And did I mention I'm being stalked by predators?"

"I'm sending Major Lorne and a backup team through," Elizabeth said.

"No, you're not," Rodney snapped. "Because I have been investigating the DHD/gate interface. And it's screwed up. The control crystals that allow the gate to talk to the DHD have been removed and the systems have been rerouted. The gate can't interface with any DHD. Not its own. Not the DHDs in the jumpers."

"What?"

"I can't dial out." Rodney pulled the microphone a little further from his mouth to permit her to hear a particularly loud jackal scream. "If I could, don't you think I would have hours ago? Right now anybody you send through is going to be trapped here with me, even if they come through with a jumper. We can't dial back."

There was a pause. "Understood," Elizabeth said. "Rodney, what's your recommendation?"

"Well, we could all just stay here on this forsaken planet forever, or I could fix the gate interface."

"What do you need to fix the gate interface?" Elizabeth asked reasonably.

"I need control crystals, ones that can be repatterned. I also need light. All I've got is a flashlight and it's midnight. I need a full toolset and a spare battery for my laptop to interface with the dialing mechanism. Oh, and I need some water! This is a desert. And there's nothing to eat or drink. Also some jackal repellent would be useful."

There was a long pause at the other end. Then Elizabeth spoke again. "Major Lorne says he's willing to come through with the supplies you need, that he's sure it's not a one way trip."

"That's really nice, but it might be. I've never done this before."

"I'm sure you can handle it, Rodney," Elizabeth said in that tone he hated, the one that meant that she expected a miracle from him and wouldn't thank him if he found one. "Lorne will be through within the hour. We need to find the control crystals for you."

"Fine," Rodney snapped. "And he can bring some dinner while he's at it. I haven't had anything in hours and I have blood sugar issues, you know."

"I know," Elizabeth said. "Lorne says he'll bring everything you need. Weir out."

The gate dimmed and the event horizon died. Rodney looked up at the endless sea of stars above. He supposed Major Lorne and a semi-automatic counted as jackal repellent.

CHAPTER FIVE

JOHN TURNED OVER restlessly for the fourteenth time. The hanging lamp guttered, the flame burning low. Teyla sat up.

"Does your head hurt?" she asked quietly.

John shrugged. "It's not awful. I just can't sleep." He was under a mound of covers against the chill of the desert night, his back to her.

"I can't sleep either," Teyla said.

"Sorry." He rolled over again and sat up, the bandage drooping down over his eye.

Teyla put her hand to his forehead. "You don't seem feverish."

"I'm fine. It just hurts."

"I think I have some Tylenol," Teyla said. "Can you take that?"

He nodded. "Should be ok. It's not very strong but it's better than nothing." She fetched the Tylenol and the remains of the tea, and he gulped the pills down. "I'm sorry to keep you awake."

"Well, I can't very well throw you out, since we're locked in," Teyla said. "So I suppose I have to put up with you." She sat back down on the edge of the bed, propping up against the headboard and pulling the covers over her feet. "We could tell stories."

"Tell stories?"

"That is what my people do when keeping watch," Teyla said serenely. "And since we must pass the cold hours of the night together, it is better to do so in companionship." She folded her hands across her stomach. "I have suggested it, so you may request the story."

"I don't know any Athosian stories," John said, settling back down, the firm pillow like a bolster beneath him. It would take some little time for the pills to help, she thought, but perhaps then he would sleep.

"Still, you must pick one," she said. "It can be anything. About a person or a place…"

For a moment he looked thoughtful, his eyes shadowed by the bandage. "How about the first time you went through a Stargate?"

Teyla looked up at the dim lamp swaying. "You do not pick an easy one," she said.

"If it's a bad idea…"

"No. You chose fairly." Teyla smiled at him. "I will tell you of my first gate."

I am springborn, so I was already weaned my second summer when my mother walked through the Ring of the Ancestors and never came back. My mother was Tegan of the Gate Field, of Emege That Was, and she was beautiful and wild both. My father loved her, and how not, when she was like the storm on the mountains or the wild birds in flight? Four years they lived together, four years they dreamed, and my second summer she walked through the gate and never returned, a smile on her lips and her pack on her back. She was Tegan, and nothing could hold her. She was meant for walking away.

My father never loved again, never chose another, and so in my childhood it was just the two of us. My father, Torren, was a trader. He was a mild man with keen blue eyes and a quiet way, the kind of man who misses nothing but says little. He represented us when people came to buy our wares, and sometimes he walked through the gate himself to sell the things we had made on other worlds, to trade them for things we could not make.

And there were many things we could not make. Plastics — these things you use so freely, even throw away — we prized them for their durability, their lightness, and most of all because we could not make them. The best came from Sateda, but we had nothing they wanted so anything manufactured by them must come through layers of middlemen, traded again and again before it was sold for Athosian grain or the furs of animals we had trapped. An energy pistol like Ronon's would have been worth a year's harvest. And so we knew what they were, but we had none.

I was six years old and a bit when I walked through my first gate. My father had business on Narara. We traded with them fairly often, for they were a good market for our furs and our pottery and in return we bought from them the richly loomed cloth that they are famous for, raw silks in all the hues of the rainbow. I loved their cloth even as a child. I could not imagine how they made such bright dyes colorfast, russets and brilliant greens, reds and lambent purples, the turquoise that is my favorite.

"It's only a short trip," my father said. "There is no reason Teyla cannot come. We will stay one night on Narada and return in the morning." I was beside myself with excitement, especially when my father got out my winter coat, now packed away neatly for the season, as it was coming to summer in the lowlands by Emege That Was. "It's winter on Narada," he said. "Their winters are cold, so you must bundle up when you play in the snow."

It is true that some parts of Athos are cold. There is snow in the mountains aplenty, but I had lived my life in the lands near Gate Field, where winters are rainy and cool, with ice in the mornings that sometimes coats the trees until they shine like glass. Real snow is rare and does not stay long. That is how we were, on Athos. You came to us in the uplands, when we had just moved to our summer pasturage with the return of the sun. In winter we were far away, in the deep valleys where the cold does not cut one to the bone. It is good that you came then. Had you come a tenday sooner, you would have found no one at all.

And so I stood beside my father in summer, bundled into my winter coat, while the great Ring of the Ancestors hummed to life, flaring blue as I waited. With good wishes ringing in our ears we stepped up, hand in hand, eager and unafraid.

I do not remember what I thought of the gate itself, of the transit, the sudden cold and the sense of disorientation, but we stepped out into snow. We stood in a broad courtyard, sculpted evergreen trees bowed beneath the weight of the snow, high mountains almost invisible, white against the pale sky. Great white flakes were falling, sticky and huge, drifting on the light wind. The stones around the gate had been cleared, and the new snow there only barely covered my boots, but the drifts around were higher than my waist. I let out a breath, and it came out steam in the frosty air. I turned my face to the sky, watching the flakes in their swirling dance, while in the distance we heard the voices of people and the sound of bells moving in the wind.

What may I tell you except that I was entranced?

We spent the day in the markets of Narada, where every good thing is sold, and my father made many trades. I played in the snow, drank warm tea on a bench beside a park where bigger children played a game I didn't know, sliding around on snowshoes with two hide balls. We stayed in a small hostel, eating beside a roaring fire alive with the crackling of evergreen wood, and went to the Temple of the Bells by starlight to watch night play on the snow, with the distant glow of lights on the mountains where people lived. We sat in the pool of a hot spring to warm up afterwards, and I was half asleep already when my father took me up to the loft where we would pass the night. I lay drowsy and comfortable, wrapped in a soft feather quilt, looking out the tiny window at the late moon rising in a silver crescent over the mountains, the snow reflecting its pale light, until waking turned into dreams.

That was my first gate, and I have never looked back. Since then I have never ceased from travel, from wanting to dare one more gate, to see one more sunrise. It makes me a bad Athosian. We are stolid people in many ways, fatalistic and accepting of *the world as it is. We have consigned our romantic past to stories, to tales of daring deeds that once were, but life is too hard for such things now. We are children of war, of a war that never ends. Most of us do not grow old, and while we tell stories of the great cities we once lived in, of heroes who once lived and dared all, we know those days are past. Such things do not happen in the real world.*

When you came to Athos, we thought you were marauders who would try our strength. What else is there to think of a group of wary armed men whose eyes are not hard but frightened, as though they did not know what waited around each corner? Your Colonel Sumner looked through me as though I were nothing, as though he had assessed the value of all he saw and found it wanting.

We are a careful people. We try not to make enemies, especially enemies with weapons that could level our village in minutes.

We did not know we were being pulled into a Story.

Once there was an Ancient city, sleeping beneath the moon, abandoned by her children, sheltered by the sounding seas. Once there was a city that came to life at her son's touch, woke from her long dream and thought of her other children, those scattered like seed before the wind.

And so the story began. It began as stories always begin, in the blue flare of a gate.

"They're in trouble," Ronon said.

Radek looked up from his laptop, its light reflecting off his glasses in the darkness. "You conclude this now?"

"Yeah." Ronon said. "Sixteen hours. There's no way they wouldn't be back by now unless something was wrong. We have to go help."

Radek closed his laptop to save the battery. He was getting tired of batting away flying insects attracted to it anyhow. "And how do you suggest we do that?"

"There are Wraith out there." Ronon got to his feet, pacing back and forth for all the world like a nervous panther he'd seen in the Prague zoo. "The cruiser probably picked up the jumper."

"And where would we look for them?" Radek asked reasonably. "Ronon, it's a very big planet. In the jumper they could be thousands of kilometers away in any direction. We are two men on foot. How do you propose we find them?"

"We can't just sit here," Ronon said in a tone that seemed to disdain Radek's cowardice.

"I did not say we should sit here. But let us not go off half cocked, as they say. We do not know where Colonel Sheppard and Teyla have gone. He said they were going to 'fly around and have a look.' We do not know where they went, or even which direction. They could be on the other side of the planet, and we will not find them this way."

"What's your suggestion?" Ronon crossed his arms on his chest, glaring down at Radek.

"We should return to the gate, get Rodney, and get another jumper through. We can search for them much more effectively from the air, and then we will have the jumper's weapons if we run into the cruiser or Wraith Darts." Radek stood up to his not very impressive height. "Otherwise we are just wasting time wandering around that might be spent getting back to the gate."

"You know where the gate is?" Ronon asked skeptically.

Radek opened the laptop. "I have the telemetry from our survey as we flew over. I was patched into the jumper's navigational computer. Yes, I know exactly where the gate is. Unfortunately, it's quite a distance, about 900 km. We are approximately 350 km from the mainland, on one of an archipelago of islands in a sub tropical sea. The coastal regions appeared inhabited, though there is an interior desert which contains the actual location of the gate. Still, it's doable."

Ronon looked at the map, his eyes darting keenly from one thing to another, fingers nimble on the keys as he focused in on first one place, then another. One always forgets, Radek thought, that he came from an industrial world. Much of Ronon's idea of technology was the same pre-war stuff he'd grown up with. Antiquated, to be sure, from the perspective of forty years later in the West, but hardly primitive. The idea of a keyboard, for example, was not new to Ronon. Did they have manual typewriters on Sateda? Presumably, if they had printing. Radek had learned to type his first year in polytechnique on a manual typewriter. Electric typewriters were for the offices of important men. He had found this manual one junked and had made it work, though there were some keys that stuck. To this day he always banged the C on his keyboards out of force of habit.

"What we need, yes? A map of where we are going." Radek said.

Ronon grinned. "Exactly what we need." He handed the laptop back. "But first we need a way off this island. There's a fishing village down at the end not too far away. We steal a boat, head for the mainland. Sound good?"

"Sounds excellent," Radek said, and grinned back. Ronon was, on the whole, less trouble to work with than Rodney. "But I believe overpowering the fishermen is your part."

In the end it was more a matter of stealing than overpowering. The fishing boats were pulled up on the beach, single masted, sails furled, and there was no guard. Who would steal them, if there was no one on the island except the fishermen and their families? About the half circle of white beach, a few houses stood above the high tide line, while more clustered back in the shade of the trees. There were no lights and no one stirred.

"Good. There are no dogs," Radek whispered, then wondered if there were dogs in the Pegasus Galaxy at all. No one had mentioned them, but it seemed that wherever people went their dogs went too, and the domestication of the dog far predated the Ancients' last contacts between Earth and the Pegasus Galaxy.

Ronon glanced at him sideways. "No guards either. Follow me."

They slipped across the sand, feeling extremely vulnerable silhouetted against the white sand. Ronon put his shoulder to the prow of one of the smallest boats, shoving. It slid backwards, splashing as the surf came up around it.

"Get in!" Ronon hissed.

Radek didn't have to be told twice. Knee deep in water, he scrambled aboard, managing to fall on his nose in the bottom in the process. Several inches of water slimy with old bits of fish sloshed around, distinctly unappetizing. A pair of oars lay in the bottom, and he managed to hoist one of them up — surprisingly heavy, he thought — nearly hitting Ronon in the head as he stuck his head over the side.

"Sorry," Radek whispered.

Ronon said nothing, only shoved. The fishing boat moved backwards into the water, scraping against the sandy bottom with a sound that seemed awfully loud to Radek. Of course it probably wasn't, with both wind and waves for company, but to him it was as loud as an alarm.

On the beach nothing stirred.

Ronon shoved again, and the boat rocked as it came free, Ronon chest deep in the swelling rollers. One broke over him, and he threw his head back, shaking water from his long hair with an expression that spoke more of exhilaration than fear.

It must be nice, Radek thought. He, on the other hand, was once again reminded why he hated to go offworld. Something always went wrong. Sometimes it was a big thing, sometimes it was a small thing. Sometimes one was bitten by ants. Other times one was lost on a strange planet with only Ronon Dex for company. But something always went wrong.

Ronon hauled himself aboard dripping. "That's good," he whispered.

The boat rocked freely on the incoming waves, bobbing up and down easily.

"We row?" Radek asked, proffering the oar.

Ronon looked at it dubiously, then at the furled sail on the mast.

The current was strong, already pulling them further out and down the beach, away from the village and possible pursuit. No doubt for a swimmer it would be dangerous, Radek thought. But fortunately they had a sturdy little boat. So it would help put distance between them and the boat's owner.

"I think we need to go that way," Radek said, pointing ninety degrees off the faint flush of dawn in the east. "Southward toward the mainland. There are many other islands, but eventually we will need to go south and west."

"Sounds good," Ronon said, leaning back against the mast and emptying water out of his boots. Instead of putting them back on he remained barefoot on the planks. "We should do that."

Radek looked at him and at the mast, furled sail waiting. "So you'll be sailing?"

Ronon frowned, and Radek thought for the first time he saw actual worry in the man's eyes. "I thought you knew how to sail."

CHAPTER SIX

JOHN WOKE, AND for a few moments couldn't remember where he was. Not this again, he thought, and then it came flooding back, the crashed puddle jumper, the desert, the doctor who had stitched up his head. Morning light came in through the small window high above. Teyla was sleeping on the other side of the bed, drawn in on herself like a child, her bad shoulder uppermost.

Right, he thought. Morning. Captured. Out of here. Very important things. By now Rodney had surely called for backup, and Lorne's team would be looking for them in a second jumper. Best to get on the radio and give them something to look for.

He sat up and a wave of dizziness washed over him. Not good. But on the other hand he wasn't nauseous. In fact, he was starving. That was good. John had been hit over the head enough times to know that was a good sign. If you're hungry, you're probably not dying.

Gingerly he got one of the energy bars out of his jacket pocket. That would help. Munching on it, he tried the radio. "McKay, this is Sheppard. Come in. McKay, this is Sheppard."

Only static answered him. They were probably out of range. The hand held radios worked less than a hundred miles, and Rodney didn't know where they were, so the second jumper would have to fly patterns broadcasting to find them. He flipped the radio to standby to save the battery. It would alert him when there was a signal.

Teyla stirred and sat up. "Anything?"

John shook his head. "Nothing yet. They'll have to fly patterns. I wish there was some way to alert them about the cruiser first."

"Lorne will be careful," Teyla said. "They will know something must have happened and will exercise caution." She shoved her hair out of her eyes.

"How's your shoulder?" he asked.

"It hurts," she said. "But it is an ache, not a sharp pain. I think it is bruised muscles, and they will heal. How is your head?"

"Better," John said. "I'm hungry anyhow."

"We must have Carson see to you when we are back in Atlantis," she said. "I'm sure he will have much to say about having you in the infirmary again!"

"Yeah, well."

The door opened to admit Jitrine with her bag. She was accompanied by a young girl in a much-washed tunic who put a tray down on the table and left. This time the soldiers did not come in, but stood outside the door until the girl left, then closed it and barred it.

Teyla got to her feet. "Why are we prisoners?" she asked. "We have done nothing, and we must speak with Tolas."

"And why are you a prisoner too?" John asked.

Jitrine's eyes narrowed. "The local officials in The Chora hate the King in Pelagia, and they resent all Pelagians, especially those with wealth and education. I was foolish enough…" She glanced away. "I will spare you the tale of my folly, but needless to say I offended Tolas, and since I am here, many *auri* from Pelagia with no means to send a letter, I am at his mercy. And he, like many others, is angry because the tribute due the King has recently increased."

John scratched his ear. "Local tax problems. I get it. What do you know about the Wraith?"

"The Wraith?" Jitrine looked genuinely confused.

"Perhaps you know them by another name," Teyla put in. "They are tall, pale men with white hair, and they feed upon humans."

Jitrine shook her head doubtfully. "I have never heard of such," she said.

"We saw a Wraith cruiser," John said, frustration in his voice.

"We know there are Wraith on this world."

"There may be," Jitrine said. "But it is a point of logic that the world is vast. Because there are Wraith on this world does not mean I have seen them."

Teyla glanced at John as if to say, true enough, so he didn't press it. "Have you seen their ships?" Teyla asked. "Small, pointed, very fast? Airships?"

"The sky streaks?" Jitrine asked.

"Sky streaks?" John said. "What do you mean?"

"We sometimes see streaks in the sky, thin clouds being etched across the heavens as though an architect drew a line on stone. Sometimes we see a silver point at the leading end," Jitrine replied.

"Contrails," John said with a nod. "They're made when the ships pass through certain kinds of weather."

"I have seen those," Jitrine said. "But I have never seen anything like the men you describe."

Teyla frowned. "Perhaps you have been fortunate," she said.

One of the guards banged open the door. "Enough time," he proclaimed, and looked past Jitrine to them. "Tolas will see you in the third hour."

"Thank you," Teyla said to Jitrine as she was hurried out. Then she looked at John doubtfully. "They have never known a culling?"

John shook his head. "It could be pretty thinly populated, if this village is any indication. Maybe they haven't been culled in a long time." He examined the breakfast tray. Something smelled very good. It smelled like… "Scrambled eggs!" He looked at Teyla and grinned in triumph.

She shook her head, smiling. "Now I know you are feeling better. We should eat before we speak with Tolas."

Dawn came over the desert. The chill of the night gave way to morning warmth. Rodney stretched and yawned and took another drink of the long cold coffee in the thermos Lorne had brought. It was the last of the coffee. Sad. He wondered if there were any of the sandwiches left.

Lorne looked around, then let the P90 rest on the sling around his neck. "The animals seem nocturnal," he said with far too cheerful a smile for someone who had also been up all night. "No more howling. How's it going, doc?"

"It's going," Rodney said grimly. "I've never tried to repattern a main gate control crystal before, in case you're wondering. It's very finicky work. Screw up and I'll damage the crystal."

"That's why I brought four of them," Lorne said.

"Yes, well, I'm glad to know you have such faith in me," Rodney said, putting his head back into the depths of the DHD. "I'll get it."

"Then we dial the gate, get a jumper and the backup team, and go hunt for Colonel Sheppard's team," Lorne said. "All in a day's work."

Rodney shone his flashlight up inside the DHD, looking for the right circuit. "Somehow I don't think it will be that easy."

Sunrise. It was breathtaking, really. The sun rose out of azure waters under a flawless sky sprinkled here and there with rose clouds. A light breeze blew out of the east, stirring the hair on Radek's forehead.

Ronon sat in the bow of the little fishing boat eating an energy bar, his eyes on the calm sea.

"We could try to get the sail up," Radek said. "We want to go southwest and the wind is out of the east. It should just push us west, don't you think?"

"Probably." Ronon stuffed the last bite in his mouth and stood up. He grinned, and Radek thought there was a flash of ironic humor there. "How hard can it be, right?"

Radek shrugged and looked at the tangle of rope on the mast. "I have never even much liked sea movies. You?"

"I watched Master and Commander with Sheppard. That's it for me. I was army, not navy, on Sateda." Ronon climbed over the benches and started untying things.

Radek looked at him sideways. He thought that perhaps they needed to untie the ropes that kept the sail furled and then find the ropes that raised it. "Yes? That is so?" Perhaps he had heard Sheppard mention something of the kind.

"Yeah." Ronon didn't look at him. "22nd Foot, the Immortals." He bent his head over the knots. "Four hundred years without being disbanded, with always a man coming back to begin again. That's over."

Radek untied the last one on his end of the mast. "You live," he said.

"That's over," Ronon said shortly and stood up, trying to shake out the sail. The heavy canvas was wet and stiff.

Radek put his head down, and after a moment pushed his glasses back up on his nose. "I tell you a story while we do this," he said. "The day is long. Why not?"

Ronon shrugged, his back to him, and Radek took that for assent.

I was two and a half years old on August 21, 1968, when Russian tanks rolled into Prague. I remember there was fear. I remember my mother was arrested. I was not there when it happened, but I remember the absence of her, the way my grandmother clutched me, a scarf over her hair and her things ready to go.

My grandmother — what is there to say of her? She was a young woman when we were annexed by the Nazis, a young woman when she got out of Prague for Plzen because of the fear of bombs. My mother was born there in the winter of '42, child of one occupation as I was child of another. So you see, my grandmother had done all this before.

I suppose I cried for my mother. I do not remember. She

was held three weeks and then released. She was one of the lucky ones. Some disappeared forever, but no one denounced her enough, I suppose. She was guilty of nothing except being in the wrong place at the wrong time, caught up in a peaceful demonstration. And so they let her go eventually. They could not keep everyone, you see.

She regretted it all her life, I think. She got away free, and so many others did not. It was betrayal to live and be happy.

My grandmother did not think so. "It is stolen," she told me. "All of this is stolen. Every moment is a moment between the wars. Every moment is snatched from death. You be a thief, Radek. You learn how to steal."

My father was different. He was nearly twenty years older than my mother, a youth rather than a baby before the war, and he was a serious man. He did not have my mother's fire. Perhaps he once had, but he never got over the pneumonia he had in '39, all winter in a work camp before they needed industrial labor too badly to keep them there when they could be building vital things for the war effort, men like my father who were neither Slovaks nor Jews. Those, they killed one way or another. Those like my father, blue eyed with German first names? He had work in a factory. You see he was lucky too. I have it on both sides, the Devil's luck.

It was not so lucky when time came to go to university. My mother had been arrested as a dissident, though she had not been sentenced. My father had been released by the Nazis. University depended on politics as much as anything, and my family was suspect. I should not have gone to university, except that I was very, very good.

And I am also very, very good at not getting caught. I am simple, you see? I am an egghead. I do not think about politics or sex or religion or any of those things. I do not even know who is in office. I have my head in a book, my mind on physics. I am a little egghead wimp, and I am no threat to anyone. I will toil very nicely in the background, doing things that make the reputations of my professors, and never ask for credit. It is good to have Radek Zelenka on one's team. He will get it done and never make trouble. I am good at getting by.

I was two and a half when the Russians came. And I was twenty three when we threw them out.

I was there on November 17, 1989. We did not know what would happen. We did not know if the army would fire on us, if the Russian tanks would come as they had before. We had learned what to do about tear gas, and how to help someone who has been beaten. I was there when the riot police came. You may not think I am much of a fighter, but that is not the point. The point is not to fight, but to make a barrier of your own body. The point is to be unmoved. Breathe through a wet handkerchief, and be unmoved. I was not much hurt, just some bruises from the scuffle. I am lucky too.

I was twenty four when we won, when we had our country back.

I got my doctorate at Cambridge, and now I am in a distant galaxy doing things my parents and my grandmother could not have dreamed of. And one day I will go home. I will teach and I will research and I will be astonished by the things that children think of.

Or perhaps I will die here. Perhaps the Wraith will have me one of these times, or any of the other innumerable hazards. If it is so, then it is, but I do not plan for it to be. I have the Devil's luck. It may be true that every moment is stolen between the wars. But you and I, Ronon, we can steal.

Ronon said nothing, but Radek saw the set of his shoulders change. "Let's get the sail up," Ronon said.

"Let us," Radek said, and stood on the bench to spread one side of the wet canvas. It would dry quickly enough he supposed, in the sun and wind. Yes, he thought, now we will do it together rather than you will do it for me because I am nothing but a package you are supposed to protect. Perhaps we have come that far.

The breeze spread the sail and the boat began to move, skimming forward over the waves a little faster. It was by no means quick, but better than it had been. They were getting somewhere at least.

Ronon grinned, the wind lifting his hair like streamers behind him. It was hard not to be caught in the beauty of it — the pleasure of an engineering problem beautifully solved, as men had done for thousands of years. How many had stood on the deck of a boat like this, looking off across an unknown sea?

"We might be the first men in the world," Radek said. "The men who discovered sail."

"Because we don't know any more about it than they did," Ronon said, but he was smiling, an unguarded look that transformed his face.

"We have theory," Radek shrugged. "That must count for something."

CHAPTER SEVEN

TOLAS WAS A BIG man with a shaven head and a very serious expression. He listened to their explanations with what Teyla thought was studious attention, though he said nothing and asked no questions, save whether or not Jitrine had given good service.

John assured him that Jitrine had tended them with every care. While he spoke Teyla was free to look about cautiously, her eyes roving though she stood beside John. Tolas had chosen to meet with them in an inner courtyard where a small ornamental pond was shaded by tall trees. Flowering plants grew around, and the pool was graced with a small statue of a boy playing the flute. Still, for all its beauty, it was secure. The walls of the house were around three sides of the courtyard, three stories tall. The fourth wall had a gate that led to another courtyard from which came the shouts of men, a stable yard or, worse, a barracks. Without some idea of where they were going, they would be running blind into a maze of rooms, or perhaps straight into the greatest concentration of soldiers. And all the while it was pretty and very diplomatic. Teyla thought that this Tolas knew his business.

John ended with an explanation of how they might be able to get the gate working, and if they did they would be valuable trading partners. Teyla was very proud of him. He had not threatened to shoot anyone once. More than once it irked her that Sheppard's team did not seem to understand that shooting was not a terribly good way to find trading partners, something which had been a standing problem and had caused endless difficulties with supply, not to mention the inability to find a safe Alpha Site. She thought that Dr. Weir had spoken to him sharply after their last adventure, so perhaps he was attempting to mend his ways.

Tolas paused for a long moment when he had finished, his chin resting upon his hand, his wrists circled by broad cuffs of leather worked with gold ornaments. "These are weighty decisions," he said, "And matters of diplomacy that reach beyond this oasis. I cannot speak for The Chora." His eyes skittered away from them, which Teyla thought a little odd. "You must speak to the King in Pelagia about this. It is his decision, as he is my overlord." Tolas looked at Jitrine, who stood beside a guardsman just inside the doorway. "In your opinion is it safe for these people to travel?"

Jitrine looked reluctant. "I would prefer that Sheppard not travel with his head as it is, however if you mean for them to go by ship it will probably be well enough. He will have no reason to exert himself that way."

"By ship?" Teyla asked. "In the desert?"

"There is a canal not far from here," Tolas said. "You will go to Pelagia by barge, which I assure you is a very comfortable way to travel." He lifted his head. "It is decided."

Teyla looked at John, but his mouth twisted as though he were not saying something else. "Fine," he said. "We'll go talk to the king."

At midmorning they sat beneath a red and white striped awning on a barge putting out from a massive stone dock. Overhead, the azure desert sky stretched uninterrupted. The green trees of the oasis behind them stood in stark contrast to the reds and golds of the desert, a thousand shades from ochre to palest yellow that shone almost silver in the hot sun. Even beneath an awning the sun beat down, and Teyla could see the sweat standing out on John's brow even as they settled onto the bench that ran along the side of the ship, the western side where the shade was deep.

"Are you all right?" she whispered.

"Fine," he said, but she thought that he looked pale beneath his tan and two days of stubble. It had only been a short walk to the barge, not something that he would even notice normally.

The barge was long and broad beamed, the back of the barge filled with livestock on their way to market, their drovers and the lowest paying passengers, while midships there was a raised upper deck with a canopy where Tolas rested in comfort. Jitrine had come aboard with him, and once in a while they could see her go to the rail looking out, but could not speak to her without calling to her.

John and Teyla were at the bow beneath an awning, four soldiers guarding them. Guests or prisoners? Somehow that continued to remain the question, and she voiced it in a low voice.

John's expression was cynical as he looked out over the desert. "Tolas doesn't know what to do with us and he's afraid to make a decision, so he's kicking it upstairs. Thinks it's above his pay grade or something. So he's punting."

"Perhaps he doesn't have the authority," Teyla said. "That is what Jitrine indicated."

"He's not sure whether we're good or not. If we're telling the truth and we can get the gate open, we're worth something and he wants the credit. If we're full of it, then he doesn't look like we duped him." John shrugged. "It's like our gear. They've left the pistol, but kept the packs and other stuff. They grabbed what they could without an actual fight. This way they can give it back if they want to make friends, or not of they don't." He lifted his hand to his eyes, shading them. "Pretty typical BS from the kind of cautious midgrade who's always watching his ass." Lines at the corners of his eyes crinkled as he squinted against the bright reflection of sun on sand.

"You could put your sunglasses on," Teyla observed.

"Right." For a second he looked blank, then reached in his pocket.

"Still having trouble with memory?" she asked.

"I'm good," John said, slipping the glasses on. Wearing them his expression became inscrutable.

She looked out over the rail. "You know, it is not helpful to obscure from me your actual condition. We must work together, and I cannot do that effectively if I misread the extent of your injuries." Teyla glanced sideways at him. "It does not make you look tough. It only makes my job harder."

His face stilled. "Right. Sorry."

A furnace breeze blew across them from the desert, a blast of hot air that did nothing to cool them.

"How hot do you suppose it gets here?" Teyla asked. She had already removed her jacket, and the wind felt good on her shoulders, but there were no more clothes she could remove in decency. Well, she probably could as far as the locals were concerned. Most of them, men and women, didn't seem to see the need for leg coverings. Tunics came to mid-thigh, a very sensible thing in her opinion. She would be comfortable in shirt and underclothing, but she imagined John would not like it if she took her pants off.

"Hot," he said. "Really hot." He licked his lips as if in memory of moisture.

"You have been in the desert before?"

"Yeah." He stood up and took a few steps away, seemingly entranced by the far line of hills. Clearly that was not working as a conversational topic. Or perhaps he was feeling worse than she thought.

The barge rocked gently on the water, drawn by placid oxen on either side of the canal, each ridden by a young boy wearing a broad sun hat. Along the canal irrigation ditches ran back, sometimes only a few dozen feet, sometimes much further. Here and there houses stood, visible from afar by the tree or two that stood around them, by the patches of green. From above, the canal must look like a lumpy worm across the landscape, the bulges of irrigated patches along it at irregular intervals.

They were moving more or less directly northward, toward the sea. Unfortunately that was in the exact opposite direction from the Stargate. On the other hand, it was in the opposite direction from the crash, from where the Wraith would be seeking them if they were. Which was another strangeness. Surely the Wraith were looking for them? If not, why not? Were they so certain that they could not leave this planet that it did not even seem worthwhile to find them?

Just before midday a servant brought them water and a tray of the ubiquitous fruit. Teyla admitted that in the heat she really did not want more to eat than the fruit, which was juicy and delicious. John came and sat down again from his endless pacing and looking at the desert as though it told him something. He looked a little better. The barge was not a strenuous way to travel at all, but it was tedious and did play upon one's nerves.

"What are you thinking?" she asked.

John bit into a ripe *sila*, juice squirting across his chin. "That it's weird. It's not that thinly populated. They're strung out along the canal, but there are thousands of people here. Presumably this isn't the only canal, either. And a bunch of this stuff, like the canal and the irrigation projects, take a lot of coordination and engineering expertise to pull off. Why haven't the Wraith bombed them back into the Stone Age? Why haven't they culled this world like they have so many others? Something's not right about this."

"I share your sense of unease," Teyla said. He had spoken the words that were behind the creeping sense of wrongness she felt. "I have seen other worlds with as much, but they were in fear of the Wraith. They had precautions, plans. These people do not even seem to know what we mean. Why have the Wraith not come?"

John shook his head.

Teyla picked up a piece of fruit and continued. "There are, for better or worse, three responses to the Wraith. To hide, as the Genii do, and hope that the Wraith will not discover the extent of one's civilization. To defy them and fight, as the Satedans did. Or to disperse and give them no targets, as my people did. All of the peoples of this galaxy that I have met do one or another of these. These people…" Her voice trailed off as the barge came upon another large stone wharf, passing a barge that lay tied up beside it, cattle being loaded aboard. "These people are a puzzle."

"Something's rotten," John said. "I don't like it." He took the radio from his pocket. The light flashed standby.

"You will try to call them again?"

He shook his head. "The battery is low. And we'll hear them when they call us in range."

"Surely by now they are looking," Teyla said.

With a sharp pop and a whiff of smoke the control crystal blew up.

Rodney jumped back swearing.

Wordlessly, Major Lorne handed him the third crystal. "Good thing I brought four of these guys," he said.

"Yes, it is good," Rodney said shortly. "Because otherwise we would be screwed more than we're already screwed, which is to say quite a lot. I've been working on this thing for twelve hours, and it's been more than twenty four hours since I started investigating the DHD. I should have solved all the major problems of physics by now! But no. I'm still working on this gate."

"Maybe you should take a nap, doc," Lorne said, scrubbing his hands through his hair. "You've been at this more than a day. Some rest would probably fix you right up."

"Oh and that will be so comfortable," Rodney said. "It's about a hundred and ten degrees and the rest of the team is lost and…"

Lorne put his hand on Rodney's shoulder. "It's not going to do them any good for you to get heat stroke. Get a couple of hours shuteye in the shade by the cliff over there, drink some water, and then get back to work. Gotta be reasonable here."

Rodney blinked. His face hurt. He probably had a sunburn, despite the SPF 50 he was wearing. And the world was starting to get a little surreal. Lorne seemed a little wavery in a way that people didn't usually get when he was just sleep deprived. Maybe he was getting sunstroke. Maybe he was about to pass out.

"Take a nap," Lorne said. "It'll work better afterwards."

"Yeah," Rodney said. He wasn't thirsty. That was probably a symptom of something. Of something bad. A thought struck him. "Snakes."

"Where?" Lorne spun about.

"There might be snakes," Rodney said patiently. "You never know. There might be some over by the cliff."

"I'll look before we sit down," Lorne said. He was looking at Rodney solicitously. Maybe he thought something was wrong. Maybe he thought Rodney had sunstroke.

"What should I do for sunstroke?" Rodney said, dismayed by the note of rising panic in his own voice. "Do you think I have sunstroke?"

"I think you should sit down in the shade, drink some water, and have a nap," Lorne said calmly. "You've got to fix the DHD, but you've been up more than 24 hours and working in the hot sun all morning. Let's take this one thing at a time."

"Right." Rodney let Lorne lead him over and waited while Lorne checked the rocks for snakes. He did feel kind of shaky. He was probably on the verge of sunstroke. That was probably what was wrong. It was more likely sunstroke than the first symptoms of a deadly alien disease.

Lorne sat down on a nearby boulder and took a long drink from his water bottle. "Besides, how much trouble could they be in, right? You said they were going to a tropical island."

"A lot of trouble," Rodney said. Lorne had only been in Atlantis a few months. He had no idea what a world of trouble there was. Yet.

Lorne held the water bottle out to him and Rodney drank. Lorne settled back in the shade, looking for all the world like the rocks were the most comfortable thing he'd ever sat on. "So where are you from, doc?"

"Canada," Rodney said shortly. Some of the rocks might not be as sticky as others. He looked for a place to sit down that seemed less sharp and pointy than the rest.

"I can see that." Lorne gestured with his chin to the Canadian flag patch on Rodney's sleeve. "I meant whereabouts in Canada."

"Vancouver," Rodney said. Which was about the last place he wanted to talk about.

"You got family?"

"Just my sister," Rodney replied testily. "We don't talk much." Which he hoped would end that entire line of enquiry.

"I'm from San Francisco," Lorne said, and seemed to take Rodney's silence for interest. "Yeah, you're probably thinking what everybody does. How does a kid from the most liberal town in America wind up in the Air Force?"

"I wasn't thinking that," Rodney said. Why would he be? Like he cared where Lorne was from?

"Or you're going to say it must be the only way to rebel, right? The only thing you can do when you grow up in San Francisco to get your parents' goat is join the military?"

Rodney sat down in the shade and took another long drink of water. It did taste good. And there was something about Lorne's very nonchalance that was comforting. "Let me guess.

You're going to tell me a long, sad story about how you signed away your life for an education."

Lorne didn't seem offended. He also didn't shut up, as Rodney had more or less intended. He looked amused. "It's not exactly a sad story and not all that long either."

I was conceived in the summer of '69, the Summer of Love, right? My dad had been drafted so he and my mom went on a road trip, one last blast before. She'd just gotten back to San Francisco and he'd reported in when she found out she was pregnant. Strange time, you know? She moved into this apartment in Haight Ashbury with this guy she'd met on the trip, my Uncle Ron. It wasn't like that. Uncle Ron is gay so they were just roommates. You know, with my dad gone and all. He got sent overseas. He was in the middle of his tour when I was born; on April 30. May Eve, my mom used to say, like that made me special.

My dad's an ok guy. It just didn't work out between them. When he got home he was too different and it was all too different. He wasn't so much into the scene, and he couldn't stand the city. He wanted somewhere big and quiet, where he could hear himself think, somewhere totally unlike the jungles of Southeast Asia. He works for the Park Service in Arizona now. Big sky and mesas, Navajo country. He was married to a woman who was half Navajo for a while, but they broke up. My sister Dorinda's a quarter Navajo, though. She's a great kid. She's married and has a baby, and she's in veterinary school in Phoenix now. She's got it all together.

My dad believes in UFOs. He thinks that there are really spaceships and that aliens have visited Earth before. People think he's kind of crazy that way. I wish I could tell him, sometimes, that he's not. That I've walked around on other planets and seen the damndest things. That there really are spaceships, and that you've never lived until you've taken the Tok'ra to a bar in Colorado Springs. Maybe one day I will. I think my dad can keep his mouth shut a lot more than he lets on.

But I didn't grow up with him. I grew up in San Francisco with my mom. She's an art teacher. She does all kinds of fabric art, painting on silk and weaving with raw fabrics, but you can't make a living doing that. So she teaches art to little kids at school. She says she really enjoys it because their minds are fresh. They haven't learned what they can't do.

I could have gone to college without the Air Force. My dad said he'd help, and Uncle Ron and Uncle Gene did too, and by then my mom was married to Boris, so it wasn't like it was just her who'd have to come up with the money. But it was what I really wanted.

No, my mom wasn't thrilled, but she wasn't mad either. See, my mom? She's the world's biggest optimist. She believes in a Star Trek future. We're going to reach this place where we don't have wars anymore, and everyone is judged on their merits, not by the color of their skin or their gender or their sexual orientation. She thinks we can get there in two or three hundred years if we really try. She says look where we've come in the last three hundred years. Nothing is impossible.

And I'm with her. I believe in that Star Trek future too. I just think you can't get there without Starfleet, without the people who go out and keep it safe, the people who explore and who make it real. They're both so sure, my mom and dad, in their own ways. They're both so sure that it could all be true. So I guess it wasn't much of a shock to me to find out it was. The first time I walked into that gateroom in Cheyenne Mountain, it was like coming home. Yeah. This is the thing. This is the real thing, the thing I'm doing. Cause anything can be true if you make it so.

CHAPTER EIGHT

AFTERNOON CAME. The barge glided onward, drawn by plodding oxen.

John had been trying to chat up one of the guardsmen, but he came back at last and sat down with Teyla beneath the awning, on the right side of the barge now, out of the sun. "Three more hours or so," he said, rubbing his stubbled chin. "If I got that right. So not too much farther to Pelagia."

Teyla stretched out her legs flexing her bare toes, her boots and socks piled neatly beside the bench. "Not much longer then."

John looked like he'd like to take his shoes off, but didn't. "Not too much." He had another drink of the lukewarm water they'd been provided and took his sunglasses off to wipe them on his shirt.

"It is your turn," Teyla said.

"My turn for what?"

"To tell me a story," she said, and gave him an offhanded smile. "I told you one last night. We have three hours with nothing to do except sit here. It is your turn to tell a story."

"I don't know any stories," he said.

It was on the tip of her tongue to ask when he had journeyed in the desert before and what had befallen him there, but Teyla thought that it was probably not a happy story, not a story for a time like this, and so she asked instead for something she thought he might actually answer. "It is your turn," she said tranquilly. "You must tell one. I would like the story of how you came to Atlantis."

Antarctica is really quiet. It's just miles and miles of snow, miles and miles of nothing. No towns, no cities, no highways. No people. Nothing. It's quiet. Even in good weather you have to rely on instruments. The ground pretty much looks the same, just mountains and glaciers, and the outposts are so small that you could miss them and just keep on flying until you ran out of gas in an endless sea of clouds and snow that all blend together. .

I liked it. Like I say, it was quiet.

My duties were pretty minimal, just flying some brass and some scientists around, a fifty mile hop out to an advance research post on the ice. Fly 'em out, sit around while they did whatever they did, fly 'em back. It's the kind of job you give a guy who's too flaky to handle anything else. I didn't mind that. It was probably true.

One time it was this guy, General O'Neill. We were just cruising along, everything pretty normal, and suddenly the radio was reporting incoming, some kind of rogue missile that could acquire a target on its own. I had a hell of a time dodging the thing, and it would have gotten us if it hadn't shut down by itself suddenly. I'd never seen anything like it.

Didn't know then that I had Carson to blame. He was messing around with the command chair and accidentally fired an Ancient drone. But at least he turned it off before he blew me and O'Neill to kingdom come.

So I was screwing around while O'Neill met with a bunch of people, got to talking to Carson, and there was this thing. You've seen our chair. You know how it looks. This one was just like it, cold and strange and eerily beautiful, like it was carved out of a snowflake.

And I wanted it. I don't quite know how else to put it. It's like it needed to be touched. It needed me to touch it. I couldn't stop looking at it. It looked like something out of a fairy tale, or like something I'd dreamed a long time ago but forgotten. And so I sat down.

You know what happened then, right? It turned on. It turned on because of the ATA gene, because I have this gene, because

I'm descended from some Ancient who went native on Earth thousands of years ago. And then everybody rushed in, and Rodney said, "Imagine where we are in the solar system," like that was some big thing. Anybody can do that, right? It's like knowing your own address.

But it didn't look like just anything, lines of force and gravity drawn in blue fire like the best heads-up display ever invented, planets and asteroids and comets tracing perfect ellipses, streaming datapoints by the thousands eager and ready and waiting. I'd never seen anything like it. Never felt anything like it, an interface that moved like my thoughts, faster than any game, faster than anything I ever flew.

I looked at O'Neill, and I saw a shiver pass over his face. He was the only one who knew. He was the only one who felt it. He was the only one who knew what it could do, and what it felt like to do it, like sitting on top of turbos open all the way, an elevator ride straight to the top, charging for the ceiling like a bat out of hell. He knew. He knew how it could eat you, seduce you, pull you in and fill you up. I can't explain what it feels like, Teyla. I don't have the right words. An interface like that — you own it and it owns you, like being one thing, one consciousness.

And so Dr. Weir decided she wanted me on the Atlantis Expedition, kind of a human lightswitch to deal with Ancient technology. She asked O'Neill for me, and I guess he figured it was her party. He must have had a look at my record, but maybe that didn't carry any weight with her. I don't know.

I almost didn't go. He tried to talk me into it. "I think anybody who doesn't want to walk through a Stargate is crazy." Sounded a lot like you, actually.

I flipped a coin.

It's how you decide when you don't care what the outcome is, when you figure why the hell not. Leave it to chance or fate or whatever. I flipped the coin and I waited a second, looking at my hand clasped against my wrist, wondering which one I wanted it to be. Stay, go back to Antarctica and fly in that quiet dream, go back to sleep and let the snow roll over me. Kind of a quiet life, actually. Stay stuck in grade until I've got my twenty years and then get out and do...something. Some kind of security work, maybe. Or be a private pilot for a corporation, flying guys like my dad from a meeting in Austin to a meeting in Tampa on their Lear Jet. That's not so bad, really.

Or walk through a Stargate. Take a one way trip to a place you know nothing about, a place that could be anything.

Most of these guys did it out of curiosity. They wanted to know something so much — these scientists and engineers and Dr. Weir most of all — that nothing else mattered. Rodney and Zelenka and the rest — they've got some balls. They signed up for this knowing they were probably going to get killed and they wouldn't even get a shot off at what took them down. Disease. Hostiles. Drowning in the gate room when the shield failed and the city died.

I did it on a coin toss. I watched it spin, and I knew which way I wanted it to fall.

Why the hell not?

He looked away, across the broad canal to the desert, shrugged.

"Do you miss it?" she asked quietly.

"Antarctica?" John stood against the side of the barge. "I don't know. Atlantis isn't exactly quiet." He looked at her sideways, the corner of his mouth twitching as though he would smile. "I guess I miss that a little bit."

"I meant your homeworld," Teyla said. "Earth. Your family, your friends."

His face stilled, but it didn't harden as it often did when someone talked about home. "I don't really have anybody to miss," he said, and his eyebrows drew together.

"You have no children, no sons and daughters?" It was

strange to think not. A man of his age ought to be the father of children well grown, daughters learning to hunt and sons to till the soil. Unless some tragedy had intervened. She hoped she had not touched on that.

"It was never the right time," he said, his eyes eliding from hers.

"Surely your mother…" Teyla began delicately. Every man has a mother who will miss him, who he will mumble for with his dying breath.

"My mom died a long time ago," he said. "Thirteen years. She died of breast cancer six years after the divorce, when I was stationed at Incirlik Air Force Base in Turkey." John looked out across the canal again, toward the fruit trees leaning toward the water on the other side, their branches almost touching their reflections in the stream. "That wasn't long after Desert Storm, and I was still overseas enforcing the no-fly zone. I was there a couple of years, actually, all through Desert Shield and Instant Thunder. I was gone the whole time she was sick."

"I am very sorry," Teyla said quietly. "I did not realize." She had thought they were different, these men from Earth with their medicines and their world of safety. She had thought they did not also stand in the shadows.

He shrugged but didn't take his eyes from the line of distant trees. "I was twenty five. It's not like I was a little kid."

"My father was taken by the Wraith when I was thirteen," she said. "But I think it is difficult to lose a parent at any age."

John shrugged again, putting the sunglasses back on. End of the conversation, Teyla thought. Though she had known John Sheppard more than a year she sometimes felt she knew him no better than she had the first day he came to Athos, the day he followed a coin toss through the blue fire of a gate.

Some kind of bird gyred in the distant sky, and she lifted her hand to watch it circle, hunting where the edge of green fields met desert. The wind blew across the canal freshened by the water, but still hot and dry. Hopefully along the coast there would be a sea breeze which would be somewhat more comfortable. I am getting spoiled by the Ancients' climate control, Teyla thought. Once I would not have missed air conditioning.

"I'm not much like her," he said out of the blue, expression unreadable in the sunglasses. "She was in way over her head about everything. My dad made a lot more money than she grew up with and she was always terrified she was going to make a mistake and embarrass everyone. She took tennis lessons and needlepoint lessons and did Jane Fonda and pretty much everything, but she always had this awkwardness, you know? Like she was some weird outsider in her own life. Like it was all an act and she was scared people would see through it. She loved us kids, though. She always wanted to protect us from everything. I think she'd have run through fire or lifted a car off us or one of those kinds of stories you hear on the news about regular suburban moms who beat off carjackers with their purse."

Teyla looked at him sideways, not chancing saying anything, as one does with a skittish animal who has finally trusted a little, waiting for him to go on.

"She kept her thoughts to herself, whatever she was thinking. She had this smile that wasn't right but you could never see behind it." John shifted from one foot to another with the slight motion of the barge as it began a gentle curve, the trees that came almost down to the water blocking the view ahead. "I don't think I ever really knew her." He glanced toward Teyla and shrugged.

Above on the upper deck of the barge there was a shout. As the canal straightened out of the curve again a body of water glistened ahead, a lake or a harbor, and beyond it was a city. White walls and white towers were stark in stone against an azure sky, massive square buildings and fortifications overlapping one behind the other, stretching as far left and right as one could see, the entirety studded with green trees. Beyond it, faint on the horizon, was the glittering line of the ocean.

"Pelagia?" Teyla asked, coming to stand at his side.

"Must be," John said. He shook his head. "It's enormous."

"Half a million people," Jitrine said with satisfaction, approaching across the deck. "There are half a million people in Pelagia under the rule of our King."

Teyla looked at John and she did not need him to speak to hear his thought. Why does the Wraith allow so many to live when they did not on Sateda, or anywhere else we have seen? What is wrong on this world? The forboding sank like ice in her heart.

"We will be there soon," Jitrine said. "And then we will see what can be done."

"Yeah," John said, but he sounded no happier than Teyla felt.

"There!" Rodney almost shouted in triumph as the gate whooshed open. "Got it!"

Major Lorne grinned, shading his eyes against the desert sun. "Great job, doc." The gate was operational again, and it had only taken Rodney the better part of a day to do it. After a nap in the shade repatterning the third crystal had been much easier. "I knew you'd get it done."

"Atlantis, this is McKay," Rodney said into his headset. "The gate is repaired. We're coming through."

Chuck's familiar voice sounded over the radio static. "We hear you," he said. "Dr. Weir's eager to talk to you."

"Let's go then," Lorne said, and a moment later they stepped through the event horizon into the Atlantis gateroom.

Elizabeth Weir hurried down the stairs to meet them, her brows knit together across her forehead. "Rodney! I was starting to worry."

Rodney spread his hands. "I can fix anything with time and the right equipment."

"Have you heard anything from Colonel Sheppard or the others?" she asked, looking from Rodney to Lorne and back again.

"Negative," Lorne said. "And that concerns me, ma'am. No hostiles, as far as we can tell, other than maybe some wildlife. But they've been gone twenty four hours. It's possible they've had an accident. They were going quite a ways north of our position, and they would have been out of radio range of the handsets."

"Or there could be interference at the Ancient ruins they were investigating," Rodney put in. "We've had that happen before. Messing up the radios."

"Still." Elizabeth frowned. "That might account for not reporting in for a few hours, but not a full day. If Colonel Sheppard couldn't get through with the radio he would have come back to report, even if they'd found something interesting enough to warrant staying to check it out. I think we have to conclude something's wrong." She looked at Lorne. "Major, get your backup team together. You're going back with Dr. Beckett and a jumper."

"And me," Rodney said. His forehead stung with sunburn. But Carson would have something for that.

Elizabeth's eyebrows rose in unison. "Rodney, you've just come in. You're probably dehydrated and…"

"Yes, I probably am," Rodney said flatly. "And I also know where I'm going, which Major Lorne does not. So once again I need to rise to the occasion and rescue Sheppard from whatever he's gotten himself into this time."

Major Lorne made a strangled sound, but when Rodney looked at him his face was composed.

"Give me half an hour," Rodney said. "I need to get some equipment together."

"Take your time," Lorne replied.

Rodney strode off toward his lab. Just like Sheppard and Zelenka to be in trouble investigating what had to be some very dull and ordinary ruins! Couldn't anyone manage without him for more than a few minutes? Really, how hard could that be?

CHAPTER NINE

"I AM NOT SURE it is supposed to be doing that," Radek shouted, holding on to a piece of rope as the sail stretched full and straining. The rope sung taut in his hands. It took leaning back on it with all his weight to hold on to it.

The fishing boat leaped over the waters, the rising wind of the approaching thunderstorm urging it on.

On the opposite side of the little boat, Ronon held onto the other rope apparently effortlessly, his head thrown back. "Probably not!" Ronon shouted back, a wide grin on his face. The speed and the movement sent his hair flying behind him, and he whooped like a boy.

Dark clouds piled up behind them, purple in the light of afternoon, the sun shining beneath them slantwise. Lightning crackled from point to point, illuminating the depths of the clouds. Thunder rolled across the water, loud and menacing.

"This does not look good!" Radek shouted over the rising wind. "I think the storm is getting closer!"

"What are we going to do? Stop?" Ronon yelled back. He grinned as the freshening wind tugged at him, like he thought this was nothing but a wild ride for fun.

"We do not know what we are doing!" Radek yelled. The rope bit into his hands, threatening to pull free. Or perhaps to just jerk him off his feet and deposit him in the ocean. Which did not seem like Radek's idea of a good time. He could swim, yes. But that did not mean he wanted to be lost in the middle of an ocean.

"Why do I go offworld?" he said to himself. "Why?" This was only his third trip, and it was beginning to look like it might be his last. Thunder rolled to punctuate the thought, even closer than before. The storm looked very big, and they very much did not know what they were doing with a sailboat.

Now would be a good time for Colonel Sheppard to show up with the jumper. Just about now. Surely any moment he would appear.

Afternoon had come and the buildings cast long shadows when the barge tied up at the dock in Pelagia. Up close, the city was even more impressive than it had been at a distance. Surrounded by sturdy walls close to fifty feet high, it boasted many buildings of four or five stories, broad streets paved with white stones, and a good many ships clustered around the docks. It looked very prosperous indeed, and more heavily populated than anything John had seen in the Pegasus Galaxy.

John was starting to get used to villages, to the kind of subsistence agriculture practiced only in the poorest countries of Earth. The Genii had a greater level of technology, as had the Hoffans, but he had not seen this level of population on either world.

As Tolas came down the steps from the upper deck, John moved to put himself in front of him. "We want to see the king," he said. "Teyla told you what we've got to offer. So let's talk."

Tolas didn't look disturbed. "You will see the king, of course," he said. "But one does not simply walk in and talk to the king. I will send word immediately that we are here, and then he will reply with an appointment that is convenient. In the meantime, we will be his guests."

John suppressed the desire to shake him. Did everything on this planet have to take forever? Strangers from an alien world ought to be an emergency! 'Get an appointment' sounded like the way the IOA would handle things. Gosh, it's nice you're here from another planet. Make an appointment.

Teyla glanced at him sideways, and he knew what she was thinking. She thought he popped off at the mouth, damaging diplomatic relationships before they even started. For that matter, that's what Elizabeth thought. She'd had a lot to say about it.

John made himself smile at Tolas. "We're happy to talk to the king whenever it's convenient for him," he said.

"Good," Tolas said, but he didn't smile. Instead he led the way off the barge and into the city.

It was further than it looked, maybe fifteen blocks in a regular city at home, but by the end of it John felt a little light-headed. He was getting pretty sick of this concussion. Back in Atlantis, Carson probably wouldn't have let him out of the infirmary yet. He'd be stuck watching the same shows twenty times on his laptop and complaining. That actually didn't sound so bad.

Teyla looked serene, if sweaty and tired. If her arm was bothering her it didn't show. He probably should be more concerned about it, even though she didn't say anything.

The palace was big. Really big. The columns in the first hall were three stories tall, and the walls and columns alike were painted with murals of flowers and trees, as though one had stepped into a painted forest. It was a pretty amazing effect, like walking through a series of pictures, animals and plants appearing at different distances as you moved. They turned left, into what might be guest quarters, another courtyard and stairs going up, four flights spiraling around the courtyard. He guessed important guests got the lower rooms, while random people who happened in got upstairs. Four flights was enough to make the vertigo come back. John concentrated on just putting one foot in front of the other. Not good. This concussion thing was starting to suck.

They stopped outside a door that opened on the landing over the courtyard, and one of Tolas' men pushed past them to open it. At least that's what John expected. Instead the guy grabbed for the 9mm in its holster.

He got John's elbow in his ribs, then a swift kick in the knees that knocked him down, the other guards crowding in with their spears. Teyla was taken by surprise, but it only took her a second to shake off the guard who'd tried to grab her and to be beside him in a fighting stance, their backs to the door.

"Hold, there," Tolas said mildly to his guards.

"What the hell is this about?" John demanded. "You said we were guests."

"I should have made it more clear that weapons were not allowed in the House of the King," Tolas said. "You will have your weapons back when you depart, but I cannot permit you to have them in this house."

"I'm not giving these to you," John said. "No way."

Tolas looked vaguely amused. "What are you planning to do? Fight your way out of the palace and city? I thought you wished to speak with the king. Surely most leaders do not allow strangers to come armed into their presence."

John could take them easily enough, even with nothing but the pistol. But then what? Tolas had a point. Even if these guys had never seen firearms before, which he was beginning to doubt, he couldn't stretch the shock and awe factor to getting out of the palace. Not with three clips and Teyla unarmed except for a hunting knife. They could probably call a couple of hundred men out if they needed to, in a place this size.

"They do not," Teyla said. "But you should ask for our weapons, not grab them. It is the kind of thing that breeds…misunderstandings."

"Your pardon," Tolas said. He held out his hand. "Your weapons?"

Teyla looked at John sideways, waiting for his cue. Was this going to be a fight or not?

Not. This wasn't the time for it, and starting something would sour any chance they had at a deal. Besides, Lorne and the rescue jumper would be showing up any second now.

Rodney must have dialed out hours and hours ago. Better to make that kind of stand with some firepower behind it if they needed to make it.

"Sure," he said, giving Tolas a charming grin. "Happy to." He handed over the pistol, butt first. Teyla passed over her hunting knife.

"Many thanks," Tolas said with a smile John hoped wasn't ironic. He gestured to the door. "Please make yourselves at home. I will go arrange an appointment with the king."

One of the guards, the one John had kicked good and hard, opened the door with a resentful look. There was something about the gesture that reminded John suddenly of a movie, of Lando Calrissian. Not good. The next line ought to be 'we would be honored if you joined us,' and then it would all go from bad to worse and probably end with him trapped in a block of carbonite, which never seemed like it would be a very fun experience. John and his friends had argued as kids over whether or not you knew what was going on while you were flash frozen in a block of stuff, and he'd argued for not. Because otherwise just seemed too awful.

On the other hand, that line of thought ended up with him getting rescued by Teyla, and he could think of worse...

She was looking at him doubtfully, waiting for him to either go in or not.

"Right," John said. "We're all good here." He ambled through the door hoping that his easy stance covered the tension. Teyla followed. And somehow he wasn't a bit surprised when the door shut behind them and he heard the bar put down.

"Why..." Teyla began.

John put his finger to his lips. "Over here," he said, leading her across the room from the door where their conversation wouldn't be heard. "We take them down, then what?"

Teyla looked at him, a tiny frown between her brows. "I agree, but it is not like you to be so prudent."

John glanced around the room. "Look, we're in no immediate danger. This thing keeps getting kicked upstairs, one guy after another throwing his weight around. By now Lorne's on the way with a team of Marines. We try something and it doesn't work and we've wasted our cards. It's better to bargain with a squad of Marines behind us."

Teyla looked concerned. "And your head is bothering you."

"I'm ok."

She shook her head, reaching up to check the bandage. "You are not. Or you would have tried something back there. Are you dizzy?"

"Just a little lightheaded," John admitted. "I'll be fine."

"You will rest," Teyla said. "In here where it is cool. I do not like you still being lightheaded. The sooner we get you to Dr. Beckett, the better." She steered him over to a chair by the window. "Sit."

It was, he thought, a pretty comfortable chair. And the view was nothing short of amazing. The fourth floor window looked out over the top of the walls to the harbor and sea, the roofs of houses and shops and the docks where lanteen sailed ships tied up, their hulls as bright as birds against the green sea. The breakwater was ornamented with fantastical turrets, and the ramparts of the wall featured emplacements for things John swore were ballistae. He'd seen a reconstruction of one once, and those looked like it. That was pretty advanced siege weaponry. He wondered who the enemy was that Pelagia stood in such a state of readiness and suspicion. Who was the enemy? Not the Wraith, surely. Ballistae wouldn't be much use against energy weapons.

The people of The Chora? Jitrine had said that there was tension over tribute, that The Chora was mad about the increase lately, resented having to send tribute to Pelagia. Was there an active rebellion? And if so, was Tolas the loyal stooge or the rebel? Was he playing his own game, with John and Teyla as pieces in it?

Teyla came and stood beside his chair, her eyes on the distant sea. "Something is wrong," she said.

"Tell me about it." The sheer curtains blew in a fresh sea breeze. It wasn't hot here, not with the wind blowing, and the desert kept the humidity low. If this were a resort, lots of people would pay good money for it.

"There is something going on," Teyla said. "And I do not think it is all about the Wraith. If it were, surely it would be obvious to them that we are not Wraith, and if they were certain we were enemies, why not kill us? They are not sure of something. But they are afraid."

"Yeah." John turned his head to catch the breeze on his neck and damp hair. "Those fortifications wouldn't stop the Wraith for five minutes. So who are they meant to stop?"

"I do not know, but we had best find out," she said. "Perhaps we can turn it to our advantage. Certainly these people seem to have plenty of food."

"Which is always an issue."

Even now that they had contact with Earth there were major issues of supply. It was quite simply impossible to supply a base the size of Atlantis with food brought by the Daedalus on her thirty-six day round trip, eighteen days out and eighteen days back. They could dial Earth, but Earth couldn't dial them, making resupply through the Stargate impossible. Therefore the bulk of their food had to be traded for locally, and it was a constant challenge finding people with enough of a surplus to trade who were also willing to trade with them. Teyla had been invaluable the last year in making the deals that kept them in supply, since she already had contacts and a measure of trust the team from Earth didn't have.

"If they have enemies…" Teyla began, and then let the sentence hang. He knew where it went. People with enemies wanted weapons, weapons more effective than ballistae and spears. A couple of guns wouldn't do much except whet their appetite for more.

"Yeah." John pulled the radio out of his pocket. It was still on standby, the battery low. Where the hell was Lorne? But it was a big planet. With no idea where they were, Lorne would have to take a broad search pattern. But even so, he'd probably been in the air for hours.

"Do you suppose Rodney had trouble with the gate?" Teyla asked.

Obviously her mind worked the same way. He'd been trying not to think about that option. "It's Rodney," John said. "He can fix a Stargate. And even if he didn't get the DHD working, Elizabeth could send Lorne and a team through from her end."

"True." Teyla frowned, putting the back of her hand to his forehead. "You do not feel feverish, but I am concerned about this dizziness."

"I'm fine," John insisted. "We just need to gather as much intel as we can and stay ready. It's not like we're chained up in a basement or something." He looked out the broad open window. Four stories up, but the stonework was rough with many possible handholds, and the top of the curtain wall wasn't far away. He could probably do it without much trouble. But Teyla would have a hard time with her injured shoulder. He bet it wouldn't take her weight. That was Plan B for certain.

"Yes," she said with an expression that looked like forcing her face to relax. "So we should make ourselves comfortable, and perhaps the king will see us soon."

CHAPTER TEN

RODNEY LOOKED at the assembled rescue team in horror. Major Lorne, of course. Lorne was ok. He was kind of growing on him, despite Rodney's general distaste for career military. Dr. Beckett, naturally. It seemed more than likely there had been some kind of emergency, so Carson was all kitted out in field uniform and flak vest rather than his usual lab coat. Six Marines, to provide some firepower. And Lt. Cadman.

Entirely logically, there was a perfectly good reason for Cadman to be there. She was, after all, a Marine. She was one of the Marines assigned to off world backup teams, which was how he had met disaster with her in the first place. Rodney had successfully dodged having to exchange more than a word with Laura Cadman the last few weeks, since Carson and Radek had succeeded in disentangling their brains, but the few days he had spent sharing a body with Cadman were seared into his consciousness forever. He put that up there with being captured by the Genii commander Kolya as possibly the worst experience of his life, one that he would never want to repeat. To be so completely, involuntarily, rawly *intimate* with someone, much less this cheerful, uninhibited woman of twenty three… It was just horrible.

And now she gave him a friendly smile, like they were cozy old friends. "Hi, Rodney."

"Cadman," he barked, glaring at Lorne, who looked oblivious.

"Are we ready?" Lorne asked.

"Ready as we'll ever be," Carson said, settling into the pilot's seat. With his ATA gene he was one of the pilots the jumpers responded to best, and after more than a year was actually getting comfortable with flying. Not that he was anywhere near as good as Sheppard, but Carson was becoming quite service-able, in Rodney's opinion.

He threw himself into the copilot's seat. From that van-tage point he wouldn't have to look at Cadman in the back. Maybe he could just pretend she wasn't here. Why couldn't Lorne have picked one of the other lieutenants for the team? Kroger or Kruger or whatever his name was? It's not like Cadman was the only Marine around. Ok, maybe she was better than Kroger, who as far as Rodney could tell had one setting — shoot it now. Cadman had a brain somewhere under that beret. Unfortunately he was too closely acquainted with Cadman's brain.

"Let's go," Lorne said, and Carson dialed the gate precisely, watching the event horizon open before them.

Elizabeth didn't say anything on the radio. There was a time not long ago when she'd have said something like "be careful" or "come back safe" but now that went without saying. Carson and Lorne wouldn't go looking for trouble. Trouble was more likely to find them.

Carson eased the indicators forward, and the puddle jumper leaped through the gate.

The seas were boiling. Not literally, of course. They were actually quite a comfortable temperature, neither cold enough to be hypothermic, or hot either. Radek thought he should know, since he had been continually soaked for the last hour. It was most unpleasant, but not nearly as unpleasant as it would be to be unceremoniously deposited in the sea. Which began to seem increasingly likely.

The little fishing boat ran before the wind. Or rather, the little fishing boat limped laboriously up waves that seemed entirely too large, while above the heavens split with lightning and the downpour soaked him to the skin. The bottom of the boat was awash, though Radek was not sure whether that was from the rain pouring down or the seawater sloshing over the sides. In either event, he was fairly sure it was not supposed to be there. Filling up with water was a bad sign in a boat.

Ronon was holding onto the sail, apparently keeping it attached to the mast by sheer physical strength, while Radek attempted to bail with a rusty bucket. A few liters of water went out, and a dozen came in. This was a battle he was losing. Still, this was a thunderstorm, not a hurricane. Perhaps they could last it out, stay ahead of the water long enough to gain a respite.

Which was more or less their entire strategy in the Pegasus Galaxy for the last year and a bit. Bail, and hope it stops raining.

Ronon bellowed something, but the wind tore away his words. Radek saw him silhouetted against sky and sea, braided hair slicked back now, holding onto the mast like some sort of pre-war engraving of Ulysses. He saw for a moment what Ronon must have been yelling about, a green dark wave rising behind them, no larger than ten or twelve feet tall, but enormous from the perspective of a small fishing boat wallowing low and half swamped.

"Shit," Radek said, and had time to take a deep breath.

And then the wave broke over them.

He struggled up through troubled water, kicking one shoe loose in the process, white foam coating the surface. He couldn't see. By some miracle, or perhaps because of the strap, he still had his glasses on but they were so streaked with sea water that he couldn't see anything but a vague impression of green sea, foam, and lowering sky.

"Ronon!" he yelled, and then took a breath as another wave climbed above him.

Relax, he thought. Remember, this is not the first time you have been in the sea. Ride the wave up to the crest and over, or dive through the crest before it breaks. Do not fight it. Do not waste your strength. Relax and go with it.

Radek stopped clawing at the water in an adrenaline fueled haze. Up and over. Try to get a look from the top. "Ronon!"

"Over here!"

He heard the shout back, but as he could not tell from which direction it came it was not as useful as that. Between his glasses and the perspective of being inches above the water, he had no idea where he was relative to Ronon.

Something brushed past his leg like a snake, and he recoiled. Surely not sharks, or hungry Pegasus Galaxy sea snakes?

It was a rope. It was a rope attached to a sail. Radek grabbed onto it, a spatter of rain hitting him full in the face. Up one wave and down the back side. Up and down. He kicked his other shoe off. Up and down, not fighting it. The rope was attached to a sail which dragged on the surface of the water, billowing out as though in unseen winds beneath the surface. Possibly the sail had torn away, or possibly it was still attached to the mast. Which was a big wooden thing that would float. That would be a useful thing to reach.

Radek followed the rope, only once getting a mouthful of water when he didn't see a wave breaking through his streaked glasses. Coughing, he let the water pull him along with the rope, along with the sail.

Yes, perfect. There was the dark smudge ahead, and he heard Ronon shout, though he could not make out the words.

"I am here!" Radek yelled back.

The sail was attached to the mast, which was underwater. The little fishing boat had capsized and floated hull up on the waves, buoyed no doubt by a pocket of air trapped beneath it. Radek let go and swam the last few meters, grabbing onto the rough wood of the hull gratefully.

"You ok?" Ronon was on the opposite side, holding on near the other end, but he made his way closer hand over hand along the hull. Radek was incredibly glad to see him.

"I'm fine," Radek said. He more or less was. No bruises, no

cuts, the water too warm for hypothermia. Other than drowning, his prospects were not bad. And finding the hull of the boat greatly increased his chances of staying afloat. He had read once that most people drown at sea when their strength simply gives out, after hours or days. With the boat to hold onto, things were better. They were less likely to drown immediately. And who knew what opportunities might arise?

"Good," Ronon said. He looked younger with his hair soaked, less certain and impervious than usual.

"We will just hold on," Radek said. "And surely they are already on the way with a puddle jumper." A thought occurred to him and he swore volubly. "The boat is capsized. We have lost my laptop." All his data. All his personal files. All sinking to the bottom of an alien sea.

"And our supplies," Ronon said grimly. Of course the backpacks were lost as well. Their food, their water…

There was a worse thought, but he could not put off voicing it. "And our radios," Radek said. Without the radios, how would the rescue team find them? They were two men adrift in a big sea, and the pilot would not even know where to look.

Night came, and the storm abated. It was no longer raining. That was a small mercy. The upended hull floated on calmer seas. Radek had managed to climb onto it, sitting on the hull rather than clinging to it, which required less energy.

Ronon held the side, despite all invitations to climb on too. "I'm too heavy," he said. "I'll tip it over."

Now, with the waves less jagged, Radek tried again. "It will not tip if you balance," he said. "You should save your strength. We will need it." He thought perhaps Ronon was abashed that strength had not been enough. It was all very well to be powerfully built, but that did not compensate actually for not knowing how to sail.

Gingerly, Ronon climbed on top, inching his way forward

to lie on the hull on his belly, just breathing for a long moment. Resting.

Radek tried once again to dry his glasses on his sopping wet shirt. It did make them less streaky. He looked up. The clouds were thinning somewhat. Through a break he could see stars. Not a bad storm, then. Just an afternoon thunderstorm of the sort that sent tourists running for the awnings of cafes, that made ship passengers cut short their jogs around promenade decks. If it had been a bad storm they would be dead. Rather than just adrift on an overturned hull, somewhere in the middle of an alien sea, with no supplies and no radios.

Still, this was an archipelago. There were other islands, and indications from the air had suggested they were populated. When the weather cleared and day came there might be other ships, or perhaps the currents would carry them close enough to another island to risk swimming.

He looked at Ronon, who rolled over on his back. He wondered if he looked that tired. Probably worse.

"It is your turn," he said.

"My turn for what?" Ronon looked up at the scudding clouds, the stars beyond.

"We must stay alert," Radek said. "It is your turn to tell me a story. I told you one."

Ronon snorted, and he thought he would not say anything. Radek drew his knees up, getting his feet out of the water. He was surprised when Ronon spoke.

My dad drowned. He was a soldier, an Immortal like me. It was the spring after I turned five. There were late snows in the mountains and then a hard spring rain. Everything flooded. Streams turned into rivers, carrying away houses and trees. The rail lines were cut above Euta when the bed washed out. Lots of people left homeless, lots of bad stuff.

The Chieftain declared an emergency and sent the army in

to help. My dad — he crawled out on a bridge. They were trying to do white water rescue, getting people out of this stream that was a hundred times bigger than usual, a family swept away in the current. The bridge washed out and collapsed.

They found his body the next day down at Hougma along with the people he was trying to save. They all died except one kid and the dog. Guess they were the lucky ones. Somebody always is, right?

I lived with my mom and my Nan in the city. There was a pool that people used in the summer time, but I didn't like it much. I wasn't really into swimming. I learned because you have to know how to swim to be an Immortal, and that's what I was going to do. Same thing with school. The Immortals only take the best. If you don't get good marks you don't get in. So I worked really hard. My mom wanted me to be a chemist or something instead, somebody who works in a lab or a hospital, not a soldier. But I would have had to find a lot of money for that, and I didn't really want to anyway.

When I was seventeen I became an Immortal. It was good. It was the thing I wanted, you know? Sometimes there's some- thing you're just right for and it all flows along, like water roll- ing down hill. When you're on and you're golden and you've got the right thing. That's what it was like.

That's what I was. That's what we were.

My Nan used to say that we live as long as we endure in the memory of our Kindred. If that's so, they're all here. Right here, in my chest. Sateda's here. We'll rise again. We have before. We know we've been laid low before, been plowed under like corpses in a field. But we come back. That's who we are. Sateda's strong. The Kindred are strong. It may not be in my lifetime. But it will happen. I'm sure. One day you'll see what we can do.

"We've got a problem!" Carson yelled just as the jumper jolted abruptly in the night sky. They had passed through the

Stargate without incident, climbing away from the desert cliffs around the DHD that Rodney could do without ever seeing again, high into the night sky. It was perfectly clear, the stars bright on a calm evening.

The puddle jumper shook, inertial dampers failing to compensate completely for some shock, and Rodney held onto his seat. "Why?" he yelled, pulling up the long range scanners. Surely somebody wasn't shooting at them.

Carson swore, and the jumper jolted again, a shower of sparks in the back arcing as something blew.

The scan was negative. They were alone in an empty sky.

Alone, except for…

"This planet has an energy shield!" Rodney shouted. "We've got to stay below it! If we get too close we're going to set off a feedback loop and it will start pulling power from us. Carson! We've got to get lower!"

"I can bloody well tell that!" Carson yelled back, struggling to control the jumper's dive. "I don't have much choice. Main power is offline!"

"Crap!" Rodney flung himself out of his chair, nearly bowling Lorne over in his beeline for the sparking control panels behind.

Secondary power, yes. That could be rerouted. They still had backup… Rodney popped the panel and started pulling crystals. The third one on the left needed to move and then…

The jumper jolted again, but it was a different kind of motion, less as though the ship had struck something and more as though it had jinked in the air, Carson struggling for control without main power. The puddle jumpers were by no means aerodynamic. They weren't meant for unpowered flight, even for a few seconds.

The crystals were hot, but he could move them with his finger tips… This. And this. Reroute the cloak's power into the main engines, and…

He seated the crystal and the jumper's inertial dampeners returned, the flight seeming completely level though he could see through the forward window that they were still plummeting. The engines came to life a second later. Rodney always found it disconcerting how you couldn't hear them, even when you knew they were only a few feet away on the other side of the hull. He could see the look of strain on Carson's face as the jumper pulled up, screaming by a scant few hundred feet above the desert.

"Bloody hell," Carson muttered. He leveled off, circling around. "Everybody all right back there?"

"We're good!" Cadman replied cheerfully. "Just a few bruises!"

"I'm going to land," Carson said. "I've got instrument fluctuations everywhere."

"Yes, and these patches are temporary," Rodney snapped, his eyes on the panel before him. He'd slapped together a reroute, but it wasn't going to hold for extended flight.

"Coming around then," Carson said.

The jumper made a wide, low turn, Carson steering clear of the cliffs and opting instead for a wide expanse of sand gleaming pale in the moonlight. The jumper settled down gracefully, only a few sparks jumping from the open panel. Not good, Rodney thought. Something else was shorted out and he was going to have to fix it.

Carson let out a huge sigh as the jumper touched down, sinking a few inches into the firm packed sand. "We're down," he said, and turned to Rodney, his face a mask of indignation. "What was that about? I've never seen anything like that. It was like hitting a wall in thin air."

"There's an energy shield," Rodney said. "Like the one we encountered on M32-3375. It protects the planet from the Wraith by basically interdicting any traffic in or out. When a ship tries to ascend or descend past a certain altitude it shorts out everything. It is like hitting a wall in the air. You'd better just be glad that you didn't run into it full on. It would have torn the ship apart. As long as we stay under it we should be fine, but the minute we got too close…"

"Could that be what happened to Colonel Sheppard?" Lorne asked from behind Rodney's seat.

"It very probably is," Rodney said testily. He should have thought of that earlier. "If he got too high he would have blown the main power in the jumper. Knowing Sheppard, he probably landed more or less in one piece. But unlike you, he does not have me aboard." Rodney stood up. "I have to run a full diagnostic and fix whatever it is that's smoking back there. Until that happens, this ship isn't flying anywhere."

Carson and Lorne exchanged a worried glance. "Fine with me, doc," Lorne said. "Let's make sure we're good before we get airborne again."

"But Colonel Sheppard had Dr. Zelenka with him," Carson said, ever the optimist. "He could fix the other jumper."

"Please," Rodney said. "It might have happened after he dropped Ronon and Zelenka off, and even if it didn't…" He stopped just short of pointing out how much more fortunate they were to have him than Zelenka, who admittedly wasn't bad, but was also not even in Rodney's league. "I've got work to do."

"Ok," Lorne said, walking into the back of the jumper. "We're grounded for now, people. Let's establish a perimeter and keep watch. We don't want any unexpected visitors while Dr. McKay fixes the jumper. We're all in one piece, thanks to the super flying of Dr. Beckett, so let's get out of the way and let them work."

Rodney heard them letting the back gate down, the voice of Lt. Cadman saying something as they went outside. He was all for establishing a perimeter. None of those jackals or whatever they were. He opened the panel behind, where there was still a thin trickle of smoke. He'd have to get the power to these circuits off before he started playing with them, and then see if any of the crystals were cracked from the heat. Once again everything was on him.

CHAPTER ELEVEN

THE LIGHTS OF PELAGIA were winking out, fires damped as people sought their beds, lamps extinguished. John and Teyla sat beside the broad window, looking out toward the sea. The hanging lamps in the room behind were unlit, giving them a better view without the backlight. Tolas had not returned.

Nor had Jitrine. Teyla had changed John's bandage herself. The cut looked long and nasty, the stitches dark with dried blood, but there was no redness of infection. Teyla had liberally smeared on her last packet of antibiotic cream and rewrapped it with the field dressing from her pocket before the sun set and she lost the light.

A short while before, the guards had opened the door to admit two servants with a tray of food, which they left on the table by the window. Her attempts to find out what was happening from them were fruitless. It was doubtful they even knew who Tolas was, much less whether he had spoken with the king.

Now they sat on either side of the table, poking at the remains of the food in a desultory fashion. There had been two wings of some sort of fowl roasted in a sweet sauce, a pottage of stewed grains and greens, bread, honey, and more of the ubiquitous fruit—a good meal, but not a spectacular one. Teyla thought this emphasized their uncertain status further. It was not what one would feed a prisoner, but given the level of wealth they'd already seen in the city, it was not fare for an honored guest either.

On the other hand, John did not seem to be fretting at the delay for once, and she said so.

He looked up from the bones he was picking at and shrugged. "Delay works for us. Lorne and Rodney will show up any minute. It's just as well if they turn up before we talk to the king. If he wants to wait until in the morning, that's probably in our favor."

"That is true," Teyla said, taking a long drink of cool water. "We do not know the reason why, if they know this world, the Wraith have left this city alone. But since they apparently have for centuries, it is unlikely that will change tonight."

John blinked. "You don't sense Wraith, do you?"

Teyla shook her head. "I do not. There are no Wraith close by, not within perhaps twenty or thirty miles. I am not certain what the range of my Gift is, but when there was a Wraith in Atlantis before the siege I had a very clear sense of him when he was entirely on the other side of the city. I would certainly know if there were Wraith within the palace or within Pelagia."

"That's good to know," John said. "Really good to know."

"I am certain," she said. "There are no Wraith close at hand."

John's eyes strayed again to the window, a slight crease between his brows. "I hope Ronon and Zelenka are ok. They should be, on the island. There was plenty of water and food. But with that Wraith cruiser around…"

"I know," Teyla said. "I am worried about them too."

"We are screwed," Radek said.

"Pretty much." Ronon's voice came out of the darkness from somewhere at the other end of the boat, which was to say about a meter away.

They lay on the upturned hull, which rose and fell in choppy seas. Above them the sky was clearing, bright stars appearing in unfamiliar constellations. Radek wondered which were the navigational stars in this world, which were the ones that men who knew anything about boats steered by. Unlike them, who knew nothing about boats. Perhaps this had been a little rash and foolish of him.

Radek sighed. "My father said I should come to a bad end if I did not stop being so impulsive."

Ronon snorted, something that might actually have been intended as a laugh. "What did you do that was impulsive?"

He sounded like he thought it was impossible, which rankled a little. "Perhaps going off to another galaxy full of creatures that eat men with no plan and no way to get home?"

There was a long silence. "Ok," Ronon said at last. "I'll give you that."

"Yes, you should," Radek said.

I heard about the Stargate years before I passed through it. It is super secret, super secure, but that does not mean there are not whispers. There always are. No matter how secret something is, there are whispers, unsubstantiated rumors, little hints here and there. I am good at putting together little hints. But I did not believe the reality of it. I thought it was a theoretical possibility, even maybe a project of the American military. I did not know there was a real, working Ancient device.

Ironically, I found that it was true not in any normal way, but through something that had no bearing at all. I had finished my doctorate at Cambridge in '97, but I did not immediately have a brilliant job waiting for me. I applied for many things, but none of the things came through by the end of the summer, and I must have work. I was offered a two month job in Paris, working for an old professor of mine who was engaged by the Louvre to take stock of some of the many things they had put away relating to the history of science. It was two months, and it was basically a glorified clerical job, but it was a paycheck and it was Paris, so I said why not?

The Louvre may be the world's greatest museum but its basements are crap. It is as though they just hauled everything down there for a century, then jumbled it up in the Second World War, and then let it sit for fifty years. My old professor was working

on a touring exhibition about the history of science, so my task
was to go through hundreds of documents and woodcuts and
engravings and minor pieces and documents donated to the
Louvre and pull out things that seemed to apply. There were
unsigned sketches of Montgolfier balloon ascensions and engravings of fanciful ice age animals based on the bones of wooly rhi-
nos found along the Danube. There were Hamiltonian obser-
vations of Mount Vesuvius and Leonardo's flying machines. It
was intriguing. It was interesting. I did not feel I was wasting
my time at all, unearthing all the starts false and true that we
have made.

And then I found it.

The sketch was by Vivant Denon, who had been the official
artist of Napoleon's Egyptian expedition. It was titled in his
flowing hand — "A rendering of the Strange Device discovered
in the Temples of Philae." It looked like a control panel, a round
pedestal of some kind of metal with broad keys on it, each key
inscribed with an unfamiliar symbol. In Denon's time, of course,
hieroglyphics had not yet been deciphered, so he had no way of
knowing these symbols were nothing Egyptian. But I knew it.

A later cataloguer, but not very late from the coppered ink,
had added "An Altar of Some Type?"

But it was not an altar. Denon had been right. It was a device.
He did not have the concept of a keyboard, but I did. This was
a keyboard in an unfamiliar system with unfamiliar symbols,
like nothing I had ever seen before. It was a round keyboard,
symbol keys and a blank in the middle. These were pushbut-
tons. It did something.

I dropped everything. I went seeking Denon's papers, his let-
ters, his work. If he sketched it, he might have written about it
as well. What I found was both brief and tantalizing.

"...a device that was perhaps an object of study in the
Renowned Museum, though it is far older in origin than the
Ptolemaic materials it was discovered with. I am perplexed as

to the metallurgy involved, as diamond cannot scratch the surface, and even hot iron does not seem to mar it..."

I am out of my field, I thought. This is not my study. But I was bored. I did not know people in Paris. I considered it an intellectual challenge. I tried to find more. Only there was little to find. A few tantalizing tidbits. Perhaps the device itself had once been stored in the Louvre, but if so it had been removed in 1941 with so many other treasures, removed to Berlin by the Nazis. If it had ever been here, a cautionary if. After the war no one knew anything of it. Perhaps it had been taken to the museum in Berlin. If so, like Schliemann's Trojan gold, it had been in turn a prize for Stalin.

Or perhaps it had never been in Paris at all. Perhaps it had been too heavy for Denon to recover with the limited resources of the expedition at the time, and had remained in Upper Egypt. Perhaps it was there still, on the island of Philae, or drowned beneath the spreading waters of Lake Nasser.

And then I was offered a job, a good one. I took it, I left Paris. But the mystery did not go away. Perhaps it was that my new job was boring, teaching first year students things older professors did not want to bother with. Perhaps it was that I had no research project of my own, but as winter turned into spring again I found myself looking at the photocopies I had made of the Denon sketch. Was I the only one who had found this odd? Was I the only one who had looked at this sketch in a century? Was I the only one who found this puzzle intriguing?

I found at last a précis of a paper that mentioned Denon and the mysterious device, a wild paper given at a historical conference in 1990 about aliens building the pyramids and ancient spacecraft in Egypt. It mentioned the line in Denon's diaries, but not the sketch. Had the author not known of the sketch? It might have made a tenuous line of reasoning more palatable. But perhaps he did not know, this Dr. Daniel Jackson.

It was difficult to find anything about him, but at last I got *an address for his current employer, somewhere in the western United States. I wrote to him asking him if he knew of the sketch, if he had considered the possibility that the device had been taken first to Berlin and then Moscow? I am a Doctor of Engineering, I said. I am not a historian like yourself. But I have found this interesting, and I wondered…*

A month later and I had forgotten. Then my telephone rang. It is Dr. Daniel Jackson, he said. I am in Paris by chance and I wondered if you might come by train and meet me. I would like to look at the Denon sketch with you, would like to meet you.

And I thought, why ever not? It is a spring weekend in Paris, and it is not so far on the train. If this Dr. Jackson is a nut, I will have dinner with him and then shove off. And if not, perhaps we will share this mystery. It will be enjoyable.

You can guess what it was, can you not, my friend?

Dr. Jackson bent over the sketch and let out a long, fervent breath. "It's the missing DHD from the Giza gate," he whispered. "They must have taken it away to make it harder for anyone to ever use it again, and it became a Ptolemaic donation at Philae. But the Ptolemaic scholars didn't know what to do with it, and they never found the Stargate." He caressed the old paper as though it were a lover's face. "The Germans must have found it in Upper Egypt in 1906."

"I think you had best explain what you just said to me," I said quietly.

Dr. Jackson looked at me, and his eyes were bright. "Dr. Zelenka, can you keep a secret?"

Most of the Marines had gone to sleep. Cadman and two men were keeping watch, patrolling in long circles around the grounded jumper, the beams of their flashlights sweeping the night. Lorne was sleeping. He'd been up all night the night before.

Of course, so had Rodney, but you didn't see him sleeping. Oh no. Rodney was running a final diagnostic on the jumper's main power. It would be a very bad thing if his repairs blew out as soon as they put any strain on them. And they were likely to put a strain on them. The way things usually went, there would certainly be a strain.

Rodney checked his watch. Five hours to fix it, about two am local time. Did Rodney ever sleep? Never. Rodney was up all one night and up all the next, because no one else could possibly do what Rodney did.

He went to the back of the jumper and looked out at the cool desert night, leaning on the doorframe tiredly. Right. Just a minute, and then he'd wake up Lorne and tell him they were ready to go.

"Are you ok?" Cadman asked softly, her P90 slung against her.

"Yes," Rodney said.

"You look really tired," Cadman said.

"Yes, of course I look really tired! I've been up for nearly 48 hours!" he snapped.

"I know," she said. "You're really persistent. I have to say that I respect that a lot, the way you stand by your friends." Cadman shrugged. "Like they stood by you when you and me… When we had that problem."

Rodney looked at her, wondering for a moment if she was making fun of him, but her eyes were entirely honest. "Thanks," he said. It wasn't like he got many compliments. Not from military and not from women. He expected her to be making fun of him, but she didn't look like it at all.

Cadman glanced at him sideways. "I guess we kind of got off to a bad start, huh?"

"You could call that a bad start," Rodney said. "But it might be the understatement of the year."

"I was actually trying to help you with Katie Brown," she said. "I mean, I know you really like her and it's not that you're a jerk. It's just that you're shy and you expect rejection."

Rodney blinked. "Did I ask you for psychoanalysis?" he managed.

"I bet you were the kind of guy who could never get a date in high school and college, which is a shame. You've got a lot going for you, under the surface." Cadman gave him an encouraging smile while Rodney stood there speechless. "Thinking about it now, maybe you thought I was trying to embarrass you or pick on you, and I just wanted you to know that I wasn't. I think you and Katie would make a great couple. And if you'd ever like any advice or anything, I'd be happy to."

"You're crazy," Rodney sputtered.

"Maybe it would help if I told Katie what happened and apologized?" Cadman said. "It's the least I can do. I'm really sorry if I screwed it up for you, Rodney."

"What, because she thinks I'm a mental case?" Rodney demanded. "Yes, that might screw it up just a little!"

"That was totally my fault," Cadman said. "I tell you what. When we get back, I'll go find Katie and explain. That way she'll know you're not schizophrenic or something."

She was probably making fun of him. She'd say she was going to do that, but it would turn out to be a big joke, and he'd think she was being nice but really she and Katie would be laughing at him behind his back. That's what always happened. You think a woman likes you, but she's really telling her friends what a fool you are, passing notes in the back of class and rolling her eyes.

But Cadman looked serious. If she was playing that game, she was really good at it.

"Sure," Rodney said shortly. "Whatever. When we get back. If we get back. I think I've got the jumper working again, but if we run into the cruiser we're screwed anyhow. It's got a lot more firepower than we do. But at least we can die in the air."

Cadman gave him a little smile. "Then I guess we're ready, huh?"

"Yes," Rodney said. "We're ready."

"Maybe you could take a little nap in the back of the jumper while we're on the way," she suggested.

"It's not that long a flight," Rodney said, but he had to admit it sounded appealing. While Cadman went outside to tell Lorne the repairs were finished, he sat down in the chair behind the pilot's seat. Maybe he could just close his eyes for a minute while Lorne herded cats.

He was asleep in thirty seconds.

CHAPTER TWELVE

IN THE COLD HOURS before dawn, Teyla woke. She thought she heard the quiet sound of the jumper's engine, but when she jolted to wakefulness it wasn't there. It was a long moment before she remembered where she was, and why there was not the breathing quiet of Atlantis' ventilation systems.

She was in Pelagia in the palace, and Atlantis was far away. The night was silent. There was the distant sound of a dog barking in the city, the rustling of the palm leaves in the garden below. Other than that, there was no sound.

John Sheppard stood beside the window, the moonlight gleaming off the white bandage on his brow, though his black shirt blended with the shadows. Whatever had wakened him, he did not perceive it as a threat. A threat would have showed in tension in every line of his body, in that questing expression he got, like a hound on a scent. Instead, he looked almost relaxed, leaning against the window frame, looking out into the night.

Teyla sat up, running her hands over her face to banish sleep from her eyes.

He looked around sheepishly. "I couldn't sleep," he said. His hair was mussed and the back was sticking up even more than usual. "For some reason it's kind of hard to settle down when you're not sure if you're a prisoner or not."

"You are worrying about Rodney and the rescue team," Teyla said.

"They would have been here by now if they weren't in trouble themselves," John said, shaking his head. "It's been thirty six hours. There's no way Elizabeth hasn't long since sent a team, whether Rodney dialed Atlantis or not."

"You think they ran into the Wraith cruiser?"

He replied, tight lipped. "It makes sense. I think the
in trouble."

Teyla nodded gravely. Of course he was imagining his people
in terrible danger, perhaps dying, while he was helpless to save
them. While he did not even know where they were.

"We're going to have to get ourselves out of this, and that's
going to involve making friends with these people," John said.
"There's no way we can get from here to the gate, a couple of
hundred miles of desert, with locals hunting us. And if the
others ran into the cruiser, we're going to have to get some
local help finding them. When we see this king, I'm going to
talk Atlantis up big."

"Make Elizabeth proud," Teyla said with a small smile.

"Yeah, that. I've seen men down in hostile country before."
He did not look at her, only out across the sleeping city. "If the
locals are against you, you're screwed. If they give you a hand,
you've got a chance of getting your people back."

Bits of things clicked together for Teyla. "And that is why
you love a good cup of tea."

"What?" he glanced around at her.

"You said it at our first meeting." Teyla sat crosslegged on
the bed. "When you came into our tents with Colonel Sumner.
He thought we were a waste of time, we Athosians. Too primitive to be of any use to him. And not worth the effort when I
said we did not trade with strangers. And you said that you
were not a stranger, that you liked Ferris wheels and things
that went very fast. So I asked if you would join us in a cup of
tea. I could see Sumner's disdain written all over him. And
you gave me a very strained smile and said you loved a good
cup of tea."

"Did I say that?" John turned around, leaning back on the
window. "I don't remember."

"You said that," she said.

"I guess I did." He shrugged. "Guys like Sumner, they don't

...gine that anyone would want to live dif-
...

..y, and that is the way of your people," she

"Nah. ...... the same way to people at home." John sat down on the windowsill. "There's one way, and it's the way of God and the United States Marine Corps. There are four kinds of people in the world — Marines, families of Marines, people not good enough to be Marines, and people who are too stupid to want to be Marines. I'm not saying all the Marines are like this. They're not. Ford wasn't. But you get these guys and they don't see anything else. They literally can't imagine any other kind of life. They don't know anything else they might do or be that would be worth anything. If you took away being a Marine they wouldn't be worth anything to themselves."

"You are not like that," Teyla said.

He shrugged again. "I'm Air Force, and it's a little different. But you get those guys in the Air Force too."

"Why are you not one of them?"

Teyla had expected he would ignore the question, but perhaps the darkness of the room and the lateness of the hour encouraged honesty. Or perhaps he was beginning to trust her a little bit.

"Never drank the Kool Aid, I guess."

There was this girl. That's a good way for the story to begin. There's always a girl, and that's always a reason. Her name was Mel, and she sat in front of him in Introduction to US/ Soviet Relations the first semester of sophomore year. She had short, short hair with a little ducktail in the back, and you could see the back of her neck when she bent her head to take notes, pale skin and that ducktail. Auburn hair, not really red. Blue, blue eyes. The kind of trim, athletic body that girls work really hard for, the body of a fencer. She was a fencer. He heard her talking about it with one of her friends. She was hoping to make the Varsity squad next year, she was that good. And that was saying something. There was a guy on the Varsity squad who was going to the Olympics in Seoul next summer unless he blew it.

Anyway, there was this girl, Mel. Melissa Hocken. He couldn't catch her eye in class and say something witty because he sat directly behind her. He couldn't sit next to her because she always sat with her friends. And there were about 200 people in the class because it was one of the big poli sci courses that fulfilled interdepartmental requirements.

John tried following her after class, trailing along with his backpack, hoping she'd go to the cafeteria or something. But it was a 9:00 class, and all he discovered was that she had a 11:00 in life sciences.

There was this girl, and that was really the start of it. That was really the reason, not anything else.

His mom called him on Monday night two weeks into the year, wanted to know if he'd come home that weekend. A long drive for almost nothing, even if she meant the house in Tahoe. "What for, Mom? You saw me two weeks ago."

"I need you to come this weekend, John," she said, and he thought her voice sounded funny, like she'd been crying. "I'll see you on Friday night."

And because it was his mom he went, even though he might have had plans. He didn't have plans, not yet, but he might have plans by Friday. Hell, he might have asked Mel out by then. Or at least talked to her. It was a theory anyhow.

He got into Tahoe late, nearly midnight. It was a seven hour drive. The lights were on and she was in the kitchen. It was spotless, tile topped counters scrubbed clean. "Where's Dad and David?" he asked, and she put her arms around him too tight.

"David's gone to bed. And I don't know where your father is."

John patted her awkwardly, let go. Something wrong, something wrong.

She held him at arms length, hair set in perfect waves, tipped and streaked just like Crystal Carrington on Dynasty. "Your father is divorcing me."

It was a really old story, not much to tell, actually. An affair, of course, but not with a bimbo like you'd expect. She was a torts attorney, thirty, brilliant, with a JD from Stanford and an undergrad from Harvard. They were going to get married. Linda was so much smarter, so much more of a go-getter. She wasn't some old fashioned boring type who played tennis at the club and supported the symphony. She was partner track.

And beautiful, of course. Sitting at the genuine antique mission table with its hand embroidered runner, hearing the whole story, John knew his mom wasn't beautiful. She kind of had been, in the wedding picture circa 1963, but that was twenty four years ago. She was fifty one, the same age as Dad. She dieted all the time, she did Jane Fonda, she used Esteé Lauder and she'd had a face lift last year. But she was dull, dull as old silver. He loved her anyway, because who wants their mom to be a blast? But she was dull. She mostly talked about tennis and wine tasting benefits for the symphony and what he and David were doing in school. She wouldn't know a tort if it bit her.

"He didn't want me to tell you. He wanted to do it himself. But I couldn't keep it from you boys."

David was fifteen. It would be hard to keep it from David, in the same house. Surely David already knew.

"It's going to be ok, mom. It'll be fine."

She gave him a brave smile. "Of course I will be. I haven't worked since we were married. He'll have to pay alimony, and I'll get one of the houses. This one, I hope, rather than the Austin house. And David…he's got to pay child support. And he'll pay it through the nose. It's you I'm worried about."

John just stared at her.

"You're nineteen. He doesn't owe you a thing. He has no legal obligation to pay for anything for you ever again."

There was this girl. That was what it was really about. Monday after class he walked up to Mel and said, "You were really smart, what you said about Prague Spring. I agree that our response should have been different, and it's a good idea to examine the difference in our reaction to Prague Spring from the Berlin Airlift in light of our commitment in Vietnam."

Mel looked at him suspiciously for a second, then put her head to the side. "Do I know you? Who are you?"

"John Sheppard," he said. "I sit behind you. That's probably why you don't see me. Because I'm behind you."

"Oh." She looked at him again as if he were some sort of interesting specimen. "You see what I mean about Johnson's political constraints?"

"Absolutely," John said. "I mean, this was totally about not wanting to tie the hands of the next president, and given the domestic situation at the time I'm not sure he could have made a military commitment to help the Czechs even if he wanted to."

"A constraint Truman didn't have."

"Right. Different time, different sitch. If it hadn't fallen apart right on top of the disastrous Democratic convention in Chicago…"

Mel was smiling at him. That was why he dared. "Do you want to get some lunch?"

"I have a class…" she said.

Duh. He already knew that. And it was ten in the morning. "I mean later. At lunchtime."

She shrugged. "Ok."

The thing with his Dad blew up at fall break. They were supposed to go skiing, but it was just him and David and Dad. Friday night they skied. It was ok. Nobody talked about anything.

Saturday they skied in the morning, and when they stopped to get lunch John went to take a shower to warm up. He put on a turtleneck and went to go meet Dad and David in the restaurant.

Only there was a woman there. She was pretty, with long brown hair like Brooke Shields, and she didn't look much older than him. She was sitting at the table, holding Dad's hand on the napkin. She'd never had a facelift, and she looked like a cat in cream in a leather coat and red velvet prairie skirt.

David looked sick. And also scared.

He came over to the table. His dad looked smug. "John, I'd like you to meet Linda."

She gave him a warm smile.

"So you're the bimbo," John said with a jaunty smile that didn't reach his eyes. "Congratulations. You've screwed your way into a lot of money."

His mom cried on the phone. "John, you can't do this."

"Mom…" Everything was like ice around him, a kind of cold fury that made everything cleaner and clearer.

"John, he's furious. You can't do this. You have your future to think about. Don't you understand that you have out of state tuition at UCLA? There's no way I can pay that out of the alimony. John, you have to behave."

She might as well have been talking to a block of wood.

He ran into Mel on Thursday, a day they didn't have class. He almost didn't recognize her. She was in Air Force uniform, tight skirt and jacket, sensible black heels, a cap pinned on her head.

"Woah, Mel!"

She came over. "I'm in ROTC. Thursday's drill day. We have to wear our uniforms all day."

"Dude." She looked like some old picture of a WAC or some-

thing out of World War II. Nobody could actually do anything dressed like that. Especially carrying her backpack in her left hand.

She saw where he looked and frowned. "We can't wear backpacks when we're in uniform. We have to carry them. Are you going to give me a hard time too, John? Because I've heard it all and I'm pretty tired of it."

"Me? No. Not me." He shook his head. "It's totally cool. I mean, whatever you want to do with your life…"

"Because I love killing babies," Mel said. "That's my big ambition. I want to go find some babies somewhere in the world to kill."

"I didn't say that!"

"Yeah, well, you looked it." She put her other hand on her hip and looked at him. "Just toss your liberal guilt right here. I'm totally responsible for Apartheid. And Colonialism. It was me. I did it all."

"You've got a chip on your shoulder," John observed.

"Yeah, well. You get asked stupid questions twenty times a day every Thursday. Try walking across the quad with people yelling Fascist at you."

"So why are you doing this?" This being the gesture at her circa 1965 outfit, little cap and all.

"Because I want to be an astronaut."

"Serious?"

"Serious."

He couldn't help but grin. "Like a real astronaut? Like Sally Ride and Judith Resnik?"

"Yeah." She grinned back. "And you know your stuff. Most guys couldn't name two female astronauts."

"Sally Ride, first American woman in space. Judith Resnik, killed with Challenger. Dude I'd like to meet is Michael Collins. And I'd pretty much pay an arm and a leg to meet Chuck Yeager."

Mel blinked at him. "I had no idea you knew anything about space. You're not…"

"A geek?"

"A geek." She grinned. "You look like a prep."

"I'm not a prep." John wasn't sure whether or not to be offended.

She looked him up and down, untucked button down shirt, rumpled khakis. "You're nineteen years old and you play golf. You're a prep."

"Ok, maybe so. But…"

"And you're a poli sci major. Geeks don't major in poli sci."

"It's for law school," John muttered. "It's one of the statistically best majors for admission."

"You want to be a lawyer?" Mel asked skeptically.

Nobody had ever asked him that before. He was surprised he knew the answer. "No."

Mel put her hand on her hip and looked at him. "Then why are you doing it?"

John shrugged. "I guess because my dad wants me to."

"And that matters a lot to you?"

"It kind of did."

November first there was no deposit into his bank account. $350 on the first of the month. That was the deal. It had been for the last year and a bit. The first. On the dot.

John walked away from the ATM, reading the slip over and over. He still had almost $200 in the account. With no beer and pizza he could manage until the end of the semester. He still had some money on his dining card.

And then what? The registrar expected $6,526 on January 4. Books were going to run a couple of hundred at least.

"I am so screwed," John Sheppard said to no one in particular.

Thanksgiving was pretty bleak. It was him and his mom and David at the Tahoe house. Dad had gone on a Panama

Canal transit cruise with Linda.

"You have to talk to your father," his mother said.

"I don't." John stared into the stuffing.

Her voice choked, and he looked up. "John, I don't have the tuition. I don't have it. Our joint accounts are frozen pending settlement. When I met with my lawyer on Monday he said your father says he's not going to pay it. That he's not going to pay for your school at all because of the way you're acting. And he doesn't have to. Don't you understand that? You're nineteen. He has no legal responsibility for you like he does for David."

John looked up. "He's treating you like crap."

"I don't want to hear that language at the table." She looked more like her old self when she said it, but with dark bags under her eyes where she wasn't bothering with the makeup.

"Mom, he's wrecked your life!"

She had always been frivolous. He'd always been kind of bored around her, since he got too big for kids' games. She wasn't interested in anything he cared about, and she was scared of skiing and hated golf. She couldn't have named two women astronauts on a bet. But there was a stark kind of dignity in her face. "That's already done, John. But I am trying to keep him from wrecking yours too."

He took a deep breath.

"If you have to drop out of college you won't be able to go back. Not for years. Lots of people say they're going part time and get a job, but it doesn't work, John. Things happen. Things come up. And they never finish. You have too much potential to waste that way. You have too much future."

He felt cold. "You're saying I should suck up to that..." He substituted an acceptable word to avoid a lecture. "Girlfriend of his for money."

His mother reached across the table and put her hand

over his. "I'm saying you should do whatever you need to do to get your tuition."

"Maybe you can get financial aid or something," Mel said.

"In the next six weeks?" John looked at her across a dining hall breakfast.

"Aren't there emergency loans?"

"Capped at $800," John said grimly. "I already looked. That would leave me with nearly six thousand dollars still to find."

Mel grimaced. "Out of state tuition?"

"Out of state tuition. My legal residence is in Nevada." He toyed with his scrambled eggs. "Aren't you paying it? I thought you were from Arizona."

"I'm on a full ROTC scholarship," Mel said, taking a long drink of her coffee. "My rich Uncle Sam is paying."

Maybe they would be better with more ketchup. "It takes two years to establish residency," John said. "So if I drop out and work, I'll be eligible for in state tuition in spring 1990. To get federal financial aid I have to be unclaimable on my dad's taxes for two years, so I'd be eligible in fall 1990."

"Two years out of school at least," Mel said. "Don't you have any rich relatives or something?"

"Other than my dad? No." John looked across at her jaunty little hat. "Maybe I should just drop out and enlist or something. It would answer the question of where I'm going to live in six weeks anyhow."

Mel shrugged. "You'd be better off trying for a ROTC scholarship."

"I thought you had to be a freshman and apply when you got into school."

She shook her head. "You can. That's what I did. But you can crash into the Professional Officers Course at the beginning of junior year. You have to do boot camp the summer before, but if they want you, you can get a scholarship then. Then you've got two years of the POC before graduation, keep your grades up and your nose clean, and you get your commission."

"What's the catch?"

"Four years active duty, ten years reserves. Minimum."

"And be an astronaut?"

Mel grinned. "Not likely. That's more of a mid-career move. With poli sci instead of a sciences degree you'd probably be a paper pusher."

"I'd rather be a fighter pilot." Four years of that didn't sound too bad.

She actually laughed. "Yeah, and I'd like to flap my arms really fast and fly around in circles! You have to get top marks on the AFOQT to even get qualified for TAC. That's tactical aircraft, the most desirable designation for a cadet. I'm TAC."

John raised an eyebrow. He'd thought she was sharp. "I thought girls couldn't fly fighter planes."

"Women can't fly them in combat situations. It's prohibited by Congress. But how long do you think that ban will last?" Mel looked at him over her coffee cup. "I'm twenty. It's not going to last my whole career."

"So can I take this test…thing?"

Her face sobered. "I don't know. They gave it in October. I'm not sure they're giving it again this semester. And we have to have our summer camp paperwork in by the beginning of break." She shrugged and put her cup down. "You could ask Lt. Col. Raymond. He's the detachment commander. I'll go with you if you want. It can't hurt to ask, can it?"

He sat in an empty classroom by himself the week before exams, listening to the clock tick, answering questions. After all the talk about it, John had thought it would be hard. But he was good with standardized tests, and some of the questions were really obvious. Ok, the military protocol ones weren't, because he hadn't been doing two years of this stuff like Mel had, but *the math and history and science were easy. And the situational questions were really totally obvious. He turned the paper in and went to catch Mel for lunch.*

"Ok?" she asked.

John slouched into a chair. "Yeah. It was just a test. I went in expecting the Kobayashi Maru."

"You are a geek," Mel said, unpinning her sandwich from the little frilled toothpicks.

"Yeah well."

"I mean that as a compliment," she said. "You have an inner geek. Underneath your preppish exterior."

"Thanks, I think."

"And you're brooding again."

"Sorry." He gave Mel a forced smile. "I was just thinking that even if this works I still have to figure something out about the spring semester. I'm betting this whole scholarship thing depends on being a full time student in good standing."

"Unfortunately, yes."

"So I'm still going to have to suck up." John closed his eyes. "Or just walk away."

"And who does that hurt?" she asked gently.

"My mom." He waited a second, a thought bubbling through. "Sucking up just hurts me."

"Then I think you know what to do," Mel said.

"Dad?" The phone connection sounded scratchy. No reason it should.

"John."

He swallowed. "I wanted to tell you I'm sorry."

There was a long pause. "That's not good enough."

"What?" John moistened his lips.

"I said that's not good enough," his dad said. "After the things you said to Linda. I'm sorry won't hack it."

He'd never considered this. He'd never imagined it. He was his dad's son, a chip off the old block. His dad had been proud of his grades, proud that he was good enough to play halfback in high school. They did stuff together. They were tight.

Something constricted in his chest. "Dad?"

"You called her a bimbo and a whore. You had the whole lodge listening while you called her a slut, a home wrecker and a high class call girl. She cried for days. She said she's never been so embarrassed and hurt in her life. I'm ashamed to call you my son."

"What the hell did you think would happen when you brought her there?" John choked.

"I wanted you to meet her. I wanted you and David to see what a wonderful person she was. I wanted you to understand why I love her."

"What about mom?"

There was a silence for a moment. "Your mom and I haven't had a lot in common for years."

"So what?" John demanded. "I mean, so she doesn't like to ski. You had to dump her because Linda likes to ski?"

"Your mom is a nice person," he said. "But she's pedestrian."

"Pedestrian?" From wherever it was he was talking from John could see his knuckles white on the receiver. "You've been married for twenty four years, and suddenly you decide she's not good enough? You've got to trade up?"

"It wasn't fulfilling me personally anymore, and that's the way it is. Your mom accepts that this marriage is over. You need to, too."

He couldn't say anything. He couldn't think what to say. There weren't any words in his head.

"Someday, John, you'll reach the point in your life where you realize that it's time to shake things up. That you've taken on responsibilities that are nothing but burdens. That you're not getting a good return on your investment."

"We're just bad investments to you."

"*You boys are good kids. But life's not about having kids. It's not that fulfilling for men. Motherhood may be some kind of biological imperative for women, but men don't really get anything out of it. You'll understand that someday.*"

"*I see.*" He was surprised his voice was perfectly even.

"*You will. You'll get it when you're forty. That's why I've told you to always use a rubber. Don't get some girl knocked up and get stuck with a burden you can't get rid of. Lots of girls are after bright young men.*"

"*Yeah.*"

"*I expect you know that already, right, John?*"

"*Oh yeah.*" As if. Why was it so freaking cold?

"*Listen, you come apologize to Linda. I want you to tell her how sorry you are, and I want you to make it good. And then if she agrees to it, I'll pay your spring tuition. That's what this is about, isn't it?*"

He didn't answer.

His dad chuckled. "*Chip off the old block, John. You've got a hard nose, just like your old man. You'll grovel and beg if it will get you the dime. Don't blame you. It's smart. It's always smart to show your neck when you're the beta dog.*"

"*When do you want me to come?*"

"*Day after Christmas? Think you can drive to Sundance? Linda and I are planning Christmas on the slopes.*"

"Sure," John said. The weather might be bad. But he'd have to go anyhow. It couldn't be that bad. "*I'll see you, Dad.*"

"Knock, knock."

John looked up from where he sat on the floor of his room, surrounded by coursepacks.

Mel stood in the doorway wearing a little black sweater. "You busy?"

"Studying."

"I see that." She came in and shut the door behind her, came and sat down on the floor, moving papers around to make room. She held out a package. "I brought you a Christmas present."

It looked pretty big, wrapped up in red paper with holly leaves on it. "Bruce Springsteen and the E Street Band Live, the complete collection? Oh man, I've been wanting this so much!" For a moment that was the only thing on his mind, how great the present was. And then... "I didn't get you anything."

Mel shrugged. "I figured. You can't afford it right now, not knowing whether you'll even be here next semester. Don't worry about it. I just thought it might cheer you up."

"It's great, Mel. It's just what I wanted and I didn't think I should get it because... But it's just what I wanted. There's some great stuff on here. Really great."

She smiled and leaned over, turning the LP boxed set. "I thought you'd like the live versions. I know you've got a bunch of albums, but this is really complete." She was sitting right next to him, and when she leaned forward he could see the edge of her bra, the slight rounding of her breasts.

"You're really great," he said. John took a deep breath. "You're kind of my best friend right now."

She looked thoughtful. "You're a really good friend too, John."

"I was wondering..."

"Wondering what?"

His shoulder touched hers, and it was just a turn of the head to kiss her, to feel her all warm and soft and startled. Curious. Assessing.

And then she drew away, a sad expression on her face.

"What's the matter?" he asked. "Did I do something wrong?"

Mel shut her eyes and when she opened them again he thought he saw tears there. "I can't."

"Why not?"

"I didn't know that you... I thought we were just friends and

I didn't mean to make you think that…"

"What's the matter? Is it somebody else?" She'd never said anything about a boyfriend. Maybe she had a boyfriend back in Arizona. Maybe she was having this long distance thing and she'd just never mentioned it and …

Mel took a deep breath. She looked like he thought he had on the phone with his father. "I don't want you to hate me."

"I won't hate you," he said. "I mean, if there's some guy in Arizona or at another school…"

"I'm only into girls." Her face was white.

"Oh." He opened his mouth and shut it again. "But you don't do lesbian things. I mean I don't see you hanging around with the student group or taking women's studies or…" He ran out of things that he thought lesbians might do.

"Because I'm in the Air Force!" Mel shouted at him. "John, do you have no sense? Do you have any idea what would happen if I got caught?"

"You'd lose your scholarship? A dishonorable discharge?"

Mel grabbed his hand and squeezed. "Having to repay four years out of state tuition is least of my worries. Try two years in Fort Leavenworth as a sex offender for crimes against nature. It's a prison sentence, John. If you actually get caught after commissioning."

"Then why the hell are you doing this? This is California…" There were a lot of lesbians in California. That kind of went without saying.

"Because I want to be an astronaut. And the way to be an astronaut is through the Air Force. I want to be an astronaut more than anything else in the world, and nothing is going to stop me from getting there." Her voice was low and intense. "I'm TAC. I'm good. And I'm going to make it." Mel blinked. "And now I've told you. I've put it all in your hands. I never tell anybody."

"I'm not going to tell anybody," John said.

She looked at him, and there was something familiar in that quirk of her mouth, an expression he'd seen in the mirror. "Good way to get back at me for turning you down."

"I'd never do that. I'm your friend."

"Seriously?"

"No, never." He patted her hand awkwardly. "Never. I promise. I'll never tell anybody. We're friends. Friends stick together. There's got to be something in life you can count on."

"Yeah."

Mel still looked like she was going to cry, and he hugged her. Not you know, boyfriend hug. Just friend hug. "You can count on me."

"I do," she said. She saw something in the papers around her, reached for it as he let go. "What's that?"

"Oh. My scores." He would have taken it, but she'd already opened the envelope.

"Jesus, John." Mel unfolded it, skimming all of it. "You're in the 99th percentile on the AFOQT. Do you have any idea how rare that it?"

"It means 99 guys out of a hundred do worse," he said.

"It means you're going to get approved for camp," Mel said. "Lt. Col. Raymond will take you for sure. You'll get a scholarship next fall if you want it. It means you might get rated TAC."

"It's kind of cool, isn't it?"

Mel looked at him keenly. "It hasn't sunk in, has it? With all the shit you've got going on?"

"I guess not."

"This is the last time you grovel," she said. "You go make nice this semester, and you'll never have to grovel to your dad again. You won't have to worry about paying for school, and you'll have a job when you graduate. You can tell him off if you want to. Like, in May."

"Yeah." It ought to make him feel better, but it didn't.

"And you'll be twenty in May, right? It's not like you're a kid. He can't do anything about it."

"Yeah." That would feel good in May, probably. It just seemed like a lifetime away. A lot further than the day after Christmas.

Mel put the paper in her lap, took his hands. "Look, John. We all make compromises with life. We have to. I have to suck it up and not date if I want to be an astronaut. And you have to suck it up and deal with your dad one more semester. Or we can walk away. That's the choice. We can walk. But you and me, I think we'd rather fly."

CHAPTER THIRTEEN

DAWN WAS COMING over the sea. Radek thought perhaps it was the slowest dawn he'd ever seen in his life. He had seen dawn many times, studying through the night for an early morning exam to sleep in the afternoon, in a bar with friends laughing or crying over the day's events, working all night to repair fried circuits while Atlantis' dawn came up pearl soft, even dawn after a night spent in love. But he had never seen dawn take so long to come as it did clinging to an overturned fishing boat in the midst of an alien sea.

Ronon was silent. Perhaps he'd gone to sleep. Radek could see his chest rising and falling in the dim light, and it was hardly cold enough for Ronon to be succumbing to hypothermia.

At last the sun rose out of the sea, a sliver of unbearable brightness sliding over the horizon, preceded by the pink and azure shades of dawn. This was why the ancients had sung praises of the sun, Radek thought. After a night as long as this, he felt like bursting into hymns himself.

Ronon stirred, one hand dipping over the side into the water. He sat up abruptly, flailing as he woke, and Radek held on tight.

"Don't move so quickly!" he said. The last thing they needed was to somehow sink their frail refuge.

Ronon grabbed on, centering himself on the hull. "Shit." The word encompassed a world of disappointment.

"Yes, we are still lost at sea. No, I have not seen a rescue jumper. No, I have not seen anybody," Radek said.

"Right." Ronon blinked, looking east into the dawn.

"They will be looking for us by now. But we do not have the radios. Fortunately it is clear and if they fly low enough they may see us."

Perhaps leaving the island had been…precipitous. Perhaps it would have been better to stay where the rescue team might reasonably have looked for them. But of course they had not meant to lose the radios. And caution had never been his strong suit.

"Yeah." Ronon considered. "I wonder if we can turn the boat over."

"We can try," Radek said. It was clear and the seas were calm. If they could flip the hull, perhaps they could have something like a working boat again. The waterlogged boat would be heavy, but Ronon was strong.

"Let's give it a go," Ronon said, and slid off the hull into the water beside.

"Ok." Radek slid off on the same side. The water was colder than yesterday, but not chill. The storm, no doubt. A thermal layer of cold rainwater that would last until the sun warmed it.

Ronon treaded water holding onto the side of the boat. "Ok, when I say lift, lift. Let's see if we can flip it over. Lift!"

Radek lifted. It didn't seem to make much difference. He could not lift higher than his chest without even the ground to push against.

They put it down and considered.

"Let me try something," Ronon said. "Can you let go and just swim a minute?"

"Of course," Radek said. He did.

Ronon took a deep breath, then pushed himself down underwater, letting go of the side of the boat. For a long moment he vanished beneath the waves.

Then one hand appeared, grasping at the side of the boat in a strong grip, though Radek didn't see the rest of him anywhere. It suddenly occurred to him that Ronon had come up under the boat.

With a massive heave, the side of the boat rose from the surface, flipping in the other direction as Ronon let go. Wallowing, it came to rest right side up. Ronon surfaced beside it, flipping the water out of his long braids.

"Fantastic!" Radek exclaimed. "You are Hercules, my friend!"

"Whoever," Ronon said, and swam the couple of lengths to the side. "Let's start bailing." The boat was half full of water, but with the seas calm surely they could bail it clear if they...

"Do we have anything to bail with?"

Ronon pulled himself over the side and pulled up the rusty bucket secured to the boat with a length of sodden rope. "Yes."

Radek swam over to the side, and Ronon reached down to help him aboard. "Perfect. Our luck has changed!"

They began bailing, and Radek considered how much better the world looked from the right side of the boat. Infinitely better. They might still be lost in the middle of an alien sea, but at least they were no longer swimming. They might get out of this yet, turn this into the kind of story that someday no one would believe. *Once I was shipwrecked with this friend of mine in a storm at night...* No one will credit it, but he would tell it anyway.

"They're not here," Lorne said.

Rodney fought his way up from strange unsettled dreams, and for a moment he couldn't remember where he was. Asleep. In the jumper. With early morning sunlight glancing off the front window. The tail gate was down, and he could hear people moving around while a cool sea breeze played around the corners of the seats.

"Dr. McKay?" Lorne shook his shoulder gently. "They're not here. We've looked all over the area around the Ancient ruins. There's no sign of them now. They were here a while ago, we think. We found some footprints and places where the grass was compressed from someone sitting or crouching, but there's nobody around at all. I've sent Cadman and a team down to the village at the other end of the island in case they went looking for food and they're hanging around down there."

"Zelenka and Ronon aren't here?" Rodney felt he was being a little slow on the uptake.

"No," Lorne said again patiently. "They're not here now." He looked at Rodney with an expression Rodney thought was almost kind. "We let you sleep while we looked around since you'd been up all night. They might have gone down to the village. Cadman's checking it out, like I said."

"You let Cadman check it out?" For some reason that sounded alarming to Rodney.

Lorne stiffened. "Look, Cadman's a good kid. Don't give her a rough time for something that wasn't her fault."

"I wasn't. I…"

"Good," Lorne said. "She's a good kid, and she'll make contact without shooting up the place. I like that."

"Yes, of course." Rodney felt himself perilously close to turning red. It was true that what had happened hadn't been Cadman's fault. She hadn't asked to be sucked up by that Wraith Dart anymore than he had. It wasn't her fault they'd been stuck sharing a body for three days while Zelenka tried to figure out how to fix it. If it was anybody's fault it was Zelenka's. Three days to reverse engineer a Wraith culling beam? He could have done it in two, if he hadn't had Cadman in his head. But if he hadn't had Cadman in his head, they wouldn't have needed to do it.

"There's no sign of hostiles or any kind of action," Lorne said. "No casings, no bullet scrapes on the walls. Ronon wouldn't go down without a fight. I'm guessing that Zelenka and Ronon got sick of waiting around and left. We just need to figure out where they went."

"The lifesign detector isn't much use," Rodney mused. "The

planet's full of humans whose lifesigns are indistinguishable from ours."

"We've been making radio calls periodically," Lorne said. "No answer yet. If we need to, we can fly a search pattern making calls, but that's going to take a while. It's a big planet."

"And it's better to pick up Zelenka and Ronon before we start hunting for Sheppard," Rodney said. "I get that. Especially since with the other jumper Sheppard could be anywhere."

"That's what I was thinking," Lorne said. He gave Rodney's shoulder a squeeze. "You did your bit fixing the jumper, doc. This is my bit."

Rodney nodded. Coffee would clear his head, but there wasn't any, and a few hours sleep had left him bleary. Just as well to sit still for a few minutes. There was no need to jump up and run around until Cadman got back from walking however far it was to the village and back. More waste of time, as the jumper could have had her there in moments. But perhaps it would intimidate the villagers the way Cadman on foot wouldn't.

Lorne sank down into the pilot's seat. He looked out the windscreen at the Ancient ruins and the pristine sky with something like satisfaction. "There's some pretty keen stuff around here."

"If you like alien planets and being shot at," Rodney said.

Lorne shrugged. "I came here from the SGC, doc. I've seen my share of alien planets and been shot at before. I was on P3X-403 when we had that little problem with the Unas." He leaned back in the seat. "This isn't all that different, except you never get to go home at night and have a beer."

"Yes, that would be a big difference," Rodney said sharply. "I was at the SGC too. It's entirely different."

Lorne cocked his eyebrows at him. "Yeah, but I hear you were a lab rat at the SGC. You weren't on a gate team."

"If by lab rat you mean scientist," Rodney began.

Lorne grinned. "By the way, what's the story about you and Lt. Colonel Carter?"

"Carter?" Rodney gulped.

"I heard you had some big thing going on."

"Oh, that thing." Rodney leaned back in his chair, assuming what he liked to think of as a worldly slouch. "Well, you know. Long distance relationships are hard to make work." He put his head back against the head rest and gave Lorne a mysterious smile. "Sam is certainly hot. And she's got those gorgeous eyes. But you know how it is. Duty calls. The Atlantis Expedition needed me."

"Oh." Lorne looked momentarily confused. "I thought she hated your guts and said she hoped you were transferred to Siberia."

"She said that?" Rodney sat upright abruptly. "No no no. She did not. It's just that our working relationship was fraught with unresolved sexual tension. It's kind of perverse, really, that her admiration for my professional acumen was seasoned both by jealousy and desire."

"I thought she said you were a jerk and Atlantis could have you."

"Obviously Sam has very strong feelings about me," Rodney said with dignity. "And I think that out of regard for her privacy we should probably stop discussing them."

"Ok." Lorne still looked confused. "Just asking. You hear all kinds of things at the SGC, and if ten percent of them were true…"

"If ten percent of them were true, every gate team would be an orgy to go," Rodney said. "And I'm here to tell you it's not."

"My team is three Marines," Lorne said. "I don't really think we're in orgy territory."

Out the front of the windscreen they saw Cadman emerge

from the trees, walking quickly toward the jumper.

Lorne got to his feet, and Rodney heard his footsteps on the metal decking in the back of the ship. "What's the story?"

Perhaps, Radek thought, they might survive this. Perhaps they might even get this well in hand. They were in a boat that was right side up, with the sodden and torn sail spread out over it to dry in the sun, and had daylight and calm seas. They had no water, and by now Radek was beginning to get thirsty, but it was not quite yet a pressing problem. Surely many of the heroes of literature had been in similar and worse positions. Edmond Dantes, for example. He had gotten out of a situation very like this one. Only Radek could not quite remember how. He had read the book so long ago.

Ronon shaded his eyes with his hand. Radek couldn't see what he might be looking at even with his glasses. "What do you see?" he asked.

Ronon squinted. "Shadow on the horizon. Might be an island."

"That would be good, yes?"

"Yeah, except for the no way to get over there part," Ronon said. "No oars, and the sail's not dry enough to get up yet."

"It will dry soon, surely. And then we can raise it again somehow."

"The sea's running pretty strong still," Ronon said. "It's hard to tell, but I think we're being pulled pretty much west at a good speed. We're going to wind up a whole lot north of where we intended."

"There is nothing for that, is there?" Radek said. "Once we have the sail to give us speed for steerage, then we can try to use the rudder. But the sail will not dry faster than it will." He looked at Ronon over the top of his glasses. "This is an exercise in frustration, yes?"

"Yes."

"Someday we will laugh about this," Radek said.

"It isn't funny."

"You know what I mean." Radek shrugged and shaded his eyes as well, looking off to the west. He could see nothing. Haze blurred into distance.

"It means you laugh at things that aren't funny," Ronon said.

"Sometimes one must laugh," Radek said. "Don't you ever laugh at yourself?"

"I'm not funny."

Radek put his head to the side, not quite certain if Ronon was putting him on or not. "Perhaps you are not," he said. "But don't funny things ever happen to you?"

"No," Ronon said flatly.

Perhaps they did not. There was very little in seven years as a runner that any sane person could find funny. Maybe Ronon's sense of humor was dead with all the rest of it. And yet he had thought he had heard, in the story in the dark, a different man than the dour one who sat before him. Once he had been a young man, fervent and generous, and perhaps that person lived in him still. He had been only a few weeks in Atlantis. Perhaps the man he had once been was not dead, but only buried within the man he had become.

"Do you like adventure books?" Radek asked.

Ronon looked at him, glancing away from the horizon. "Why?"

"There is a book you might like. I will loan it to you when we get back. I think it will appeal to you."

He thought Ronon might snort, but instead he shoved his hair back out of his face in the freshening wind. "What's it about?"

"It's about a man who is sent to prison for eleven years for a crime he did not commit, accused by his faithless friends. And it's about how he escapes from prison and gets revenge on them."

Ronon's eyebrows rose. "Is there fighting?"

"Quite a lot," Radek said. "And there is an honor duel. And pirates. And bandits. And a beautiful woman. And a treasure."

"Ok," Ronon said.

It took Radek a moment to realize what he meant. "Ok, you'd like the book?"

"Yeah." Ronon lifted his hand to his eyes again. "That sounds pretty good."

"Then, my friend, when we get back I shall introduce you to the Count of Monte Cristo," Radek said triumphantly. "There is even a point in it where he is lost at sea, just as we are now."

"How'd he get out of it?" Ronon asked.

Radek twisted around, something in the opposite direction catching his eye. "He was rescued by a passing ship. Just like that one over there! Look!"

Ronon spun about. To the east there was a distant sail spread white against the hot horizon, a fairly large one it seemed, though it was still quite some distance away.

Radek cheered and nearly made the mistake of jumping up and down.

"Help me get the sail up," Ronon shouted. "Even if it won't move us, they'll see it!"

"And we will be saved!" Radek yelled, grabbing armloads of the sodden canvas. Literature always prevails in the end.

"They don't know anything about them, sir," Lt. Cadman said, her back stiff as she made her report to Major Lorne. "None of the villagers have seen them. No strangers, no aircraft, nothing. I don't think they're lying, Major. They were almost worshipful when they saw us. I think if they had seen Ronon Dex and Dr. Zelenka they would have told us. Also, everything seemed fine. If they'd gotten into a fight with Ronon you'd think he would have done some damage."

Lorne nodded slowly. "That's true. He would have."

"Then where are they?" Rodney demanded.

"I don't know either!" Cadman snapped. "I can tell you where they aren't."

"Like that does any good!"

"People." Lorne held up a hand. "If they're not here, and they're not at the village, then somehow they left the island. Either Colonel Sheppard picked them up in the jumper before whatever it was happened to him, or they left another way."

"There is no other way!" Rodney said.

Lorne's voice was patient. "It's an island, Dr. McKay. Cadman, go see if the villagers are missing any boats or if there have been any ships calling at the island in the last day or so. If they didn't leave by air, they left by sea."

"Yes, sir." Cadman turned smartly and started off with her detachment again, back through the underbrush toward the village.

"A boat?" Rodney said. "Do they know how to sail a boat?"

"I don't know that, do I?" Lorne said quietly. "For all I know, Ronon was the Sailing Champ of Sateda and Dr. Zelenka used to go boating every weekend. Or maybe they hitched a ride with someone. If a ship called at the island, maybe they bartered for passage back to the mainland. That would be a really sensible thing for them to do, and the people who talked to them wouldn't be here for us to ask about it. We need to find out, not jump to conclusions."

"Ok," Rodney said. He felt pulled up short by Lorne's calm. Off kilter. He was definitely off kilter. Which probably had a lot to do with I'm-In-Your-Brain-Knowing-Your-Innermost-Thoughts Cadman.

"And we don't know that Sheppard didn't swing back and pick them up before he ran into the energy shield or whatever happened. He could have. Which is probably what happened if we don't find out they left by sea."

"And then?"

"Then we start flying a search pattern while you call them on the radio," Lorne said. "We'll find them. Even if the jumper ditched at sea, we can still latch on to the electrical traces. But it's a big planet and without knowing where they were, it's going to take us a while. So let's take this one step at a time and be methodical." He gave Rodney an encouraging smile. "Scientific."

"Right," Rodney said. That should sound comforting, but somehow it didn't.

CHAPTER FOURTEEN

TEYLA WOKE to the bolt on the door being drawn back and was on her feet before it opened. John stood by the table and, while he made no sudden move, she saw his feet shift quietly into a guard position. A chair was not a bad weapon under the circumstances, if such became necessary.

Unsurprisingly, it was Tolas.

"Let me guess," John said. "The King will see us now."

"No." Tolas looked serious, as though he hadn't realized that might have been supposed to be funny. "The King acknowledges that your visit is important, but he is unable to meet with visitors during the Great Festival of Renewal."

"Oh for the love of…" John started.

"We understand that there are times and places that are inappropriate," Teyla said swiftly. "How long is this festival and when will the King meet with us?"

"It is three days," Tolas said, "And the King already left last night for the Holy Island."

John rolled his eyes. "Just like us to get here on a holiday weekend when all the bigwigs are out of town."

"It is three days to play the Games of Life," Tolas said. "It is our most sacred festival, celebrating our compact with the gods. The High King will be there, as will our King Anados, and all the other kings of the world. Together they will renew their oaths of peace and friendship to one another, and their fealty to the High King. Together they will celebrate the Gift of Life that the gods bestow upon us."

"Some kind of Olympics?" John looked sideways at her. "Ok, so a big festival and all the brass there."

"All of the kings will be present," Tolas confirmed. "There to renew their vows of brotherhood and to present their lands' tribute to the High King. It is he who governs the world, and it is to him you should appeal if you do, as you say, represent another world entirely. The High King, the representative of the gods themselves, is the one who has the authority to treat with you. If our King Anados did hear and approve your requests, you would still have to make them again to the High King. So it seems best to me to send you along to the Holy Island where the gods dwell, that you might without delay make your pleas to the High King and all the kings assembled in pious celebration of the Games of Life."

"Cutting out the middle man," John said. "Fine. We'll go talk directly to the High King. But how are we supposed to get there?"

"Fortunately, the tribute ship has not yet sailed," Tolas said smoothly. "I have had it held in the harbor pending your arrival. It will not even be a full day's journey to the Holy Island, and you will travel in all comfort as passengers on the tribute ship."

"We have only the greatest thanks for your consideration of our comfort," Teyla said diplomatically.

"That sounds super," John said with a friendly smile, but she thought there was something in his tone that didn't exactly match his words. Maybe she imagined it, as he seemed all affability and charm. Or perhaps that was the problem in itself. When he smiled that way something was badly wrong. She had seen that smile before. "Shall we get started?"

It was the work of a moment to gather up their jackets and a few other small things. They followed Tolas and his careful honor guard through the corridors of the palace and across the wide plaza that separated the palace from the city. John said nothing, though she could see from his watchful stance that he was looking for something.

An opening for escape? That seemed unlikely in a foreign city surrounded by guardsmen. What was he looking for?

Unfortunately, Teyla could not read his mind but only follow his cues. For the moment at least he seemed determined to play along with this.

It was not yet hot, and the city was bright and clean in the morning, white walls and streets washed down with water and just starting to dry in the sun. A cool breeze came off the harbor. It lifted her hair on her brow gently. It came to Teyla that she had, in the entirety of her life, never stood in a city so big.

In terms of size it was not as big as Atlantis, but Atlantis was nearly empty. The not quite four hundred people of the expedition, even swollen as that number was since contact with Earth was reestablished, disappeared into the city's vastness like nothing. They might give a building to each person and still have left over. Each person on the expedition might have a palace of fifty rooms, and there would still be city to explore. As it was, they clustered nervously in a few towers together, but even so by Teyla's standards their quarters were palatial. Each person, regardless of their rank, might have a room of their own and a private bath. Some had balconies, sitting rooms, views of sky and sea that showed vast vistas. And each had running water at a touch, temperatures that suited them exactly, lights and windows that opened at their will.

Teyla had never imagined so much room. Her own bath, with its twin showerheads and golden tiles, was a luxury beyond compare. She did not think the Earth people were used to it either, or Rodney would not go on about garden tubs and choice real estate. Even by their standards, Atlantis was sumptuous. The Ancients had taken for granted unbelievable comfort.

And yet they stood in danger every moment. There was something surreal about being besieged in a palace. There was something disorienting about watching the sky light up with the Wraith bombardment, energy flaring against the shield, while one had clean hot baths and elegant chambers, soaring architecture and good food. There was something decidedly disorienting about fighting for one's life with hand and knife in beautiful and pristine places, stalking death through spacious white rooms.

These things belonged in darkness, in underground shelters where one went to earth like the prey animal one was, only to be hauled out at last, filthy and starved, to be food. One could almost expect it, then.

She wondered if the Ancients had. She wondered if, in their pride and their luxury, they had ever really understood that they were defeated. If they could possibly have understood that the future lay not in their clever and mannered civilization, but in the hands of their human children scrabbling in the dirt, left to the Wraith.

Compared to the majesty of Atlantis, Pelagia was primitive. And yet she had never been in a city with so many people. There might be half a million people in the city. That almost made Teyla's head spin. Half a million was the population of a healthy planet. She could not imagine that there had ever been half a million Athosians in the entire world. Perhaps stronger worlds like Sateda had boasted populations in the millions, before the Wraith decimated them, but she had never set foot there. She had never breathed the same air as half a million people. She was not Ronon, who understood cities and the kind of people who lived in them.

It was almost claustrophobic. On some level, the idea of so many people assembled raised the hairs on the back of her neck. It was asking for the Wraith. It was providing an irresistible temptation. To put so much food so close at hand, clustered like fruit on a vine for the taking...

How could this world not have been Culled? It was impossible.

She found herself walking closer to John, as though staying in his shadow possessed some virtue. He glanced aside and saw it, reassurance in the slight lift of one eyebrow as if he had put a hand on her shoulder. Yes, he was disturbed too. And no, this was not the time. He was determined to play this out, and she must as well.

Together, they went up the gangway onto one of the ships, Tolas beckoning them aboard before him politely.

Three massive banks of oars waited in their ports. Above, the stern deck was fitted out with a canopy that let the sea breeze in while providing shade. Tolas and the dignitaries repaired to the cabin, while John and Teyla were escorted to the stern deck. A servant came around with bread and fruit, and they sat on the bench that ran around the edge of the deck while the ship cast off. The oars beat in unison to the sound of a drum as the ship moved out into the open water, making for the harbor entrance, and John frowned.

Teyla took a bite of her fruit, moist and cool in the bright daylight. "Yes?"

"Galley slaves?" He looked forward, but they could see nothing. The rowers benches were below decks. Who the rowers were, and what their conditions were, could not be seen.

"There are probably slaves," Teyla said. "I do not see how they could build all this otherwise."

"Yeah." John frowned again. "It kind of goes with the territory, doesn't it?"

"I do not like it either," Teyla said. "But when there is much wealth and less technology it seems inevitable."

"You've seen it before in this galaxy?" John looked at her, his hand hesitating over the bread in the basket.

"Yes." Teyla took another bite of fruit. "There are many worlds and many ways in the Pegasus Galaxy, John, and you will not like many of them. There are worlds where the sons of the poor are castrated and worlds where women live in seclusion. There are worlds where one may be executed for failing to worship the right god or failing in obedience to one's chief. There are worlds where I am an abomination and worlds where

I am a goddess. You will find that every way that humans can live is tried by someone, somewhere."

"An abomination or a goddess?" His mouth twitched, as though trying to get his head around the thought.

"Oh yes." Teyla looked out across the busy harbor, little boats paddling away from their wake as they cleared the breakwater. Ahead, the sea stretched azure and calm. Tolas had gone in the cabin, and no one else seemed close enough to hear. "My Gift has its place on Athos. But most of the others who suffered the same fate as my ancestor were killed, remember? People would not allow them to live among them, different as they were, touched by the Wraith." She took a deep breath. She had spoken of this to no one in the months since the origin of her Gift had become clear, not even to Dr. Kate Heightmeyer. But John was a stranger to their ways. The hatred of the Wraith did not go bone deep within him. Other prejudices, other hatreds perhaps. But not this one. "You do not understand, John. You do not know how it is."

"You're saying if people knew about your Gift you'd be in danger," he said.

Teyla pushed her hair back from her face, looked into the eye of the wind. "I am saying that in some places I would be killed. Not among Athosians. There, I am different, and perhaps there are some who would recoil if they knew where the Gift came from, as Charin and my father feared. They would not kill me, certainly. But there are places where I should be burned alive."

She heard John take a deep breath. "That's not going to happen."

"I certainly do not intend for it to," Teyla said evenly. "But I also do not speak of my Gift outside of Atlantis and outside of my people." She looked at him. John sat tight lipped, as always fiercely protective of his friends. "I am fortunate," she said. "The ways in which I am different do not show in my face."

He nodded slowly, the sea breeze pulling at his hair. "I get that," he said.

"Perhaps you do," she said. There was always something of the outcast about John, no matter how well he tried to fit in. "I am a bad Athosian," she said.

"Bad?" He took up a fruit and looked at her over it. "Everybody likes you."

Teyla laughed. "Oh, I wish that were so! In any group there are currents and counter currents, jealousies and gossip and trouble. We are no different or more virtuous than any other group of human beings! Admittedly right now I have a good amount of what you might call social capital, but I am not a good Athosian."

"What's a good Athosian?" John looked bemused.

"Is it so easy to define your people?" Teyla put her feet up on the bench in front of her. "I will try, though." She looked out to sea and her face sobered. "We marry. We all marry, husband and wife tied together in work. We all marry, and we all have children. I am thirty four and childless, John, and it is a long, long time since I was married."

"I didn't know you were married," he said.

Teyla shrugged. "Why should you know that? It ended long ago, long before your people came to Athos. But I have never Chosen another, and that is unusual."

"Being divorced sucks," John said. He took a bite of the fruit, his eyes avoiding hers entirely. "But so does being married."

"I am not the kind of woman who marries," Teyla said. "I am Teyla Who Walks Through Gates. I do not have room in my life for someone. I am too selfish, at the heart of it."

"You're not the only one," John said. "It's kind of a disaster. You know. People wanting things and being disappointed."

"There are things I do not have to give," she said. "It is better to make no promises I do not intend to keep."

"It's better not to make a lot of promises." John lifted his hand to shade his eyes, looking ahead to the sea, squinting.

"Your sunglasses," she reminded.

"Oh, right." He got them out of his pocket and put them on. "I think there are some other ships out there."

"There probably are. If this is a major festival, it would not surprise me if there were ships converging from all the islands and ports," Teyla said. She did not glance around, as that would draw attention, but she already knew there was no one close by. "And I do not like this. Something is wrong here, John. Something is badly wrong."

"I know." His expression didn't change and he didn't look at her. Anyone observing would think they still spoke of other things. "There's no way the Wraith haven't discovered this world, as much stuff as they've got. You remember Olesia, right?"

Teyla tried not to twitch. "Since that was a week and a half ago, yes."

"Elizabeth thinks that the Magistrate had some kind of deal with the Wraith. That it wasn't just that the Wraith took the first humans they ran into, the prisoners on the island, but that they actually had a deal about it. The Olesians gave some people to the Wraith in return for the rest being left alone." John looked out to sea, unreadable behind his sunglasses. "Nice deal if you can get it, I guess."

"Like the warren of bones in Watership Down, the book you gave me," Teyla said, making a connection. "Where the rabbits know there are snares in the grass but nobody ever talks about it. Nobody ever mentions the ones who've been taken." She grimaced. "We are wild rabbits, we Athosians, all risking the same dangers. At least that way our hands are clean of one another's blood."

"Yeah." John's mouth was set in a grim line beneath the shades. "That. I'm starting to wonder what the deal is here."

"You think it's something like that?" It made sense. Teyla

could see how it might be. "Tolas is definitely hiding something, but I would guess that most of the Pelagians don't know, anymore than most of the Olesians did."

"The answers are on that island ahead of us," John said, gesturing with his chin. "This business about a High King and games in honor of the gods. The Games of Life?"

"What if the gods are Wraith?" Teyla blurted. She stopped, thinking about it.

John nodded slowly. "It makes sense. We've seen that before, back in the Milky Way. Alien predators setting themselves up as gods to get a never ending stream of stuff without having to do any work. Only in this case, the tribute isn't stuff. It's people."

"Food for the gods," Teyla breathed.

"I'll bet you my last cigar," John said.

"What is a cigar?"

"Never mind." He shook his head. "Why run around Culling when they can sit on their asses and have the locals bring them tribute? Lazy bastards don't even have to get up and do any work."

Teyla smiled grimly. "We, at least, make them work for it."

"They've got the technology to carry off the god thing. You've got to have a big technological gap to do that. Any sufficiently advanced technology is indistinguishable from magic," John quoted.

"Who said that?"

"A guy on Earth named Arthur C. Clarke. The Wraith have that kind of advantage here, and it's the perfect place to do it. It's got a big population, but unlike Sateda these people don't have the technology to get it. Ronon would see through their stuff and know it was Wraith tech, not magic. You couldn't pull that kind of scam there. You couldn't pull it on the Genii. But these guys aren't there. They could get by with it."

Teyla leaned on the ship's rail. "So now we are being taken to the gods."

"They're not sure whether we're the real thing or not," John said. "If we really are from another planet, the Wraith will want to question us. If we're not…" He shrugged. "We're tasty and crunchy."

"I will know," she said. "I will know when we are close enough if you are right and there are Wraith here."

John nodded seriously. "That will give us an advantage. We know what they are, but they don't know what we are. They'll think we're just more little rabbits."

"Not El-ahrairah himself." Teyla could not help but smile. "O prince of rabbits!"

He glanced at her sideways. "I hope I've got a few tricks up my sleeves."

"We have the radio," she said.

"And we know Wraith tech. They don't know that we know it. That's a big thing." John put his elbows on the rail and leaned beside her, as if also admiring the view of the sea. "We need to wait for the right opening, gather the intel and make the move when we're ready."

"Hopefully that will be with Lorne and a squad of Marines behind us," Teyla said.

"Hopefully." John lifted his head, looking toward the distant horizon. "I hope Zelenka and Ronon are doing ok."

"So do I," she said.

CHAPTER FIFTEEN

RADEK AND RONON watched as the ship came closer, leaving off waving their arms when it became clear that the ship had seen them and altered its course to intercept them. As it came nearer, they had a better look at it. It was most probably a merchant ship. A single bank of ten oars on each side swept in time, and it was low and not particularly streamlined. An upper deck perched awkwardly astern laden with cargo lashed on with ropes, while on the forward deck a bunch of small livestock in crude cages made a variety of alarmed noises. Some of them looked like pygmy goats.

The men on deck were lean and bearded, wearing sweaty linen tunics that came to their knees, but they called out readily enough as they came alongside the little fishing boat.

"We have been shipwrecked!" Radek called back. "We are the only survivors!" Which sounded much better than 'we are aliens from another planet who have stolen this boat without knowing how to sail it.' That seemed a potentially problematic story. Stealing boats might be as illegal here as it was on Earth. It probably was.

In no time at all the sailors threw down ropes, and Ronon climbed up easily. Radek looked at the swaying rope with trepidation. This had never been his favorite part in the gymnasium. In fact, he'd never managed to climb the rope in his life.

Ronon leaned back over the side. "Give me your hand," he said, and pulled Radek up as though it were nothing.

Towering over the sailors on the deck, his massive forearms bared, Ronon looked like some hero out of legend. They gave him a wide berth.

The one who might be the captain, a little better dressed, spoke. "You don't look like fishermen," he said doubtfully.

"My friend here is a warrior of great renown," Radek said, pushing his glasses back up on his nose. "We took passage with the unfortunate fishermen, but last night there was a terrible storm."

The captain eyed Radek skeptically, though he seemed to accept readily enough that Ronon was a mighty warrior. And certainly they knew there had been a storm. That was absolute truth.

Ronon looked dour and flexed a few muscles for effect.

"I am a scribe," Radek said, waving his forefinger about. "I tell his mighty deeds." He was suddenly very grateful that his polytechnique school had required ancient history. He could manage all these cultural things as well as Teyla. And certainly he could play the scribe.

At that there were a few nods and grins. The captain looked at Ronon, or rather looked up at Ronon. "He's yours?"

"Yeah," Ronon said.

The captain shrugged. "To each his own! It's good luck to rescue the shipwrecked. After all, one day it may be us. We're bound for the Holy Island with cargo. We'll take you and your boy there if you like, and then you're on your own."

"Sounds good," Ronon said gruffly.

Radek felt the blood rush to his face. Oh really. That sort of ancient cultural thing.

One of the crew looked at Ronon speculatively. "You're not planning to enter the Games of Life are you? Because I'd put some money on you."

"I might," Ronon said even more dourly. Apparently he thought the role required extreme taciturnity.

Rather than…whatever Radek's required.

"Tell me of these games," Radek said chipperly. "My friend is ever anxious to try his sword against new opponents."

From the gales of laughter that broke forth Radek gathered this was a worse double entendre in their language than in his native Czech, and he cursed the Stargate's translations for the millionth time. It probably didn't bear repeating in Satedan either, from the way Ronon gave him an absolutely incredulous look underneath his brows.

"You are ambitious, little man!" the sailor who had mentioned the games said.

The captain frowned, however. "You do not know of the Games?"

"We've come a long way," Ronon growled. "I'm not looking for trouble." He frowned in a way that suggested that anyone who helped trouble find him might not be made very happy. "And if you've got any water it would be a good thing."

At that a skin bag of water was produced, and Ronon drank before he passed it to Radek. The water was stale, but Radek hadn't realized quite how thirsty he was. Yes, it had only been ten or twelve hours, but they had been exerting themselves quite a lot, swimming in the towering waves and then bailing. He stopped himself before he finished the skin, both because he remembered that it was a bad idea to drink too much at once, and because Ronon might also want more. He had not drunk deeply before he passed it on.

Most of the sailors had lost interest and gone back to their work, and even the captain was forward looking up the mast at something.

"What the hell?" Ronon said in a low voice.

"I do not want to say we are from another planet," Radek said. "That might be very imprudent."

"No shit, with Wraith here," Ronon said. He hunched his shoulders as though the transmitter was still there beneath his skin, a habit that would no doubt die hard. But Carson had removed the transmitter more than a month ago. The Wraith could no more find Ronon than any other individual human on this world. "Did you have to say…"

"I do not need to know what I said," Radek said quickly. "We need to know how long it is going to take us to get to a port and what is going on and how we can get passage from this island to the mainland where the gate is. Unfortunately we have nothing to trade at the moment."

"Nothing you'd like." Ronon grinned wolfishly, and it took a moment for Radek to realize that was a joke.

"Very funny," Radek said.

Ronon stretched his arms and cracked his knuckles. "Wonder what these games are. Maybe I could win us some money."

"If they have a coinage based economy," Radek said. "Perhaps some sort of gladiatorial combat?"

Ronon nodded. "If it's to the touch it might be worth a try. I don't know what these guys think is good."

"You are very good," Radek said. He'd heard Sheppard all but wax rhapsodic about the Satedan's fighting skills, and it took quite a lot to impress the colonel. "If it is not mortal combat it might be worth a try. It sounds as though these people have gambling, and perhaps you could win passage."

"Everybody has gambling," Ronon said. "I'd try it. See what you can find out." He stood up and leaned on the rail in the wash of the wind.

"I should find out?"

"You're the talker, aren't you?" Ronon looked at him sideways. "What do I keep you for?"

"You are getting too much into this role," Radek grumbled, but he ambled back along the deck to try to strike up a conversation with the captain.

The jumper took off from the island very precisely. Carson was being incredibly careful. Which suited Rodney just fine. He was all in favor of not crashing the jumper again. And not repairing the jumper again. He would really like to find everyone, go home, have dinner, and sleep in his own bed sometime this year.

"Ok," Major Lorne said, coming forward and sitting down in the shotgun seat ahead of Rodney. "Let's head back toward the gate. We'll start there and fly concentric circles going out, starting with, say, a ten kilometer radius and working our way out in 20 km increments."

"That's going to take quite a bit of time," Carson said.

Lorne nodded. "Yep. But if they're on hand held radios we need to make at least a couple of passes within range or we may miss them, and the range varies based on weather, humidity, and whether or not they're indoors. It's more likely they'll be close to the gate than on the other side of the planet, so let's start near the gate and work our way out. That way the other side of the planet is the last choice."

"That actually made sense," Rodney said.

Lorne looked over his shoulder at him. "Thanks, doc. I do try to make sense sometimes."

Carson shook his head. "Where could they have gone?"

"They got off the island somehow," Lorne said. "We're just going to have to make radio sweeps. Unless Dr. McKay can do something with the life signs readings?"

"Sorry, no," Rodney said shortly. "Dr. McKay cannot. The people on this planet are human. Which means there's no possible way to tell the difference between our people and them on the life signs detector. And the EM fields given off by our equipment are too faint to pick up unless we're right on top of them. At which point we would have had them on the radio for ten minutes already."

"I can't believe they're missing again," Carson said.

"Yes, well," Rodney snapped. "Maybe it's time to face the facts that we aren't very good at this. Week before last we were taken prisoner by the Olesians and tied up in a hut. The week before that Cadman and I got sucked up by a Wraith Dart. Two weeks before that we spent 24 hours running around the woods in deadly solar radiation trying to catch Off-His-

Gourd Ford while Ronon wanted Carson to operate on him in the wilderness with a penknife and a toothpick like something out of MacGyver. Before that…oh yeah. Before that we were besieged by an incredible number of pissed off Wraith. It's just possible that we're doing it wrong!"

Carson looked at Lorne as if to say, what did you expect?

"Well, what do you suggest, doc?" Lorne said. "Pack up and go home?"

"No." Rodney set his jaw. "There's too much to learn here."

"Then we take some chances," Lorne said. "I'm sure if you don't like being on the gate team that Dr. Zelenka wouldn't mind taking your place."

"Zelenka?" Rodney could hardly believe his ears. "Zelenka doesn't even like to go off world! And he's agoraphobic or something."

"You're claustrophobic," Cadman pointed out from behind Rodney's seat.

"Was anybody talking to you? I think not," Rodney snapped.

"I'm just saying," Cadman said.

"It's much worse to be agoraphobic than claustrophobic, from the point of view of a gate team," Rodney said. "After all, we don't do a lot of spelunking. But we do kind of have to be outdoors under the sky."

"I thought you didn't like that," Lorne said.

"Only when there's dangerous solar radiation," Rodney replied doggedly. "You were incredibly careless. I bet if Carson checked your sperm count he'd be appalled."

Cadman made some noise that sounded like a stifled sob.

"I don't need his bloody sperm count!" Carson said. "It's not a fertility clinic around here!"

"My sperm are just fine," Lorne said, but he didn't sound too confident. As well he should not. It was no laughing matter.

Cadman made another strangled noise.

"Look," said Carson in his best consulting physician tone, "It's not as though he won't make more. The kind of long term radiation damage you're talking about, Rodney, is not something you're going to get in a day from solar radiation on a habitable planet. The human body is a lot more resilient than you think. In eight to ten weeks Major Lorne's sperm will be entirely normal. Unless he were planning on impregnating someone immediately, he'd probably be fine. And you know that sperm quality doesn't necessarily have any physiological side effects. Most men with poor sperm motility don't even know they have a problem."

"Do we have to keep talking about this?" Lorne asked.

They were all spared replying by Cadman interrupting. "Look!" she said, pointing ahead. "That can't be good."

They were passing over desert and scattered oases, the green of the canopy of groves of palm trees bright against the sands. One, however, was different. A dark line cut across the green, a trail of broken trees and snapped off branches, culminating in a dark spot nearly at the edge of the desert.

"Something crashed," Cadman said.

Rodney cursed.

"They hit the energy shield too," Carson said. "Oh, hell." He had already begun the turn to investigate. Even from this distance it didn't look good. This was not a controlled landing like theirs. This was much, much worse.

"Ok," Lorne said, standing up. "Everybody, it's search and rescue time. Cadman, you take the perimeter."

Rodney felt ill. They passed close over, seeking a landing site just beyond the trees, and he saw what was left of the other jumper. It lay half buried in dirt and sand, the windshield broken and one of the drive pods completely missing, its side scorched as though by fire. If Sheppard and Teyla had been lying injured in that thing for two days... He couldn't help but imagine, though he would much rather not. If they'd been lying dead in that thing for two days, while he couldn't get the crappy DHD to work...

"Dr. Beckett?" Lorne said.

"As soon as we're down," Carson said grimly, and Rodney knew he was thinking the same thing. Or perhaps blaming himself for the time lost when they skimmed the energy field themselves. "I'm on it."

Lorne clasped his shoulder briefly. "I know you are, doc," he said. "Let's move out!"

CHAPTER SIXTEEN

SHORTLY AFTER THE SUN passed its zenith a servant came along the stern deck with water and bread and cheese, which John and Teyla ate sitting along the rail. John cast an eye forward to the canopied section where presumably Tolas and the most important passengers were. "They're not starving us anyway."

"Which makes sense if they're not sure what we are," Teyla said. The seas were calm and the skies blue. The galley skimmed over the waves light as a sea bird. It would be an enjoyable adventure, were it not for the end they now suspected waited for them — the Wraith, set up as gods over a captive people who literally provided them nourishment. "Thank you," she said to the servant, taking the cup from his hand. "May I ask you who the people are on the very forward deck?"

He glanced in that direction. "They are participants in the Games. Competitors in the Games of Life." He nodded quickly and hurried away, as if he had been told not to spend overly long.

"Competitors in the games?" Teyla said.

John shook his head. "No way."

From where they were it was easy to pick out Jitrine among the passengers on the forward deck, but she was not the only one who was elderly. There were two men who seemed older than she was, one of whom was crabbed and bent. There were five or six others, a tall bearded man who stared out over the sea, a boy and girl who couldn't have been more than twelve or thirteen, and several women who didn't look like athletes.

Teyla shook her head. "Those people cannot be competitors. Can you imagine Jitrine and that young boy in some kind of sport against the others?"

"Foot races, track and field…" The crease between John's brows deepened. "Any kind of boxing or wrestling… Can you see Jitrine boxing or wrestling?"

"She is an elderly woman, and she is hale, but no," Teyla said. "Either these games are not tests of strength and speed, or…"

"They're a hoax," John said. "Some kind of excuse to give these people to the Wraith. Jitrine was clearly Tolas' prisoner too and she said there was a long story about why, about tribute and how the people in The Chora didn't want to pay it."

"Because it was too heavy," Teyla said. It made a grim sort of sense. "The tribute is people, John. Those participants in the games are the tribute. Unwanted people."

"People somebody has a grudge against," John said. "Nice. The Olesians at least bothered to accuse people of a crime before they stocked the Wraith's feeding pen. These guys pretend they're sending them to compete in the games."

"It causes less resistance, I imagine," Teyla said. "After all, if one is not being sent anywhere bad, why should people object?"

"But they do," John said grimly. "That's what Jitrine was talking about. Too much tribute. Too many people just disappearing. Too many friends and family asking too many questions. It gets dicey for a ruler to have lots of people disappear."

"And then we just wander in to fill the quota?" Teyla's eyebrows rose. "We take two spots and that is two less local people Tolas has to find. No wonder he wants us to behave. If we start raising a fuss, people will wonder about what is going to happen, where people are going. If we are just traveling along nicely, it is nobody's problem."

John nodded. "Very convenient. If we don't turn out to be useful, we count toward Tolas' tribute."

"We will have to see what opportunities present themselves," Teyla said.

John looked at her. "How's your arm?"

She flexed it experimentally. "It hurts, but it seems that the swelling is better today. I will not be able to fight two handed, but it is my left arm. I can certainly use a pistol, and if I have a stick I will fight one handed."

He looked as though that was better than he'd feared. He'd seen her fight one handed before with her sticks, and she could usually beat him. And a stick was usually an easy weapon to find.

"How is your head?"

John winced. "Ok."

"Truly?" Teyla prompted. "Do not tell me you can do things you cannot."

"I'm still a little dizzy," he admitted. "It comes and goes."

Teyla nodded. "We will take this as it comes." If John admitted to being a little dizzy, he was truly not well. But then it had been less than forty eight hours since he had a concussion. He probably would still be in the infirmary back in Atlantis. "Dr. Beckett would have you still in the infirmary."

"Yeah, well. Carson's not here. And if he were, we'd be out of this soup."

"Let us hope so," Teyla said.

"There's some dried blood on the dash," Carson Beckett said. "Not too much." He was bent over the console of the wrecked jumper. Through the broken windscreen the air was thick with the birdsong of the oasis, hot and dry. "A bit on the dash and some smears on the armrest, like a man with blood on his hands put them there."

"How bad is it?" Rodney asked, climbing over the rear seats coming forward.

Carson raised his head. "I'm cautiously optimistic. No bodies. No large amounts of blood. No bullet holes or spent casings. This much blood? Someone injured, yes. But certainly not losing blood in a life-threatening amount. From the location, on the control board, I would guess it's Colonel Sheppard's."

"Wonderful," Rodney said darkly.

"No sign of Teyla, no blood anywhere else. What have you got back there, Major Lorne?"

Lorne leaned around the door that divided the cockpit from the back. "Two P90s gone, two packs gone, survival gear gone. Teyla's jacket's gone. Paper from a field dressing on the floor. Somebody was hurt, but not so badly they didn't bandage it up with a field dressing and get moving. They took weapons and survival gear, and there's no sign of a fight. I'm guessing they walked out of here."

"Why?" Rodney demanded.

"I don't know," Lorne said. "How would I know? But it doesn't look like they were prisoners when they left. They had time to get all the stuff they'd need. They had water, food, medicine."

"Perhaps they hoped to make it back to the Stargate," Carson said. "I know that's what I'd do."

"Me too," Lorne said. "And the colonel's done desert survival before. When I was at the SGC somebody said something about it. Afghanistan, I think?"

"There's a lot of desert between here and the gate," Rodney said. "And it's hot. Did I mention it's a desert?"

"That's our next thing," Lorne said. "We'll check out the desert between here and the gate. The most likely thing is that they took the survival gear so they'd have a good shot at walking back to the Stargate. Chances are they're somewhere along the way. If not, we'll recenter our search pattern here and continue radio calls. They can't be too far."

"Not on foot," Rodney said.

"We'll find them before lunch," Carson replied.

"When have I heard that before?" Rodney asked.

Radek strolled along the deck of the merchant ship, wiping off his glasses on the hem of his shirt. Not that it did much good. His shirt was soaking wet with salt water, but at least it got some of the streaks off his glasses. Other than wishing for a hearty lunch, Radek felt — actually, pretty good. He had never thought he was the sort of man to be shipwrecked and spend the night clinging to an overturned boat in a storm and come out of it fresh and cheerful. Perhaps fresh was stating it too strongly, as a hot shower and a very large bowl of soup would be welcome just now. They weren't dead, and that was quite a lot. Maybe there was something to this action hero adrenaline high that others talked about.

Radek ambled up to the captain where he stood astern and put his glasses back on. He waited for the man to turn to him before he spoke. "So, these games," he began casually.

The captain gave him a broad grin. "You think your friend might win? There is only one winner."

Radek put his hands in his pockets. "One winner? How do the games work?"

"It's one game," the captain said. "The Games of Life. It's a game of skill and strength both. It's good to be a big strong fellow, but that's not enough." He tapped his temple. "You have to have it here. You have to have brains. Skill and strength both, or you will not survive."

"Survive?"

"It can be deadly," the captain said with a shrug. "If you're not fast and clever enough."

"How does it work?" Radek asked. "An arena or…"

"A labyrinth," the captain replied. "There is a huge maze underground. It has traps, it has dangers, it has monsters in it, they say. There are obstacles and that does not even count the other competitors. The first person to get all the way through the maze is the winner."

Radek waited, but the captain didn't go on. "That's it?"

"That's it. You go in with no weapons or tools, and you come out at the other end. The first person who makes it is the winner and they are rewarded with a big purse and sent on their way. There are lots of bets placed on who it will be. The gods themselves like to bet. The thing that's hard, you see, is that you have to solve the obstacles which requires cleverness, but you also have to hold your own against the other competitors in a fight, and there are traps that only a strong man can defeat. So it is a very special champion who can do both."

Strength and cleverness at once. Radek had a thought. "So do competitors never team up? If my friend and I, for example…"

"One winner," the captain said. "One of you walks out. That's the catch. One of you is a rich man and one of you belongs to the gods. People have tried it before, teaming up, but someone always betrays the other at the end. So now everybody knows better than to do it. Why help someone who will stab you in the back at the finish line?"

"Belongs to the gods? Is that a euphemism for death?"

The captain blinked. "No. Belongs to the gods. The competitors are dedicated. They become the property of the gods. One man walks away the winner. The rest belong to the gods to serve them."

"Not such a good bet then," Radek said. A very neat way of getting people to place themselves in slavery. Diabolically clever, actually.

"Not if you want to walk away, little man," the captain said. "You help your friend, but do you think he'll be the one to let you walk out at the end while he stays?"

"I do see your point," Radek said. He ambled away, back down the deck to where Ronon stood. Ronon looked up as he approached and he leaned on the rail beside him and related what he had learned.

When he finished, Ronon frowned. "That's not a plan."

"Indeed not," Radek said. "Very clever, of course. A labyrinth, a maze, lots of obstacles… I'm sure it is intriguing."

"If you could see it."

"What?"

"If you could see it. How do the spectators see it?" Ronon asked.

Radek blinked.

"Look," Ronon said. "A bunch of people go underground. They fight. Somebody comes out the other end. So what? That's boring. It's only interesting if you can see the fights." He leaned on his elbows, his eyes on the sea. "On Sateda we had radio, just like you guys do. There were people who narrated sporting events on the radio so if you couldn't get there you could hear what happened, but it wasn't the same as being there. Five, ten thousand people would come out for big championships. Huge crowds. That was part of the fun, being there with your Kindred yelling for your champion. If nobody could see it? If it all happened underground and you never had any idea what was going on, just waited for somebody to come out? That's not exciting."

Radek nodded slowly, his eyes on Ronon's face, his mind whirling. At last he said, "My friend, there is something very wrong here. Something on this world is not at all as it should be."

Ronon looked at him sideways, curiously.

"They are not supposed to have the technology to do this, but they must have a way of seeing what is happening in the labyrinth."

"They have cameras, like the Genii?"

"Maybe. That is not out of the question. We have seen that the Genii have achieved analog broadcast." Radek looked around them, up at the mast and forward to the livestock on deck. "But do you see anything to suggest this society has that level of technology? Or that these people know anything about it?"

"No." Ronon shook his head. "The Genii tech — it's maybe fifteen or twenty years ahead of where we were on Sateda.

Not a full generation. Your stuff is maybe a couple of generations. It's better."

Radek snorted. "You mean the stuff you've seen is. I did not grow up with this. Do you think we had cell phones and laptops in Czechoslovakia in 1980? I grew up in a house with a wood-stove, and then one with a pre-war oil furnace. I did not see a computer except when I went to polytechnique. Nobody had computers at home, not even in the West. In the East? Perhaps a great university would have them. We had the radio and the streetcar. If you were very lucky you might have a TV, and then if you could make the rabbit ears work for you, you might pick up German broadcast television." Radek smiled. "The station in Nuremburg showed Star Trek in reruns. That is how I saw it, grainy from the mountains, on a black and white television set. But we did not have these things. I was not running around with my laptop talking on my headset then. There is hardly a moment in time of difference between the technology I grew up with and that which you did."

Ronon blinked. "I thought you guys had all this stuff."

"It is all new." Radek shrugged. "Even the Americans did not grow up with all this, though they had more tech in their homes in the West than we had. And much of what you are seeing, Ronon, is Ancient technology. We've had it a year, and some of it we can make work. Lots we cannot yet." He looked out to sea once more. "But it is wrong and you have found it. They must have some way of watching the games. And if they do, they are lying about a great deal, like the Genii, or…"

"Or we're in a lot of trouble," Ronon said.

CHAPTER SEVENTEEN

THE MERCHANT SHIP did not so much glide into the port of the Holy Island as creep, sails reefed and oars out, making its way very slowly through the heavy traffic. Two great stone quays shielded the harbor filled with smaller boats, while above on the steep hillsides of the town, buildings clustered. The ones nearest the water were somewhat ramshackle houses of wood, but the ones higher up were stone, with painted columns and wide porches offering vistas of the sea that must be simply stunning. The highest tiers were reserved for palaces and temples, bright with red and gold paint. The symmetry and beauty reminded Radek of the Dalmatian coast, or possibly of how the islands of Greece must have looked in their heyday. He had never been to the islands, but perhaps it was like this — tier upon tier set in lavish greenery, while beneath it the blue sea glittered in the sun.

Certainly the scene looked like a spectacle out of Plutarch. Beside the largest quay, a massive galley with scarlet canopies was tying up while musicians played a fanfare. Soldiers marched off in gilded array, spears catching the sunlight, headdresses sparkling with gold. In their midst a number of officials walked, shaded by fans held by half-naked servants. Behind, in procession between lines of guards, others walked to the music of drums.

"What is all that?" Radek asked the captain.

"Tribute ship," the captain said, glancing across the water. "From King Anados of Pelagia, to tell by the markings. The Pelagians always put on a fine show! They're very rich, and the king likes everyone to know it. Of course that means their tribute is more too, so it's not all good."

It was indeed spectacular. Radek expected pacing cheetahs

any second. It was something, he thought, to see these things as so few on Earth ever did, to see things that no one would believe even if he could ever speak of them. There was a bit to be said for going off world, really.

"Who are those people?" Radek asked, gesturing to the cluster of assorted people at the back of the procession between guards.

"Tribute," the captain said. "They're contestants in the Games." He shrugged and went back to yelling incomprehensible nautical things at the sailors, who were trying to bring the merchant ship in to a smaller dock.

Ronon came and stood beside Radek. "Impressive," he said.

"Those are contestants," Radek said, taking off his glasses and cleaning them on his shirt. "But something is not right there. That boy is very young. And that old woman? Surely she is not an athlete? It does not seem likely that she has wagered her life on a contest in a labyrinth."

"*They* haven't," Ronon said flatly.

"Who?" Radek put his glasses back on again.

"There," Ronon said, pointing, but the gesture was hardly necessary.

Toward the back of the procession among the others were two unmistakable figures—Sheppard and Teyla.

"Don't react," Ronon said, squeezing his arm.

"Right." It was good to see them alive and in one piece—at least they seemed to be in one piece, walking bareheaded up the street in their black BDUs. Sheppard had a white bandage over one eye, but they did not seem badly hurt. Radek had begun to wonder if they were dead, and had troubled himself in the night keeping that thought at bay. Not dead, and not badly injured. But just as surely prisoners. The guards around them carried spears and they seemed watchful.

"They must have been captured," Ronon said.

Radek nodded. "And something is not right. You had a good point about seeing the contest, and this…" He shook his head. "We must find out what is going on here."

"We need to rescue them," Ronon said.

"Of course we do," Radek said. "But first we must find out what is happening. All is not as it appears, and we must not walk into a trap. If we do, we will not be able to help them or ourselves."

Ronon's brows rose and fell. "Excuses?"

Radek sighed. "Do you think I am such a coward as to just leave them? Is that what you have decided?"

Ronon regarded him steadily for a moment. "No," he said. "You're ok."

"I am glad you think so. And I am not suggesting for a moment that we leave them. But we must think how to do this. We are in the middle of a strange city, and they are surrounded by guards. We have no weapons except your pistol, and no way off the island. The games do not start until tomorrow, and Colonel Sheppard and Teyla are both strong. We must do this by stealth, Ronon, so that we have the best chance of success. It will do them no good if we are merely captured as well."

"Ok." Ronon crossed his arms. "We need to know where they're going."

"Then let us depart this ship as soon as it comes to the dock and follow the procession," Radek said. "We are strangers, but since there is a great festival there must be many people here who are oddly dressed and known to no one. We mingle with the crowd and find out what we can."

"It's a plan," Ronon said, but he plainly hoped the plan turned into action soon. Radek only hoped that action would not be precipitous.

Teyla looked about the Holy Island with interest. She hoped that would not seem odd. After all, they were travelers who had never been here before, and the sights were indeed impressive. Surely a certain amount of curiosity would seem natural.

John had lifted his head and was walking straight ahead in the procession with a firm step, but she saw how his eyes darted one way and another, saw the tension in the set of his shoulders. Then he glanced at her, one eyebrow quirked, and she knew what he meant. When there was an opportune moment in the crowded streets, they would try to break away.

The way uphill was very crowded indeed. Hundreds, perhaps thousands, of people lined the narrow streets, looking out from windows and porches of houses, cheering and shouting at the spectacle. Tolas and the other officials walked in great state beneath fans, surrounded by guards in glittering array. From time to time one of them would wave, or toss something into the crowd that set off screeches and a scurrying frenzy — small coins or candies, treats or amulets — Teyla could not tell. But whatever it was, it stoked the crowd to an even greater volume, pressing in on the procession and being pushed back in turn by the cordon of guards.

Where they were, toward the end of the procession, this was having a very salutary effect. The number of guards directly around them had diminished from eight to four, two walking on each side. The crowds were loud and people pushed one another, trying to get closer to see better, or to be in a better position for the tosses of goods. Once they got among the crowd it would be difficult to get to them, and from what Teyla could see the city was a rabbit warren of houses and lanes crowded closely together, leaning over one another on the steep hillsides, with terraced gardens and walls of various heights protecting buildings and streets. Fruit trees and growing plants filled the gardens, providing still more cover. If they could slip away from the guards, it would be very difficult to find them again. And perhaps it would not occur to Tolas to look until they reached their destination.

John stopped and bent down as though to retie his boot laces, and Teyla nearly ran into him. She saw, beneath his bent head, how he swiftly untied it before he made a production of tying it again.

Only one of the guards hung back. "Come on, now," he said. The last of the other contestants passed them, two guards bringing up the rear.

"Sure," John said with an affable smile as he stood up, ambling along behind them. Teyla had to admire the grace of it. They were now in the very back, with only one man behind them.

He did not need to say anything. She saw the set of his shoulders change an instant before he moved, and she was ready.

They were at a turn of the street, where it proceeded steeply uphill. Two small lanes ran into it, and there was a little square with a fountain, crowded tight with people pressed together. Behind the procession the crowd was breaking up.

John bent again, as though reaching for his boot, but this time he came up with a roundhouse that connected squarely with the last guard's jaw, knocking him backwards just as Teyla seized his spear and broke it across her knee. Six feet long it was of no use to her, but a three foot section was very useful indeed. John darted back down the processional way with Teyla a step behind him before there were even shouts of alarm.

Dodging among the startled spectators, the broken shaft held to her side, there was no need to actually strike anyone. Most of the calls were not screams for help, but simply cries of startlement, with the occasional comment on how rude it was to shove past people.

Behind them, up the street, there were cries of alarm, but it had all happened so quickly, and at the end of the procession, that most of the guards now had to get through the crowd of spectators.

John dodged down a side street and Teyla followed. He did

not even wait a moment before he took the first side turn, then leapt up a low stone wall covered in creeping vines and clambered onto the terrace above. Teyla followed. They slipped through the branches of three small fruit trees that hung low, then climbed over another wall into the alley behind a large house that faced the street above. No one was around. The inhabitants were probably in the front of the house watching the procession, or if this street was not one of the processional ways, perhaps they had gone down to watch. They hurried around the corner of the house and John flattened himself against the rough stone wall. He was breathing more heavily than she might expect, but he put his finger to his lips. She slipped in beside him and he leaned out a fraction, looking back.

There were no sounds of near pursuit. Away beyond the walls were shouts and music, but whether alarm or just the normal sounds of the festival she could not tell.

"It appears we have gotten away cleanly," Teyla whispered.

John nodded. He turned away, checking in the other direction up the narrow space between houses, high walls rearing on both sides. It appeared this space was used as a refuse dump and sometime privy, as it stank badly. At the front of the houses it was masked from the street by a large bush and a dwarf fruit tree. They peered out.

The street ran steeply downhill to their right, presumably to join the lower street the procession passed on, while to the left it twisted around the side of the hill, houses and garden walls abutting it.

"Come on," John said, and stepped out sharply, strolling along the side of the street going uphill. Teyla followed. It was true that if no alarm had reached this area it would be more suspicious to dart across people's gardens than to simply walk along the street purposefully.

Around the curve there was a drop to the left, a stone restraining wall along the edge of a bank that went down steeply toward the port. Above, to the right, a magnificent house took full advantage of the view, porches spread to catch the breeze.

"Over the wall," Teyla said. "Let us stop and plan." The wall was nearly as tall as she, and John had to help her up with her hurt shoulder, but once they sat in the shadow on the other side of the wall they were perhaps as safe as they could be. They could not be seen from above unless someone leaned over the wall and looked down, and the wall covered them from the houses above. Below, rough scrub and rocks made it a tough clamber of about forty feet to the trees and garden walls of houses. From the flat roofs of the houses below they would be visible, but at a distance that would make it difficult to tell who they were or what they were doing. Beyond, the sea stretched, the port off to their left. A few clouds littered the sky, perhaps signs of thunderstorms to come in the night.

John let out a long breath. "Ok."

"That was well done," Teyla said.

"I thought so."

For a few moments they sat there companionably.

"Now what?" Teyla asked.

John pulled the radio out of his pocket and checked it again. It was still on standby, the low battery light on. If anyone had called they would have heard it. Which was in itself worrisome. What had happened that there had been no rescue team? Had the rescue team likewise run into the Wraith cruiser? Were even now Rodney and Lorne prisoners of the Wraith or, worse yet, dead?

John brushed his hair back from his bandaged brow. "There's one flyable ship on this planet. The Wraith cruiser."

Teyla twisted around to look at him. "Do you have any idea how to fly a Wraith cruiser?"

"No. But it has a comm board. And maybe I can figure it

out. We captured that Dart a few weeks ago. I've had a look at the tech."

"That Dart was blown to pieces," Teyla observed. "I did not know there were anything like operable systems."

John made his so-so gesture. "Not really. But Zelenka figured some of it out."

"Radek isn't here. And we have no idea where he is," Teyla said. "I am sure if anyone could figure out how to operate a Wraith cruiser it would be you and Radek, but to take the ship and fly it, the two of us?"

"Maybe," John said. "It's a thought." He lifted his hand to his eyes, looking out to sea. "But I'm done waiting to be rescued. If they could have, they would have by now. We have to assume we're on our own."

Teyla nodded slowly. "Then we need a plan."

"First we need to find the ship," John said. "They must have it parked somewhere. If most of the people don't know about it, we're looking for a hangar or a private airstrip of some kind. This island isn't that large. If it's here, it's close by."

"If I were the pilot," Teyla said slowly, "I should want it in the palace complex. It would be easier to conceal that way, and it would be possible to reach it quickly in the event of an emergency. I would not want to put it somewhere I must then reach on foot, which might take some time."

"You've got that right," John agreed. "It looked like that Wraith cruiser on Olesia was capable of a vertical takeoff. Which means they could be in pretty close, tucked away in a building or a courtyard or something. They wouldn't require a runway, like a 302 does."

"Is that a big advantage?" Teyla asked.

"Oh yeah." John leaned back against the wall. "There's no question that a helicopter, or a plane with a vertical takeoff, like a Harrier, can go places most aircraft can't. The problem we've never been able to solve is payload size. Even the biggest copters are a fraction of the size of a big plane. The vertical takeoff requires too much power. You can't get something the size of a C-40 in the air from a vertical takeoff." He shrugged. "Apparently the Wraith can. Which is going to be a big, big problem to us in the future."

"So even though the cruiser is quite large, it may be in a fairly small space?" Teyla thought she had followed all that.

"Bingo. And you're right that around the palaces is our best bet. The question is how to figure out where." He looked around, back toward the higher ground behind them, where the villas and palaces clung to the terraces of the island. "We need to get up to the top," he said. "If we can get an overview, we can probably spot it."

"That area looks crowded," Teyla observed. "There are many houses, and surely there are many people about."

John nodded. "We wait until later." She followed his glance out to sea, to the spreading clouds rising in white billows in the afternoon sunshine. "It looks like we're going to get a thunderstorm later on. We can move under cover of the weather. And that will give them a while to hunt around for us, maybe spread out and think we've gotten back down to the harbor or aboard a ship. Let's stay put for a while, and make a move when we've got weather and evening to help us."

"I agree," Teyla said, though her agreement was not really necessary. He was in charge, and she had little reason to ever dispute his professional decisions. Whatever else John Sheppard might be, he was an excellent commander. She had thrown her lot in with the men from Earth out of necessity, but she stood by her decision. If she had had all the time in the world to consider, she could not have done better. "We will wait," she said.

CHAPTER EIGHTEEN

THE MIDDAY SUN beat down on desert and Stargate. Rodney stood in the shade of the back of the jumper, the open wormhole shimmering like a mirage before him. He put his hand to his headset and glanced at Major Lorne as he spoke into it. "I'm telling you, Elizabeth, we've been back and forth for hours."

"We've flown a full, low-altitude grid between the crash site and the Stargate," Lorne added. "It's only about 40 miles. No radio signals, no life signs, nothing. Most of it is flat, open dunes. From 600 feet we'd see them, even if they were dead."

"What do you recommend, Major?" Elizabeth Weir's voice was crisp, but it betrayed her concern.

"Subcutaneous transmitters," Rodney said. "We all need to be outfitted with them."

"I'm talking about a solution for now, Rodney," Elizabeth replied by radio.

"If they didn't walk back toward the Stargate, they went in a different direction," Lorne said. "Probably toward the canal or river. If it were me, I'd follow the water, especially in this heat."

Rodney decided to ignore the fact that Lorne had said before that if it were him, he'd walk back to the Stargate. "There were settlements along the river visible from the air," Rodney broke in. "If they were hurt they might have gone to the locals for help."

"Our next step is to expand the search along the river and canal," Lorne said. He glanced at Rodney as though expecting argument, but Rodney wasn't about to give him one. "We'll make another low altitude search, this time going northward. We'll find them, Dr. Weir. Dr. Beckett said he didn't think that the amount of blood in the jumper suggested a life-threatening injury. They're probably holed up somewhere with shade and water. And there's a good chance that an expanding sweep will locate Ronon and Zelenka too."

"All right," Elizabeth said. "Stay in touch. I'll expect a check back in six hours."

"Yes, ma'am," Lorne said and nodded at Rodney, who tapped the ship's controls to release the gate. Its blue glow snapped off.

Carson shook his head. "Aye, I'm with you about the sub-cutaneous transmitters. Next time."

"Provided there is a next time," Rodney said darkly.

"The problem is," Radek said, looking about the busy marketplace, "that we are very conspicuous."

"I thought the problem was that we were lost on a strange planet with no gear, no money, no laptop, no radio and no way to get home," Ronon said.

"That too." Radek pushed his glasses up on his nose again. "But you must admit that our appearance is memorable." Or rather, that Ronon's was. Radek's shirt and pants might be odd, but the scientist himself did not look entirely out of place on the Holy Island. His hair, his size, his demeanor were all nondescript. On the other hand, Ronon turned heads wherever he went. Six foot four and built like a brick wall waiting for someone to punch it, Ronon was the kind of man who made people get out of his way and remember his passing. "You look like a warrior, my friend," Radek said. "You would be less noticeable if you were dressed as the warriors here are."

Ronon shrugged. "Not like we can buy clothes. And I could mug somebody, but that would start trouble."

"Yes, I should think it would," Radek said quickly. "The last thing we need is whatever passes for the police looking for us. That will make it considerably harder to find Colonel Sheppard and Teyla."

"Enough standing around," Ronon said. "It shouldn't be hard to find out where the procession went. Everybody saw it. We go that way, we see where they're keeping them. We figure out a way to bust in. Let's do it." He strode off up the street in the direction of the imposing buildings at the top of the hill.

Radek blinked. "This is like stealing a boat, isn't it?" he said as he followed. "The same sort of foolproof solution." Still, he supposed this was how the action hero thing worked.

The marketplaces around the palaces were busy, crowded with festival goers, and to Radek's surprise no one paid them much attention. There were variously dressed shoppers, presumably travelers from many different lands who had come to the Holy Island for the games, and perhaps everyone assumed they were from some place on the edges of their known world. Or maybe they thought that they were just odd. In any event, they moved freely through the crowds, and a few judicious questions about the upcoming games gathered some useful information.

Radek excused himself from a conversation with a potter selling his wares in an open stall and made his way back to Ronon. "I have found where the contestants come out of the labyrinth," Radek said in a low voice. "Down the other side of the hill from the port, behind the palaces, there is a rough gully. There is a place down there where select spectators and the High King go to watch the end of the course. Other than the King's guests, the others are chosen by lot and there are people who resell their chits for huge amounts. Very expensive tickets to scalp!"

"That sounds about normal," Ronon said.

"Yes, it does." Reassuringly normal, in fact. "There is a path that goes to it. It is not secret at all."

"Which means it's guarded," Ronon said thoughtfully. "Probably not as much as it will be once the games start, but they've probably got some guys down there to keep people from going in and hiding stuff that will give contestants an edge."

Radek nodded. "That is what I would do. I would hide things already inside to make sure my contestant won." He looked at Ronon, the beginning of an idea forming. "So we go in?"

"It's the place we know Sheppard and Teyla will be," Ronon said. "Could work. But I'd rather get them out of someplace less guarded. Once the games start, every guard in town will be around making sure nobody interferes. I've done security for big festivals before."

Radek looked at him sideways. One more snippet, he thought. One more hint of who Ronon had been before Sateda fell. He could see that Ronon had been the kind of young man put on crowd control at festivals, flexible and with good judgment. "It is a thought," Radek said. "The contestants are in the palace now, going through some kind of dedication ceremony." He shrugged. "That would be hard to get them out of."

"Yeah." Ronon scratched his beard absently. "Let's work our way over to the palace and get as close as we can. See how many entrances and guards. Tell you what. You stay here, talk to people and find out as much as you can about the opening of the games and where the contestants are kept tonight. I'll take a look around. Meet you back in an hour."

"That works well enough for me," Radek said.

John looked down from the sparse shelter of a twisted cedar tree on the hillside, squinting into the gathering dark. By dint of a laborious climb, he and Teyla had worked their way to the top of the hill behind the palaces, slipping through alleys and yards, climbing over walls and refuse heaps. They didn't smell very good, but they had at last gained the top slopes, left devoid of buildings for obvious reasons. It was too steep to build, and the rocky, precipitous slope had nothing to recommend it except the view it gave of the city and sea below. If this island were on Earth it would probably be a scenic overlook, but here it was nothing. A few struggling trees clung between rocks, stunted by the continual winds off the sea..

Dusk was falling early. Massive cumulous clouds piled up to the west, hiding the sunset and flashing with lightning in their purple depths. This would not be a very nice place to be in the coming thunder storm. They were going to have to come down before it broke. Too many of the trees bore the marks of being struck by lightning, hardly a surprise considering this was the highest point for miles around.

John wished he still had his binoculars, but he didn't need them to see what he'd come to see. "There it is," he said with satisfaction. "Tucked in nice and neat. They are pretty ships, aren't they?"

Teyla nodded.

The wedge shape of the Wraith cruiser was unmistakable, parked in one of the colonnaded courtyards of the palace below. It wasn't the largest he'd seen, but it very nearly filled the courtyard, a nice job of flying to land it without clipping the buildings around it. Which meant it would be a nice job to take off without hitting them either. John had spent too many years as a helicopter pilot not to appreciate the difficulty of that.

The ramp was lowered and the cruiser seemed to be powered down, resting on its landing gear with its running lights dark. There were no signs of crew about it.

"Standing down," John said. "Must be feeling pretty secure."

"If one of the inhabitants of this world did get aboard they could not fly it," Teyla said. She looked at him, a wrinkle between her brows. "Are you sure you can?"

"No." John didn't particularly like the idea of taking a ship out of that kind of tight parking the first time in the cockpit of a new class. For that matter, the first time in the cockpit of a Wraith ship at all. He'd seen the bits and pieces Zelenka had been putting together of the downed Wraith Dart, and a lot of it was totally unfamiliar. Of course it wasn't, really. There are only so many ways to put things together so they'll fly, but it was possible for the interfaces to be so different that it took even a good pilot months to adapt. He'd learned to fly an Osprey, once, but he'd never gotten used to it. And if he'd tried to take off like this the first time in the seat, even without the approaching storm, John knew he'd have bought the farm. "But we can get to the communications gear. If we can send a signal to our folks, we're good."

Teyla looked like she liked that idea a little better. "At least we can warn them the Wraith are here," she said. Her face looked faintly strained.

"Are they?" he asked.

"Oh yes." Teyla nodded without hesitation. "There are Wraith here, in the palace below. I do not know how many. More than one, less than a hundred. I feel many minds, but not a full ship's compliment." Her eyes unfocused, as though looking at something beyond the immediate.

"Don't," John said, and grabbed her wrist. He'd seen her try this before, with results both good and bad. "There's nobody to snap you out of it, and you might give us away."

Teyla let out a deep breath and looked at him sideways. "You are right," she said with a relieved expression. "I would not get anything very useful, and they might sense me."

"Let's save it," John said. "And concentrate on getting to the communications gear."

In the distance there was the first faint rumble of thunder.

"I do not think I can climb down this side of the hill," Teyla said. "Not with my shoulder useless. We will have to go around."

John had already figured that. It was way too steep. Teyla couldn't do it with one hand. "We'll go down the way we got up and then go around the side. It looks like there's some kind of garden there. I can't tell from here how high that wall is, but with trees on both sides we can probably get over there. They build everything in this rough stone with lots of footholds."

Together they climbed down the hill in the gathering dark. For a moment, as distant lightning flashed and they scrambled around a large boulder, John felt the world shift in a moment of vertigo. Perfect, he thought. That was all he needed. Between his head and Teyla's messed up shoulder, they weren't up to their usual standards at all.

"Are you all right?" Teyla asked, her hand to his shoulder.

"Fine," John said. "I'm good." She probably didn't believe him. But he didn't have energy to waste arguing.

It was almost full dark before they reached the trees along the garden wall. John stopped in the shadow of the wall, ostensibly examining the best way up. If everything would stop tilting it would be easier. He fought back a wave of vertigo induced nausea. It's not real, he told himself. It's just your body not being able to match what your eyes see. Just hang on and it will stop, trees and wall and sky all tilting together.

Teyla was examining the wall, exploring the stones with her good hand. "I think we can manage here," she whispered. "It's lower toward this end and there is better cover."

The vertigo was subsiding. "I think you're right," he said, and took a step toward her.

Teyla spun around, the broken staff she'd taken from the guard in her hand. There was a flash of silver in the trees, the glitter of long, white hair. Teyla caught the Wraith in the throat with the stick, sent him spinning backward among the scattered leaves beneath the trees. Her next movement turned toward him, dropping into guard again as her eyes widened.

She saw what he didn't, but in the next instant he felt the cold muzzle against the back of his neck.

"Drop it," the other Wraith said.

CHAPTER NINETEEN

"I AM MOST UNHAPPY," Radek Zelenka said to no one at all. He stood under a flimsy awning which did little to keep off the pouring rain, while lightning flashed so close that the thunder seemed almost simultaneous. Instinctively he counted as his father had taught him as a child, one thousand one, one thousand two…

Crash. Less than a kilometer away, including vertical distance. "Radek", his father had said long ago, "you should learn how fast sound travels, how far from the flash you are. It is not for lightning. It is for artillery shells. The muzzle flash warns you. The count tells you how far you are away and whether the shells will reach you. I remember once…" His voice had trailed off, his face closing in a way Radek knew too well, not tight but blank.

"I'll remember," Radek had said. "I'll learn."

And he had, of course. The first time he had watched the Wraith bombardment flashing against Atlantis' shields, he had started counting. It gave him the circumference of the shield with comforting accuracy. He wished his father were still alive and that he was not cut off from Earth forever that he might tell him. It is as useful in another galaxy as it was over the Vltava.

The lightning leaped again, illuminating the square in front of the palace on the Holy Island like a strobe light, the thunder a second behind. One thousand one…

On the other side of the square a party was coming around the corner of the buildings, not hurrying as people will do who have been caught out in a storm, but walking slowly and purposefully. Soldiers, he thought. In the intermittent flashes their shields might have been riot gear. Soaked to the bone, his hair plastered to his scalp with rain, Radek watched. The square was almost empty. Of course it was. Most people had fled inside. Only he, who had no home or lodgings to hurry away to, huddled under this dripping awning, his back against the wall. But then he had watched like this before, in cold rain.

Escorting prisoners, he thought. Their careful gait, their measured distance from someone in the center of the rank — prisoners.

The next flash of lightning showed what he wanted to see and what he dreaded. Sheppard, head down, his hands bound behind his back, the rain dripping off his sodden hair. He did not look up. Closely guarded indeed — four men tight around him.

And Teyla. Her arms were also bound, but she lifted her head as though he had shouted, as though he had called her name in a voice audible over even the crashing thunder, her eyes unerringly seeking his. They widened, as though she could not believe she saw him and he wanted to jump up and down, to assure her that it was really he. But of course he didn't. When someone you know is being arrested you must not react. You cannot help them if you are also arrested. Their life may depend on you staying free.

And so Radek did nothing. He stood beneath the awning and watched while the rain dripped down from his soaked pants to his bare feet, wishing for the hundredth time that his shoes had not been lost along with his laptop and radio. Running about the island barefooted on the uneven paving and questionable refuse was not at all comfortable.

Up the steps, Sheppard first. Under the portico. Through the broad doors, the guards still with them.

Radek took off his glasses and squinted into the rain and gathering dark. As wet as they were, they were next to useless. Sheppard and Teyla did not seem injured, and they were prisoners in the palace. They were tightly guarded, but seemed alert. Now he had only to wait for Ronon to get back from his scouting expedition and they should plan what to do.

It would be very nice, of course, to have some dinner. The bit of bread and rough wine they'd been offered on the merchant ship as a courtesy to shipwrecked men had been at midmorning, and it was now after dark. A lovely bit of beef, or even one of the mess hall's ubiquitous hot dogs would be extremely welcome just now. For that matter, Radek thought he could tuck into an MRE with unfeigned enthusiasm. But. They had no money, and there did not seem to be the sort of public feast that accompanied some festivals. Or perhaps there usually was, and the rain had put an end to it. In any event, food did not seem likely unless Ronon had an idea better than armed robbery.

Well, Radek thought optimistically, perhaps the rain would be their friend in any event. It would be very hard for sentries to keep careful watch, and they might be careless. They might prefer to shelter inside rather than stand guard properly, whether Ronon and Radek tried the palace or the maze. It might after all serve them.

Sticking his hands in his wet pockets, Radek leaned back against the wall. Ronon should be along soon, and they would move on to the next thing.

"This is more like it," John said, twisting around as the guard held him at spearpoint while another untied Teyla's hands. He had to duck not to hit his head on the ceiling. The cell was low and dark, with no exterior window and a door of solid, heavy wood.

Teyla grunted, and he knew the roughness of being untied had jerked her injured shoulder painfully. There were four guards, and with the spear point against his chest there were few options at the moment. Teyla seemed to have concluded the same thing, as she backed away from the guard who had untied her instead of stepping forward into a kick. The one with the spear to John's breastbone backed off, and an instant later slammed the door behind him. The heavy sound of the bar on the outside falling into place was clearly audible.

"John?"

"Yeah." He reached out a hand, groping blindly. With the door shut and no lamp, in the absence of a window the cell was pitch dark. He felt her hand on his arm and knew she must have reached too. "Are you ok?"

"I am well," she said. "It only hurt when he jostled it." He imagined that she shrugged. "We may as well sit down and be comfortable," Teyla said, carefully drawing him down to sit beside her on the floor.

He flailed out with one hand searching for the wall and was rewarded with barked knuckles. Yes, the wall was close. John turned around, leaning against the wall. "Much more homey," he said. "Kind of predictable, actually."

Teyla laughed. "I am glad to see that our current lodging suits you better than the last two!"

"It just seems more honest," John said.

He heard her shuffle around and her shoulder brushed his as she settled back against the wall beside him. "I would prefer the other lodging," Teyla said. "Somehow I am not expecting that this will come with a nice dinner and Jitrine to look at your head."

"My head is fine," John said stubbornly.

"Then why were you dizzy earlier?"

"Because I have a concussion."

"I had noticed." Her voice was smiling.

John leaned his head back against the wall. "They're going to let us out of here tomorrow if we're in these Games. It's just overnight. So we might as well try to get some sleep." If he closed his eyes he couldn't see the dark.

"Radek is here," Teyla said.

His eyes popped open. "What?"

"When we were being taken through the square in front of the palace I saw him," she said. "He was across the square, and I'm sure he saw me."

"Are you sure it was him? It was raining pretty hard." John hadn't seen him, but he'd been concentrating on putting one foot in front of the other. It would have been bad to have to puke from dizziness in front of a pile of guards.

"Yes, I am sure it was Radek," Teyla said, but her voice didn't sound certain. "I saw the reflection off his glasses. It might have been a man who looks like him, but we have not seen anyone in this culture with glasses. And he was watching me."

"No Ronon?" If Zelenka and Ronon were here that was the best news he'd had in days.

"I did not see Ronon, but surely Radek could not have gotten here by himself. And he was not a prisoner. He was just standing there under an awning of a shop in the marketplace along the main city square." Her voice was stronger now. "They must be here," she said. "Ronon must be here too. And if they know where we are they will try to get us out."

"Big if," John said, but he couldn't help but feel his spirits lift. Ronon trying to get them out was worth a good deal. And while Ronon was new to the team and he couldn't be a hundred percent certain he'd been right about the Satedan, he was sure that Zelenka wasn't about to give up on them. He and Teyla were good friends, and he'd shown a remarkably stubborn streak the few times John had worked with him. They might get some backup here after all.

Unless Ronon and Zelenka walked right into the Wraith.

"They will try," Teyla said.

"The Wraith."

"I know." He heard her sigh in the darkness. "But Ronon has been fighting the Wraith for years. He will not underestimate them."

Which was true. "We'll just have to stay sharp and be ready for an opportunity when it comes," John said.

"And for that we must sleep," she said.

"Right." There was a long silence.

John stretched out his legs in front of him stiffly. Ok, maybe this escape attempt wasn't the best idea he'd ever had. He'd managed to trade a comfortable room for a hole in the ground. Not an improvement. And his chances of sleeping were about nil. Somehow sitting in a cell waiting for something to happen wasn't really relaxing.

Teyla let out a long sigh.

She wasn't sleeping either. Probably for exactly the same reasons, possibly coupled with an inner monologue of all the things she'd like to say about what an idiot he was to stage an unsuccessful escape attempt that not only didn't get them away, but also left them in a worse situation than they'd started with. But she wouldn't say it. It took a great deal to get Teyla to openly criticize him.

Like the time he'd disobeyed Elizabeth's direct order and hauled Teyla into the middle of a plague that it turned out he was immune to and she wasn't. She'd had a sharp word about that.

But mostly when she thought he was being a total ass she'd just look at him with one eyebrow quirked, as if to say, "Is that your final answer?" That expression always gave him pause.

Of course, if he hadn't crashed the jumper in the first place, then they wouldn't have been captured and none of this would have happened.

"Look," John burst out. "I'm sorry, ok?"

"For what?" Teyla sounded mystified.

"For crashing the jumper."

"You did not intend to crash the jumper," Teyla said reasonably.

"If I'd done a better job flying, we'd be fine," John said.

"If you had done a worse job flying we would be dead," Teyla said.

They sat there in the dark in silence for a long time. He wished he could see her face. He had no idea what she was thinking. Maybe she was asleep.

Teyla sighed, and he heard the sound of cloth rubbing against stone as she shifted position. Not asleep. They couldn't sit here in silence for ten hours until morning.

"Your turn," John said.

"My turn for what?"

"For a story."

He heard her let out a long breath, her shoulder almost against his. "It is, isn't it? What kind of story do you want?"

He shrugged. "Any kind of story."

"I know lots of stories," Teyla said. "You have to pick something."

It came to him, the story he wanted. He wondered if it were taboo, something she shouldn't talk about. But if it were, she'd probably just say so and he'd apologize. This was Teyla, after all. "Tell me about the dead city," John said. "The one across the water from the Stargate, from the camp where I met you on Athos."

She paused a long moment, and when she began again her voice was low. "There are many stories about Emege That Was."

"Is it wrong to ask?"

"No." He could almost see her shake her head. "But there are so many that I must decide which ones. So many stories of my people are about this city, and about those that lived there long ago." Teyla paused again. Then she spoke again, in the formal cadences of what he had begun to think of as her storyteller's voice.

Once and away there was a city called Emege. Once, when the Ancestors ruled, it was a city like any other. People lived in it and worked and raised families and grew old, all under the protection of the Ancestors. And the Ancestors gave to the people of Emege great treasures, and for a while some dwelled there, shedding their grace on their children.

But shadows come, as shadows always do, and the Dark Bird stirred. One by one the Ancestors went from Emege, drawn by troubles far away. "It will not affect you," they promised. "It is only that we have a war to fight, one you cannot understand."

You are thinking now, John, that this story is true. I did not know whether it was or not, until I came to Atlantis, but now I think it is. I think it has a seed of truth, the kernel of that long ago war between the Ancients and the Wraith, as the Ancients were pushed back and back, until all they held was Atlantis.

You see, then the Wraith came. Their cruisers swept over the planet and their vast hive ships, Culling and Culling and Culling. The people of Athos were food for the great armada that besieged Atlantis.

Emege held for a very long time. The Ancestors had given to the people of Emege a great and powerful gift, and beneath the virtue of its power many refugees crowded into the city, the last, safe place on our world. A year and a day, the poets say, Emege held against the Wraith, but at last the virtue was gone from the gift and the city fell. Queen Death stalked the streets and she slew for the love of it, men, women and children alike. Her men dined on the children of Emege, that it might never rise again.

And we cried out to the Ancestors, "Why have you abandoned us? We are your children! We are the daughters and sons of your house! Why do you not come through the Ring with your weapons and your ships? Why have you left us?"

There was no answer. There was never any answer, only the sweep of black wings as the Wraith hunted and hunted. In their wake starvation walked, abandoned markets and abandoned fields scoured by frail scarecrows in rags, gleaning half spoiled food by night. It hardly mattered that the Wraith came less and *less.* There was nothing left to destroy.

And then in the ruins of Emege a young man came up, and his name was Arda. "I have been their prisoner," he said. "I have stood in the feeding pens of the Great Armada, and have returned to tell of it. Death was slain by the power of the Ancestors, but in doing so it has taken all their power and virtue from The World That Is. They are gone, and they will never return. It is of no use to plead for them. We speak to a dead gate, and the waves that reached up and consumed Death have also swallowed them. We are alone, the last children, all that is left."

"I have stood in the feeding pens," he said, "and they have released us, for they are glutted on our brothers. They have put us out to pasture, as a man will let his flocks run loose to forage when their fodder is too expensive, knowing that he can always round them up again later, when he is hungry. What use to keep us aboard their ships, more than their chambers can hold, when left to ourselves we will forage? We can always be hunted at will."

And at that the Last wept, knowing they were the last people in the world, and in time they too would be hunted.

"Do not despair," Arda said. "They will not come here again for a long time, for even evil must sleep, and when they do we will be ready for them. The Ancestors are gone, and their magic and virtue. Now we live in the world of men. But men will not prove so weak as the Wraith may think."

And they said to him, "If the Ancestors could not prevail, with their might and wisdom, surely we have nothing? Surely we are kine who will be harvested in our time."

Arda spoke again, and his words were hard and true. "Does it not come to every man, that in time his mother is gone from him? When we are children we cling to her skirts and seek her for every good thing. She is our happiness, and without her we will starve or die of cold. Every man is born of woman, and we need her with all our strength. But to each of us comes a time, *late or soon, when his mother is gone. Sometimes it is that death takes her soon, leaving us mewling and weak, hoping that some other will take us in and care for us. Sometimes it is that death waits, and our grandchildren sit on her knees when, honored, she passes into that night with her century. But sooner or later, every man stands alone. Sooner or later, his mother cannot save him. The Ancestors are gone, as a mother from us all. We must stand like men, like men and women of good age who are bereft but not cowed. We are not infants who will die without her touch! We are not crawling children, who do not know right from wrong! We are youths, perhaps, who should have known her wisdom and care for many years, but who must stand as men even before our time. And stand we shall."*

And so we did. In time, the towers of Emege again pointed to the sky. In time, her streets lived again, and lights blossomed behind the windows of her houses. The Wraith slept. Two generations passed before they came again, and then three before the next time. Sometimes as much as a century passes between Cullings. Sometimes it is only a few years. Sometimes the Cullings are light, a Dart or two through the Ring, a dozen people lost. Sometimes thousands die, cities falling in flame and sorrow.

But always we know this—this is the age of men. We live, and living hope. Our mothers cannot save us. The Ancestors will never return. The world is what we make of it.

And in that some of us find nothing. That which will be, will be. There is little point in striving, if our efforts will be brought to nothing. And some of us find instead hope. We are not weaker than the Wraith, nor stupider. In time, we will find a way, for everything there is under the sun changes.

That is the story as I learned it, but now I will tell you another. Stories are truth. Stories are life. This is the story Elizabeth Weir told me, and in it she adds another thread to the loom.

Once there were a beleaguered people, forced back and back and back by the Wraith, their warships lost, their numbers trimmed to the bone. Once, the Ancestors submerged their city beneath the sea, that they might stand a little while longer as the last of their kind. Once, they listened to the last of their transports destroyed, their kin screaming their last breaths into vacuum, and they knew they were alone. They could not save their children. They could not save themselves.

Their story ends, as stories do, in the blue flare of a gate. They left their city to sleep beneath the sea and walked through a gate with their children and their bundles, with their parents and foodstuffs for the journey. They walked through a gate.

They walked into your world, into the light of your sun, with their children and their bundles, their parents and their stories. They came to places familiar and strange, and they walked the lands of your world as the last of their kind, the elder children of time.

And where they went, stories followed them. They taught men to build and taught them to govern, and here and there they left something else, for they were not so different from us. They left their cast of face, the shape of their hands, a river of blue-black hair, a pair of green eyes. They dwindled and they vanished, leaving mystery behind.

The story begins, as all stories begin, in the blue fire of a gate. There was a chair beneath the ice, and she woke at her son's touch. There was a city beneath the sea, and she came to life when her son called her. All that ever was, still is. All that may be, yet may be.

As orphans separated by tragedy and war seek each other across the decades, so we seek each other now, your people and mine, brothers and sisters, children of the Ancestors.

So I believe.

Silence fell, all the darker for the visions conjured by her voice. For a moment John had almost seen it, the Giza gate open in hot sun, the Ancients stepping through with their parcels and their sleeping infants, glancing behind as though they could see what they left. They stood in his world, not at the end of their story, but at the beginning of his history.

Once, in the Neolithic, some farmers along the Nile became what we call the Nagada culture. The first line in the textbook, the first slide in the presentation, the opening credits of the documentary.

They came from this gateroom, walked through his gate, leaving Elizabeth to cover the consoles carefully with plastic, and walked into his world as exiles. They left the systems on standby, powered down instead of destroying the city, because like Teyla's people they hoped.

They hoped that sometime their children would walk back through that door.

"Hope is the White Bird," Teyla said. "And her wings beat with unbearable strength."

"Yeah," John said, and squeezed her hand in the dark. White snowfields of Antarctica and the chair glittering like polished glass, a tossed coin rising in the air and flashing as it fell. He had no words for this thing. He was not like Teyla or Elizabeth, who could conjure visions in the dark, make people believe the impossible. But he saw it. He understood, her warm hand clasped in his. "The apple doesn't fall far from the tree," John said, and hoped that made sense.

"No," she said. "It never does."

CHAPTER TWENTY

TO THE NORTH out to sea there were spectacular crashing thunderstorms, but here the skies were clear. Carson Beckett set the jumper down lightly among the dunes along the beach, where a narrow belt of seagrass separated ocean from desert. He cut the power, letting the lights dim to board and emergency lights, and sighed. "We need to talk about this," he said.

Rodney rubbed his forehead. "There isn't anything to talk about, Carson! We keep looking until we find them."

"We can't search the whole bloody planet!"

"Yes, we can!" Rodney shouted. "And we're going to until we find them."

Major Lorne stepped up, standing behind Rodney in the copilot's seat. "Look," he said. "We're not giving up yet. But we've got to think this through. Dr. McKay, we've been at this more than 48 hours. This is the third night with no sleep for you and me. We're making mistakes. We're not making sense. If we keep this up we're going to fly right over them and miss them, or botch the search and have to cover ground we've already covered. We can't search through the night."

"Then what do you suggest?" Rodney snapped. "Just go home?"

"That we go back through the gate, switch out for Dr. Kusanagi flying the jumper with Cadman and a second team on board, and the rest of us stand down for ten hours. Dr. McKay, you've been going for three days. That's about the limit." Lorne put his hand on the back of the chair. "We're not going to find them by wearing ourselves out and crashing this jumper."

"Dr. Kusanagi? Please! She's no pilot," Rodney scoffed.

"Neither am I," Carson said. "But nobody seems to remember that. Miko does all right." He looked at Rodney, his face uplit by the board, dark circles under his eyes. "Rodney, be reasonable. We'll do a better job coming back fresh in ten hours."

Rodney closed his eyes. Going back through the gate felt like defeat. It felt like giving them up, abandoning them. They'd never give up on him. When he and Elizabeth had been the prisoners of the Genii leader Kolya during the storm, Sheppard hadn't even considered ditching him.

And yet he knew he was exhausted. Even with the handy stimulants Major Lorne had asked Dr. Beckett for, he knew he was just about at the limit. This was the point where the mind started to play tricks.

"Ten hours," Carson said. "Do I need to make it a medical stand down?"

Last year he would have battled it out with Carson, but that was before he'd seen quite so much of other planets. Before he'd been nearly killed quite so many times. This was not a piece of cake, and a mistake could doom his team. Rodney swallowed. Carson was probably right. Rodney shook his head. "No. Back to the gate, people. Let's radio ahead and tell Kusanagi to get her butt in gear."

"Cadman, you'll lead a fresh team," Lorne said. "You've had some sleep in the back, right?"

"I'm good, sir," Cadman said brightly. "And I've been watching the grid. Dr. Kusanagi and I will stick to the grid and report in every hour."

"That way we'll keep covering ground," Lorne said. "And you guys may find them. We've covered the entire length of the canal from the crash site to the ocean. It's time to start expanding the circle. Center on the crash site and make sweeps out at twenty kilometer increments. That ought to get a couple hundred miles out before we relieve you again in the morning."

"Will do, sir," Cadman said.

Carson eased the jumper back into the air again, the minutes elongating over the desert in swift flight. When Rodney dialed the gate, the flash of blue fire was visible for miles. It should have been welcoming, but to Rodney it was defeat. I'll be back, he promised silently. I will be.

It seemed like centuries before Ronon returned, but according to Radek's watch it was only an hour and twelve minutes. The rain had slowed to a drizzle, but Radek was soaked to the skin and long since past wishing for a warm fire or a hot bath. A warm fire seemed likelier, but probably still out of reach.

Ronon walked casually around the edge of a building. He knew better than to creep when such would seem more alarming than simply strolling. The city was full of strangers who might be abroad, but only thieves would be sneaking. "Come on," he said.

"Come where?"

"Come on." Ronon disappeared back around the corner of the building, and throwing his hands up in the air, Radek followed.

"Would you care to tell me where we are going?" he hissed.

"This way." They made their way along the slick streets, dark between the buildings. There were of course no modern streetlights, and only the occasional lit window provided any light outside. The pavers were as uneven as those he'd grown up with in the old parts of cities not wrecked by war, and he liked them no better here than there. They were a pain in the behind quite literally on a motorcycle. He'd skidded into a signpost in rain like this, in Old Town Prague, and torn a ligament in his knee that kept him on crutches for a month.

It was full of these cheerful thoughts that he almost ran into Ronon when he stopped and eased a door open. From within came the distinct smell of goats.

"Lovely," Radek said.

Ronon ducked in and Radek followed, pulling the door shut behind him.

"I found this place," Ronon said. "I think the people in the house are gone. The goats are gone. So it's a good place for us to hole up for a few hours." It was dark, but Radek could hear the sound of Ronon moving around.

"It is dry," Radek said optimistically. And if no goats were currently in residence that could only be to the good.

Some dim light came in from a window in the back, showing hay and a coil of rope on the wall, a trough containing stale water.

Ronon sat down on one of the bales of hay. "Here," he said, reaching under his coat. "I found us some food."

"As in stole?"

Ronon shrugged. There was half a loaf of brown bread and what seemed to be four hardboiled eggs.

That was not too bad after all. It wasn't as though he were likely to steal a bowl of stew.

Ronon handed over two of the eggs very fairly, and Radek sat down beside him and began peeling one of them. It really did smell amazingly good, and it tasted even better.

"I found Sheppard and Teyla," Radek said.

Ronon looked up and blinked. "What?"

"While you were scouting," Radek said with some satisfaction. "They were prisoners. They were being escorted into the palace under heavy guard. Their hands were tied, but they did not seem injured. Teyla saw me, and I am almost certain that she recognized me. They know we are here."

"How many men?" Ronon asked, tearing off a chunk of bread and passing the rest to Radek.

"Eight," he replied. "They were going in the main entrance very heavily guarded. Perhaps they had tried to escape."

"I would have." Ronon bit off a bite. "Wish we knew where they were held."

"I could hardly follow them in," Radek pointed out. "I thought it best to wait and tell you."

"Yeah." Ronon pushed a sodden braid back out of his eyes and nodded thoughtfully. "It doesn't matter where they're held tonight. We know where they're going to be tomorrow. I found the exit from the maze and checked it out."

Radek leaned back on the hay. It was nice and dry in here. "So what do we have?"

"There's a courtyard in front of it but no seats. Pretty strange, because you'd think people would want to sit and see the winners come out."

"Unless they are watching from somewhere else," Radek said. "As you pointed out before. Which suggests something very strange is going on here."

"Yeah. The entrance itself is just an archway. There are two guards there now, but they weren't standing outside or anything. They were sitting inside playing a dice game." Ronon shrugged. "Not a big thing, to stand in the pouring rain, guarding an empty room. No wonder they're slacking. I couldn't see very far inside, but it seemed like there was a complex — a bunch of tunnels running in various directions."

"It's a maze," Radek said. "We expect that."

"Yeah, but did we expect power cables?" Ronon paused to let that sink in. "There were a bunch of power cables running along the ceiling. They've got microphones or video or something in there."

"Which means there is something we can use," Radek said thoughtfully. Power cables meant a power source. And any power source could be a source of trouble in his hands.

"So here's the plan. We go down an hour before dawn and slip in. If the guards are outside, I'll take care of them. If not, we just get past them and get inside. Then we figure out what's going on, grab Sheppard and Teyla, and get out of here."

"That works," Radek said. "But first we get some rest, yes?"

"Yeah." Ronon settled back in the hay. "Didn't get any sleep last night hanging on to an overturned boat. We can get a few hours now and be rested when we go in before dawn." He looked over at Radek, who was contemplating his second egg. "Better than the boat."

"Here." Radek handed the egg back.

Ronon looked at it but didn't take it.

"Go on," he said. "You are much bigger than me. I have one egg and some bread, you have three and some bread. It is fair."

"Ok." Ronon took it back and started to peel it thoughtfully.

Radek burrowed down in the hay, though his stomach still growled. Tomorrow they would rescue Sheppard and Teyla. And then what? He shoved that thought back down. Perhaps Sheppard would have some ideas. He usually did.

Rodney awoke in darkness, struggling up from dreams that vanished even as he grabbed at them. Just as well, really. He probably didn't want them. Rodney groaned, rolling over and looking at the clock. He'd slept just over three hours.

Great. Six more hours of the stand down. He should sleep more. He should sleep. That's what he was here to do. Sleep. In and out. Breathing. Sleeping.

Only not. He was wide awake, his blood surging with adrenaline to run away from something that only existed in his dream. When he needed to sleep. Because it was important for him to sleep. So that tomorrow he could go save everybody from whatever it was they'd gotten themselves into this time.

Not really tomorrow. It was a little after 9 am, Atlantis time. Days and nights didn't match where he'd spent the last three days. Sleep. He needed to sleep. He was supposed to be sleeping. Because later today he'd have to be brilliant.

He should think about something nice. Not sheep. Sheep

weren't nice. Sheep were dirty, smelly and stupid, three things
he didn't like. He should think about something that wasn't
dirty, smelly or stupid.

Sam Carter came to mind. She was neither dirty, smelly
nor stupid. Ok, perhaps there had been occasions in the past
in the field when she had been dirty and smelly, but she was
never stupid. And when he'd last seen her she'd been reasonably well washed.

"Do you want the Lost City?"

*Rodney blinked at her. "Huh?" he said. She wore an over-
sized black t-shirt with drab BDUs, and somehow the effect
was pretty stunning.*

*Stunning in the sense of she'd like to shoot him with a zat
gun. She looked irritated. "I said, do you want the Lost City?
Dr. Weir is going to be heading up a team that looks at the fea-
sibility of an expedition to the Lost City of the Ancients, based
on the information recovered from the Antarctic outpost. Are
you interested in being on her team?"*

*Rodney straightened up, putting his laptop on the desk in
front of him. "This is another excuse to send me somewhere
other than the SGC, isn't it?"*

Sam's eyebrows rose. "Why would you think that?"

*"Because you had me sent to Siberia for six months? To go be a
special liaison to the Russian program? Maybe because of that?"
Rodney snapped. "Now you want to send me to Antarctica? I
think you just can't deal with the competition around here."*

*Her arms came up, crossing over her chest. "You can think that
if you like," Sam said. "I was actually trying to do you a favor.
Dr. Weir's expedition may not pan out, but if it does you'd be
the chief scientist on what might turn out to be the most exciting voyage of discovery that mankind has ever attempted. At
least that people from Earth have ever attempted," she amended.
"But don't let that get in the way of your ego. Of course I'm just*

*trying to get rid of you because I think you're going to upstage
me somehow." She turned to leave. "Never mind. Forget I said
anything, McKay. I'm sure there are plenty of other people who'd
be happy to do it. I'll just call Dr. Weir and Dr. Jackson and tell
them you're not interested."*

"Wait wait wait." Rodney hurried around the desk to get in
front of her at the door. "Dr. Jackson?"

"Dr. Jackson is in Antarctica right now working on the Ancient
database, since he has the most complete reading knowledge of
Ancient on Earth. He thinks that he may be able to derive a gate
address soon, but of course he's not a scientist. He's having a great
deal of trouble with the technology. But if you're not interested,
I'm sure that General O'Neill can find someone..."

"Who knows more about Ancient technology than I do?"
Rodney gave her a jaunty smile. "Wrong. There's only one person on the planet who knows more about Ancient technology
than I do."

"Me," Sam said, uncrossing her arms.

"Actually, I meant General O'Neill, but he's probably forgotten it again," Rodney said quickly.

"Are you interested or not?" she asked. "Because if you're not
up for it, that's ok."

Rodney gave her his most charming smile. "If Dr. Jackson is
having trouble with the Ancient technology, I'm sure I can give
him a hand." That was smart. After all, Dr. Jackson was a good
friend of hers. She might appreciate him playing nice. Jackson
was just a social scientist, and couldn't be expected to figure out
anything complicated. "So," Rodney said, "How about dinner
tomorrow night? We could grab a bite after work..."

"I'm engaged," Sam said shortly.

"Ok. How about Wednesday, then? Wednesday would work
for me."

She stared at him. "Engaged. To be married."

"Oh." Rodney felt the blood rush to his face. "Engaged. As in *married. Not as in have an engagement tomorrow night."* He blinked. *"To who?"*

"Detective Pete Shanahan, with the Colorado Springs PD." She put her hands on her hips.

"Oh." Rodney blinked again. *"You, um, like action hero types then. Shoot 'em up stuff."*

"He's a police officer, not a cowboy," Sam said.

Rodney nodded. *"Detective. Smart guy? Smooth, suave, that kind of thing? Laconic? Dark past? All kinds of unspeakable suffering revealed in his gaze?"*

"Not so much," she snapped. *"Pete is a nice guy. He's outdoorsy and playful and..."*

"You're deliriously happy?"

"Yes."

Rodney leaned back on the desk. *"You don't sound like it. Deliriously happy, I mean."*

"I am."

"Oh come on!" Rodney exclaimed. *"Nice, outdoorsy and playful? He sounds like a golden retriever!"*

She pursed her lips, and he thought for a second that she was really mad, madder than maybe she'd ever been at him, but then he saw the laughter in her eyes and she broke. *"There you have me, Rodney,"* Sam laughed, biting her lip in what he thought was an absolutely adorable gesture. *"He is kind of like a golden retriever."*

"So you'll have dinner with me?" It always pays to press the advantage when you're winning.

Sam grinned at him, her head to the side, and turned for the door. *"No."* She stopped just inside and looked back. *"What about the Lost City?"*

"I'm going," Rodney said. *"What did you think?"*

And he had, of course. It's not like you can live with yourself if you say no, spend your life wondering what would have happened if you'd been one of the few who dared to do something really extraordinary. After all, even the best of the best have to stretch a little, reach for a prize that's really worthy of their talents.

Tomorrow — today — he'd find their missing people. He promised. He wouldn't quit until he did.

And with that thought, Rodney fell asleep.

CHAPTER TWENTY-ONE

RADEK JERKED AWAKE at a cry, but before he was even properly conscious it stopped. He lay there in the darkness, wondering what it was that had awakened him. Not goats, though the shed smelled strongly of them. Perhaps a dog in a different yard, or a sound outside in the street.

Ronon was awake. He could hear his breath in the dark, quick gasps half stifled.

Radek rolled over. In the dim light that came in from the window he could see Ronon lying open eyed on the straw, his pupils huge and dark in a face rendered paler in silhouette. It came to him in that moment that Ronon was still young. How old had he been when he became a runner? Twenty, perhaps? Like Edmond Dantes, tragedy had stolen his youth, made him older than his years. He looked terrified, as though surfacing from some terrible dream Radek did not even care to speculate upon. He would not want Radek to know it.

And why should he not be frightened? One ought to be, trapped without resources hundreds of kilometers from the Stargate, on an alien world full of Wraith. Surely this was not the first time Ronon had been in such circumstances, all the more reason to be afraid. All the more reason to be plagued with bad dreams.

Loudly and distinctly, Radek stretched, turning over and reopening his eyes as though for the first time. "Ronon?" he whispered.

"Yeah?" His voice sounded almost normal.

"I cannot sleep," Radek said, allowing a note of apology to creep into his tone. "Nerves, you know. Talk with me."

"What do you want to talk about?"

A distraction, at least. He would not be able to dwell upon whatever it was while keeping up a conversation. "It does not matter," Radek said. He waited a moment, as though the idea were suddenly striking him. "It is your turn for a story."

"I don't remember any," Ronon said.

"A poem then," Radek said.

Ronon turned his head and looked at him. "Are you a poet?"

"Me? No." Radek shrugged. "I am an engineer, and I have no gift for words. But there are some I learned in school that stick with me, and some others I carry around here." He tapped his temple. "My father said that the ones you know are the ones that can never be taken from you. You can pull them out and enjoy them wherever you are, whenever you wish, no matter what may happen around you, with no one the wiser. And so there are a few I know. So few, I am afraid. I am a scientist, and I have no gift of memory."

Ronon nodded, rolling onto his back, looking up at the low ceiling of the shed. It was a long time before he spoke, and Radek had almost decided he would not. "We learned some in school too. A lot of them. I used to know the first fifty lines of the Yennam Cycle straight off. But I've forgotten them now." His eyes were shadowed in the dimness. "You wear them out when you think them too much. They get holes in them and you forget them."

Radek nodded. "I can see how that would be," he said gently. He is like the old men, Radek thought, the ones who tell you they do not remember the war, and perhaps they are not lying.

A silence fell. Ronon cleared his throat, his voice almost a whisper, but growing stronger.

Rushlight, quick-bright
Glimmers soft and fair,
Swamp glade, music laid
Trembling in the air.
Marsh weed, strife seed,
Memories in the water,
Crippled lark, moondark
Presage the coming slaughter.

> *Greyfish, death wish*
> *To light the rising dawn,*
> *Nightshade, broken blade*
> *Sinking, sinking, gone.*

When he had been silent a long moment Radek spoke again. "That is lovely," he said. "What is it part of?"

"It's about a king a long time ago," Ronon said. "He was murdered by his brother while they were hunting in the marshes." He shrugged. "It's not just the Wraith who fight wars. We're pretty good at killing each other too."

"I know," Radek said. He wondered if it would be too much to reach out and clasp Ronon's shoulder. Probably it would. So he did not. "I shall sleep better now," he said, but did not close his eyes until after Ronon did.

"We can find them," Rodney said. "We're not giving up on them." He felt only a little better for a few hours sleep, but surely coffee could fix that. Coffee could fix anything.

Elizabeth Weir folded her arms across her chest. The door to her office was shut, so that no one could hear her conversation with him and Lorne. "I'm not saying we should, Rodney. But you've been searching for two days and found nothing. I need to hear a plan that's going to work. Your present plan seems to be to fly around in circles and hope you bump into them. I think you need to rethink this."

Major Lorne straightened his shoulders. "We are following a search grid, ma'am."

"And following that search grid, how long will it take you to complete a full survey of the planet?" Weir asked.

"Six days," Lorne said, and Rodney winced. "Give or take a little."

"Six days." That was Elizabeth at her most skeptical. "Six more days flying around the planet twenty four hours a day."

"With all due respect, ma'am," Lorne said, "It's not going to take six days to find them. They're not going to be on the other side of the planet, and we're proceeding methodically outward."

"Do you know they're not on the other side of the planet?" Elizabeth asked. "You don't know where they are or how they might have gotten there. You've already searched the area near the crashed jumper, near the Stargate, and near where Zelenka and Ronon were supposed to be."

Rodney leaned forward on the desk. "Just what are you saying?"

"I'm saying that you need to consider indigenous modes of transportation. And you need to consider the planet's inhabitants. They're human. Don't you think it's likely that our people have made contact? Don't you think it's more likely that they might have sought assistance and food from the people who live there than that they would be wandering off in a random direction? Why would Colonel Sheppard or Dr. Zelenka go stand in the middle of the desert or a trackless forest? Give our people credit for a little common sense. Let's apply some logic as well as method to the search."

"I'm doing this by the book, ma'am," Lorne said. "A search grid is the recommended way to find people."

Elizabeth pulled Rodney's laptop toward her. "I know you're doing it by the book, Major. But we need to be a little more flexible, and take other factors into account. We know our people. We know what they're likely to do. Now let's look at this together. Where were the population concentrations that you observed?"

It seemed that only moments later Ronon was shaking his shoulder, that Radek must have barely closed his eyes. "Time to get up," Ronon said.

Radek blinked and scrabbled for his glasses, which had

slipped off. "Yes, yes. I am coming," he said.

Ronon stood up, stretching his arms. It was still raining, though not nearly as hard as the night before. A chilly, gray morning — not the best for games. But perhaps it would distract the guards from their duty. He certainly would not want to be standing out in the rain for hours.

In the pre dawn darkness they made their way through the sleeping city, down a broad, curving path that led along the edge of a sharp drop. Poles marked the sides of it, sodden banners dripping from each one. Radek was sure in bright sunshine it made a fine show, but in the damp dawn it looked rather sad.

Ronon stopped ahead of him, holding his hand out. "There," he whispered.

Below, where the path curved around, was a small paved area delineated with more banners. Beyond it, in the side of the hill, was an archway of white stone that gleamed in the dim light. He did not see any guards.

"This way," Ronon whispered again, and slipped effortlessly off the path and into the jumble of rocks on the steep hillside, moving from one to another with surefooted grace.

Radek shook his head. He was likely to break his neck that way. Still, the best he could do was try to follow.

He must have been loud, for several times as they worked their way closer Ronon looked back at him with annoyance, but the sound of the rain covered all. A gloomy, dark morning with little to recommend it, Radek thought. He slipped on a jagged rock, sliding half way to his knees and banging his left elbow painfully. Ronon looked around again. He made a hand motion that Radek chose to interpret as 'stay down,' and so he did so while Ronon crept closer, almost invisible against the stones.

It seemed to Radek that Ronon was gone for a very long time. When he did return, climbing back toward where Radek waited, his expression was grim.

"What is it?" Radek whispered as Ronon sank down beside him.

"Wraith," Ronon said.

"What?"

"There are Wraith here," Ronon said. "That Wraith cruiser we saw day before yesterday? It must be set down somewhere around here."

"It has not sounded like a Culling," Radek said. Though admittedly his experience in such things was limited, he imagined it would involve a lot of shouting and fleeing.

"It's not a Culling. These people are working with the Wraith like the Olesians were," Ronon said. "Which explains where they're getting this tech stuff. The two regular guards were down there and there was a Wraith with them. One of the masked guys, not one of the long haired guys."

Radek sat very still. A horrible thought had occurred. Looking at Ronon, he saw the same thought written on his face. "Tribute," Radek said.

Ronon nodded slowly. "Wraith like games. That's why they make Runners."

"This is a game like that," Radek said. "A contest where everyone loses."

"They let one guy go at the end and feed on all the others," Ronon said. "It makes sense. They like to play with their food. I bet they've got a nice comfortable TV room somewhere and are watching the whole thing on camera, making their bets. It's how they do with Runners, when they can. They send these video feeds after you, drones to follow you around and catch the action on tape."

Radek shuddered. This man had spent seven years on the run from this. He could not even begin to imagine what that must have been like. "And they have Sheppard and Teyla," Radek said.

"And a bunch of other people too," Ronon said grimly. "Those people we saw on the ship. The old lady. Those kids."

Radek shook his head. Truly, he should not be surprised by the scope of evil. But it was nice to think it less than it was, a constant mistake of the optimistic. "What are we going to do?"

Ronon smiled, and it was not a nice smile at all. "We're going to screw up their little party. Are you with me, Zelenka?"

"Absolutely," Radek said.

Teyla dreamed, and in her dream she was in Atlantis. She walked through the corridors like mist or smoke, the way it seemed to her when she reached out to the Wraith during the siege, when it seemed to her that she stood upon a hive ship. She walked through Atlantis, and doors opened ahead of her as they always did for John. They opened at her thought, live and bright in her mind.

Teyla came into the control room, the banks of machines humming quietly to themselves. The room was light and cool. Only the people were gone. Wraith manned every console. The daylight through the tall stained glass windows gleamed off long white hair.

She recoiled, backing into the doorway, as the nearest one turned. "Welcome home," he said. Before she could scream, before she could so much as move, he bent his head, hair falling forward like a torrent of silver.

At the communications console the other Wraith did the same, ornamented leather whispering as he inclined his head in deference.

"The Osprey queens are always the most beautiful," the first said, raising his eyes to her. "And the strongest. Atlantis is yours. What is your will, My Queen?"

She froze, horror creeping upward in her throat. She stretched out her arms, tight sleeves of white leather ornamented with silver, long greenish hands, the backs of them protected by bracelets of silver mesh fastening to wrist and first finger, ornamented with tiny gemstones. A Wraith queen's hands.

A third Wraith stepped around the last console, his chin high and eyes bright. "Welcome home, My Queen," he said. "You see we have saved the best for you." He reached back behind the console, jerking someone forward into the light. With a swift motion, he shoved Sheppard to his knees, a torn gag stoppering his mouth beneath his eyes glittering with fear and pain. His shirt was open at the collar, the pulse jumping in his throat, ready and waiting...

CHAPTER TWENTY-TWO

TEYLA SHRIEKED, struggling in pitch darkness with something that held her fast, gripping her shoulder and her wrist. She twisted, trying to get her weight behind it. She must fight it. She must get free.

"Hey! Hey, stop it!" It was John's voice. "Teyla! It's a dream!"

It was John, this thing she struggled against, one hand of his behind her head to keep it from banging against the stone wall.

"It's ok," he said. "It's just a dream."

"A dream." They were surrounded by impenetrable darkness. The cell. A cell on the Holy Island. That's where they were. There were no Wraith in Atlantis. She was no Wraith. It was nothing but the stuff of nightmare.

"It's a dream," John said again. "You were thrashing around. It's a dream. Stuff like that happens."

"I dreamed I returned to Atlantis and it was controlled by the Wraith," Teyla said, her heart still pounding in her chest. "There were Wraith everywhere." She could not bring herself to say more. It was so vivid before her still — John on his knees, her hand flashing with silver and gems as she reached for his chest to take the life from him.

She wondered if he looked concerned, for he stilled. "Have you had dreams like this before?"

Teyla started to shake her head. " No. And yes." Her pulse was slowing a little, no longer pounding in her ears. She took a deep breath. She had dreamed that she was Wraith before, seen her own face in the mirror and had it be that of a queen. "I dreamed about the Wraith often during the siege, before we knew what the Gift meant." That was when she had a dream like this before. It was a warning.

"Yeah, but that time there was a Wraith commando loose in the city," John said. "You weren't imagining it. There really were Wraith close by." He shifted heavily, letting go now that she was no longer flailing. "Are there Wraith close now?"

That coldness in the pit of her stomach, the overwhelming urge to flee rendered impossible by confining walls…

"Yes," she said, trying to focus it, to control it rather than have it control her. "There are Wraith very close by. Several of them. They cannot be more than a few dozen yards. Upstairs, perhaps, in the rooms overhead. That is why I feel this so strongly." She gripped his hand. It was a warning, but one she could not act upon. "John. It is hard not to react, when every bone in my body screams that we must flee."

"I'd love to," John said. "Only there's the little problem of this cell…"

She laughed, as no doubt he meant for her to. Yes, easier to come down this way. It was a dream, like the ones before, a manifestation of her Gift. That was all. "It is like in this book you gave me, Watership Down. When the rabbits are not able to flee and freeze with terror instead, because what approaches is so terrible, and yet there is no way out."

"We're big rabbits," John said. "Maybe the Wraith should be worried instead."

"Only you would say that when we're locked in a hole in the ground."

"What? Because I'm the bravest guy you know?" He was teasing, but she appreciated it all the same.

"No. Because you are utterly insane," she said, intending the same spirit.

"Probably," he said quietly, and perhaps it was the darkness that caused him to say more than that. "My ex-wife thought I was. Some of the stuff when I got back from overseas… It wasn't anything Nancy bargained on coping with. But you know. It comes and goes. You deal with it."

"I do know," Teyla said. His words were very offhanded, and yet she held her breath. She hardly knew what to make of honesty from him, of things that were so raw. He was not a man who spoke easily or often, and she felt as though the wrong word might silence him, might end this tentative trust.

"What do your people do? You know. After a Culling," he said quietly.

Teyla took a breath. Talking about this was steadying, and perhaps he did indeed want to know. Perhaps he truly was curious, as eager to learn as to teach. "We sing. We cry. We remember." There were Wraith just overhead. Many of them. "We mourn. Sometimes it is too soon to speak of the Lost, or the situation is too dangerous. We are still in peril, and there is no time for mourning. But when there is, we drink and we scream and we lament." She stopped, wishing she needed to say no more, but honesty deserved an honest answer. "And then when that is done we suffer in silence." She waited, but he did not speak. "And you?"

"I've never been through a Culling," he said, and she thought of those she had met in his imagining of home, when they had been trapped in an alien mindgame rather than on Earth. When she had gone to visit a place of John's that had never existed, drunk beer with men who were dead. Teyla had not met those friends. They were gone long before the Earthmen came to Athos. They lived now only in John Sheppard's mind, at that illusory party by a swimming pool in a place he had never actually lived. Home was an imaginary apartment full of ghosts where the beer was always cold and the lost were found.

"No, I suppose not," she said softly. "I am sure you do not in the least understand what I mean."

There was the sound of footsteps outside, and the bar on the door rattled. Teyla jumped to her feet, managing not to run into John in the process, as he was doing the same.

The door opened. Four human guards stood outside. The

first reached in with spear leveled. "Come on."

Blinking into the light, John stepped forward. For a moment Teyla wondered if he were going to grab the spear shaft, but he did not. It was possible, but probably not the best plan. If they did fight their way clear of these four men, the spear would give them little against Wraith with energy weapons. Better to wait for an opportunity where they had more latitude, and more chance of success.

"Come out," the guards said, gesturing again.

John walked out, his hands held well away from his body, and she followed. One of the guards eyed him suspiciously. "Special prisoners?"

The first guard looked John up and down. In his dirty BDUs, three days growth of beard on his face, a stitched up cut across his forehead, he did not look particularly formidable. Nor particularly alien. There was nothing about him, other than his basic style of dress, which made him stand out at all. Nothing that screamed "Take me to the Wraith!" Teyla fervently hoped her own appearance was equally unnoteworthy.

The first guard shrugged. "No, just send them out with the others." He looked at John evenly. "Better for you if you don't make trouble. After all, you might win the Games. You look like you can handle yourself."

"Thanks," John said. Some time in the night he'd removed the old bandage, and the dark stitches were clearly visible against his skin. Still, it seemed to be healing.

Teyla took a step toward him, hoping that the direction to send them with the others meant her as well. She could not help but worry that as strongly as she felt the Wraith they must be aware of her too.

The guard's eyes fell on her, then flicked back to John. "Your wife?"

"No," John said.

"Good. It's everyone for themselves inside the maze. You

hang back and wait for somebody, you lose." He gestured for them to walk ahead of him down the corridor.

They did, spear points at their backs. At the end of the corridor was a courtyard full of people milling around. A couple of them might have been warriors, but most of them were a mix of ages and professions, men and women of different lands, the youngest a girl and boy of twelve or thirteen who stood together nervously, the oldest Jitrine, her white hair clearly visible in the sun.

John glanced at Teyla as they were herded in with the others, and his eyebrow quirked. "Everyone for themselves?"

"Of course," Teyla said, glancing around. There were perhaps a dozen guards, and five archers on the wall above. "Otherwise a single rush would take them down."

"But these people aren't going to do that," John said. "Look at them. A crowd of civilians. People don't act like that. They don't act together. They haven't got the training to take the chance. If I yelled 'get them!' they'd all just stand there."

Teyla nodded. "Most people are afraid of getting hurt. And so they will go to their deaths rather than risk pain. It is the first thing you must learn in stick fighting. You must learn how to be hurt. And once you have mastered the fear of being hurt, you realize it is only pain." She looked at him sideways. "That is why you are a good student. You aren't afraid of pain."

"I'm good with pain, actually," John said.

Teyla froze as a new figure appeared on the wall above.

His long white hair almost glittered, and the somberness of his black leathers were relieved by a cloak of silvery blue that snapped and waved against the clearing sky. He wore a circlet across his forehead set with heavy blue stones, and a fancy mesh of gold and jewels covered the back of his feeding hand. His face was proud and haughty, and he lifted his chin like a god or king.

The guards did not bow, but most of the people around John

and Teyla threw themselves to their knees. "It is the High King!" someone whispered, tugging at Teyla's sleeve.

She shook his hand off. She would not bow to any Wraith.

John remained standing too, as well as a handful of others, though it would have been wiser for him to blend in. "I've got a problem with my knees," he said out of the corner of his mouth, and Teyla almost smiled.

She had not paid attention to the beginning of his speech, which seemed to be laying out the rules of the game. Contestants would enter the maze in small groups a few minutes apart. There, they would face challenges and obstacles. The person who exited first was the winner and would be set free with a fabulous prize in gold. There was no mention of what would happen to the rest of the contestants, though Teyla thought she could guess far too easily.

She could see John sizing up the other players. They fell into two groups, those who hoped to win and those who already despaired. Some, like Jitrine, knew they had little chance of beating out warriors in a trial of strength and endurance. Others eyed the contestants thoughtfully, as if deciding who to get out of the way. More than one pair of eyes lingered on John, though fewer did on her. She did not look as obviously prepossessing as he did. With three days growth of beard and the cut across his forehead, he looked like a ruffian to watch out for.

Those were the contestants angling their way toward the front. Obviously the first groups would have an advantage in getting through the maze. It did not seem that the contest was only one of skill, but also of speed.

John seemed in no hurry, content to hang back as the speech ended and the eager ones crowded forward, so she remained beside him.

At the Wraith Lord's signal, two guards stepped forward with gold staves in hand. They stretched them over a section of pavement. With a grinding sound, the stones began to part smoothly, exposing a dark hole between them that might be deep as an abyss.

A moan rose from the crowd, except for the contestants who still pressed forward eagerly, intending to be the first. Unsurprisingly, there were six men at the fore, big men that Teyla had marked for warriors. Of course they would want to be first. The cordon of guards parted and three of the six were chosen out, matched with three random people from the crowd, two women and an old man.

Some pushed forward and some pushed back. In the milling around, Teyla saw that Jitrine had come to John's elbow. "How is your head?" she asked.

"Better." John put his head to the side. "Why are you here?"

"I told you," Jitrine said simply. "I have enemies. And it seems they were more powerful than my friends. So I take my chances in the labyrinth."

"Those chances are slim," John said. He glanced over to the pit, where already a shout came from below. Some of the first group were losing no time in beginning to eliminate rivals.

"There will be those below who are injured," Jitrine said, and her chin rose.

"Yes," John said. His face looked serene. Teyla had seen that expression before when he flew, when he was judging to a nicety the distance from obstacles, avoiding shots by a hair. She had seen it fleeing the Wraith armada with Orin's family aboard, dialing the gate with that look of concentration that was almost rapture. "Don't worry," he said to Jitrine. "Just stick with us."

"That is not wise, Sheppard," Jitrine said with dignity. "You know that only one can win. You, by yourself, might have a chance."

"We're not going there," he said. "Teyla's my team. We go together. You stick with us, and we'll get you through."

"People have tried that before," Jitrine said. "It does not work.

Those who make common cause are destroyed."

"We'll take our chances," John said. He looked at Jitrine keenly. "Will you?"

"I am a doctor. I will go with you so far as I may, as much as the ethics of my profession allow."

"Fair enough."

The second group had gone down while they waited, and it was not lost on Teyla that the Wraith Lord had disappeared. Probably to join his fellows wherever they intended to watch the games from, for surely they meant to observe what happened underground! She shivered. If the Wraith had noticed her he had not acted. Probably he had not noticed her. She had not reached out with her mind, and when she did not she might seem as ordinary as any other human. Certainly when she had been captured by the Wraith before, in the Culling Sheppard and his men had interrupted, they had paid her no special attention. Perhaps they had not noticed anything at all.

The third group went down, and they moved forward, John carefully keeping her and Jitrine one to each side.

"Play it like it goes," he said in a low voice. "Let's not pick a fight. But if they jump you..."

"I will take care of myself quite adequately," Teyla said.

He had the good sense to look abashed. "I know. I meant with your shoulder and all."

"We will look after one another," Teyla said, and gave him a small smile to indicate that she was not really angry.

"Yeah."

There was no one in front of them. The guards gestured. Before their feet there was a steep stairway running down into darkness.

"Here goes nothing," John said.

CHAPTER TWENTY-THREE

THE STEPS LED down into darkness. John went down carefully, Teyla and Jitrine behind. Presumably there were another three people to make up their group following. The ones eager to be in the labyrinth had already descended in the first groups.

There was the glow of firelight ahead, and the corridor broadened. John looked about and nodded with satisfaction as the others came down behind. "You enter a ten by ten corridor," John said. "It's lit by four brackets with torches in them. Ahead of you, a ten by ten corridor runs straight ahead. There are also ten by ten corridors going off to the left and the right." He grinned. "It's perfect."

Teyla looked confused. "What are you talking about?"

"It's a roleplaying game. I used to play it as a teenager. The dungeons always start exactly like this." Jitrine was also looking at him with bewilderment. The other three people pushed on ahead, glancing back nervously at his smile and heading straight down the center corridor. They might think his amusement was a little odd, under the circumstances.

Teyla shook her head. "I have no idea what you are talking about."

"It's a puzzle. A game. I used to play a game like this," he said.

Now she looked alarmed. "With people?"

"No, not with people!" John shoved his hair back out of his eyes. "Well, with pretend people. My friends and I had these characters…" This would take a week. "Look, it's a really complicated game. But it's just like this." He looked around the smoothed stone walls, the iron brackets with torches. Yep. Just like the game. Except for that.

John took a step around, getting his back to it so no one could read his lips. "Teyla, look over my left shoulder. Up where the wall meets the ceiling."

She breathed out. "A camera."

"Yeah."

Jitrine shook her head. "I do not understand."

"They've got to track their bets," John said. "Otherwise the Wraith can't follow the game. I'll bet there are cameras all over this maze."

Teyla nodded. "And of course most of the contestants have no idea what they are."

"Before we do anything too weird we're going to have to take out the cameras," John said. "And make it look like an accident for as long as we can."

"You know those men in the first groups are going to ambush us," Jitrine said. "I heard them talking. They will wait in some appropriate place and then ambush the other groups coming through."

"That will not be as easy as they think," Teyla said, reaching up for one of the torches. She brought it down and ground the flame out on the stone, leaving only the smoking bundle of wood. Despite the smoke, she got a second one and did the same. "Sticks," she said, holding up the wood.

John nodded. He'd seen how lethal Teyla could be with sticks. But now she only had one good arm. "I'll take one."

Instead of saying 'Get your own' as he'd half expected her to, she handed one over with a smile. "Let us see what you have learned," she said.

Jitrine looked at the three identical corridors, all of them leading off into darkness. "Which way?"

John thought for a second. "Teyla, which hand is a Wraith's feeding hand? Usually, I mean."

Her brow furrowed. "Right, I think. Why is that important?"

"Then we go left," John said. "Look, the game master always wants you to turn right, so that's where they've fleshed out the dungeon the most and that's where the most dangerous traps are. Straight is second, and then left is the fastest way through."

Her frown deepened. "I still have no idea what you are talking about, but left looks as good as any other way."

"Then we go left," John said. "And poke the ground ahead of you for traps." He thought better of it. "Here, let me go first. You take six. I'll do the poking."

Teyla stepped back and let him pass her, and he jauntily started poking the floor ahead of them with the butt of the torch. Pit traps would be about par for the course.

"What about ambushes?" Jitrine said behind him.

"Where another corridor crosses or there's a turn," John said. "Right here there's nowhere to hide." About every thirty feet there was another torch in a bracket, but even the dimness between them wasn't enough to conceal a man. Poking ahead, he casually looked up at the walls. And where there was a torch, on the opposite side there was a camera. In fact, he wasn't certain that there weren't small recessed lights in the ceiling itself, turned off now.

Glancing back, he saw Teyla looking as well. "It's like a set," John said. "It's pretty scary looking, but it's nothing but a set for their games. A maze for lab rats."

"Or rabbits?" Teyla asked, and he was glad to see her smile. She didn't seem unnerved by the deliberate spookiness.

"Or rabbits," he said.

Jitrine looked at him keenly. "You are not afraid because you have seen something like this before?"

John shrugged.

Jitrine squared her shoulders. "Then we may yet live."

"I told you we would live, doctor," Teyla said gently. "I have been in far worse places with Colonel Sheppard and come out alive."

Ahead, the corridor opened out into another chamber. It was dark, suggesting that someone had had reason to remove the torches. "A pretty unsubtle ambush," he murmured to Teyla. "These guys ahead of us aren't great brains."

"Stay back in the corridor," Teyla said to Jitrine quietly. "We will handle this."

John eased up toward the entrance. He could see how to play this, but it would involve Teyla doing the heavy lifting. He counted off on his fingers, one, two, three… On three he plunged through the entrance at a run, far out into the dark chamber beyond and then spun around.

Taken by surprise, the two men who had been waiting on either side of the door ran after him, one of them catching him around the knees in a flying tackle. The other one, a step behind, got Teyla's stick across the back of the head, sending him staggering to his knees.

John rolled, laying about with the stick in his own hand. It contacted quite satisfactorily with the guy's arm, a stinging blow that probably didn't break bones but sure hurt. That was good enough to get his feet free, and a swift kick got the guy to let go.

Meanwhile, the third man circled Teyla warily, all too aware of his friend unconscious on the floor. She played him, the stick rising and falling in whirling patterns, silhouetted against the light of the corridor beyond. John saw her movement coming an instant before it happened, the result of practicing with her a lot. A feint, a spin, and the stick hit twice, hard on the top of his right shoulder, just on the muscle, and then the return to the groin. Her opponent collapsed to the floor moaning as the guy John had kicked gathered himself up. Wisely, he turned and ran away, skittering away into the darkness, in loud retreat.

John picked himself up, stick still held at the ready. Teyla's opponent was rolling around on the floor groaning.

The other one, the one she'd hit over the head, was unconscious. Jitrine bent over him.

"Come on," Teyla said. "We cannot stay here. Another group will be coming along behind."

John gestured to the guy groaning on the floor. "What about him?" Armed as they were, with only sticks, they couldn't take prisoners. But leaving this guy in their rear didn't seem much of a plan.

Teyla looked down at him. "We must leave him. What else is there?"

John shrugged. "You mess with us again, we're not so nice, ok?" He glanced at Teyla. "You're lucky she likes you."

He glanced up. There were two doors out, one opposite the entrance they'd come in, and the other in the same wall but off to the left of the door.

"Empty room, twenty by twenty. Two doors. Just what the game master ordered. Look around and see if you see anything useful," John said. There were no furnishings or even the trunks he half expected.

"Up there," Teyla said. At ceiling level on opposite sides were two cameras.

"Right," John said. "Wonder how our betting odds just changed."

"I have no idea what you're talking about," Jitrine said.

"Those things in the wall are cameras, doctor," Teyla said. "They allow the Wraith — the High King and his soldiers — to see what happens here."

"Using optical lenses and electricity," John said, trying to think of the things her society might at least have words for. "Trust me, it's complicated. I couldn't even tell you exactly how a video camera works. But it's so they can watch the games."

Jitrine frowned. "It's a machine?"

"Yes," Teyla said.

"And these games are not a sacred rite, but merely entertainment for them? For these you call Wraith?"

"Yes," Teyla said grimly. "And when we have entertained them, they will kill us. We do not intend to allow that to happen."

Jitrine stood up. "What do you intend to do?"

Teyla looked at John.

"We're going to shut this place down," he said. "I don't know how yet, but we will. No more death games."

"You are one man," Jitrine observed. "How do you think you can do such a thing?"

Frankly, he had no idea. But Jitrine and Teyla were both waiting for an answer. John shrugged. "Theseus was only one guy too, but he killed the Minotaur."

Teyla's mouth twitched, and he wondered if he were really putting anything over on her. "That is a story of your people I do not know," she said.

"Yeah, I'll have to tell you sometime," John said. "I've got another book you could borrow, called The King Must Die. But first, let's get out of here."

Teyla looked around. "Which way?"

"Door in the same wall," John said, looking at the less obvious one. "When the game master thinks they're being clever."

This passage was dark, and he poked ahead of them carefully with the butt of the torch. Jitrine was right behind him, and in the dark she almost ran up on him several times. It was a good thing he was feeling ahead, because a flight of stairs down began abruptly. How far he'd have fallen down if he'd missed the first step was a really good question.

"Stairs," John said. Behind him he heard Teyla halt. He felt around. "There's a rail on the left hand wall."

Cautiously, they descended. Twenty two steps. Not quite two stories, maybe a story and a half. There was a faint glow ahead, as of another room torchlit.

Something moaned.

There was something lying at the foot of the stairs. No, someone. As John came closer he saw that it was the boy from the ship, the one who had been in the first group to enter the labyrinth. He was curled at the bottom of the stairs.

Before he could say anything, Jitrine pushed past him and knelt beside the boy. He was cradling his wrist, and there was an open cut down the side of his forehead back into his hair. "What happened?" Jitrine asked gently.

He looked up at them, his eyes wide and frightened. "The man in our group, the big one… He said he was going to win and he hit me with something. I don't know… I turned around and ran, just trying to get somewhere he wasn't." His eyes flicked up to John and back down to Jitrine. "I didn't see the stairs in the dark. I guess I fell all the way down."

"We must get him into the light," Jitrine said.

John hesitated.

"I am a doctor," Jitrine said. "This boy has not harmed us, and I am bound to render aid. Now will you help me or not?"

"Yeah." John bent down and helped her get the boy up, while Teyla checked ahead.

"It is another empty room," she said. "Two cameras. But this time there is a table and two chairs."

"Don't touch anything," John said. He got the kid and hauled him along, Jitrine hurrying after. There was blood all over her hands where she'd touched the kid's head.

There were four torches, one on each wall. In the ceiling, hidden among the rough stones, were three or four recessed light fixtures, though they weren't turned on.

"Set two," John said. He put the boy down under one of the torches.

"Let me see," Jitrine said, kneeling down.

"Am I going to die?" the kid asked. There was blood all over his hands too.

"No," Jitrine said firmly. "Head wounds bleed a lot, but may not be very serious. Why, Sheppard there bled all over me when I stitched his head a few days ago, but he's perfectly fine now!" She looked at John. "Show him your wound."

John obligingly pushed his hair back. "See?" he said. "Not so bad."

"It will give you a very manly scar," Teyla said with a smile.

The boy stopped shaking quite so much, enough to let Jitrine examine it. To John it looked pretty dramatic, but Jitrine didn't seem concerned.

"Long and shallow," she said. "I should stitch it to make sure it doesn't pull, but it is not as bad as it looks. When we get through this, I will want to tend to it, but it is already stopping bleeding. Let me see your wrist." As she took his hand he groaned.

"What is your name?" Teyla asked by way of distraction as Jitrine felt it carefully.

"Nevin," he said. "We're not getting through it, are we?"

"Yes, we are," Teyla said.

Jitrine met his eyes matter of factly. "Your wrist is broken. I will need to set it and splint it when we are done. I am sure it is painful, but I do not have anything to give you. They have taken my medical bag."

Teyla fished in the pockets of her BDUs. "I have another bandage. Perhaps that would bind it for the time being?" She pulled out one of the long field dressings.

"That will do very well," Jitrine said.

John paced back and forth. "We need to get a move on, people."

"This will only take a moment," Teyla said, and gave him what he was beginning to think of as her quelling look. He could say they were going on without the kid, but then Jitrine would insist on staying with him, and Teyla would insist on staying to guard Jitrine, and at that point...

It was easier just to shut up and not play that out.

John walked over and glanced up at one of the wall cameras. "Yeah," he said.

CHAPTER TWENTY-FOUR

THE STARGATE WHOOSHED open in a burst of blue fire, and the jumper leaped through, climbing into the morning sky. Carson Beckett eased back on the controls, mindful of the problem of altitude. They mustn't get too close to the energy shield that protected the planet.

Major Lorne pointed to the map on his laptop, as Carson never could get the heads-up display working properly. "Cadman said they'd gotten as far as this."

Rodney, leaning over the back of the copilot's seat, snorted. "That's not very useful. Half our flight path will be over ocean that way."

"And we've established that Ronon and Zelenka left the island in a boat," Lorne said patiently. "Don't you think it might be a good idea to look for them at sea?"

Rodney allowed that might be wise. The problem was that there were so many small boats at sea on a clear day. They made low approaches over a dozen small fishing boats and transport ships laboring over the clear blue waters, but the radio stayed ominously quiet. Even Rodney was beginning to find Lorne's continual radio calls irksome.

"What the hell is that?" Carson asked. He must have answered his own question, because a moment later he put the controls over, diving sharply toward the sea and pulling up at what looked to Rodney like a dangerous few hundred feet, driving hard toward the coast.

"What?" Lorne looked up from his laptop, where the search grid was connected to the jumper's sensors. "What?"

"A Wraith cruiser," Carson said shortly. "Our sensors were picking it up at extreme range. It was almost masked because it was grounded and not powered up."

"A Wraith cruiser?" Rodney said disbelievingly. "How could this mission get any worse? Oh, I know! There could be Wraith here!"

"Did it see us?" Lorne asked.

Carson's hands moved nervously over the board. "I don't see how. It was grounded with minimal systems using power. That would suggest to me that it was parked and that they didn't plan on taking off anytime soon."

"Great," Lorne said.

"How about we engage the cloak instead of running like scared bunnies in the opposite direction?" Rodney asked. "You know, we don't actually have to run away. The Wraith can't detect us cloaked."

"Oh. Right then." Carson engaged the cloak. "Forgot that for a minute."

Rodney rolled his eyes. "How long have you been flying this thing, Carson? A year?"

"I don't fly it very often," Carson retorted. He turned back, banking long and low over the sea.

"Keep flying the grid," Lorne directed. "We want to make sure we don't miss spots searching the sea. If Ronon and Zelenka took off in a boat, we need to make sure we don't miss them. And cloak or no cloak, if we start transmitting right on top of that cruiser they'll notice. It masks our ordinary electronic signature, not an outgoing signal. So let's take this easy, one step at a time."

For once Rodney wanted to swat Lorne for his methodical, calm style. Sheppard would just charge in and blow up the Wraith cruiser or something. But he had to admit that Lorne was more likely to find their missing people. Just not as quickly as Rodney would like.

Rodney checked the ordnance. Two drones. Two ought to take out the cruiser at most. Well, unless they were unlucky. Certainly even Carson ought to be able to hit a sitting duck, with the cruiser parked and powered down.

"One thing at a time," Lorne said softly. "First we find our missing people. Then we deal with the Wraith. Remember what we're here for."

"Two doors," John said. "The old two doors, one to the left and one to the right." They were more like openings, really, leading into another pair of torchlit corridors. No doubt they had the obligatory cameras too. Down the one to the left he could see another door thirty feet or so along.

"Left?" Teyla said.

Nevin was standing beside Jitrine, looking the worse for wear but a bit stronger since Teyla had given him one of her granola bars and told him how well he was taking his injury.

"Yeah," John agreed. He led the way down the hall, poking the floor every few feet as he went, Jitrine and Nevin behind him. It seemed a little odd that none of the groups behind them had run up on them while they had paused, but maybe taking the door in the same wall a ways back had been an unpopular choice. It was fine by him if they went through the entire maze without running into anybody.

The floor seemed solid and good, and listening at the door produced nothing. John flung it open, then laid about on the non-hinged side with the stick, whacking the bare wall with great enthusiasm. Nothing. Jitrine looked at this little performance skeptically.

"Ok, then." John sauntered into the room. "Just checking."

Another made to order dungeon. Ten by ten, with two torches and two cameras.

"You'd think these guys could do better than this," he said to Teyla as the others filed in. "Maybe a large chest to check for traps."

Teyla crossed her arms across her tank top, her head to the side. "Because spandex can be dangerous?"

"Trunk!" John said quickly. "Chest like trunk! A trunk kind of chest."

Teyla looked like she was going to laugh. "I do not see any trunks in here. Why would there be one?"

"They just…go in dungeons." John shrugged. "To hold treasure. Or magic weapons. Or giant poisonous snakes."

"Why would a giant poisonous snake be in a trunk?"

John blinked. She had a point. "You know, I've always kind of wondered that."

Jitrine looked at Teyla curiously. "And you're not his wife?"

"I have better taste than that," Teyla said seriously, but the way she looked at him sideways took the sting out of it.

John looked up at the ceiling. "You know, this is pretty lame." The cameras were right there where they ought to be. "No traps, no special effects, nothing more lethal than a stairway. This isn't right. This isn't legendary danger."

"Perhaps we are not to the dangerous part yet," Teyla said.

John nodded thoughtfully. "Maybe. Maybe they figure these first rooms are for the contestants to thin each other out a little bit. The obstacle is the other contestants. And then further along comes the good stuff. This is all totally straightforward. Nothing to it."

"Empty rooms," Teyla said.

"There's only one way out," Nevin said, looking at the door in the opposite wall.

"Then I guess we go that way." John opened the door and half turned toward it when a fist connected with his face, spinning him around. The floor came up with amazing speed.

"Cameras," Radek whispered.

"I see them." Ronon crouched in a shadow just ahead of him.

"They are on both sides of this corridor," Radek whispered,

craning his neck to see. "I do not think there is a way to pass that is not in view of one camera or the other."

"Backtrack again," Ronon said.

Radek shook his head. "We cannot. There were only two converging corridors at the end, and we have tried them both. Unless we go back to the very beginning by the guard post, we must go through one or the other."

Ronon's brows twitched, and he moved back quietly to Radek's side. "Any bright ideas?"

Radek looked up at the cable running camouflaged along the ceiling. "We could cut the electric cable. I cannot reach it, but if you lift me up I will be able to. We must be far ahead of the contestants, since we are working this back to front, so perhaps they will think it is a camera malfunction if they lose the visual on a corridor that no one has come to yet. I doubt they will send someone to fix it, with contestants in the maze."

"Sounds like a plan," Ronon said.

Radek looked at the cables again. "I have another thought."

"What?"

"If we trace the cables we should be able to find the control room. It might be a remote routing center. They may have this running on automatic so that they can sit back somewhere and relax while they watch it."

Ronon nodded. "Or it might be full of Wraith."

"I thought that was your department, my friend," Radek said with a smile.

Ronon loosened his energy pistol in its holster. "I'm beginning to like the way you think."

Feet spun around him. Teyla's feet. Teyla's feet in her black boots were doing an elaborate dance, forward and backward, now advancing, now retreating. Other feet were dancing too, four other feet in leather sandals. Some of them belonged to someone who said, "Ooof."

That would be Teyla getting him in the stomach with a stick.

John reached out and grabbed the nearest foot and yanked as hard as he could. It slid out from under its owner, and the person attached to the foot came crashing down, landing hard on the floor with a crack. The other feet retreated.

"Sheppard?" It was Jitrine kneeling beside him, helping him to sit up. "Sheppard, can you speak?"

"Yeah," he managed, turning over. His jaw hurt. A lot. He moved it experimentally. "That was not fun."

"I should think not," Jitrine said.

There was a flurry of blows behind him, and then a strangled noise. "Mercy," a man's voice groaned. "Mercy, please…"

John twisted around.

Teyla had the other man down, her foot on his back forcing his throat down on the stick. Much more pressure and he would surely black out. "Why should I do that?" she asked, tossing her hair back from her face. "You will just try to ambush us again."

"No… I swear…" he croaked.

John got to his knees. "I'm ok," he said to Jitrine. "I'm good." Nevin watched, wide-eyed.

"I see no reason to trust you," Teyla said, but she did ease the pressure of her foot enough to let him breathe.

"I just want to get through this thing," the man mumbled. "That's all."

"As do we all," Teyla said. "But we do not do it by ambushing others." She jerked the stick from beneath his throat, letting him sag to the floor as she took a few steps away. "Get up."

Jitrine's hands were under John's arms, but he shook her off to get to his feet himself. "I'm ok. Really."

The other man got up rather more slowly and laboriously. The way he clutched his side suggested Teyla might have cracked some ribs too. John knew the feeling. But then, one of his friends seemed to be out cold on the floor.

"What is your name?" Teyla demanded.

"Suua," he said. "Look, I'm a fisherman. I mean, I'd rather be a fisherman. I just want to get home."

"Why did you do this?" she asked.

"I ran into those guys, and they said I was with them or against them, so I said I was with them." He rubbed his throat with one big hand. "We heard you coming up behind. We didn't see you. I didn't know that you had a kid with you."

Nevin bristled visibly.

The guy's eyes strayed to Jitrine. "You're a doctor. I don't go around attacking doctors."

"No, just me," John said. "So why shouldn't she lay you out again?"

"I can help!" he said. "Look, I can help you through. Most of the rest of them ran away, so they're still ahead of us. Don't you want some more muscle on your side?"

"And how can we trust you?" Teyla asked. "If we take you with us, how do we know that you won't turn on us the moment we run into your friends again?"

"Um, you don't?" He was thinking hard about that.

John walked over to stand beside Teyla. "This guy's not the brightest bulb on the tree," he said out of the corner of his mouth.

"I am a Pelagian doctor," Jitrine said. "Do you think that I lie?"

"No, ma'am," Suua said respectfully. Clearly that meant something to him.

"These people are not from our world, and they have come to release us from the service of these false gods," Jitrine said, "The High King and his men are nothing but parasites demanding tribute. Is that not how you got here in the first place?"

Suua's face turned red. "I owed a lot of money," he said. "And they said one of my family needed to be tribute so I figured better me than my wife or my daughter."

"We will have no more tribute when they are done," Jitrine said. "Sheppard has promised it, and he is a hero sent by the Ancestors."

Teyla looked at John and her eyes widened a little. He could read that as if she'd spoken. Pretty tall order, and no idea how they were going to deliver on those promises. But he'd better figure out a way.

"Sure," John said, trying to look nonchalant. "We're going to shut this place down."

Suua blinked. "No more tribute? Ever?"

"No more tribute," Teyla said. "Now will you come with us, or stay behind and not hinder us? If you wish, you may, and nothing ill will be done to you by our will."

Suua looked at Nevin. "What about that kid?"

"He's with us," John said.

Nevin swallowed.

Suua nodded slowly. "All right. If that's how it is."

"That's how it is," John said. "We're all going to get through this thing together."

"Then I'll come with you," Suua said. "For no more tribute."

"No more tribute," Jitrine said. "This will be the end."

"Ok," John said. "Welcome aboard." This was turning into a regular party — cleric, fighter, kickass ranger, random kid, and now dimwitted bruiser. "What's next?" he asked aloud. "Vampires? Mummies? Ghouls? Gelatinous Cubes?"

Teyla looked at him quizzically. "I thought gelatinous cubes were those things Rodney liked so well in the mess hall? Why are they frightening?"

"Those are gelatin cubes," John said. "A gelatinous cube is…different." There was really no explaining this one. "It's a long story."

"Oh."

"They're a kind of monster."

"I think we already know what monsters we will face," Teyla said. "Wraith."

CHAPTER TWENTY-FIVE

"WELL, THIS IS nice," John said. The corridor sloped down, the walls not squared now but shaped like natural rock, the floor not entirely even. Ahead, there was the sound of rushing water. The torches were further and further apart, so it was necessary to go slower, checking the floor ahead constantly. John took the point, followed by Suua where he could keep an eye on him, followed by Jitrine and Nevin, with Teyla bringing up the rear.

Before him the corridor opened out into a large chamber, the sound of the water louder yet. Taking the nearest torch from the wall, John held it up to take a look. "Oh man," he said.

The corridor opened into a cave, the ceiling some twenty feet above their heads. Through the middle of it ran a swift stream, white water rushing quickly past in a steep bed. Two pillars stood at the edge, and an identical pair stood on the other side. From the ones on the other side dangled the remains of a rope bridge. The main ropes had been cut, however, leaving the rest dangling in the stream.

The others crowded out onto the ledge over the water with him.

Suua blinked. "The guys I was with who got ahead? They must have gone across and cut the ropes so nobody else could follow."

John swore.

Jitrine shook her head, looking down into the stream bed. "The water flows underground again before long, just there. Who knows where it goes?"

"It does not matter," Teyla said, kneeling down and reaching toward the water below, spreading her fingers to the spray that rose from the whitewater. "It is bitterly cold."

"And running like a fire hydrant," John said. "There's no way that's natural here. They've got this under pressure."

"Very probably," Teyla said. "But if the bridge were still intact, it would not be difficult. It is only about twenty feet across."

"And if the ropes weren't all on the other side," John said.

"Too far to jump," Suua said thoughtfully.

"I could swim across," John said. "And then throw the ropes back. If we tied the ropes back to the post on our side, we could all get across."

Teyla stood up, her hands on her hips. "Colonel, I should be the one to do it. You are injured."

Colonel, he thought. We're back to Colonel instead of John. With the addition of Nevin and Suua, this had turned into a large enough group to warrant formality. Or perhaps it was the addition of people she didn't trust.

John shook his head. "Not with your shoulder. My head's not as bad as that, and you know you can't climb up the other side with your shoulder messed up." On the other side, the ropes hung down into the water about ten feet from the pillars they were attached to. Ten feet of wet, slimy jumbled stones making a dangerous slippery surface. Whoever swam across would have to climb up the ropes, and there was no way Teyla could do it with her torn up shoulder. She hadn't been able to get up a dry stone wall the day before without help.

Teyla opened her mouth and then shut it again, her lips pursed together. "The current is very strong," she said. She didn't argue. She had more sense than to claim she could do things she couldn't.

"I know." John looked at it. "But the thing's not that wide. Twelve, fifteen feet across the actual water. If I start upstream of where the bridge was, it's a couple of good strokes and the water will carry me down to the ropes."

"And if you miss you will be swept away," Jitrine observed.

"I'm a good swimmer and it's not that far," John said, taking off his jacket and handing it to Teyla. "It's cold, but I'm only going to be in the water for a minute. It won't be bad."

He walked around the pillars, checking out the steepness of the bank upstream. It wasn't as steep as he'd feared. The stones were broken and there were good hand and foot holds. Carefully, with Teyla holding the torch above, John started climbing down.

The spray was icy. Definitely under pressure, he thought. And definitely chilled. It might be cool here, but this temperature was too low not to be artificial. Just above the surface of the water he stopped, taking a good look across. There were probably rocks just beneath the surface. The water couldn't be more than a few feet deep. Shallow water was more dangerous than deep water. This current could throw you against rocks hard enough to break bones. He'd broken his foot that way, whitewater rafting on the Snake River when he was sixteen.

So he wouldn't dive. He'd just try to paddle across as quickly as possible. A couple of good strokes, maybe only one if he kicked off from the wall hard enough.

John lowered himself the rest of the way down, up to his hips in the icy water. The torch wavered as Teyla bent over, a worried look on her face.

"It'll just take a second," John said. Damn, this was cold!

With one last glance at the other side, he let go and pushed off strongly.

The water shocked him, and all he could see was white foam. The current buffeted him, half rolling him on his back. Don't panic. Keep going across the current. One stroke. Two. Three. Where was the other bank? The stream wasn't this wide.

John flung his arm out in a fourth stroke, and cracked it hard against rocks, grabbed onto the stones with all his strength, pulling his head out of the water. He scrambled forward, barking his shin, then got a foot up on that rock and pushed.

He took a long breath and shook his hair out of his eyes.

He was on the other side just below where the ropes from the broken bridge dangled down. To his right, it was only a dozen feet before the torrent went underground again, into a camouflaged drain opening.

"It's ok," John called back. "I'm good."

He hauled himself back a few feet against the current, then pulled himself out with the ropes. His teeth were chattering by the time he reached the top, and he stomped around to warm himself. The water was very cold. Good thing he'd only been in it about thirty seconds.

"Are you all right?" Teyla called across.

"Just cold." John started hauling the ropes up. There was a tangle of them tied to a few boards which must have once served as a footpath across the stream. "Not a problem."

Jitrine screamed.

"Look out!" Teyla shouted.

John spun around just quickly enough to catch movement out of the corner of his eye. Then something heavy and flat hit him in the back, hard and solid, pitching him forward into the raging water.

"There you are," Carson said. "Tucked in there nice and snug."

The jumper made a long, low altitude pass over what was clearly a heavily populated island. In the courtyard of a large building, screened on every side by porticos of white stone, was a Wraith cruiser. It was essentially parked indoors. Other than from a vantage directly above it, it could not be seen from the ground. And since presumably it was the only aircraft on this world, it was effectively invisible.

Lorne nodded over the sensor readings. "Powered all the way down, all systems in standby mode. They weren't planning on going anywhere soon."

"So shoot it," Rodney said. The idea of leaving a Wraith cruiser alone didn't sit well with him.

Carson frowned. "It's smack in the middle of a building full of humans, Rodney! If I hit the cruiser with a drone, it will blow up half this city. In case you haven't bothered to read the sensor report, there are fifty thousand human beings on this island! The collateral damage from air to surface missiles here, and the resulting fires, would be in the thousands! You're essentially asking me to bomb a city full of helpless people."

"Fine." Rodney said shortly. "So what are we supposed to do? Ignore the Wraith? Is that a better plan?"

"Chances are we'd also be bombing our own people," Lorne said quietly.

Rodney looked at him. "How do you get to that?"

Lorne met his eyes frankly. "Look, we've had no luck reaching them by radio. They probably don't have access to the radios anymore. Which means there's a good bet they're prisoners. And where do you think the Wraith would hold them?"

"On the cruiser or in the complex around it," Rodney said reluctantly. "I hear you."

"So let's find out if our people are on the cruiser before we blow it up," Lorne said.

Carson's brow furrowed. "Let me have a look around and see if I can find a place to set down. Can't you scan for our people?"

"For the forty-ninth time, Carson!" Rodney snapped. "I have no way to tell our people apart from any of the other fifty thousand people on the island!"

"We're going to have to do this the hard way," Lorne said. He looked toward the Marines in the back. "Cadman, issue out the P90s."

There was dark and there was water. It turned him over and over, his hands scrabbling for purchase on the smooth curved surface above.

A drain, John thought, fighting not to breathe. A round plastic drain. The water was rushing through pipes, filling them completely. There was no distance between the surface of the water and the pipe. He was going to drown in here.

No sooner had he thought that than the pressure of the water eased as it spread, opening up. His hand broke the surface and he struggled up. His legs hit something solid, then his chest. John dragged himself up in pitch darkness, his hands encountering stone instead of plastic, his greedy chest sucking in breath.

There was a splashing and coughing, and he flailed out, grabbing for whatever it was and getting a handful of soggy cold cloth.

Coughing. That was Teyla's cough. "Teyla?" And the cloth he had was the leg of her BDUs. He pulled her out of the rushing water onto the ledge he perched on. "Teyla? What the hell happened?"

She coughed again. "One of the other men, the ones who had gone ahead, was waiting. He hit you with one of the bridge planks and knocked you back in the water."

John took a deep breath. "But you were on the other side of the stream from him. What are you doing here?"

Teyla sounded almost amused. "Well, I had to go after you, did I not? Would you expect that I would just say, 'Too bad that Sheppard is swept away?' I thought that perhaps we could climb back up."

"What about Jitrine and the others?" he asked.

"I told them to wait on the same side of the stream," Teyla replied. "We did not have much time to talk. I had to act quickly."

"Yeah, I see that." There was not the slightest glimmer of light. So there probably wasn't a camera to give themselves away to either. And the handful of pants he'd grabbed a moment earlier gave him an idea. "Do you still have that flashlight buttoned up in your pocket?"

"I have not taken it out," she said. He heard movement, and then was almost blinded by the pure white light of the LED lighting.

Teyla played the light over the water and the chamber around them. It was not big enough for them to stand up, perhaps four feet in height above the water and little more than ten feet in length, a crevasse carved out of natural rock. Perhaps it was a fissure that had widened when the Wraith put in their drains, blasted out or fractured further by the rushing water. There was no way out except the water where it flowed through, filling the smaller entrance tunnel and leaving perhaps five or six inches of space at the top of the exit drain.

John swore again. "This is so not good."

"The water is freezing," Teyla said.

He looked at the inrushing water. "We can't climb back up that," he said. "The current's too fast and there isn't anything to hold onto. It's plastic, not stone. It's totally smooth."

"I know," she said. "I had expected stone, like the stream bed."

"It's just a set," John said. "Anything that isn't going to show they didn't bother to make look natural."

Teyla glanced around the small cave. "And of course there are no vents here."

John nodded. "Which means we've got air for what? Maybe fifteen or twenty minutes in a space this big?"

"Possibly," Teyla said, shining the light around again. There were some tiny cracks, but none large enough to even get a hand through, much less to provide a means of escape. She flashed the light over the water. "We are going to have to go down."

John nodded slowly. He was cold from the water, though in the enclosed space their bodies' warmth took off the chill. "The drains have to go out somewhere. As fast as the water's moving, there's a pump. So it has to go into a pool to recycle. With plastic drains instead of rocks, there's less chance we're going to break bones on the way down."

Teyla took a deep breath. It was clear she did not care for the freezing water any more than he did. "I see no other way," she said, glancing the light around again, as if hoping some other way out had magically appeared. "I will turn it off and button it back in my pocket," she said, "So that we do not lose it."

"Right." John looked at the water, a last look before the light switched off and left them again in utter blackness. He heard the sound of wet cloth as she put the flashlight away.

In the dark, Teyla took his hand. "Ready?" she asked.

"Ready," John said. "Three deep breaths and then we go."

"All right."

One. Two. Three.

They plunged into the frigid water and were swept away.

CHAPTER TWENTY-SIX

"GET BACK!" Ronon whispered.

Though he was already pressed tightly to the stone wall, Radek attempted to make himself even smaller. He could see very little ahead of them through the bulk that was Ronon, but Radek could hear the others.

There were voices coming down the corridor that their corridor branched off from, three or four men's voices raised in argument.

"I said we should have gone that way."

"Shut up, twerp. Unless you'd like to take me on, ok?"

There were heavy footsteps. Radek could see Ronon's shoulders tensed, his stun pistol at the ready. If the strangers turned into their corridor they would get a surprise.

"How about that way?"

The footsteps paused and they considered.

"No, this way!"

It seemed that they decided to stick with the main corridor. They went past, the sounds of their passage loud in the dim light.

When the last noises had faded away, Ronon moved, holstering his pistol again with a grin. "Not so bright. Any enemy would hear them a mile away."

Radek let out a deep breath. "They would be the first contestants, it seems. We are beginning to reach the part of the maze where the games are being played."

"Or they're beginning to reach us," Ronon said. "These are the guys in front. They're probably the most dangerous because they probably screwed over plenty of other people to get here, and they'll turn on each other before the end." He straightened. "Ok. Let's get back in the main corridor and keep following the cables."

Radek looked up. "They are bundled now," he said. "See how they are tied and painted over? We must be getting close." He set off down the corridor, in a hurry to reach the control room.

Ronon grabbed his shoulder. "Stop!" he said. "Watch where you're going!"

Just ahead of Radek the floor disappeared. Instead of smooth corridor floor there was a drop of seven or eight feet to a second floor lined with spikes of bright steel cut in sharp snowflake points. And on them…

Radek looked away, swallowing hard.

"One of those guys was careless," Ronon said. "We can't be."

Radek very deliberately looked over at the floor on the opposite side, not glancing down at all. "How can we get across?" Ronon could probably jump, fit as he was, but Radek harbored no illusions about his ability to jump across the pit without the same unfortunate consequences as the contestant below.

Ronon grinned wolfishly. "You know that movie Sheppard had us watching last weekend on DVD? The really good one?"

"I do not," Radek said. He tended to avoid movie night unless something he particularly liked was playing, as two hours of watching cars blow up bored him senseless.

"Where the guy says, 'Never toss a dwarf' and the other guy just picks him up and flings him?"

"Oh, that movie," Radek said with a sinking heart. "You are not seriously considering…"

"No problem," Ronon said, picking him up under the arms. "Easy peasy, as Beckett says."

"Put me down! Put me down right now!" Radek shouted. "Do not…"

And then he was flying through the air, then smacking face down on the floor on the other side, his arms flung out to protect his glasses. The wind knocked out of him, Radek lay on the floor trying to catch a breath. Behind him he heard a scuffle, and Ronon knelt down beside him.

"Sorry. Maybe I threw you a little too hard."

Radek rolled over, hoping that no bones were broken. "That was not funny."

"It got you across, didn't it?" Ronon offered a hand to help him up.

Radek gingerly uncurled. His legs seemed to work. He glared at Ronon over the top of his glasses. "Do not ever do that again."

"You could jump," Ronon said.

"I cannot."

"Then don't complain," Ronon said. "You're across, aren't you?"

He hauled Radek to his feet. "Come on. We're following cables, right?"

"Yes."

Unfortunately, the body in the pit was not the last one they found. A little further along they found a man who had been hit over the head with something large and heavy. Perhaps, in the infirmary in Atlantis, he might have been saved, but here his breath had already stopped.

"This game is not so much fun," Radek said grimly.

"Neither is being a Runner," Ronon said. "Unless it's fun for the Wraith." He ranged ahead, checking the floor and walls for more traps. Radek sincerely hoped he found them without tripping them. But perhaps the men who had already passed this way had tripped any booby traps that had been set.

There were cameras, of course, and now it was impossible to avoid them entirely in the main corridor. Hopefully, the Wraith would conclude they were just regular contestants in the confusion of criss-crossing corridors. Still, they moved swiftly and tried to stay out of the light.

"Stop," Radek directed. "I need to have a look at this." Along the ceiling the mass of cables ran into a small box and then exited on the other side. They ran a few feet further along, then disappeared in a small hole in the side wall at ceiling level.

"What is it?" Ronon asked.

"That is what I am trying to ascertain," Radek said. He craned his neck to see better. "The cables disappear into a solid stone wall? That does not make sense. Why would they go to such trouble? Drilling through stone is very difficult, and they have just fastened the cables to the ceiling elsewhere."

Ronon came back. "Are we out of the cameras?"

Radek glanced down the hall. "Just barely. I do not think that one can see us." He put his hands to the wall as far up as he could reach beneath the drilled hole. Yes. As he thought. "Ronon, put your hand to this wall and tell me what you feel."

"Nothing," Ronon said, running his hands over the uneven surface. "What am I supposed to feel?"

Radek took his other hand and put it to the wall three feet away, smiling. "Do you see?"

Ronon nodded cautiously, looking at the section of wall in front of him. "It's not cold. The stone is cool over here."

"Stone does not heat easily," Radek said. "In fact, the temperature in most deep caves stays around ten degrees Celsius year around. It does not vary much, away from the surface. It does not get much colder unless it is in a very intemperate climate, nor much warmer. But this section of wall…" He ran his hands along it beneath the cables. "This section of wall is warmer. It is not made of stone."

Ronon ran his hands over the surface. "Plaster painted to look like stone?"

"We have found our door," Radek said. "This is a false surface. What is beyond it I do not know, but something has been hidden."

"The control room?"

"Possibly. Or a technical closet, which would be nearly as good." Radek looked at it speculatively. "If it is a server closet or one where the camera cables attach to a power source, we are in business."

"If it's the control room there could be Wraith in there," Ronon said, drawing his pistol. "You get back around the corner."

"What are you going to do?" Radek asked.

"If it's just plaster I'm going to blast through it," Ronon said. "So get back."

The water tossed Teyla, throwing her around and around like a leaf in a stream. She had thought that she could hold onto John, but that proved impossible. The strength of the water ripped their hands apart in seconds.

She had no idea how long she was underwater. It seemed forever, but it could hardly have been long, as her lungs had not yet begun to burn with the need to breathe. Suddenly there was nothing beneath her, no sides to the drain, and for a second there was the sickening feeling of falling. From how far up, she wondered? How far down?

And then she smacked the water full on her back, came up struggling. She kicked for the surface and gulped in a huge breath. Just one. And then John landed right on top of her.

She had a moment's panic, pressed beneath him, the shallow bottom of the pool scraping along her arm, pinned beneath his weight beneath the surface. Then he twisted, and she bounced up like a cork, the spray from the incoming freshet in her face.

"What a ride!" John said, and he was grinning as he tossed the water out of his eyes. Teyla had the momentary urge to slap him.

"We did not do this for fun," Teyla snapped.

"I take my fun where I can get it," he said.

She did not need to tread water. The pool only came up to the middle of her chest. Teyla looked around.

About five feet above her head the drain poured from the wall in a torrent of white water. Two other drains did the same to her right, one larger and one smaller than the one they had descended, presumably feeding from traps and settings in other parts of the maze. The pool they stood in was broad and shallow, with a grate covering a drain at the far end from which came mechanical sounds that were loud even over the flowing water — presumably the pump which recycled the water through the system. The ceiling was high, perhaps thirty feet above, of natural stone. Dim emergency lights hung on cables, illuminating the room with fitful low fluorescents.

"I do not see anything that looks like a terminal or a workstation," Teyla said, frowning.

He looked around too. "Me neither," he said.

There were no banks of lights or panels, no screens or anything that looked like heavy equipment, just the drains in and out, and the loud sound of the pump that recirculated the water.

John pushed his sodden hair back out of his face and started wading toward the edge of the pool. The water wasn't as cold as it was further up, but it was still quite uncomfortable. "It must be controlled from somewhere else," he said. "After all, contestants must wash up in here occasionally still alive." He gave her a shrug replete with gallows humor.

"We are alive," she said, clambering out of the pool as well. The air was cool but not chilled — a little warmer perhaps than the caves above, but still far from comfortable when one was soaked and cold. "And we need not fear we will suffocate here."

"That's true," John said, looking up at the vents in the wall far above. This room was lit and ventilated, even if it was rarely used.

Teyla sat down on the stone and tried to wring out her pants. The leg pocket had a soggy copy of Watership Down in it, and she hated that she had probably ruined it. He had brought it to her from Earth aboard the Daedalus only a few weeks ago, and said it was a story of his people that he had loved and thought she would enjoy. Perhaps it would dry. Perhaps all the pages would not stick together and the ink run as so many of the books she had seen did.

John paced around. "Here's a door," he said. Instead of the ordinary wooden ones they had encountered in the maze, this was a metal power door with no visible hardware on it, obviously meant to open electronically. John waved his hand over it and around it, but nothing happened.

"Perhaps it is locked," Teyla said.

"No kidding!" John grinned to take the sting out of it. "Why don't you come over here and see if your Wraith gene opens doors the way the ATA gene does for me?"

"It never has before," Teyla said, but she came and tried anyway. The door remained stubbornly closed. "No lock mechanism," she said, examining the sides of the door. "Perhaps this is meant to be opened from the outside."

"If this is just a water treatment trap, probably," John said.

"And now it is a trap for us," she said. "I do not see any other way out." The vents were small and high in the wall, and no doubt the drain was only the cover on the pump that recycled the water. It would not actually lead anywhere.

"We can't climb back up," John said thoughtfully. "But there's got to be a way to get this door open."

While he considered the wall beside the door, Teyla walked around the edge of the pool. The larger of the other two drains that fed it was not entirely full to the top of the pipe, and the water was not running as hard. It flowed rather than erupted in the bubbles of white water under pressure. But she could not get a better look without getting back in the frigid pool.

Casting a glance at John still examining the door, she waded into the water. It was very cold. Knee deep. Waist deep. From there she could see up the pipe, even though it turned. There was a strange blue light, as though it were not far to a chamber lit electrically with colored lights, and she thought she could even see the end of the tunnel perhaps fifteen feet ahead at a gentle slope.

"John!" Teyla called. "Come look at this!"

He waded out to join her. "What?"

"Do you think that could be a way out?"

Wincing at the cold, he waded over to the end of the pipe. It ended just about at the level of his shoulders, definitely a curved pipe with a low gradient. The water splashed over his whole body as he put his hands on the pipe and pulled himself up, looking. It made her colder just looking at it.

"I think you've got something," he said. "It looks like there's a pool that's draining down this pipe, and the drain is in the side of the pool, not the bottom. I don't see a cover on it either."

"Perhaps they are just as happy to let all the bodies aggregate in one place," Teyla said grimly.

John nodded. "Probably. It would be a pain in the neck to have to hunt for them all over this place, even if they can turn the water off and drain the pools." He let himself back down. "I think we can get up there. It's not too steep to climb."

"Then we had best do it," Teyla said. "This cold water saps our strength. The sooner we are done with it, the better."

"I'll boost you," he said, and put out his knee for her to climb on, his hands on her waist. With that it was easy to get up in the end of the pipe, though crawling forward through the water sent stabs of pain through her shoulder. Even on all fours her shoulder would not easily take her weight.

The pipe gave a little as John came up, his head just behind her buttocks in the tight space. "Need a push?" he said.

"I think I can manage," Teyla said. The pipe was a gentle

curve, and it was only the flowing water that made it difficult to climb. Her hands were numb with cold before she reached the top, and it was an effort to haul herself out of the pool onto the ledge just above the drain. She sat there, rubbing her chilled hands together, while John pulled himself up beside her.

"Well, this is different," he said.

Above them the ceiling soared eighty feet, festooned with stalactites. From somewhere in the darkness around its final peak, blue lights shone out at intervals, casting eerie shadows among the stones, as though they were sharp teeth. On the far side of the pool a waterfall plunged down some half the distance to the ceiling, green lights below the water casting a nacreous uplight, turning the flowing water into a mysterious glittering green and blue curtain. For those who had never before seen colored electric lights, the effect must be beyond unsettling. It must be terrifying.

The pool itself lapped against the sides of the chamber, filling it nearly entirely except for the ledge they sat upon. Other ledges jutted out over the water at intervals, dark corridor entrances opening onto each one.

"This is very impressive," Teyla said. It was no doubt designed to impress, and she could appreciate the workmanship even if she wished to be gone. It was beautiful, in a strange way.

"Yeah." John looked around them. "That's one word for it."

On the far side of the cavern and far above three figures appeared at the cavern entrance, looking out across the expanse.

"Should we call out to them?" Teyla wondered.

John shrugged. "And ask them to do what?"

"You have a point," she said. They were far across the chamber, and the entrance they stood upon looked out over a bare drop of thirty feet to the surface of the water. Teyla twisted around, looking up. There was another ledge about fifteen feet above where they were, but the sides of the chamber were steep and slick with spray from the waterfall. "I do not think I can climb that," she said reluctantly.

"I figured that." John scratched his head. "We'll figure out another way."

The people on the other side of the cavern disappeared from the corridor entrance, no doubt concluding that they could not go this way.

"I'm getting pretty tired of this game," John said.

CHAPTER TWENTY-SEVEN

THE BLAST from Ronon's pistol was loud in the confined space, but Radek didn't cover his ears. He wanted to hear what happened next.

The initial blast, Ronon shooting his way through the false wall, was followed by five sharp shots and then silence. The corridor was full of plaster dust, and pressed against the wall around the corner, Radek wondered what to do next. Unarmed, he was of very little use charging in if there were Wraith. But if Ronon had been stunned, he could not stand by and do nothing. He must do his best to rescue him somehow.

"Zelenka?" Ronon called out softly.

"It is about time," Radek said, pushing through the plaster dust to the irregularly shaped hole in the false door.

Ronon shrugged, shoving pieces of door out of the way.

"Ah, now this is more like it!" Radek said happily. On the other side of the door was a control room, several banks of monitors and computers half obscured by dust. Two dead Wraith lay on the floor, taken care of by Ronon's energy pistol. Doubtless they were the technicians who managed the machinery of the maze. Radek sat down before the nearest workstation, lit up with three screens and five or six glittering leads coming in.

"Can you get it to work?" Ronon said, leaning over his shoulder.

"It is already working," Radek said. His fingers flew over the panels of touch sensitive electrodes that made up a Wraith keyboard. Data was streaming in from dozens of locations. "The problem is getting it to stop."

"You can figure it out, right?" Ronon sounded worried. Perhaps the screens upon screens of data in Wraith made him a little nervous.

"Of course I can figure it out," Radek said testily. "But it takes some time. I figured out how the rematerialization phase booster on a Dart worked, didn't I? Otherwise Rodney and Lt. Cadman would not be alive. But it is not simple or quick. Wraith tech is not intuitive to the human mind."

"I got that far," Ronon said. "Can you find Sheppard and Teyla?"

"I am sure that I can in a few minutes." Radek tried a combination of keys with familiar looking figures, glancing up to see if the display screens changed. They did. One screen showing an empty section of corridor shifted to a view of an empty room with a table and two chairs in it. "Ah!" he said.

"What?" Ronon leaned over, his chin almost on Radek's shoulder.

"I have found a camera toggle. It changes between different cameras live in the maze. But I do not know how to tell it which ones…" Another touch, and it showed a view of different corridor, a body at the far end lying very still. "I think I am making it cycle through the cameras."

"Can you get the corridors around us to see if anybody's coming?"

Radek turned his head and gave Ronon a quelling look over the frames of his glasses. "I can, in time. I do not tell you your business. I do not tell you how to blast things or kick things. Please do not tell me how to do computers! I will work much faster if you will back off and let me."

Ronon looked abashed. "Ok." He took a step back. "I'll just stand here by the door and guard."

"Thank you," Radek said, and bent his head to the board. Truly, one would think there was nothing to it, as little respect as his work garnered! Why there is nothing more simple than to crack an alien computer system in an unintelligible language in order to gain access to the security systems of a large complex!

A combination of touches brought up what must be another menu. Some of the labels were plain enough, even with the very limited Wraith vocabulary that Dr. Weir had worked out. Some were similar to the controls of the Wraith Dart that he had worked on, as little as there had been of that left. The cockpit interfaces had been almost destroyed.

But yet there were some things that made sense. Lights must control the artificial lighting in the maze, presumably leading to a submenu that broke lighting out into locations. Water? That was mysterious, but presumably the complex had plumbing. Steam? Perhaps he was not reading that right. Or perhaps the contestants were in worse trouble than he had imagined.

"Perhaps if we go around the pool," Teyla said, "We might be able to get up on one of the ledges on the other side."

John squinted across the dimly lit water. "I don't think it's any better over there. The walls are pretty steep. And the water's awfully cold."

Teyla thought that he might be shivering, though he tried his best to hide it. A long swim in icy water was not exactly what the doctor ordered for a man with a head injury. Swimming across the pool would chill him to the bone again, and in truth the sides of the pond did not look any easier to climb over there. All of the ledges on that side looked as though they were at least ten feet above the water. If they gave onto corridors that was all very well, but she did not see how they would get up to them. "I suppose we could go back down the drain and try the door again," she said.

The alternative was to sit right here, trapped on this ledge, until the games ended and the Wraith came to round up the losers. That also seemed like a bad plan. Going back down the drain involved another plunge into the icy water, but the room below seemed warmer. Even if they could not get the door open, it might be a better place to be stuck. And perhaps they would find a way to get the door open in time.

"Sheppard!"

Teyla's head jerked up.

Jitrine stood on the ledge above them with a torch in her hand. She turned and looked back down the corridor. "They're here," she called excitedly to someone. "Come on!" In a moment Nevin and Suua hurried out onto the ledge.

"What the hell?" John said to Teyla.

She shrugged. "I do not know."

"We found you!" Jitrine said triumphantly. "We knew if we followed the water we would find you eventually."

Suua began lowering down a rope ladder made of the ropes from the bridge. His hair was plastered wetly to his head, and his clothes were dripping. "Come on up," he said with a grin.

Teyla began laboriously to climb up. Without the rope ladder it would be impossible, and as it was it was both difficult and painful.

"Why did you look for us?" John said, a note of genuine confusion in his voice.

Jitrine reached down to put her hand beneath Teyla's good shoulder and help her up. "Did you think that after you had fought on our behalf we would desert you?"

"Kind of, yeah," John said.

Jitrine gave him a stern look. "You have much to learn of Pelagia, Sheppard. You underestimate us."

"A hero's got to have friends, right?" Nevin piped up. "Those guys who are in the story too."

John looked abashed. "Thanks," he said.

Suua gave him a hand up the last few feet. "No problem," he said. "We're going to get out of here, right?"

"Right," John said. "And when we've shut this place down, we'll get you home to your wife and daughter. I promise."

"Then we have a deal," Suua said, and shook John's offered hand.

Teyla blinked. It was like him to remember Suua's family, in case he needed to know that. But then she had seen him send far too many messages to families, messages to break hearts and rend lives.

She turned instead to Jitrine. "How did you get across the stream?"

"After you and Sheppard were swept away the men on the other bank laughed at us, saying we would never get across and we had lost already. We waited until they left, and then Suua swam across. He threw the ropes back for us, and Nevin and I crossed on them," Jitrine explained. Her face was serene, as though she had never had any doubts that Suua, who had so lately attacked them himself, would keep his promise to throw the ropes to them once he was across. Perhaps it would have made no difference, and Jitrine would have stayed with Nevin regardless. Or perhaps she truly had never had any doubts.

"After that Jitrine said we needed to follow the water," Nevin said brightly. "She said that it all flowed downhill, and that we needed to get to the place where it came out. That all cisterns have a basin."

Teyla looked at Jitrine in surprise.

"I am a Pelagian scientist," Jitrine said firmly. "Do you think we do not have cisterns and sewers? Do you think I have no idea how they work?"

"Of course not," Teyla said. Perhaps John was not the only one to underestimate the Pelagians. Perhaps she had, too.

"How did you get here?" John asked. "Do you know where these corridors go?" He craned his neck, looking back in the direction they had come.

"There are many corridors back there," Suua said. "It seemed like they were coming together, but we heard the running water so we backtracked up one of them until we found this ledge."

"We came out first on the other side," Nevin said helpfully,

"And we saw you, but we couldn't get across."

"That was you?" John said.

Jitrine nodded. "So we backtracked and found another way down. I think Suua is right. The maze is converging. I think we are coming to the end, or at least to some major obstacle that they wish all contenders to face."

"Great," John said. "The big monster."

Teyla looked at him swiftly. "The big monster?"

"There's always one," John said. "The big guy with all the hit points. The penultimate challenge of manhood and strength, an epic adventure the like of which has never been seen before!"

"Why has your voice gotten funny like that?" Teyla asked.

John dipped his head. "It was like a dramatic voice over. In a preview. Oh, never mind…"

"You mean when it says, 'Next week on Star Trek, Jean-Luc Picard takes his shirt off?" Teyla asked. She could not help breaking into a broad smile. No matter how cold and wet and hungry and miserable they were, she could always rely on John to keep everyone moving by whatever means worked best. It took a great deal to dampen his spirits. He was, perhaps, the most resilient man she had ever met.

"Yeah, like that," John said. "But I don't think they actually say the part about the shirt. And there's always a plot-related reason for it. Like he's dead for the fourteenth time or something, or he's about to be impregnated by shrimp."

"That observation is very meta," Teyla said.

"I have no idea what you're talking about," Suua said. "Again."

"This is the witty banter," John said. "I don't know why, but she likes it."

Jitrine looked at Teyla seriously, though a smile played about the corners of her mouth. "I see why you do not marry him."

Teyla shrugged. "There is only so much of this one can take."

"The big monster," Suua said. "Is there really a monster, do you think?"

"If there is, we'll take care of it," John said. "Can't be much in here you and me can't handle, right?"

Suua nodded seriously. "That's true."

Teyla bit her lip, refraining from saying, 'Except about forty Wraith!' That would be extremely counterproductive. John was doing a fine job of countering the strangeness and spookiness of the labyrinth with humor, and it would not be a good idea to deflate him. Especially as the one most in need of something to keep him going with was probably John. He ought to be lying down resting, not swimming across icy streams and climbing walls.

"Onward and downward then!" He took the torch from Jitrine and started down the corridor, back into the heart of the maze, leaving wet footprints on the floor of the corridor behind him. His boots made a distinct squishing noise.

Suua came just behind him. "To the left," Suua said. "And then down the stairs. That's where we came from before we doubled back here to come to the water."

"Got it," John said. "Teyla, on six."

She took up her usual place in the rear, behind Nevin, who turned and smiled at her. "Do you want this back?" He held out her jacket, the one she had shed before leaping in the stream after John.

"Yes, thank you so much," Teyla said, taking it and putting it on. It was warm and dry, and she felt it improve her morale on the spot.

Ahead, John froze silhouetted against the faint light that came around the corner from the corridor ahead.

"Shhhh," Teyla whispered to Nevin, who had begun to say something. She held up a warning finger as they all came to a halt.

John looked back at her, meeting her eyes, and passed the

torch to Suua. He was going ahead to scout.

From around the corner ahead came a scarlet glow, as though there was a vast inferno. Or a bunch of red lights. Teyla shook her head. These kind of mindgames with the credulous were so characteristic of the Wraith, who loved to torment their prey.

Anger began a slow burn in her belly. Anger is good, she thought. Anger keeps you strong. Anger makes you warm.

John slipped off down the corridor ahead, a dark shadow against the ruby light. It was some minutes before he returned, and when he did he herded them all back up the corridor and behind the first turn.

"What is it?" Teyla whispered.

"The big monster," John said grimly.

CHAPTER TWENTY-EIGHT

TEYLA CREPT FORWARD, peering around the corner. The corridor broadened out into a large chamber, though she could only see part of it from her vantage point. It looked like another cave, but instead of being partially filled with a frigid lake, this one seemed to be filled with pits of fire. The floor was uneven, marked with narrow paths between sharp stalagmites, though even those paths were broken and a person crossing them would have to stop and carefully climb over the stones. Here and there, among the stalagmites and stones, vents of steam emerged unexpectedly from the ground, shooting into the air in great gouts, rendered pink and red by the lights below.

No, thought Teyla, there were no real fires. Those were lights. But the steam was real, as was evidenced by one of the men leaping backwards from the edge of a vent, holding his scalded arm.

At the edge of the chamber were the four thugs they'd encountered before, now armed with the butts of torches they'd picked up along the way. They had a prisoner with them, the girl who had stood with Nevin on the ship from Pelagia.

Crowding up behind Teyla, he let out a gasp. "That's my sister," he whispered urgently. "That's my twin sister, Ailan!" He turned, clutching at John's arm. "You've got to do something!"

John grimaced.

Two of the thugs were arguing, apparently debating the best way across the chamber. On the other side, a darkened doorway with carved lintels made it plain what the goal was. As they watched, more vents erupted in steam, almost obscuring completely the narrow, winding paths.

"This is a wretched place," Teyla whispered to John. "I am not sure there actually is a safe way across it, except by chance."

"Tell me about it. These guys have been going crazy with the hydraulics." John hefted the butt of the torch himself, then ground out the flame against the stone.

"You're not going to challenge those men," Teyla said, her brows rising. "Four to one?"

"I don't have much choice, do I?"

One of the men seemed to have prevailed to his companions, and now he and another thug converged on Ailan, pointing to the maze. She shook her head. One of them hit her hard across the face, snapping her head back. He pointed to the path, his hand raised for another blow.

Nevin scrambled up, Suua catching onto him. "Let me go!" Nevin pleaded, struggling hopelessly against Suua's strong grip. "I have to help my sister!"

"They want her to walk the path for them," Teyla said grimly. "To find the safe way through. That way, if there are traps to be tripped it is she who will be badly burned."

John looked from Teyla to Suua. "Let's take them," he said.

Carson Beckett eased the jumper around in a long turn while Major Lorne leaned over the back of the pilot's seat. The skies above the island had cleared of the night's rain, and it was a lovely, bright day. "Having trouble finding a parking place, doc?"

"Just a bit," Carson said. "This island is heavily populated. I don't want to set it down in the middle of the street. Even cloaked, people will notice the ship when they walk right into it."

The cloak did nothing to render the jumper immaterial. Anyone who touched it would know it was there. The island was rocky and a great deal of it that was level enough to land on was covered in trees. Some of the city streets were wide enough, but they were also busy. Crowds of people were out and about, bustling from place to place or doing their marketing in the city's squares and streets. The chances of landing without making most of the city aware of them were slim.

"Unfortunately," Lorne said. He tightened his grip on the back of the seat. "How about we go around the other side again? Some of those orchards over on the back side of the island might be spaced enough that we could set down without hitting trees."

"If you say," Carson said. "I don't think there's enough room anywhere except in the big plazas and such. But we can't do that without people seeing us."

"What if we don't land at all?" Rodney said. Carson twisted around to give him a dubious look, but Rodney persisted. "What if we just hover? Can't we let some people out?"

"Sure," Lorne said. "If you don't mind jumping." Carson swept back over the city at a couple of hundred feet, wide plazas and narrow streets opening before them, all studded with trees and market stalls.

"I was thinking like on a roof or something," Rodney said. "There are all these big, wide roofs. Carson could hover a few feet above the surface and we could get out. Climb out on a roof and then get down from there."

Lorne's face broke into a wide smile. "I think you've got something there," he said. "Nobody's going to walk into us by accident if we're parked on the roof!"

"Hey you!" John shouted. It wasn't the most memorable speech he'd ever made, but they weren't really giving him points for that.

It did get the guy's attention. The biggest of the thugs turned around. "You got a problem?" he yelled.

John nodded. "Yeah. I've got a problem. You."

The thug didn't seem disturbed. "Yeah? You and what army?"

"This army," Teyla said serenely behind him. She and Suua stepped out, one on each side, each with a torch stick in hand. "I would let go of that girl if I were you."

Instead he gave her a vicious shove and Ailan went sprawling on the sharp stones beside the path. Behind Teyla and Suua, Nevin lunged out, Jitrine holding on to his injured arm.

The guy laughed. He was almost as big as Ronon, only hopefully not as fast. "Women and a little kid. Yeah, you try it."

"Suit yourself," John said, stepping forward into guard, covering Teyla's left so she could attack with her good side. Teyla's good side with sticks was better than both his sides, any day. Three on four wasn't bad odds. Time to plow on in. He rushed forward, stick in hand.

By himself. Three of the thugs bore down on him, and he barely countered their moves.

"What the hell?" John yelled.

Teyla waded in next to him, smartly rapping with her stick the guy who had nearly decked John. "I am sorry! I thought it wiser to let them come to us." She spun around in a flurry of kicks and movement, letting the momentum of her attacker carry him past her straight into Suua's fist. One down.

"Let them come to us?" John was incredulous. "They're on the edge of a steam pit!" He ducked under the flailing club of one of the thugs, unfortunately catching the second man's blow right across his back. That hurt.

Teyla reversed direction, coming around in a long kick that barely missed John and connected with the man's knee, dropping his leg out from under him. "We had the better ground," she said serenely.

"So what?" John hit the man in the back of the head, knocking him sprawling. He didn't seem inclined to get up.

He heard rather than felt the blow coming, in the rush of air preceding it. The third man's torch butt connected with his left side, full force and momentum behind it, right on the sore ribs from the crash. John staggered backwards, unfortunately completely fouling Teyla in the process. It was about all she could do not to hit him with the attack she had half completed.

The man's second blow hit Teyla as she backpedaled, catching her in the upper left arm. The cry that escaped her lips was unexpected. He'd never heard her cry out, no matter how hard she was hit. This blow hand landed on her bad shoulder.

John lowered his head and butted the man in the stomach, which did in fact distract him from Teyla. Unfortunately, it also brought the man's club down on his back again. John staggered, the world spinning around him momentarily. Bad plan, hitting something with his head, he thought belatedly. Very bad plan.

He raised his head in time to see Suua catch the man around the throat, shaking him like a terrier with a rat.

John took a deep breath, straightening up. Oh yeah. Bad plan. The dizziness made the room seem to swoop around him. Teyla had stepped back, her lips white, her arm once again at an odd angle. The blow had popped her shoulder out again.

"Stay back!" The fourth thug had retreated to the edge of the steam pits, and he held Ailan before him, a stick against her throat forcing her head up. "Don't come any closer!"

He could break her neck that way, John thought, without very much effort at all. It would be a stupid thing to do, because then he wouldn't have a hostage, but the wild look on the man's face suggested that maybe he wasn't thinking that clearly. He could kill the girl in a panic, even if it doomed him with her.

"Stay back! I mean it!" Inch by inch, he backed out onto the narrow path, dragging Ailan with him.

"John," Teyla said warningly, probably some prelude to

something about asking him if his head were bothering him or did he need his sunglasses.

"These things always seem like a good idea at time," he said. "I'll get her." Suua was still holding on to the third man, the best fighter, and Teyla's shoulder was out again. "I'm fine. It's no problem." He advanced onto the edge of the path.

Yeah, that was real steam. He could feel the sticky heat on his arms, condensing on his forehead and hair. The vent screens were backlit with eerie red and yellow and orange lights, as though he walked on a narrow path over a pit of flames. The flames weren't real, but the steam could scald and burn. And the vents turned on and off.

John jumped back as one opened to his right, sending a jet of steam taller than his head. If he'd been standing over that, he'd be very sorry right now.

"You get back!" the thug yelled, dragging Ailan with him. He was awfully close to a vent, the girl twisting as she tried to get away from the heat she could surely feel.

John held out his hands, the stick in his right. "I just want the girl," he said. "You can go. Run. Sure. I don't care. I'm not trying to win."

"Course you're trying to win!" The guy's eyes were slitted against the steam. "You want to take me down, is what."

"Just give me the girl and you can go," John said. "Nobody's going to win, don't you see? We're all going to be food for the Wraith."

"The gods said the winner goes free a rich man!" Back and back, into the heart of the maze. One of the vents opened behind him, just missing him and Ailan, John creeping cautiously after.

"They're not gods," John said. "They're Wraith. They're parasites who live on you people, feeding on you when they want to. This is just an excuse to get some suckers in here and harvest them."

He didn't buy it. John could see that in his face. So much for talking. "Look, just give me the girl."

Ailan squeaked as he grabbed her tighter, her feet almost off the ground.

"Take her then!" The guy shoved Ailan at him hard, and they both went over, falling among the sharp stones and steam vents. Fortunately, they didn't land on a live one, but the hot grate was enough to burn his hand where he'd flung it out to catch himself, the rocks digging bruisingly into his side.

Ailan screamed, which pretty much covered up any other noise. Like the noise of the guy rushing him with his stick.

John caught the blow on his left forearm. It missed Ailan's head, but he felt the shock all the way to the tips of his fingers. The momentum shoved him back on to the vents.

John rolled to the side, orange and red lights playing as he rolled over them. If the vents opened right that second, he'd be steamed like dry cleaning.

He hooked the guy's feet with his, trying to trip him while evading the blows from the stick. Not good. There was a rock to his left. He couldn't roll any further.

Heat blasted just behind him, a vent opening.

So not good. He had to get up. He was never going to win this way.

Grabbing the big rock, John staggered to his feet, blows raining down on his back. This guy didn't hit as hard as Teyla, but he hit pretty hard. He was barehanded, his stick lost in the scuffle on the floor. Beneath his feet the vent hissed, the panels starting to turn.

And suddenly the lights came on. The entire cave was flooded in light of bright fluorescents. The red and orange lights died, the steam switching off at the same moment.

The guy blinked owlishly in the sudden brightness, and John clipped him in the jaw with a roundhouse. He went down like a sack of grain. Got to go ahead and win.

In the bright lights the room was transformed. It no longer looked like a chamber from hell, but instead a kind of cheesy stage set, with big boulders concealing what was no more than a bunch of lights and effects.

Their party seemed as confused as the thugs, looking around incredulously. Only Teyla seemed to have taken it in stride, half way out on the path toward him, her left shoulder clutched in her right hand. "John? Are you all right?"

"Great," John said, aware that he was rolling like he was drunk. "It's all good here."

She clearly didn't believe him, but Teyla bent down and helped Ailan to her feet instead. "Are you hurt?"

The girl shook her head, her eyes wide, a long mark down the side of her face where one of them had hit her.

Nevin ran out, Jitrine following him as quickly as she could, her robes caught up in her hand.

"Ailan! It's all right!" Nevin called. "You're safe! These are my friends! We came to rescue you!" He threw his arms around his sister, and she buried her face against him.

Jitrine stopped beside John, looking up at him, an expression of concern on her face. "What did you do? Why did it stop?"

John shook his head, drops of condensed steam and sweat falling from his hair. "I don't know," he said. "It didn't look good for a minute there. I don't know what happened."

CHAPTER TWENTY-NINE

IN THE CONTROL ROOM, Radek slumped forward over the key panel, his eyes on the monitor. "That was almost not in time," he said.

"You've got them, right?" Ronon asked.

Radek's fingers flew over the symbols on the unfamiliar touchscreen. "I've turned the steam off and the overhead lights on. I haven't turned the cameras off for that room yet. It seemed less of a priority."

"So they know," Ronon said. "The Wraith know somebody spoiled their party. They know we've got the control room. Which means they're on their way down here."

"There is that," Radek said. He didn't take his eyes off the monitor. "Shutting down the water, that is it there. Main pump off. Backup pump off. I am leaving the special lights on and bringing up the general safety lighting throughout the complex." He stroked the board with satisfaction. "Locking the movable floors in the safety position. All traps turned off, in the maintenance mode."

"Right." Ronon hauled him out of his chair by the back of his shirt. "Time to go."

"I think you are correct," Radek said, grabbing onto his glasses as Ronon let forth a salvo with his energy pistol into the servers and monitors. They exploded most satisfactorily in clouds of sparks and smoke, and he flung up his hands to shield his eyes from the glare.

"Here." Ronon thrust the two Wraith stun pistols taken from the dead controllers into Radek's hands. "Let's get out of here. Do you know how to shoot one of these?"

"Um…" Truthfulness was probably the better part of valor. "No."

"Then stay behind me." Ronon plunged into the hallway, pistol at the ready.

"Where are we going?" Radek demanded, following after.

"To find Sheppard and Teyla," Ronon replied. "Where else?"

Radek shrugged. "Where else indeed?"

They dashed through the halls, not bothering to dodge cameras now, though some of them were no doubt active. Even if the cameras were still operative, without the control systems the Wraith would not be able to use them to spy on what happened within the maze. They might not know where the Wraith were, but the Wraith were also now essentially blind. They could not track them, or the contestants. Radek thought with satisfaction that many of the traps, like the steam room, could not be reactivated without the controls that were now destroyed. Presumably the water hazards would all empty swiftly, the water flowing downhill to the storage cisterns without the pump to bring it to the upper levels. In a few minutes the maze would be oddly silent, the flowing water stilled. Perhaps this would save more than a few lives, those of contestants still trapped within the maze. Whether they might have a chance of escape, or would simply be hunted down by the Wraith later, he could not guess.

Ronon dodged around corners, checking ahead with a speed that Radek did not understand. How could he tell so quickly if the corridor ahead were full of Wraith or not?

Fortunately, it was not far to the steam room. The big set piece trap of the maze, it was near the end, with only a few corridors leading on from there, providing a last opportunity for any teams that had beaten the steam room to betray one another. No doubt this was very entertaining for the Wraith. It seemed the sort of game they would enjoy.

Ronon barreled ahead of Radek into the steam room. "Wraith! They're on the way!"

Sheppard looked around with an expression of utter amazement. "Ronon?" Then he saw Radek and boggled again. "Zelenka?"

"We gotta get out of here," Ronon said. "The cameras were still live when the steam went off. The Wraith will be coming."

Teyla looked at Radek with a gratifying expression of thanks, putting two and two together quickly. "You turned the steam off?"

"I did," Radek said modestly. "We are quite a good team, Ronon and I."

To his surprise, Ronon nodded solemnly. "That's true."

Sheppard looked from one to the other, questions like 'how' and 'why' dancing in the air over his head, then apparently decided that all explanations could wait until later. "We're glad to see you," he said. "Are those spare stunners?"

"Yeah. One for you and one for Teyla."

Radek passed them over gratefully. Better nearly anyone else than him.

The elderly woman Radek had seen on the monitors came over, standing beside Sheppard. "Is there a moment for me to see to Teyla's shoulder? She will be in much less pain and better able to fight if I do it first."

Radek looked at Teyla, only now aware of the drawn expression on her face. The drape of her jacket mostly hid the shape of her left arm, but now that he looked something wasn't quite right.

"I can go on," Teyla said, her words sharply enunciated.

Sheppard looked from her to the older woman and back. "Do it," he said. He forestalled Teyla's protest with a hand on her sleeve. "It only takes a minute, and you'll feel a lot better if you let her pop it back in."

She gave him a hard look. "If you think we have a minute."

Carson Beckett came around for another pass at the roof he

had selected, a broad expanse only a block or so from the court-yard where the Wraith ship was parked. It looked like it was part of the palaces. Below it, a hillside dropped sharply away, though a road meandered along it. Halfway down there was a courtyard ornamented with bright, waving flags, as though for some sort of festival. There were people in the streets, a busy market set up.

However, the palace roof itself seemed safe enough, quiet and deserted. There were no guards on the roof, which made sense as there was really no way for anyone to get up there from the ground. Clearly the Wraith were not expecting any kind of assault from the air.

Major Lorne looked over the Marines in the back. Cadman was adjusting the chin strap on her helmet. "Everybody ready?"

"Ready, sir," Cadman said.

Rodney checked his P90 for the millionth time, trying to ignore the sinking feeling in his stomach. This was so not going to be fun. In fact, experience had taught him exactly how not fun it could be. This was one of those occasions where ignorance was indeed bliss.

"You stay back, doc," Lorne began quietly, then broke off as Carson started swearing under his breath, his head going up like a hunting dog's. "What is it?"

Carson put the ship over again lifting to circle around rather than set down. "The Wraith cruiser just started powering up."

Rodney snapped around. "Why?"

"I don't know, do I?" Carson said grimly. "But it's not good news."

Her shoulder did indeed feel better, Teyla thought, letting John help her put her jacket back on and taking up the Wraith stunner in her right hand. There was no question the muscles were torn, however. If and when they got back to Atlantis she no doubt had several weeks of anti-inflammatories and physical therapy ahead of her. When, not if, she corrected herself. Surely it would be possible. Surely, if Radek and Ronon had found them, with all of a strange world between them, anything might now be possible!

"Get down!" Ronon yelled from by the door, and Teyla flung herself behind one of the ornamental stalagmites that littered the floor of the steam room, Radek to her left and John to her right.

John was crouching on the grate of a big steam vent. He looked down doubtfully. "They can't turn this back on, can they?" he said to Radek.

"Not a chance." Radek shook his head. "We did a very thorough job, Ronon and I."

A blue Wraith stun beam cut the air above the stone he sheltered behind, heralding the arrival of the Wraith. Beside the door, Ronon's energy pistol spoke loud. Ronon was flattened against the wall beside the door, and ducked out to get off one shot. He pulled his head back in time before a barrage of blue fire answered.

"Four to six," Teyla guessed aloud. "Based on the concentration of fire."

John nodded, and she saw that he'd come to the same conclusion himself.

"There will be more," Radek said. He looked decidedly scared. Teyla thought Radek was not used to being pinned down by enemy fire. It had not happened on the few occasions he had been offworld before.

She looked at John. "Is there a plan?"

He nodded sharply, his eyes on Ronon, waiting for a move that would cover him to get off a few shots. "We take the cruiser."

Radek swore in Czech. "How do you think we will fly this Wraith cruiser?" he asked.

John glanced back and forth between them, Teyla with her Gift that allowed her to interface with Wraith technology, Radek with his knowledge of systems and the beginning of a reading knowledge of Wraith. Surely with their help he could figure out how to fly it. He believed he could fly anything. Unfortunately, she was uncertain whether or not that was true.

"We'll manage between us," John said. "Now let's get out of here. Radek, stay back with Jitrine and the kids until we've cleared them out. Teyla, go left."

"You do not have to tell me twice to stay," Radek said fervently.

She waited until Ronon fired again, and then in the moment when the Wraith would assuredly have their heads down, dashed left and closer, to the shelter of a boulder nearer the door. As she dove behind it, she got off two sharp shots into the doorway. It was impossible to see what she might be shooting at, or if she'd hit anything, but at least fire from a different direction might confuse them.

One second, and John was moving, right and forward, to a new position. The stalagmites that had afforded the Wraith such pleasure as obstacles to the humans were now providing them with cover. Turn about was fair play. Not that Teyla ever cared much about playing fair.

Ronon glanced back, then with John covering him ducked out again. The stun beams narrowly missed him. They would have hit, if he had ducked out at full height, rather than with his head two feet lower than normal. He got off several shots before he got back.

The volume of fire had decreased markedly. One or perhaps two shooters were firing now. Teyla pegged another three shots through the doorway, but whether or not she hit anything was impossible to tell.

Ronon looked back at John again, and she saw his almost imperceptible nod. John rocked forward on the balls of his feet, ready to go. Ronon lunged for the doorway, John a step behind, going for the frame as Ronon threw himself flat just inside, laying down a thick barrage.

Teyla moved, left and forward again, coming to the edge of the doorframe under the cover of Ronon's shots. So close to the Wraith. She barely even had to try to get a sense of them. She could hear them speaking mind to mind as though they were shouting.

Fall back! Fall back to the entrance and pick them off when they come out!

The Wraith Lord who commanded them had better sense than to get into a situation where his men must rush out of a narrow entrance against defenders. Better to turn it around. There was one exit from the maze. Sooner or later they would have to chance it. They would have to rush from a doorway against five or six times their number armed with energy weapons. There were no other options.

Or they might wait, stalemated. But even then sooner or later they would have to do something. There was no food in the labyrinth, though there was water aplenty. Sooner or later, the people in the maze would have to try to break out, and they would be waiting for them.

"Ronon!" Teyla shouted. "They are backing off!"

Ronon rolled out of the doorway, landing almost against her foot and getting swiftly to his feet. "How do you know?"

"I hear them," she said.

He looked skeptical. Of course. Ronon did not entirely believe in her Gift, had not really seen her use it.

"John! The Wraith are withdrawing!" she yelled. Even on the other side, he should hear her.

He looked at her and nodded once, keeping up the occasional shot into the doorway.

The incoming fire from the Wraith dwindled, then finally ceased.

Teyla closed her eyes. A moment, a touch… She could risk so much. She would not have to go deep or far. They had pulled back to the entrance, one hapless spectator outside chosen to be fed upon so that a wounded man might regain his strength. She could feel the outside wind on her face, the bright sun cutting at last through scudding clouds…

"Teyla?" John was beside her, his hand on her sleeve. "Are you ok?"

She opened her eyes. He looked concerned and unshaven, but at least he was not wobbling on his feet. "They have pulled back outside, to the doorway. They know we have to come out that way, and then we will be emerging from a small space into a wide field of fire. They have us. This is not the first time someone has rebelled in the maze, though this is the first time anyone has reached the control room. They are uneasy. They do not know why this has happened, how someone could have known what to do."

Beyond John, Radek looked decidedly self-satisfied.

John scratched his ear contemplatively, while Ronon cast glances through the door. He didn't seem entirely confident in Teyla's pronouncement of what the Wraith were doing.

John glanced over at Radek. "You're absolutely positive there's no way they can turn the traps back on?"

"Positive," the scientist nodded.

"Do they know you turned everything off?"

Radek put his head to the side. "Almost certainly not. They would not have been able to see anything except this room on the cameras after I began. I did this room first, as you were in here, and then did the cameras before I moved on to the other systems. They would have lost the cameras first, and unless there is some sort of entirely independent secondary internal sensor system, which I doubt, they would have no way of getting any information from inside the labyrinth."

John nodded slowly. "So they can't see us or what we're doing, track us, or tell what the status of their traps is."

"Essentially, yes," Radek said. "They may be able to reset some of the traps manually, like the pump for the water, but I think they would have to get to the pump room and do it from there. I have fragged the interfaces, as you would say."

Ronon looked back at him. "What's the plan?"

John nodded to the hallway. "We can't go that way. They're waiting for us, and we can't get out through that kind of fire with three stunners. So we need to go another way."

"What other way?"

Jitrine broke into a wide smile. "The door we came in!"

"Exactly," John said. "It ought to be easy to go back up, with all the traps disabled and the lights on. We go back up to the courtyard of the palace, rush that door, and go for the cruiser."

"That's a plan," Ronon said. "You know the way?"

John winced. "Teyla and I got here…kind of a roundabout way. Jitrine? Suua? Do you guys know how to get back up there?"

Suua nodded gravely. "We can retrace our steps."

"I remember," Nevin piped up. "I remember exactly."

"Ok." John picked up one of the fallen sticks and handed it to Suua. "Let's go. Teyla?"

"I know. On six." She couldn't help but smile. Yes, they were still trapped in the labyrinth, but things were decidedly looking up.

CHAPTER THIRTY

THE PUDDLEJUMPER came to rest on the roof of the palace, Carson carefully letting it come down easy, just in case the roof wasn't strong enough to hold it. At the first sign of buckling or damage he could lift again. But the stone pillars seemed sturdy, possibly stronger in terms of loadbearing than most modern architecture on Earth allowed, and the jumper settled without problems at all.

"Still cloaked?" Major Lorne asked.

"Still cloaked," Carson confirmed. "They shouldn't be able to see us or otherwise detect an EM signature." He eyed the radio in Lorne's hand. "Unless you start using that radio. The cloak isn't going to hide an outgoing signal."

"I know," Lorne said. "But my team needs radios to keep in contact. You stay with the jumper, doc." He looked around. "Dr. McKay? This is your call. If you'd like to stay with Dr. Beckett…"

"I'm going," Rodney said. He swallowed hard. "You'll probably need me."

"Yeah, probably," Lorne agreed. "Ok, we're on then." He hit the release on the rear door and led the way out.

The maze looked different with the lights on. Nevin and Jitrine came just behind John up the passages, showing him how they had gotten there. Overhead lights in the ceiling rendered them about as spooky as any hallway anywhere, which was to say not so much. At one point they passed through a gallery high above what had been the waterfall room. Now, lit by bright fluorescent lights dangling from the ceiling, with the waterfall silenced, it was just a big room with a very shallow pool at the bottom, three feet or so below the level of the drain. Anybody could wade across it.

"Not so impressive now," John said.

Jitrine nodded. "It was beautiful and eerie both. I do not know why the waterfall glowed as it did."

John pointed down, showing her. "See those blue and green things just below the water? They're spotlights and they shine up the sheet of the falls. It was a pretty impressive effect, but they're just lights with colored covers on them."

"Like silk screens placed before lamps in the theater," Jitrine said. She shook her head. "Nothing but theatrical effects."

"Pretty much," John said.

Radek had fallen back beside Teyla. "What is the matter with your arm?"

"I dislocated my shoulder in the jumper crash," Teyla said quietly. "When Colonel Sheppard hit his head."

"You crashed the jumper?" Radek sounded incredulous. "Again?"

"The Wraith cruiser attacked us," Teyla said. "They outgunned us considerably. The Colonel lost them, but we had taken such damage that he could not keep it in the air. We crashed in the desert. Fortunately, we were not more seriously injured."

Radek blew out a breath. "That is bad news," he said. "That the jumper is gone. I had hoped you might have it, or have supplies. We lost all of ours two nights ago, radios, food, everything."

"You have not had food since?" Teyla sounded concerned.

Radek shrugged. "We had some bread. And a hardboiled egg."

"John? Hold up for a moment," Teyla called out.

He stopped immediately. "What's wrong?"

"Radek and Ronon have had almost nothing to eat in two days," Teyla said. "Give me a moment to get out what I have left of the emergency supplies."

There wasn't much left. They'd eaten the fruit leather and some of the crackers for breakfast, washing it down with the two juice packets. There was a granola bar and a bag of salted corn kernels, and two rather mashed packets of peanut butter crackers.

Radek looked at the small spread hungrily. "Might I have the granola bar?" he asked hesitantly, as though he did not wish to be greedy.

Teyla handed it over. "Of course."

"I'm good with the corn kernels," Ronon said, popping the bag open. "Save the rest for later."

Radek glanced at him in surprise. "Don't you want more?"

"Shouldn't eat too much right before I fight," Ronon said. "Just a little bit to give me energy. I'm set."

Teyla offered the crackers to Jitrine. "Are you hungry?"

Jitrine looked at Suua, Nevin and Ailan. "We had breakfast," she said firmly. "The contestants all were offered reasonable food at daybreak in the palace. We will not take anything from your meager stores."

Suua looked like he wanted some crackers, but he shrugged. "We're fine."

John thought it wasn't such a great sacrifice, as at least he'd had breakfast. That couldn't have been more than five or six hours ago. Of course, they could have had breakfast too, if John's escape attempt hadn't landed them in solitary.

"Time to go, people," he said.

They turned a corner and ascended another flight of stairs. There were voices ahead, a woman's voice raised in anger. In the room above four other contestants stood about arguing, three women and a man who had lagged behind or been left by others intent on victory. Seeing the strong and well armed party, they didn't wait. With a scream, one fled down the entrance corridor, followed by the others.

"Wait!" John yelled.

"We mean you no harm!" Teyla called after.

They were talking to their backs.

Jitrine shook her head. "They think we are one of the parties that has been killing people in the maze. I cannot blame them for running."

"Yeah." John looked around in frustration. "We'd help them get out of here too, if they'd give us a chance."

"They are too frightened to do that," Jitrine said sadly.

"I know."

It wasn't long until they came to the hazard that had given them so much trouble the first time, the swift flowing stream with the broken bridge. Five people were sitting against the wall on the other side, knees drawn up. The water was off, and had long since drained down from this part of the labyrinth. There were overhead lights on, and the stream bed was dry.

It was still dangerous, though. The bridge was missing, and to get over they'd have to climb down the loose stones of one side and back up the other. This was much easier without the cold, fast running current, but John knew it was still going to be tough for Jitrine, and for Teyla with her bad shoulder and Nevin with his broken wrist.

"I've still got this," Suua said, holding out the rope ladder he'd made from the bridge ropes. It looked...pretty good.

"Where'd you learn to do that?" John asked, testing the knots, though he'd already put his weight on it, getting up from the ledge at the waterfall pool.

"I'm a fisherman," Suua said patiently. "I make nets. Out of rope."

"Well, great."

One of the women on the other side stood up and called across, "Who are you and what do you want?"

Before John could think of an answer better than 'I'm a guy from outer space here to kill the gods,' or 'I'm an immortal hero here to slay the minotaur' Jitrine forestalled him.

"I am a Pelagian physician," she said. "We are returning to the entrance. We do not wish to harm anyone."

"Why are you going to the entrance?"

Jitrine glanced at John. "We think we may be able to get out that way. Will you let us cross without hindering us?'

They consulted together. John saw some gestures at the kids, at Jitrine, at Teyla with her injured arm and Nevin with his taped wrist. "I guess we don't look too scary," John said quietly to Teyla.

Her mouth quirked in a smile. "You look very scary. You look like an unkempt madman."

"I do not."

"You do too." Her smile broadened. "You look like a thug. Try looking friendly."

John smiled weakly, and she burst out laughing.

"The Smile of Wrongness!" Teyla said. "I did not know you could do it on purpose!"

"The Smile of Wrongness?" he asked, laughing. "What's that?"

Teyla shook her head. "It is an expression you get when you feel that you must smile, but you do not in the least want to. When someone is threatening you, or when you have to deal with Colonel Caldwell. You did it when you first came to Athos. 'Yes, let us talk about ferris wheels and drink tea while stranded in a galaxy far from home with the city about to flood while I am on my very first alien world and Colonel Sumner is gunning for my ass!' That smile!"

John ducked his head ruefully. "Was it that obvious?"

"Not then." Teyla's eyes danced with mischief. "Then, I just thought that you were disturbed."

"Disturbed?"

"Insane," Teyla clarified. "Perhaps in a good way, but more than a little unbalanced."

"Maybe I am," John said. "Maybe I've just gotten better at covering it up."

Her smile faded, but not the warmth in her eyes. "Maybe you are," she said quietly. "But we all have our scars. What defines us in life is not what happens to us, but how we bear it."

There was something in her face, in the tilt of her chin, that made him want to ask, want to know what she carried beneath her usually serene and unruffled surface. "Teyla…"

"You may come across!" the woman on the other side of the dry stream bed shouted. "If you leave us alone, we will not harm you or hinder you!"

John snapped around. "Ok, we're in business! Suua, can you hold the ladder on this side and let me down? Then I'll go up the other side, you get everybody down this side, throw me the ladder, I'll get everybody up that side, and then you climb down this side and then up the ladder."

Suua blinked. "You lost me."

"Let me down this side," John said patiently. "And then I'll climb up the other side. Let's start with that."

"And hope that no one turns the water back on," Teyla said darkly, looking at the dry stream bed where he had been swept away before.

"That is not possible," Radek said patiently. "I told you. I have turned off the pump."

"Might they not reach a manual override in the pump room?" Teyla asked.

John looked around at her, hoping he didn't look alarmed. "We didn't see one when we were down there, did we? If we had, we would have turned the water off."

"I am sure that there is one somewhere," Radek said sensibly. "But they will have to get to it, which will take them some amount of time."

"No," Teyla agreed. "We did not see one, so perhaps it is even deeper within the maze."

"Or in a pump control room somewhere we have not discovered," Radek said. "It is possible. I did not have time to examine all the systems from the central control room."

"Great," John said, and started to climb down. He was absolutely not thinking about a wave of cold water rushing down the dry stream bed. Absolutely not.

Besides, it wouldn't start like that, would it? It would be more of a trickle as the pumps came back online. It was a long way down to the pump room. It would take a while to get going. Surely even if they turned it back on, it would take a long time for the water to recirculate. They'd have some warning.

John scrambled across the bottom of the stream bed. Ok. Now back up the other side. He'd climbed it soaking wet, with the stones slippery and shifting and the current dragging at him. It was, in fact, a lot easier to get up it dry. The side had a definite slope, so it was much easier than the wall yesterday.

John stood up on the other side. "Ok. Everybody down."

With a glance back at the others to encourage them, Jitrine began descending the ladder. When she got to the bottom Ailan started down, and then her twin, Nevin, cautiously descending one handed. His broken wrist couldn't take any weight at all.

That would be the bad, John thought. Not him down in the middle, but everybody else, while he watched safe above the water. That would be the really, really bad. His hands were sweating and he swung his arms, pacing back and forth. Got to breathe through this.

Across the stream bed, Teyla caught his eye, and he figured he wasn't fooling her.

"I am ready," Teyla said confidently, and she started down the ladder, holding on with her left hand, the Wraith stunner stuck in the back of her waistband.

Ronon waited above, his eyes on Suua. That was good. Ronon would keep an eye out. Ronon always did. He'd be the last one down, usually Teyla's place, but with her bad shoulder she needed the ladder.

Ronon saw him watching and nodded. He'd be nervous too, if everyone were down in the middle except him. He probably was nervous.

Teyla. Then Zelenka. Then Suua. Ronon last, climbing down without the ladder.

"Catch, Sheppard!" He tossed it up and John caught it, tying it to the pillar the rope bridge had originally hung from. "Everybody up," Ronon said. He boosted Ailan onto the ladder surprisingly gently.

"Thank you," she said quietly, almost the first thing John had heard her say.

Ailan. Then Teyla. Nevin. Jitrine. Zelenka. Suua.

And then Ronon last, watching everybody's backs, his eyes on John as he climbed. He knew how to do this, John thought. He was completely patient with the civilians. And then they all stood on the right side together.

"Piece of cake," Radek said to Ronon.

"Yeah." Ronon glanced at Radek in a way that seemed almost friendly. "It's all good." Which was a little baffling, since Radek was likely to be scared of climbing in and out of things, while Ronon didn't seem like he was scared of anything, much less climbing through watercourses that might turn into raging streams at any moment.

"Let's head for the surface," John said. "Ronon, come up here with me. We need to check out what's ahead of us."

It wasn't far to the surface. At the first chamber below, where John and Teyla had checked for traps a few hours earlier, they paused. It looked little different with the lights on, a boring ten by ten room.

"This is it," John said. "Everybody, you stay with Teyla while

Ronon and I check things out. Just stay here."

Carefully, with Ronon on his heels, he slipped down the corridor toward the stairs. Everything was well lit. The stairs to the surface went steeply up, ending in the sliding doors set in the ceiling. There was a door panel on this side, but it was dark. Probably because Radek had cut the power.

"We're going to need Zelenka up here," John said quietly to Ronon. "He's going to have to hotwire the panel."

"Yeah." Ronon crept up the stairs to the very top, and John knew better than to interrupt him while he had his ear to the door. After a few minutes he came back down. "There's a couple of people up there. I hear two sets of footsteps. Can't tell if they're Wraith or Wraith worshippers. No big crowd or anything though. It's quiet."

"There was a big crowd this morning," John said. "But they've probably gone down to the exit to catch people coming out. If this door is locked, they won't see any reason for more than a couple of guards."

"So we get Zelenka to open the door and we rush them?"

"That's the plan," John said. "And then head for the cruiser. If we take their ship, they can't exactly follow."

"Makes sense," Ronon said. He looked at John skeptically. "You really think you can fly that thing?"

John was saved from answering. "Go ahead and zip her up, doc." A voice crackled behind him, and it took John an incredulous moment to realize it was his radio, hooked on his belt on standby, useless for days.

"Closing the back then."

"That's Carson!" John grabbed for the radio. "What the hell?"

"Underground," Ronon said. "We've been too far underground to pick up a radio signal for hours."

John flipped the radio out of standby. "Beckett? This is Colonel Sheppard."

"Bloody hell! Lorne, did you hear that?" Oh yeah. It was Carson all right.

"Colonel Sheppard?" Major Lorne's voice was loud and clear. "What is your position, sir?"

"Give me that!" Rodney said. "Sheppard? Where are you? I want you to know that I've been looking all over this god-forsaken planet for three days for you. You don't even want to know what I've endured!"

"You're right. I don't." John felt a huge grin plaster itself to his face. "Rodney, what's going on?"

"I'm here with Carson and Major Lorne," Rodney replied. "We came to rescue you, you dumbass."

"Good to talk to you too," Ronon said.

"Is that Ronon? How is that Ronon? Wasn't he on the island with Zelenka?"

"Yes, but…" John began.

There was the sound of a scuffle at the other end, and Lorne's voice returned. "Let me do this. You can complain about your sunburn later. Colonel, where are you? We are on the roof of the palace overlooking the main courtyard. Dr. Beckett has a cloaked jumper parked just behind me."

"You're right above us," John said. "You see a pair of double doors set flush in the pavement? We're in the chamber right below them. I've got Teyla and Ronon and Zelenka, and a bunch of civilians we've rescued from the Wraith."

"I see the doors," Lorne said steadily. "There are two Wraith guards almost over your heads. Sir, do you know there's a Wraith cruiser here?"

"That's what shot me down," John said. "I'm aware of it."

"The Cruiser has powered up," Carson said, presumably from the jumper's sensors. "But hasn't started lifting off."

"Probably because Radek tore up their power grid," John said. "They've got quite a complex down here, but Radek already turned off everything below ground level. If I were them, I'd power up the ship too." He glanced at Ronon. "So much for taking the ship. We can't do it if they've got their shields operative." An idea was beginning to form. "Go back and get Zelenka. I've got a better plan."

CHAPTER THIRTY-ONE

"THAT'S YOUR clever plan?" Rodney said indignantly. "Rush them?"

"It's a classic," John insisted into his radio. "Two guards. Me, Ronon, Teyla. Plus you, Cadman, Lorne with a P90, and six Marines."

"So that's six to one odds in our favor? You call that a clever plan?"

"I like six to one odds in my favor," John said indignantly. "Less chance of somebody getting hurt."

"How about we shoot these guys, you get Zelenka to get the door open, and we all get out of here?" Lorne put in. "How hard can that be?"

"That was my plan," John said. "Well, except that I thought Zelenka could get the door open first, and we'd rush these guys together."

"I think me, Cadman, and six other guys can take two guards," Lorne replied dryly. "Sir."

"Ok," John said. It would be kind of embarrassing if they couldn't. Lorne plus seven Marines on two guards. Yeah. He looked at Ronon and shrugged. "You do that. Ronon, go get Zelenka. Let's get this door open and get out of here."

He waited, crouched on the stairs beneath the door for what seemed like several very long minutes before the familiar sound of fire above rattled across the metal and stone. Lorne wasn't taking any chances with those Wraith, or sparing any ammunition.

Ronon came back up the stairs with Zelenka, everyone else crowding into the corridor below.

"Can you get the door open?" John asked.

Zelenka shrugged and started prying the cover off the

control panel with Ronon's knife. "Certainly. Give me a moment."

Teyla came up the stairs and crouched beside John. "Ronon told me that Rodney was here. What is the plan?"

"Lorne and his guys took out the guards. Radek gets the door open, and then we're out of here. Carson has a cloaked jumper parked on the roof. We just run for the jumper."

"On the roof?" Teyla's eyebrows rose. "Do you think these people can climb up onto the roof?"

John looked at her bad shoulder, the one she hadn't mentioned. Teyla probably couldn't climb onto the roof, much less Nevin or Jitrine. "Ok. No. Hang on." He flipped the radio back on. "Carson? Can you bring the jumper down here in the courtyard with Lorne covering you? We've got wounded who can't climb."

"It's pretty tight," Carson replied. "But I'll give it a try."

"Oh come on!" Rodney's voice came over the radio. "It's not that small of a courtyard!"

"I said I'd give it a try, didn't I?"

John listened for the sound of the jumper's engines above, hearing nothing. Of course he heard nothing. Carson had the jumper cloaked. He looked at Zelenka. "The door?"

"I am working on it." The scientist had his head bent to the door panel. "It would help if I could see what I am doing."

"Here." Teyla switched on her flashlight and shone it at the panel.

Zelenka looked around with a quick smile. "Thank you."

"Are you going to take all day?" Rodney asked over the radio. "You know the Wraith heard when we started shooting?"

"Rodney, keep your pants on," John snapped.

"Keep my pants on! After I spend three days hunting your sorry ass all over this planet? No sleep, wild animals…"

The doors shook, a strip of daylight showing between them.

"It is unlocked," Radek said.

Ronon put his shoulder to the left hand door. "Ok. Let's get this thing open."

John took the other side and pushed, the doors opening slowly on well greased tracks. They were heavy, but reasonably well balanced. As the gap between them grew, he saw Rodney's face staring down with a concerned expression that changed to irritation as he saw them.

"Oh really," Rodney said to Zelenka. "You didn't leave the doors powered?"

"No, Rodney. I am sorry I have not done this as brilliantly as you would," Zelenka snapped, climbing out into the sun. "I am sure you would have done a much better job."

"I would have," Rodney said, crossing his arms on his chest.

"I should like to see you try, you claustrophobic weasel!" Zelenka snapped. "Down in those caves you would have been calling for your mommy!"

"At least I wouldn't have screwed up something as simple as opening doors," Rodney snapped back. "Or been a complete dead weight."

"Dead weight?" Zelenka's glasses were trembling on the end of his nose, which was roughly level with Rodney's chin. "I do not even have expletives enough for you!"

John stepped between them. "Not now! You can do your Lois and Clark imitation later! Everybody, get in the jumper. Rodney, help Teyla up the steps. She's dislocated her shoulder." He looked down at Teyla, who was coming up behind Nevin and Ailan. She didn't seem to need any help.

"Oh." Rodney elbowed past Nevin to grab Teyla's good arm. "It's ok. I've got you." He put his arm under hers helpfully.

"Thank you, Rodney," Teyla said sweetly. Her eyes flicked up at John with a look of amusement.

Zelenka headed for the jumper, spewing what were no doubt

words he wouldn't find in a Czech to English dictionary, followed by Jitrine and Suua.

Ronon had his energy pistol in hand and had taken up position next to Cadman. He glanced at her sideways. Cadman did look awfully small with a P90.

Cadman grinned at his pistol. "It's not the size of the boat. It's the motion of the ocean."

It must have taken a moment to translate, but then Ronon roared with laughter.

There was a sudden blast of fire from one of the doorways around the courtyard, and John threw himself to the ground, returning fire with the Wraith stunner. Three, maybe four. He saw one of the Wraith move, coming forward to just behind an ornamental planter. Great. Stun beams were very effective on flesh, but much less so on ceramic. He could probably shoot at that thing all day and not bother the guy behind it.

Fortunately, that wasn't an issue with a P90. Lorne laid down fire that sent the planter flying in a hundred fragments, the Wraith behind it diving for cover.

"Where is the jumper?" Teyla shouted. Suua and Jitrine and Teyla and Rodney were flat on their faces, trying to figure out which way to go. With the jumper cloaked, they couldn't see exactly where it was, and under fire they couldn't afford to wander around looking for it.

With a warping of air like a mirage coming into focus, the jumper decloaked. The back was down. "Come on!" Rodney yelled, dragging Teyla up. "Come on, kids!"

Ailan and Nevin scrambled after, running for the jumper as fast as possible.

Returning fire. John rolled out of the way of a stun beam, only to see it catch Ronon's legs. It was a partial hit, and rather than rendering him unconscious, just dropped his legs out from under him.

"We retreated to the jumper under fire," John muttered.

"Why do so many of my reports end that way?"

Cadman's fire laid out one Wraith and flushed another. John's stun beam caught him and flung him backwards, buying at least a moment's time.

"Ronon?"

Teeth gritted. Ronon was dragging himself along the pavement toward the jumper with his arms, his legs apparently paralyzed by the beam.

John swore, and scampered over the stones, staying as low as possible. He grabbed Ronon around the waist and yanked him along. "Come on, buddy. Let's get this thing done."

Pulling and scrambling, he got Ronon in the jumper, rolling onto the floor in the back. Behind them, Lorne was laying down covering fire as the last of their team got aboard.

John tried to get up, tried being the operative word. He was completely hemmed in by feet. Boots. Feet. More feet. Suua's feet were big and wearing sandals. He stepped back enough, wedging against the seat, for John to get up, pressed tight between Cadman and a Marine lance corporal, who looked apologetic.

"Sorry, Colonel," he said.

"How many people are in this jumper anyhow?" John asked over the general din as the back gate began to rise.

"Eighteen!" Rodney shouted from the front. "Six Marines, Lorne, Cadman, me and Carson. Plus you, Teyla, Zelenka, Ronon, and four people you picked up."

"Like sausages in a can," Radek put in.

Carson glanced back at him. "Don't you mean sardines?"

"You have your fish, and I will have my sausages," Radek said primly.

"Eighteen," John tried to push his way between Marines to get to the front. Whether or not that would be a weight issue was something he'd have to find out. He'd never had eighteen in the jumper before. "Carson, can you lift this thing?"

"Just a moment," Carson said. "I'm having trouble getting the back gate closed." The blue fire of Wraith stunners glanced off the windscreen as John shoved his way into the forward compartment, stepping on Radek in the process.

"Ow, ow, ow," muttered Radek, who was inexplicably bare-footed.

"Well, hurry up," John said. "They'll get something with heavier firepower out here any minute."

In the front co-pilot's seat, Teyla pointed. "They just did." Above the colonnade, the Wraith cruiser was lifting into the air.

"Not good!" John elbowed past Rodney, who was standing in the aisle. "Carson, let me take the chair. Rodney, get that back gate closed!"

"Anytime," Carson said fervently, sliding out of the pilot's seat, which involved nearly sitting in Teyla's lap as John shoved past him into the seat.

John's eyes flicked over the board. "Somebody's standing on the manual release," he yelled. "Rodney!"

The cruiser began to rotate on its landing jets, its guns tracking toward them.

"Crap." John got the shields up just as the first barrage of shots from the cruiser hit them, rocking them sideways, one of the jumper's drive pods scraping along the stones of the courtyard. Indicators lit red. Running into the ground wasn't recommended.

"Rodney!"

"Got it!" The back gate locked into place, a really important thing if you didn't want to spill your seventeen passengers out the back of the jumper when you hit the gas. He'd learned that the hard way in a pickup truck once.

The jumper shot into the air, dodging around the next fire in a surprisingly clumsy fashion. The scrape to the drive pod seemed to have damaged one of the lateral thrusters. Well, no time to worry about that, and not much need to. He could hold it steady and compensate manually if he needed too, as long as nobody expected anything really tricky. John eased the indicator for the cloaking device to full.

And nothing happened.

A quick glance at the indicators — the port cloaking emitter was damaged.

"Rodney!"

"What?" shrieked Rodney from the very back.

"We've lost the cloak." John spared another look at the heads up display. "It says the emitter is damaged on the port drive pod."

"Do you expect me to climb out and fix it?" Rodney yelled. "I can fix power problems inboard. I can't fix an external emitter that you bent up with your lousy take off!"

The cruiser's next shot shook the jumper, sending Carson flying into Teyla's lap. "Sorry," he said, trying not to squash her, her nose against his chest.

At least the inertial dampeners seemed fine. John banked the jumper steeply to the right. Not so hot. It was definitely pulling. That lateral thruster was important. He'd fought the cruiser before, in the other jumper, but he still didn't remember a moment of it.

John gave it full speed, streaking out over the sea at low altitude. He'd done this before. This was what Teyla said he'd already done. And it hadn't been a good plan before. With the energy shield above he couldn't go for altitude, and with no cloak he couldn't disappear.

The sea blurred past beneath him, no more than a vast expanse of blue. Behind, the cruiser was gaining, and had still not achieved her full speed. Flat out, she'd probably have the advantage, especially as heavily laden as the jumper was. He spared a glance for the heads up display. The little jumper could handle the weight, but it was definitely slowing them down.

The coast of the mainland was coming up ahead, Pelagia on the far eastern horizon. This was exactly what he'd done before. He was sure of it. No need to make the same mistakes twice.

John pulled the jumper around in a steep turn, banking hard and coming onto a new course at full speed, closing on the cruiser at better than nine hundred miles per hour as they ran toward each other.

Shots streaked out, closer and closer, splattering off the forward shields.

Straight toward the cruiser. Holding steady. Holding steady. They couldn't go any higher. Even the slightest deviation...

"Forward shield at 20%," Teyla said quietly, her eyes on the readouts.

"What are you doing?" Carson squawked.

"A game I used to play in a pickup truck," John muttered.

The cruiser grew larger and larger, fragments of a second elongating, seeming to take forever to close the distance between them.

"Oh God," Carson said.

Another shot splashed the shield with blue, rocking the jumper wildly. They were going to hit. They were going straight into the forward superstructure...

And the cruiser pulled up. The instant it twitched John dived, one hundred percent power in a ninety degree dive toward the sea.

Above, there was a tremendous explosion as the cruiser hit the energy shield, pulling away from the jumper and fatally into the shield above. Pieces fell toward the sea, caught in gravity's inexorable grip.

The jumper pulled out at two hundred feet, skimming along over the waves as detritus rained down.

Teyla let go of her white knuckled grip on the chair arms, but said nothing.

"It's called chicken," John said, euphoria surging with adrenaline through his veins. He knew he had a silly grin on his face, not the kind of expression that you ought to have at a moment like that. "You drive at each other as fast as you can and see who blinks first."

"This is a way of killing your friends," Teyla observed.

"It's kind of a rite of passage," John said. "I never wound up in the reservoir. But I did bend the gas gauge all to pieces once." His hands felt light and fine as fire, like he could move at the speed of sound.

"Lovely," Carson said.

"My mom wasn't happy," John said. "She ran out of gas when the tank looked full. Man, you could put a lot of weight in the back of that car! You could actually get it airborne if you took a hill at about seventy."

"And this is how people die on your world," Teyla observed.

Carson nodded. "I hope someday you have a boy to keep you up nights doing crazy things like that. Your poor mother!"

He was coming down now. Each breath seemed to take a normal amount of time. John put the jumper over carefully, looking at the screen to reorient himself to the heads up display of the mainland coast that the jumper helpfully provided at a thought.

"Ok, folks," John said. "Next stop, taking our guests home. Suua, can you get up here? I need you to show me where to go."

Behind, the slow rain of smaller particles descended to the waves and were swallowed up.

CHAPTER THIRTY-TWO

EVENING WAS FALLING over the sea, and the first stars were showing, the sparks from the campfire flying like fireflies before the wind. John stood behind the beach dunes, the wind tugging at his hair, taking a sip of the local beer that Suua offered him.

"Is it good?" Suua asked hopefully. He was taking playing host to the visitors very seriously indeed.

"It's good." John said. "It's really great beer." It wasn't his taste so much, malty and dark, but at least it was beer here, not tea. On a good day that was how it turned out, drinking tea in a place you'd never been before with some would-be enemies turned friends. Behind Suua, a vast number of his relatives and friends were spit-roasting fish over a fire, turning them quickly so that they wouldn't burn. It smelled wonderful.

"I never thought it would work," Suua said, glancing back as well to the figures limned by firelight. "I'm home. My wife, my daughter… I never thought I'd see them again. Thank you. Thank you."

"You're a good guy in a fight," John said. "I'm not sure we would have made it without you."

Jitrine came and joined them, her white robes much the worse for wear over the last few days. "You should not be drinking alcohol with a head injury," she said disapprovingly.

"It's just a few sips of beer," John said, but he handed the jar back to Suua. He looked at the doctor. "What are you going to do next?"

"I'm going back to Pelagia with Ailan and Nevin," Jitrine said. "The children are orphans, which is why they were sent as competitors for the Games in the first place. No one wanted them. So they may as well stay with me as anything else. There is much to do in Pelagia." Jitrine looked west, toward the distant port city far out of sight along the coast. "With the High King killed aboard his airship, King Anados of Pelagia will have need of me. Perhaps it is our turn to rule the waters, without some High King in the islands who stands above us all. Perhaps it is time for the rule of men, and for us to shape this world as we will."

"A Pelagian empire," John said.

"It may be." Jitrine's eyes were serene. "And who is to say if that is good or ill?"

"Not me," John shrugged. "It's one of those things. One of those things about being human. Somebody's going to step into the power vacuum, and it might as well be your King Anados. It's got to be better. I figure he's not going to feed on people anyhow."

"You can be sure of that," Jitrine said.

Teyla and Rodney came to join them, leaving Ronon and Radek tucking in to the first fish off the fire. Ronon was getting a whole fish to himself, and Radek was laughing as Suua's wife tried to cut a piece off for him, catching it with his fingers.

"I don't want to hear about how much I eat ever again," Rodney declared. "Ronon and Zelenka are going to eat these people out of house and home."

"There are many more fish where these came from," Suua said. "Even your big friend cannot eat all the fish in the ocean."

"Probably not," John agreed. "But he might try." Ronon was actually smiling. He wasn't sure he'd ever seen that before.

"Have you decided what we're going to do about the DHD?" Rodney asked.

"What about the DHD?"

"I fixed it," Rodney said. "That means anybody can use the gate to go in or out. Which is a problem, because it means the Wraith will be back. We can dial in and out, but so can anybody else who wants to."

John felt Teyla stiffen beside him. "Ok, so what's the alternative?" he asked.

"There's the energy shield," Rodney said. "It protects the planet like it has for thousands of years, just like the other ones we've encountered. The Wraith can't come in from space. If I take the control crystal out and bring it with us, any Wraith who come through the gate will be trapped and never be able to return to their hive ships. They won't be able to dial out, and they probably don't have a supply of spare control crystals, so they'll be stuck here." He looked at Jitrine. "Your people can probably take care of a few scouts, right?"

Jitrine nodded gravely. "King Anados will put a guard on the gate day and night. You may be sure of that." She looked at Rodney, one eyebrow rising. "But if I understand correctly, if you do this we will not be able to use the gate either."

"Well, you haven't been using it now," Rodney said. "I mean, the Wraith have controlled it for centuries. So you wouldn't be losing anything."

"Except the opportunity to be part of the rest of the galaxy," Teyla said quietly.

"Part of the galaxy that has Wraith all over it!" Rodney said. "The Ancients set these shields up to protect worlds that weren't advanced enough to protect themselves, a kind of a time capsule to nurture cultures and make sure humanity survived. These people can't take on the Wraith! If it weren't for the energy shield, this world would have been Culled a long time ago."

"And if you take these control crystals," Jitrine said keenly, "The Wraith will not be able to Cull us, but we will not be able to use the Stargate either."

"Yes," Rodney said, putting his hands in his pockets. "Your world will be free to develop at your own pace without outside interference. Like the Prime Directive."

"Without any knowledge of the battles fought outside on

our doorstep. Without your medicines and your technology. Without your people and your things changing us," Jitrine said. "We will remain as we have remained, in a time capsule, kept in willful ignorance." She shook her head, and her eyes came to rest on Teyla. "Is this what you would choose for your people?"

Teyla took a deep breath. "In exchange for no more Cullings, at least for a long, long time until the energy shield eventually fails? That might be centuries, you know. You might have five hundred years of peace. It is a very great opportunity." She took another deep breath, and her eyes avoided John's. "I would not make that choice. Many Athosians would, and would call me traitor or criminal for speaking as I do. But I am Teyla Who Walks Through Gates. To be bound to one world, ignorant of the struggles of all humanity outside, waiting for the day when the choices of others at last determine my fate? I could not choose that." She raised her face, the sea wind pushing her hair back from her brow. "Better to face the world with courage. Better to risk all, knowing that you will be changed, knowing that the struggle is in itself worthy."

John swallowed.

Teyla looked at him sideways, a fleeting glance. Then her eyes met Jitrine's. "But I cannot make that choice for you. We have the control crystal, and you must tell us what to do with it based upon the beliefs of your own people, based upon the things you think are right."

"Why us?" Suua said, casting about uncomfortably. "How can we decide for our whole world?"

"Because you're the ones who're here," John said. "That's how it usually works."

Jitrine looked at Suua. "What do you think, fisherman?"

Suua's brow furrowed. "I think it's stupid to close a door without seeing what's on the other side."

"A ton of Wraith are on the other side," Rodney observed.

"Rodney," John said.

Suua looked at Jitrine. "But what do I know? You are a learned Doctor of Pelagia. You know better than me."

Jitrine nodded slowly, and her eyes met John's. "In the Colleges of Pelagia we are taught this, first and above all — to seek knowledge, and to scorn no source of wisdom that there is under the sun. To choose to remain ignorant of all that happens in the rest of the galaxy in order to cling to a tenuous safety…that is a betrayal of our deepest values." She looked at Teyla, and her smile was rueful. "But Pelagians are not all the people there are in the world, nor even the largest part. And yet we must decide for all. Perhaps this is the moment where future generations will say we went astray, and I stand now as the greatest evil our world has ever known. Perhaps I will be reviled, and perhaps the Wraith will come and I will die with the blood of thousands on my hands. But still I must choose knowledge. Leave the Stargate open. Leave the control crystal where it belongs."

"I don't think…" Rodney began.

"Rodney," John said quietly. "It's their decision. We're not going to deactivate their Stargate without their permission. We don't have the Prime Directive, remember?"

"We probably ought to," Rodney said. "Future generations may not think much of us, either."

"And that will really suck. But they weren't here," John said. He looked at Jitrine. "We'll leave your Stargate intact. But you might want to tell your King Anados to get some guards over there pronto. Not everybody who comes through the gate is going to be friendly."

"We understand that, Sheppard," Jitrine said. "And we are not soft as you might think."

"I didn't think that," John said gravely. "You're one tough old bird."

Jitrine broke into a wide smile, then leaned up and put her

cheek to John's. "Take care of yourself," she said. "And tell your wife to rest that arm."

"She's not my wife," John said.

Jitrine released him and went back to the fire, sliding onto the bench beside Carson, who was putting a fiberglass cast on Nevin's wrist. He greeted her cheerfully, and she leaned in to see what he did, pointing at something about Nevin's hand.

"She is a fine doctor," Teyla said, watching Jitrine examining Carson's work.

"She pretty much is," John agreed. "Carson said she did a good job on my head, and that he's not even going to keep me in the infirmary. That if I were going to die I would have by now."

"That is Carson indeed," Teyla said. Stars were glittering and the sea breeze was freshening. She pulled her jacket on one arm and he held the other side for her to slide her injured arm into the sleeve, gently working the binding over her wrist so that he didn't jostle her shoulder too much.

"He looks like he is having a good conversation with Jitrine," Teyla said.

"I imagine he'll want to come back," John said. "You know Carson. He'd be lecturing in Pelagia next week if Elizabeth would let him."

"She might," Teyla said.

"She might at that," John said thoughtfully.

Rodney hunched his shoulders against the wind which ruffled his hair. He looked uncomfortable, as though he'd rather not say anything, but was doing it anyhow. "I'm glad you guys are, you know…not dead. I thought…when we saw the wrecked jumper… There were all those jackals and I had to hunt for you all over the planet and you'd gotten yourselves captured by the Wraith and…"

"We love you too, Rodney," Teyla said. "Thank you."

Rodney opened his mouth and shut it again. "You're welcome," he said quietly. He looked about, as if suddenly surprised by something. "I'm going to go see if there is any food left." Hands in his pockets, Rodney hurried away.

Teyla looked after him. "Sometimes Rodney is very strange," she said. "Why would he not want us to know that he was worried about us?"

"That's just Rodney," John said. "He's a good guy."

"I know," Teyla said with a smile.

John zipped up his jacket. The nights could get cold, here on the edge of the desert. But they wouldn't be staying the night, thanks to his team. Maybe they were all getting better at this. "We're all in one piece, anyhow."

"More or less," Teyla agreed with a quick glance at his forehead. "I am afraid my book is ruined."

"Your... Oh, Watership Down." It took him a moment. "Well, if it is I can probably find you another copy or get it sent out on the Daedalus' next run."

"It is not right to ask for another gift because you have ruined the first one," she said.

"It is if you ruined it saving the ass of the guy who gave it to you," John said. He stopped, hesitating. "I'm glad you like it."

"The stories of your people," she said, tilting her chin up as though she could see his world among the distant stars. Of course she couldn't. They were too far away. "It is through one's stories that you come to know them, through the stories they love and the stories they tell, the ones they embrace close to their hearts. Stories are powerful things."

John looked up at the alien stars, so close in the velvety darkness, moving in their unfamiliar courses. He'd dared to imagine this once, long before life intervened, a different story, an impossible one. He cleared his throat. "There was this kid who loved Star Wars," he said. "And he wanted to be Han Solo. The stars over his back yard might be the stars of Hoth or the Tion Hegemony or Corellia. Gotta find you a copy of Han Solo and the Lost Legacy next time I'm on Earth."

"I will look forward to it," Teyla said formally. Then something in her face changed, stilled. "This Han Solo. Did he die young?"

John shook his head. "Nah. He had some close calls and some really bad ones, but no, he didn't die. He had the fastest ship in the fleet and he married the Princess and she became President of the New Republic and he was her consort. And they stuck together through thick and thin, a whole lot of work healing the galaxy after the Empire."

"That sounds like a very good ending," she said thoughtfully. "I suppose if he had wanted to die he would have."

John shrugged. "There are always plenty of ways to die if you want to." The sea wind lifted her hair, pulling it back from her face as though baring a question. "What story… What story did you want to be in?"

Teyla looked at him sideways, a warm smile spreading across her face. "Once there was a queen, and she walked out of darkness, and Death made a cloak around her to guard her passage, and thus they came to the City of Emege where every tower was alight for joy. I will tell you the whole story one day."

"It's a deal," John said. He glanced back toward the cooking fires. "As soon as Carson's done, let's pack up," John said. "If we can pry Ronon and Radek away from the food, that is. Let's go home."

ABOUT THE AUTHOR

Jo Graham is the author of three historical fantasy novels of the ancient world, *Black Ships*, *Hand of Isis*, and *Stealing Fire*. She lives in North Carolina with her partner, their daughter, and a spoiled Siamese cat.

COMING SOON
STARGATE ATLANTIS: Homecoming

By the author of Death Game, Jo Graham, and renowned
sci-fi/fantasy author Melissa Scott

Published October 2010

SNEAK PREVIEW
STARGATE ATLANTIS:
HOMECOMING

Book one of the Legacy series

by Jo Graham & Melissa Scott

AZURE STREAKS FLASHED AND DANCED, blue shifted stars shapeless blurs in the speed of her passage. Atlantis cruised through hyperspace with the majesty of Earth's old ocean liners, her size impossible to guess in the infinity of space. Her towering spires and thousands of rooms were nothing compared to the vast distances around her. Atlantis glided through hyperspace, her massive engines firing white behind her, shields protecting fragile buildings and occupants from the vacuum.

Behind, the Milky Way galaxy spun like a giant pinwheel, millions of brilliant stars stabbing points of light in the darkness. Atlantis traversed the enormous distance between galaxies, hundreds of thousands of light years vanishing swifter than thought. Even with her enormous hyperdrive, the journey was the work of many days.

It was nine days, Dr. McKay had predicted, from Earth to Lantea, Atlantis' original home in the Pegasus Galaxy, deserted these two and a half years since they had fled from the Replicator attack. Of all the places their enemies might seek them, they were least likely to look where they were certain Atlantis wasn't.

Of course, no one person could stay in the command chair that controlled the city's flight for nine days, not even lost in the piloting trance that the Ancient interfaces fostered. Not even John Sheppard could do that. Lt. Colonel Sheppard had come to Atlantis five and a half years ago at the beginning of the expedition, and the city had come to life at his touch. The City of the Ancients awoke, long-dormant systems coming on slowly when someone with the ATA gene, a descendant of the original builders, came through the Stargate. Atlantis had been left waiting. Though it had waited ten thousand years, humans had returned.

But even Sheppard could not spend nine days in the chair. The Ancients would have designated three pilots, each watching in eight hour shifts, but the humans from Earth did not have that luxury. Sheppard was First Pilot, and Dr. Carson Beckett, a medical doctor originally from Scotland, was Second. Twelve hour shifts were grueling, but at least allowed both men time to eat and sleep.

Five days of the journey gone, 20:00 hours, and Dr. Beckett was in the chair. His eyes were closed, his forehead creased in a faint frown, his arms relaxed on the arms of the chair, his fingers resting lightly on the interfaces. Nearly six years of practice had made him a competent, if reluctant, pilot. And so it was Dr. Beckett who noticed it first.

It was one tiny detail, one anomaly in a datastream of thousands of points, all fed through the chair's controls and interpreted by the neural interfaces that fed data straight into Beckett's body, as though all of Atlantis' enormous bulk was nothing more than the extension of himself.

It felt like…a wobble. Just a very faint wobble, as when driving an auto along the highway you wonder if one of the tires is just a little off. It might be that, or it might be the surface of the road. Nothing is wrong on the dashboard, so you listen but don't hear anything, and just when you've convinced yourself you imagined it entirely, there it is again. A wobble. A very small movement that is wrong.

Perhaps, Beckett thought, if you were borrowing a friend's car you wouldn't notice it at all. You'd just think that was how it was. But when it's your own car, lovingly cared for and maintained every 5,000 km, you know something is not quite right. Perhaps one tire is a little low. Perhaps you've dinted the rim just a tad, and the balance is not entirely even. It's probably not important. But if you're the kind of man who keeps your car that way, you know. You notice.

Beneath the blue lights of the control room, Beckett's eyes opened. The young technician monitoring the power output looked around, surprised. It was very quiet, watching someone fly Atlantis.

His tongue flicked over his lips, moistening them, reminding himself of his own physical body, and then he spoke into the headset he wore. "Control, this is Beckett. I've got a wobble."

There was a long moment of silence, then his radio crackled. "Say it again. You've got a what?"

"A wobble," Beckett said. "I don't know a better word for it."

"A wobble." The voice was that of Dr. Radek Zelenka, the Czech scientist who was, with Dr. McKay, one of the foremost experts on Ancient technology. Certainly he was one of the foremost experts on Atlantis, having spent most of the last five and a half years repairing her systems.

"It doesn't feel right," Beckett said. "I don't know how to put it better, Radek. It feels like a tire about to go off."

"Atlantis does not have tires, Carson," Zelenka replied.

"I know it doesn't." Beckett looked up toward the ceiling, as though he could see Zelenka in the gateroom many stories above, no doubt bent worriedly over a console, his glasses askew. "That's what it feels like. That's how my mind interprets it."

"He says we have a wobble. Like a flat tire." Zelenka was talking to someone else. "I do not know. That is what Carson says."

"A wobble?" That was McKay, the Canadian Chief of Science. "What's a wobble, Carson?"

"It feels wrong," Beckett said. "I don't know how to explain the bloody thing! It feels like there's something wrong."

"I am seeing nothing with propulsion," Zelenka said. Beckett could see how he would say it, his hands roving over the control board, data reflected in his glasses. "Everything is well within the normal operating parameters."

"I think I would interpret a propulsion problem as an engine light," Beckett said slowly.

"And a tire is what?" McKay would be putting his head to the side impatiently. "Do you think you can give me engineering, not voodoo? Your vague analogy is next to worthless."

Lying back in the chair, Beckett rolled his eyes. Five and a half years he'd put up with Rodney bullying him over this damned interface. "Something to do with the hyperdrive?" he ventured.

"The hyperdrive. That's very informative. The hyperdrive is a major system, Carson. It has literally tens of thousands of components."

"I don't know any more than that, all right?" Beckett snapped. "If you want a second opinion, get Sheppard down here and have him take a go at it."

"He has only been off duty for two hours," Zelenka said, presumably to McKay. "He is probably still in the mess hall. I can call him." McKay must have nodded, because his next words were not addressed to Beckett. "Colonel Sheppard to the command chair room. Sheppard to the command chair room."

He should love being pulled away from his dinner after a twelve hour shift. Beckett felt vaguely guilty about that. He sat up a bare ten minutes later as Sheppard barreled into the room, an open bottle of soft drink in his hand, his dark hair ruffled.

"What's the problem?" Sheppard said. He couldn't be too worried if he'd brought along his drink. Soft drinks were rare in

Atlantis, since they had to be brought from Earth, and though they'd laid in a limited supply it could be expected to run out soon. Sheppard was unwilling to abandon his short of murder and mayhem.

Beckett smiled ruefully. For all their differences of background and skills, he had developed a considerable respect for Sheppard in their years of working together, a respect he thought was mutual. "Sorry to take you from your dinner. I've got an anomaly I can't pin down." He sat up, letting the chair come upright, the sticky interfaces disengaging from his fingertips. "It feels like a wobble. You know. When you've got a tire about to go."

Sheppard frowned and put his drink down on the edge of the platform. "Ok. Let's have a look," he said with the air of a man about to look under a friend's hood.

Beckett stood up, catching himself for a moment on the arm of the chair. It always felt very strange to settle back into his mere physical body after some time in the interface.

Sheppard slid into the chair and leaned back, his eyes closing as the interfaces engaged, the chair lighting around him as power flowed, a profound expression of peace on his face. Beckett knew better than to interrupt. Sheppard's fingers twitched lightly in the interface, then stilled. He would be diving into it now, the pathways of the city's circuits and cables mirroring the neural pathways of his mind. Done right, impulses flowed like thoughts, data streaming effortlessly into easy interpretations. Beckett usually did not find it quite that simple. Practice and diligence had made him a competent pilot for the city, but he had never quite gotten the knack of thinking in three dimensions, of visualizing so many moving points completely. He wasn't a pilot. He was a medical doctor who through some trick of genetics had the particular piece of code that the city responded to. Sheppard was in his twentieth year in the Air Force, a man whose natural talents ran this way, honed by years of experience in high speed aircraft. He could get a lot more out of the interface than Beckett could.

It was nearly fifteen minutes before Sheppard surfaced, his eyes opening and the chair tilting halfway up. His glance fell on Beckett, but he spoke into his headset. "Control, this is Sheppard. We've got an anomaly in the number four induction array."

"The east pier," Zelenka said. "*Zatracenĕ!* Will we ever get that piece of trash fixed?"

"Carson's the one who tore it up fighting with the hive ship," McKay said. "And I thought we had it. I ran a stress test on it the night before we left."

"Well, you must have missed something," Zelenka said. "Because here we go with it again."

"It doesn't look like it's that bad," Sheppard said, cupping the headset and straightening up completely in the chair. "It's a wobble, like Carson said. It's not a flat. It's just a variance in output."

"A crashingly small one," McKay said. "I've got the power log in front of me now. Five one hundredths of one percent."

"After running at full power for five days?" Zelenka was probably leaning over McKay's shoulder, looking at the numbers. "No wonder you didn't catch it. That is nothing. We cannot expect every system to run at optimal for days on end. It would not show up in a stress test."

"Give me the summary." That was a new voice, Richard Woolsey, Atlantis' commander. "Should we drop out of hyperspace?" He was probably hovering over the two scientists by now.

It was McKay who spoke, of course. "And do what? We're between the Milky Way and the Pegasus Galaxy, right in the middle of a whole lot of nothing. I'm not seeing any kind of damaged component that we can repair, or quite frankly anything that amounts to a problem. Carson, it's nice of you to tell us about every little wobble, but this is just that. A little, tiny wobble."

Sheppard looked at Beckett and shrugged. "That now we know about. So we can keep an eye on it. It's just exactly like a tire. You may not need to run and do something about a little dent in the rim, but you keep an eye on it."

Beckett unhunched his shoulders, putting his hands in his pockets.

"Yes, well. We will keep an eye on it," McKay said. "But I think we can all take a deep breath and put this away."

Sheppard stood up, flexing his hands as he withdrew them from the interface.

"I'm sorry to put you to trouble," Beckett said. "I hope your dinner's not cold."

"It's ok." Sheppard picked his drink up off the floor. "Better safe than sorry. And we should keep an eye on that. You have a little wobble in your tire one minute, and the next thing you know you have a blowout doing eighty."

"And that would be bad," Beckett said, imagining what the analogy to a high speed blowout might be piloting a giant Ancient city through hyperspace between galaxies. It would put a pileup on the M25 to shame.

"Damn straight," Sheppard said, taking a drink of his soda. "See you at 06:00, Carson."

"This turn and turn again is getting old," Beckett said. "What I'd give for another pilot!"

"We couldn't exactly bring O'Neill with us under the circumstances," Sheppard said.

"Four more days," Beckett said. "Over the hump." He slid back into the chair, feeling the interfaces clinging to his fingertips in preparation. "See you in the morning." He closed his eyes, sinking into Atlantis' embrace.

A new danger lurks in the Pegasus Galaxy

STARGATE ATLANTIS

HOMECOMING
Book one of the LEGACY series

Jo Graham & Melissa Scott

Based on the hit television series created by
Brad Wright & Robert C. Cooper

Series number: SGA-16

STARGATE ATLANTIS: HOMECOMING

Book one in the new LEGACY SERIES

by Jo Graham & Melissa Scott
Price: £6.99 UK | $7.95 US
ISBN-10: 1-905586-50-7
ISBN-13: 978-1-905586-50-9
Publication date: October 2010

Atlantis has returned to Earth, its team has disbursed and are beginning new lives far from the dangers of the Pegasus galaxy. They think the adventure is over.

They're wrong.

With the help of General Jack O'Neill, Atlantis rises once more – and the former members of the expedition must decide whether to return with her to Pegasus, or to remain safely on Earth in the new lives they enjoy...

Picking up where the show's final season ended, Stargate Atlantis Homecoming is the first in the exciting new Stargate Atlantis Legacy series. These all new adventures take the Atlantis team back to the Pegasus galaxy where a terrible new enemy has emerged, an enemy that threatens their lives, their friendships – and the future of Earth itself.

STARGATE ATLANTIS: BRIMSTONE

Series number: SGA-15

**by David Niall Wilson &
Patricia Macomber**
Price: £6.99 UK | $7.95 US
ISBN-10: 1-905586-20-5
ISBN-13: 978-1-905586-20-2
Publication date: September 2010

Doctor Rodney McKay can't believe his eyes when he discovers a moon leaving planetary orbit for a collision course with its own sun. Keen to investigate, he finds something astonishing on the moon's surface – an Ancient city, the mirror of Atlantis...

But the city is not as abandoned as he thinks and Colonel Sheppard's team soon encounter a strange sect of Ancients living beneath the surface, a sect devoted to decadence and debauchery, for whom novelty is the only entertainment. And in the team from Atlantis they find the ultimate novelty to enliven their bloody gladiatorial games...

Trapped on a world heading for destruction, the team must fight their way back to the Stargate or share the fate of the doomed city of Admah...

Ronon's past catches up with him

STARGATE ATLANTIS

HUNT AND RUN

Aaron Rosenberg

Based on the hit television series created by
Brad Wright and Robert C. Cooper

Series number: SGA-13

STARGATE ATLANTIS: HUNT AND RUN

by **Aaron Rosenberg**
Price: £6.99 UK | $7.95 US
ISBN-10: 1-905586-44-2
ISBN-13: 978-1-905586-44-8
Publication date: June 2010

Ronon Dex is a mystery. His past is a closed book and he likes it that way. But when the Atlantis team trigger a trap that leaves them stranded on a hostile world, only Ronon's past can save them — if it doesn't kill them first.

As the gripping tale unfolds, we return to Ronon's earliest days as a Runner and meet the charismatic leader who transformed him into a hunter of Wraith. But grief and rage can change the best of men and it soon becomes clear that those Ronon once considered brothers-in-arms are now on the hunt — and that the Atlantis team are their prey.

Unless Ronon can out hunt the hunters, Colonel Sheppard's team will fall victim to the vengeance of the *V'rdai*.

STARGATE ATLANTIS: DEAD END

by Chris Wraight
Price: £6.99 UK | $7.95 US
ISBN-10: 1-905586-22-1
ISBN-13: 978-1-905586-22-6
Publication date: June 2010

Trapped on a planet being swallowed by a killing ice age, Colonel Sheppard and his team are rescued by the Forgotten — a race abandoned by those who once protected them, and condemned to watch their world die.

But when Teyla is abducted by the mysterious 'Banshees', Sheppard and his team risk losing their only chance of getting home in a desperate bid to save Teyla and to lead the Forgotten to a land remembered only in legend.

Order your copy directly from the publisher today by going to www.stargatenovels.com or send a check or money order made payable to "Fandemonium" to:

<u>USA orders:</u> $10.95 ($7.95 + $3.00 P&P).

<u>Rest of world:</u> $13.95 ($7.95 + $6.00 P&P)

Send payment to: Fandemonium Books, PO Box 2178, Decatur, GA 30031-2178 USA.

Or check your local bookshop — available on special order if they are out of stock (quote the ISBN number listed above).

STARGATE ATLANTIS: ANGELUS

by Peter Evans
Price: £6.99 UK | $7.95 US
ISBN-10: 1-905586-18-3
ISBN-13: 978-1-905586-18-9

With their core directive restored, the Asurans have begun to attack the Wraith on multiple fronts. Under the command of Colonel Ellis, the Apollo is dispatched to observe the battlefront, but Ellis's orders not to intervene are quickly breached when an Ancient ship drops out of hyperspace.

Inside is Angelus, fleeing the destruction of a world he has spent millennia protecting from the Wraith. Charming and likable, Angelus quickly connects with each member of the Atlantis team in a unique way and, more than that, offers them a weapon that could put an end to their war with both the Wraith and the Asurans.

But all is not what it seems, and even Angelus is unaware of his true nature — a nature that threatens the very survival of Atlantis itself…

Order your copy directly from the publisher today by going to www.stargatenovels.com or send a check or money order made payable to "Fandemonium" to:

<u>USA orders:</u> $10.95 ($7.95 + $3.00 P&P)

<u>Rest of world:</u> $13.95 ($7.95 + $6.00 P&P)

Send payment to: Fandemonium Books, PO Box 2178, Decatur, GA 30031-2178 USA.

Or check your local bookshop — available on special order if they are out of stock (quote the ISBN number listed above).

STARGATE ATLANTIS: NIGHTFALL

by James Swallow
Price: £6.99 UK | $7.95 US
ISBN-10: 1-905586-14-0
ISBN-13: 978-1-905586-14-1

Deception and lies abound on the peaceful planet of Heruun, protected from the Wraith for generations by their mysterious guardian—the Aegis.

But with the planet falling victim to an incurable wasting sickness, and two of Colonel Sheppard's team going missing, the secrets of the Aegis must be revealed. The shocking truth threatens to tear Herunn society apart, bringing down upon them the scourge of the Wraith. Yet even with a Hive ship poised to attack there is much more at stake than the fate of one small planet.

For the Aegis conceals a threat so catastrophic that Colonel Samantha Carter herself must join Sheppard and his team as they risk everything to eliminate it from the Pegasus galaxy…

SG-1 unearth an ancient evil

STARGATE
SG·1.

OCEANS OF DUST

Peter J. Evans

Based on the hit television series developed by
Brad Wright and Jonathan Glassner

Series number: SG1-18

STARGATE SG-1: OCEANS OF DUST

by Peter J. Evans
Price: $7.95 US | £6.99 UK
ISBN-10: 1-905586-53-1
ISBN-13: 978-1-905586-53-0
Publication date: March 2011

Something lurks beneath the ancient sands of Egypt. It is the stuff of Jaffa nightmares, its name a whisper in the dark. And it is stirring…

When disaster strikes an Egyptian dig, SG1 are brought in to investigate. But nothing can prepare them for what they find among the ruins. Walking in the dust of a thousand deaths, they discover a creature of unimaginable evil – a creature the insane Goa'uld Neheb-Kau wants to use as a terrible weapon.

With Teal'c and Major Carter in the hands of the enemy, Colonel O'Neill and Daniel Jackson recruit Master Bra'tac to help track the creature across the galaxy in a desperate bid to destroy it before it turns their friends – and the whole galaxy – to dust…

STARGATE SG-1: SUNRISE

by J.F. Crane
Price: $7.95 US | £6.99 UK
ISBN-10: 1-905586-51-5
ISBN-13: 978-1-905586-51-6
Publication date: February 2011

On the abandoned outpost of *Acarsaid Dorch* Doctor Daniel Jackson makes a startling discovery – a discovery that leads SG1 to a world on the brink of destruction.

The Elect rule Ierna, ensuring that their people live in peace and plenty, protected from their planet's merciless sun by a biosphere that surrounds their city. But all is not as it seems and when Daniel is taken captive by the renegade Seachráni, Colonel Jack O'Neill and his team discover another side to Ierna - a people driven to desperation by rising seas, burning beneath a blistering sun.

Inhabiting the building tops of a long-drowned cityscape, the Seachráni and their reluctant leader, Faelan Garrett, reveal the truth about the planet's catastrophic past – and about how Daniel's discovery on *Acarsaid Dorch* could save them all...

Order your copy directly from the publisher today by going to www.stargatenovels.com or send a check or money order made payable to "Fandemonium" to:

<u>USA orders:</u> $10.95 ($7.95 + $3.00 P&P).

<u>Rest of world:</u> $13.95 ($7.95 + $6.00 P&P)

Send payment to: Fandemonium Books, PO Box 2178, Decatur, GA 30031-2178 USA.

Or check your local bookshop – available on special order if they are out of stock (quote the ISBN number listed above).

STARGATE UNIVERSE.

Original novels based on the hit TV
shows **STARGATE SG-1**,
STARGATE ATLANTIS and
STARGATE UNIVERSE

AVAILABLE NOW
For more information, visit
www.stargatenovels.com